GRAND THEFT

ALSO BY TIMOTHY WATTS

Steal Away
The Money Lovers
Cons

TIMOTHY WATTS

GRAND THEFT

G. P. PUTNAM'S SONS   New York

G. P. Putnam's Sons
Publishers Since 1838
a member of
Penguin Group (USA) Inc.
375 Hudson Street
New York, NY 10014

Library of Congress Cataloging-in-Publication Data

Watts, Timothy, date.
  Grand theft / Timothy Watts.
    p. cm.
  ISBN 0-399-15099-4
  1. Automobile theft—Fiction.   2. Organized crime—Fiction.
3. Criminals—Fiction.   I. Title.
  PS3573.A88G73   2003   2003043213
  813'.54—dc21

Printed in the United States of America
10 9 8 7 6 5 4 3 2 1

This book is printed on acid-free paper. ♾

Book design by Victoria Kuskowski

1

IZZY FELDMAN SAID, "Enough is enough," took the Jericho 941 nine-millimeter pistol out from underneath his armpit, and shot Philadelphia mob boss Dominic Scarlotti between the eyes with such studied noncha-lance that even Anthony "Little Anthony" Bonica—who had been expecting it—jumped and said, "Holy fuck, you didn't even want to *talk* to him first?"

Anthony was dark, southern Italy, in his late thirties, going to fat, with strange eyes, one of them going a little bit off center. Izzy had heard he was half blind, but it didn't appear to affect his ability to double-cross anyone.

Izzy put his pistol back in his shoulder holster and looked at Anthony like he was some kind of idiot. "Talk about what? You already did enough talking for both of us."

Anthony had a reputation as a wild man, a hair trigger, but Izzy hadn't seen anything to be impressed about yet, except that Anthony was just as emotional as Saul Rubin had said he was.

Izzy towered over Anthony Bonica, his crew-cut hair—worn just a shade longer than when he'd been in the Israeli Army—and dark clothing calcu-lated to have precisely the effect they were having on the smaller mobster. Izzy had grown up an orphan, eventually adopted by his boss, Saul Rubin. Since that time Izzy had traveled to many parts of the world, doing Saul

Rubin's bidding. To remain anonymous, he used one of five passports, depending on where he was headed, what he was doing and, most important, who he was dealing with.

In the past twelve years he'd advised government troops in the Philippines fighting Islamic fundamentalists. He'd trucked armaments into Afghanistan for the mujahideen factions blacklisted by the ISI, the Pakistani intelligence service. After the Gulf War, Saul Rubin had devised a way to help Saddam Hussein beat the UN economic sanctions, and Izzy had traveled to Baghdad to oversee the project. After six months he had returned to the States and immediately—again on Saul's orders—sold strategic information about the viability and progress of Hussein's chemical weapons program to the CIA. Then he had hopped a cab to the J. Edgar Hoover Building and resold the same information to the FBI, knowing that the two agencies would never compare notes. Izzy had interrogated Hamas warriors in the jails of Jerusalem and taught Palestinian terrorists the art of making bombs small enough to fit in the sole of a shoe without either side knowing the double role he was playing.

Izzy did exactly what Saul Rubin said to do. Over the years it had put millions into Saul Rubin's various bank accounts. In turn, Saul Rubin had made Izzy himself a rich man. Saul Rubin was a man of few loyalties, but Izzy knew Saul's history and had learned that the loyalties he *did* form were worth more than what any team of high-priced attorneys could ever concoct.

Saul Rubin was an old man, Izzy only in his mid-thirties, and Izzy felt an awesome responsibility toward his benefactor. He watched TV with Saul until late into the night, fed Saul's dog, oversaw the day-to-day running of Saul's house and did whatever else it was that Saul wanted done—from shampooing the dog to putting a bullet in the head of a man like Dominic Scarlotti.

Izzy could disassemble any weapon made without conscious thought, but he carried his Jericho 941, partly for its stopping power and partly because it was made in Israel. He considered it to be *some* sort of a link to his heritage, a nod to his ancestry without getting carried away. Keeping things simple worked well for Izzy Feldman, be it a reliable, old handgun or his black pants, black turtleneck, and black jacket. Keeping things simple let Izzy keep his mind on other things, like shooting Dominic Scarlotti squarely between the eyes so that he didn't have to check to see that he was dead or waste another bullet putting him out of his misery.

Killing Scarlotti was the easy part. The difficult part would be dealing with his heir apparent, Little Anthony Bonica. Izzy considered the mob a bunch of bunglers—the late Dominic Scarlotti less so than most—small-time crooks who dealt drugs, turned women out onto the streets, and more often than not sent lifelong friends to jail to save their own skins.

Anthony Bonica had not only said he'd gotten the hit against his boss sanctioned by the New York Families—he'd hired Saul and Izzy to do it. But Saul hadn't sent Izzy on this errand for the money—$50,000. Fifty thousand was a parking ticket. Saul had okayed it because Dominic Scarlotti had gotten wind of a big project Saul was involved in. The next step, Saul knew, would be for Scarlotti to try to shake Saul down. The solution was to take Scarlotti out, but the problem for Saul and Izzy was, if they nailed Scarlotti, they ran the risk of starting a war with Anthony.

Izzy and Saul had been discussing exactly this the day, just two short weeks ago, when Anthony had shown up at Saul's door, a shit-eating grin on his face and a wild proposition to present to them. Saul had listened carefully, sighed, and then pretended he was trying to decide whether he wanted to get involved.

Anthony had said, "You know how it is, those guys up there, New York? They want a hitter with no connection to the Families."

Saul had pretended to think some more. "I suppose I *could* spare Izzy to do the job. A favor among friends." Saul had paused and smiled benignly at Anthony's treachery before adding, "Plus the fifty thousand, naturally."

Saul had told Izzy that Anthony was what the pot at the end of the rainbow looked like, a chubby Italian mobster with garlic breath who had inadvertently stopped by to solve their problems. Izzy wondered now if Anthony would even believe it if Izzy told him the only reason this thing was going down was that Saul Rubin thought Anthony's skull was a vacuum compared to Dominic Scarlotti's. Saul could work Anthony Bonica and play solitaire at the same time, whereas Scarlotti had had the brains *and* the balls to squeeze Saul over a sensitive, $12 million deal that was set to take place in the most volatile place on earth. Anthony? Izzy bet Little Anthony didn't even know where the Middle East was.

The hit on Scarlotti was arranged so that Little Anthony drove Dominic Scarlotti to the half-renovated restaurant they owned. Izzy would be waiting inside. When Little Anthony and his right-hand man, Tommy Inzarella, escorted Dominic Scarlotti through the door, Izzy did things according to Anthony's plan. He stepped from behind the front door and put the barrel of his Jericho against Tommy Inzarella's skull so that he could go through the charade of checking everyone for weapons and wires.

Little Anthony said, "What the fuck?" like he was pissed and scared at the same time. Then he made a production. "Okay, *okay* already." Opening his shirt and turning all the way around. Pulling his pants down to reveal red silk boxers. He pulled the waistband out. "You wanna look down there, Izzy?"

Izzy shook his head. "I'll take your word for it." Then he turned to look at the person who he'd come to kill.

Dominic Scarlotti unbuttoned his jacket without being asked. The old man was cool about it. Izzy had to give him that. Scarlotti opened his shirt and dropped his trousers without changing expression. When he was buttoned back up he calmly pulled a gold cigarette case out of his breast pocket, extracted a cigarette, tapped it on his thumb, lit it with a gold lighter, and said, holding up the cigarette case, "You mind if I keep this, or are you afraid I'm gonna beat you to death with it?"

Izzy said, "No, go ahead."

Scarlotti lit the cigarette. No shake to his fingers. The old man had known exactly what was happening. Known it was his last smoke.

Now Anthony waved his hand through the gun smoke and walked over to touch the corpse with his shoe. "Jesus Christ. You fucking Hebes, you don't give a shit. Just come out and *whack* the motherfucker. No talking, just *bang*."

Izzy looked at Tommy Inzarella, a broad-shouldered, slender man who had just become an underboss—the second most powerful criminal in Philadelphia after Anthony. You couldn't tell it from looking at his face. There was nothing there.

Izzy moved next to Anthony, ignoring what he'd just said. "I did this first part. But the next part is yours. Are you listening to me, Mr. Bonica?"

Anthony said, "Yeah, I'm listening. But I'm not sure I'm hearing anything."

"My boss," Izzy said, "Mr. Saul Rubin, he was willing to do you this favor."

"*Favor?* I pay your boss fifty large and you call it a fucking favor?"

"You came to us. You could've had one of your own crew do it. Was there a reason you didn't?"

"Don't worry, you'll get your fucking money."

"I'm afraid Mr. Rubin is going to want more than fifty grand."

"The fuck you talking about, you prick? You fuck with me now, Tommy there'll put you on the floor next to Dominic."

Without bothering to look at Tommy, Izzy said, "You misunderstand me, Mr. Bonica. Saul Rubin okayed this. And it's done. Finished. The only thing he wanted me to mention was this: Mr. Scarlotti here, it's important that he gets found."

"*Found?*" Little Anthony looked from Izzy to Tommy Inzarella and got no response. "Why?"

Although it had little to do with the real reason, Izzy said, "Mr. Rubin just thinks it would be best for everyone concerned, especially you, if Mr. Scarlotti there—his body, that is—were discovered."

Anthony shook his head. "Fuck that. He disappears." He gave the body another nudge with his toe. "You know how close I came to not even getting that piece of shit *here*? He tells me—we're driving by City Hall—all of a sudden the prick tells me he's gotta make a fucking stop." Anthony looked at Tommy Inzarella. "Tell him, Tommy."

Tommy sounded like he didn't give a shit. "Dominic wanted to get laid."

Anthony nodded. "That's right. So don't go telling me, I got to this, I got to do that, with the fucking body. I had enough shit convincing the motherfucker to take the fucking ride. I tell him," Anthony pointed at a stack of drywall leaning against the far wall, " 'Dominic, you gotta come see the repair work. Make sure it's what you want.' All he does, halfway here, he says, 'I gotta make a stop.' Apparently he's got some piece of ass stashed at the Sheraton over by Rittenhouse Square. He's got a helluva fucking set of balls, making me wait on what I planned out."

"Are you finished, Mr. Bonica?" Izzy didn't act mad or like he was arguing, because—dealing with this man's mentality—what was the point? "Mr. Rubin simply thinks it would be less confusing if Mr. Scarlotti's body turned up, say, in a few days. There'd be less speculation."

"Listen to me. What the fuck are you talking about? Dominic's body turns up, I got every cop in Philly up my ass."

Izzy shook his head. "Mr. Bonica, please. Originally the plan was for you to be out of town. I believe you mentioned Florida. Well, you didn't do that. Instead you insisted you wanted to be here. See it happen. But still, we both know you're relying on some sort of an alibi or none of this would have taken place. All I'm doing is relaying some information from my employer. He believes that Mr. Scarlotti's body should be found within a day or two. That way you avoid the confusion of people not knowing that Mr. Scarlotti is deceased. Do you understand?"

Anthony looked furious. "I understand I don't take orders from your boss. Fuck him and fuck you. That's the end of this fucking discussion." He jerked a thumb at the corpse. "I'm gonna put that *thing* in my car, drive over to New Jersey and bury him someplace in the fucking Pine Barrens. You? You should be thanking me for not making you do it."

Izzy was determined to remain polite. He'd been hired to do a job and he'd almost completed it. All he had to do was make sure Saul Rubin's wishes were taken care of. "Mr. Bonica, I can understand how, on other occasions with other people involved, that might be the prudent thing to do. Bury their body so you don't have to worry about the police ever finding it. But I don't think you're giving this the proper amount of thought." He didn't think Anthony ever gave *anything* the proper amount of thought, but they didn't have all night to discuss *that.*

Anthony laughed loudly. "Why the fuck do you talk like that?"

Izzy realized he'd rather be dealing with the remnants of the KGB, the Saudi Security Police, or even with political prisoners in the interrogation wing of the Governor's Building, Israel's high-security prison on the West Bank. At least people who ran those spots or ended up there could be original. He wondered just how long Little Anthony would last in one of *those* places.

He took a deep calming breath and said, "I beg your pardon?"

Anthony turned to Tommy. "Hey, you ever hear anyone, wasn't some kinda asshole on TV, talk like that?"

Tommy shrugged.

Anthony said to Izzy, "Like *that.* 'I beg your pardon.' You go to some fucking private school or something?"

Izzy pictured taking his Jericho back out so that he could put Anthony right there on the floor with his dead boss. He knew Saul would be disappointed, so he couldn't do it. Instead he said, "Why don't we keep our conversation to what's germane to our situation?"

"Are you fucking with me?"

"Absolutely not, Mr. Bonica." Izzy had to stifle a sigh. "I just want you to consider this: If Mr. Scarlotti simply disappears then what are people going to say? They're not going to know, is he on vacation somewhere? Maybe he's spending some time in that beautiful house he has down at the New Jersey shore, coming out at night to head up to Atlantic City to gamble at the casinos. They're not going to know who's in control."

"I'll *make* sure they know who the new boss is."

Tommy Inzarella said, "Anthony, he's got a point."

Anthony turned to stare at him. "Don't you fucking—"

Izzy interrupted. "If people aren't absolutely sure what happened to Mr. Scarlotti, ask yourself this: How are you going to convince everybody that *you* are the new head of the family? Try to understand, they won't even be asking themselves the question. You see? I'm saying, for your own sake, and to make things easier, his body *has* to be found. Not in any way that the police could tie it to you. No one wants that. But just so the people who need to know are left with no doubt that you are now in charge. Just like you said a moment ago. The new boss."

Anthony seemed to think about it, even rubbed the scar tissue around that lazy eye of his. Izzy wondered for just an instant, was Anthony actually going to see that there might be a whole other level to this that Izzy wasn't mentioning? The real reason Saul wanted Scarlotti's body found? But then Anthony smiled and Izzy could see that, once again, Saul had been right. Anthony Bonica couldn't see beyond his own vanity.

Anthony's expression brightened, and Izzy could picture him running the word over and over again in his head:

Boss.

Now Little Anthony was smiling. He said, "Fuck, Izzy, your boss wants the body to show up? All right, what do I care? I would be delighted to accommodate him. Abso-fucking-lutely. Tell Mr. Rubin not to worry. Tell him I got the perfect place to put Dominic. The *perfect* motherfucking place."

Little Anthony knelt to look at the corpse, still laughing. By the time he stood up, Izzy had slipped out of the place unnoticed.

TEDDY CLYDE'S FENCE, Johnny D, called him up to tell him that Davey-Boy, Teddy's younger brother, was in serious danger of screwing up their lives. Johnny D ran a chop shop out of the back end of his auto body shop in Northeast Philly during the off-hours, and his sixty-four-year-old voice had a Marlboro rasp on the other end of the phone.

"I get a call," he told Teddy, "this was ten minutes ago, your brother Davey-Boy saying he knows where a Porsche is and would I hang around a little while so he can steal it and bring it on over? I know it ain't exactly my fucking business 'cept for maybe on the off, *off* chance your brother actually shows up with an intact, drivable vehicle. But I thought you'd like to know what Davey's planning. He said not to tell you, it's supposed to be a surprise—which is the main reason why I'm calling. Plus which, he could get us both in a shitload of trouble."

Teddy didn't like surprises in his line of work. They never had a good ring to them and—if they involved his brother—never had a good anything to them. He thanked Johnny D, hung up the phone and decided he'd better go do something about it. He was wearing a Hard Rock Cafe T-shirt and jeans and he went into his bedroom to come up with what a Porsche owner would wear at this time of night. The closet was full of different types of clothes and accessories. Teddy's working attire ranged from business suits, tennis warm-up outfits and golf clothes to a beautifully hand-tooled leather brief-case that was full of file folders stuffed with important-looking documents and also had a false bottom where he stored every key made for whichever car he was going to boost next. There was even a set of golf clubs in the back of the closet—Pings—leaning lazily next to two Prince tennis rackets that Teddy had never done more with than carry around occasionally if he was going to cop a vehicle from somebody who spent a fair amount of time out at Merion or the Philadelphia Country Club. There were some serious automobiles in *those* parking lots. Teddy inventoried his closet every six months or so and added enough upscale outfits to keep up with whatever image he might need to portray and, hopefully, fool the odd cop who might stop to ask him some otherwise embarrassing questions.

Porsche . . . He put on a golf outfit—forest-green Polo shirt, khaki slacks and Cole Haan loafers with a nylon U.S. Open jacket to go over everything. He knew it was warm out, but it wasn't late enough in the spring to be too hot. A quick look in the mirror told him that he was looking at a fairly handsome, successful, mid-thirties, confident kind of guy. Brown hair that had just a touch of gray at the temples. Someone who could do business with you, smile at you the whole time, so that you might never figure out he was screwing you out of your money. He saw the embodiment of a guy who'd just hit a lazy eighteen holes. A six handicapper because that's how much time he had to play. But also, now, after presumably leaving his buddies at the nineteenth hole, he was going to go on out, hop in a Porsche—if Teddy could find Davey-Boy before it was too late, that is—and look like the fucking thing belonged to him. He already knew what Davey-Boy would wear, and that was why he was rushing just that little bit. Get to Davey and tell him he was way out of line before some squad car noticed that Davey didn't quite fit the image of the successful Boxter, 928, Turbo Carrera owner—or whatever model—he was looking to boost.

He was tempted to take a golf club with him, both to complete the outfit and also, depending on where Davey might have picked to steal the car, as a potential weapon if things went crazy. Maybe Davey would run into the owner of the car and the guy would turn out to be a linebacker for the Philadelphia Eagles. Teddy picked a nine iron out of the closet so he'd be able to wave it in the guy's face if the occasion came up. But at the last minute he left the club propped against the wall next to the front door of his apartment because he decided taking it along might jinx things.

Teddy Clyde had a few rules about his profession. The first went something like this: If you are going to steal something, act like it belongs to you in the first place, hence the closetful of different outfits. Another one: Always shave, keep your hair trimmed, and act like you graduated from Princeton University. Also, a huge one: Have another job. One just like the mopes who owned the cars he was boosting would have. Teddy had given it a lot of thought. He wasn't a doctor and he hadn't passed the bar exam. He didn't know shit about nuclear physics. But he had to come up with *something*. What kind of business was it that you could put a tie on, wear a nice suit to work and have people look at you in a respectable way?

After running that one around in his head for a few days, Teddy became a stockbroker. He had the looks. He could talk to people about their money with a Kevin Costner I'm-here-for-you-twenty-four-seven look on his face. And he knew enough to bullshit his way through the market until he found out more.

He rented an actual office out at Three Bala Plaza, right off City Line Avenue up from Route 76, the Schuylkill Expressway. Two floors above him was Salomon Smith Barney and Teddy hung around with a few of those guys, bought them drinks at a place called Sherri's out in Overbrook, a place that glistened with polished mahogany and the sound of brand-new money trying to act old. Teddy listened mostly to what the other brokers said after their third or fourth scotch, skipped the bullshit about their ski trips or who was banging their secretary. He put out four grand a month for the smallest space in the building and paid a good-looking call girl he knew to dress the part and go out there twice a week, sometimes three times, to pick up the mail, answer the phone and pay the bills.

He did actually have customers. Four of them. Little old ladies. A cliché, he knew, but they were easy to please, bought him presents at Christmas and remembered his birthday in ways that they thought were very sly. Teddy went with Exxon Mobil, Long Island Power & Light, General Motors—the heavy hitters—and stayed away from the techs.

But probably Teddy's number-one rule was this: Don't put your faith in the hands of anyone else. Not Johnny D—although they were friends of a sort and respected each other—and especially not your brother if he had the kind of record that Davey did. It wasn't personal. It was business. If you were going to go to the trouble of stealing something—if it was how you made your living—don't make the mistake of letting someone else, even your brother, decide what it was you were going to take. Teddy's was definitely a one-man operation, and he meant to keep it that way. Davey had made a big mistake tonight whether he realized it or not, and the people Teddy dealt with—who paid him a good wage—got frightened when amateurs appeared on the scene. Sooner or later, instead of taking hot items off Teddy's hands, they would find somebody else to do their work for them. Teddy averaged between three and four hundred grand a year boosting high-end Mercedeses, Porsches, Ferraris, Caddies, BMWs and Lincolns.

But it wasn't like he could apply for unemployment if he lost his job.

DAVEY'S APARTMENT was in a seedy neighborhood. Red brick buildings, shitty, poorly lit, roach-infested apartments surrounded by warehouses on three sides and low-end retail shops along the opposite street—two adult bookstores within sixty feet of each other. Teddy didn't have to look long. He found Davey-Boy, dressed like a half-assed Harley-Davidson freak, trying like crazy to steal a Porsche GT-2 no more than a half a block from where he lived. Teddy had to wonder, did Davey just happen to see the car that afternoon, decide to boost it right away? Or had he actually waited on the thing, at least developed *some* idea of the owner's habits? Did the guy live nearby, park it regularly and not usually come on out except for the next morning?

If it wasn't such a pain in the ass it might have been interesting. Teddy sat in his own car, a gleaming black Acura Legend, and watched his brother fuck everything up in a matter of minutes. He thought he knew *why* it was happening. Davey, out here on the street, trying his damndest to steal a car he probably didn't even know how to drive. For what? So that he could call

Teddy up, tell him what he had done to impress him. Ask Teddy could he just this one time be introduced to Johnny D in person? Teddy could picture Davey's face, eager, saying, "Come on, Teddy, introduce me. Maybe I can make it a regular thing. Make some money." Making Teddy regret the day, it had been almost a year ago, when he had let Johnny D's name slip into a conversation with Davey. It had been yet another time that he was trying to straighten Davey out about something but had only managed to get Davey's curiosity going: How was it that Davey-Boy could be more like his older brother? Hold on to a regular job even if it involved being a crook? Davey-Boy was intent on two things: improving his income and, as he put it, being as cool about it as Teddy. Teddy didn't know whether his work involved "cool" or not. It wasn't something he gave a lot of thought to because he'd long ago figured out that if you were going to steal high-end automobiles for a living it paid not to think about *anything* else while you were on the job. Teddy could understand Davey-Boy's point of view, but he wished his brother would stop. Stick to what he did and be happy with it because if Davey kept this kind of bullshit up, it was an odds-on bet that he would end up calling Teddy from jail before too long and probably bring Johnny D and Teddy down with him.

Teddy watched Davey pull something out from underneath his jacket. Davey seemed to struggle with whatever it was and Teddy finally realized it was a coat hanger. *A coat hanger!*

Davey stepped to the driver's door of the Porsche and began to work the hanger past the top of the driver's window. What did Davey think he was doing, stealing a Model T? A '77 Subaru?

Jesus Christ.

Johnny D and Teddy had a lot of years of working together behind them. Teddy stole extremely high-end automobiles because anything else wasn't worth the risk. Johnny D took them off his hands and paid Teddy ten percent on the retail dollar. It didn't sound like much, but when you added the fact that Teddy was a pro, could steal a car—once it was properly staked out—generally in under a minute, it was a fairly nice way to make a living. Except, unlike his brother, Teddy had been perfecting his art since he was fourteen, viewed it as an honest and honorable career, and disliked clothes hangers enough that he got nervous picking up his dry cleaning.

Davey-Boy, on the other hand, had always been a piece of work when it came to crime. The first time he'd been busted had been for shoplifting at a Woolworth's five-and-dime when he was seven. Davey had somehow managed to snag a goldfish out of one of the tanks they kept in the rear of the store near the hardware supplies, and had been mostly—and profoundly—surprised that the fish was dead by the time the store's security dick made him empty his pockets in the rear office of the store. It was the same summer that their old man had taken off with the semipro hooker, leaving not only a bitterness in his mother's soul that she had tried to drink away, but a serious inferiority complex in Davey's mind. Teddy had entertained the idea of beating the crap out of Davey for the fish thing but had cut him a break because of what their dad had done. It was a thing he'd been doing ever since, rescuing Davey every few months, thinking, each time, should he give it up? Leave Davey to his own devices? But every time the thought came up he knew he couldn't, because it was exactly what their old man had done and that had started the whole thing. Teddy figured it was a thing he had to keep on doing, some kind of penance so that he wouldn't get carried away with the idea that *his* life was going fairly well.

The problem was genetics. The luck of the chromosomal draw. That plus a lousier upbringing than Teddy had gone through because their mom had been emotionally up a wall, reeling with the impact of their old man's deception. Davey simply couldn't do too many things very well. It was a shame but it was also too bad that it didn't stop him from trying. Like tonight, out here on a Thursday night attempting to steal a car that, even if he pulled it off—somehow managed to get it to Johnny D's chop shop—he wouldn't get the time of day out of Johnny. Johnny D only dealt with a few tried and trusted people, Teddy being one of them. Johnny D didn't give a fuck about too many things or too many people, but he had cared enough to call Teddy and tell him what was happening.

THE GT-2, a convertible, was sitting at the curb near the corner of Cypress and Seventh Streets. If Teddy got out of his Acura and walked a hundred feet to his left, he could look down Seventh and see the Tomb of the Unknown Soldier. More important, the precinct house for the Sixth District, Philadelphia Police, was only nine blocks over at 235 North Eleventh Street. Teddy wondered if his brother even knew that one.

Davey-Boy wore leather jackets even when it was hot out. He tried never to complete a full sentence that didn't have the word *fuck* in it. He'd bought himself a Macintosh computer and made a half-assed living buying controlled-substance drugs—Class II pharmaceuticals—over the Internet from doctors who knew a quick buck when someone threw it at them and were willing to perform online "consultations" and dispense anything from Xanax to Vicodin. Davey doctor-shopped, told everybody he had a bad back and was stressed out, and timed everything so that he had a steady stream of pills coming in. He dropped important people's names to his customers like he was spastic. If you read the papers you knew who he was talking about— Tommy Inzarella, Dominic Scarlotti. Davey could be dumb but he was no fool. It protected him from getting ripped off because what if he *was* connected to Anthony Bonica, one of those guys? Teddy had told him often enough that the whole thing could land him in prison, or worse, and why didn't he give it a ride.

Then again, it was better than Davey getting into the preowned automobile business.

To keep himself from driving away, Teddy had to think about their mother.

He tried to picture her long before she had died. Familiar but just a little bit old-looking. Run-down from working hard her entire life and trying to be attractive way past the age when she was any good at it. Then he thought about her on her deathbed, the ravages of her life and the cancer itself having eaten away at her features until Teddy had trouble looking at her, just like he had trouble remembering to breathe in through his mouth, suck on the peppermint Lifesaver he always took with him because the smell of her dying was that bad. And the last night, the night she died, her grabbing his jacket, pulling him down so that he could hear her finally, the whisper at his ear as loud as she could and interrupted every three seconds by a wracking cough. But there was a deadly seriousness to her eyes. Pinning him there while she made him promise—hell or high water—to look after Davey-Boy. Neither one of them had to go into it more than that—they both knew Davey was a frog, leaped from one mud hole to the next and was going to land in real trouble eventually.

Teddy had come up with as much as he could, telling her, "I'll try, Mom. I really will. See if I can get him to find some kind of direction." At the time Teddy hadn't believed it. His brother had caused a shitload of trouble already and Teddy didn't think their mom dying or much of anything else was going to change him. But maybe it didn't matter because by the time he had finished promising his mother she was unconscious again. She died three hours later, never saying another word and Teddy had tried, off and on, to live up to his promise. But, lord, sometimes it got old.

From where he sat, Teddy could see that Davey-Boy had a look on his face like he had swallowed something the wrong way. A Michael Jordan way of sticking his tongue out as he tried to work the coat hanger past the rubber grommet of the window. He was having no success whatsoever. Davey paused while a young couple walking hand in hand down the street toward the Porsche took one look at him, crossed the street and picked up their pace. As soon as they turned the corner, Davey went back to work on the car. Three seconds later the car's alarm blasted into the night.

Teddy had just enough time to hope that his brother hadn't brought one of his goddamn guns with him—he certainly didn't want to get shot by a skit-

tish Davey just because it was suddenly noisy as hell and Davey was panick-
ing and might just mistake him for a cop.

Teddy climbed out of his Acura and stepped to his trunk, finding the ring
that had his sixteen different Porsche keys on it. He walked the fifty feet to
where Davey stood, seemingly paralyzed on the pavement, five feet away
from the blasting sound of the sports car with a look on his face like he just
done number two in his underwear.

When Davey saw Teddy he jumped, said, "Holy shit," and looked like he
was going to go into a long explanation. Teddy ignored him while he found
which key worked this particular Porsche, opened the door, popped the
hood and then ripped the wire out of the alarm horn.

In the deafening silence that followed, he turned to his brother. Davey
had the same younger-brother-fucked-up look on his face that he'd had for
most of his life. Davey said, "I was only going to—"

Teddy reached out, touched his shoulder and then squeezed just hard
enough to make sure he had Davey's attention. "Why don't you close your
mouth so we can get the fuck out of here, talk about your sudden career
change later."

Davey pulled his arm free and said angrily, "I was only trying to show you
that—" He shut up again when a siren sounded in the faraway distance, getting louder by the second. Davey went bug-eyed and Teddy had to speak
sharply to keep his attention.

Teddy said, "Davey, let me ask you something. Which side are you on?"

"What? The fuck you mean, which side am I on?"

"I mean this. You've been standing by this car going on fifteen minutes
now." Teddy pointed back to where his Acura sat. "I've been sitting there
watching you. *Fifteen* minutes. Easily. And you're *still* on the outside of the
goddamn car, trying to get in. Only reason the alarm stopped wailing is
'cause I yanked the wire. Fifteen fucking minutes. In that amount of time
you should've had the fucking thing to the chop shop. Johnny D would be
halfway done putting a new VIN number on it."

Davey looked at the car. "I was thirty seconds away, man. A minute, max."

Teddy took the coat hanger out of Davey's right hand and said, "With this? Jesus." Teddy had the cops about forty seconds away. He took a quick glance at the Porsche. Pure black and looking like a Stealth fighter except that the Porsche gleamed like a neon light. Sleek lines and three inches of road clearance. A tiny scrape on the front bumper, white paint on the black that Johnny D would fix in five minutes. Worth easily—depending on how far the guy had gone with aftermarket add-ons, a beefed-up sound system, tires, wheels—in the neighborhood of a hundred and ninety grand. If Teddy was working, had been contracted out by Johnny D to go get this specific car, not only would the thing be long gone by now but Teddy would be putting ten percent of that back-end price in his pocket. Nineteen large.

He said, "Listen close, 'cause here's what I'm gonna do. We're going to forget this ever happened. I'm going to take you over to Palisades and buy you a drink. I told you sometime I'd go there with you and now's the time."

Davey scuffed one shoe on the pavement and turned away from Teddy to say, "You don't got to take me anywhere."

Teddy said, "The fuck I don't. You hear that?" pointing to where the sirens were getting louder. "We got maybe ten, twenty seconds. So do what I say. Stop whining and stop thinking. We make a quick stop and then you and I head over to that topless bar, have a couple of cocktails and maybe try to figure out which one's have had their boobs redone. But—you understand me—we got to do it *now*."

Davey said, "What do you mean, 'a quick stop'?"

And now Teddy made himself grin, sensing the exact amount of time he had before the squad car came squealing around the corner. He punched Davey-Boy lightly on the shoulders to show that there were no hard feelings and said, "Well, hell, kiddo, you found the thing," nodding at the GT-2, "so what the fuck, it's not like we're going to leave it sitting here, now is it?"

He had to wait for Davey-Boy to brighten up and begin to nod his head like one of those fake dogs people put on the back shelves of their cars, only faster, saying back, "Fucking-A, Teddy."

Teddy wanted to leave it there. He knew it wasn't any use, but still, he couldn't help himself. He opened the door of the Porsche—gonna drive it over to Johnny D's, explain to Johnny that Davey was going to have a memory loss. Forget his phone number and never bother Johnny again. Then Teddy was going to do like he said. Take Davey over to the topless club and buy him a drink or two. Let him stare at the dancers and dream impossible dreams. Within a couple of hours, maybe less, the whole thing could be filed away and Teddy could head on back to his apartment, get some sleep, which was what he'd originally wanted to do before all this bullshit went down.

He could've stopped it right there, but he didn't. He paused just short of climbing into the Porsche, waited just long enough for Davey to look into his eyes one more time. Then he said, "I have to tell you, watching out for you all these years—sometimes it's an ordeal."

The cop pulled up three seconds later, eyeballing Teddy carefully, but then rolling his window down without too much suspicion on his face. Teddy waited until the cop was even with the Porsche and then got a relieved expression on his face. "Officer, thank God," he said, pointing at a tall building on the next block. "I heard screams and then I saw two black guys. They came out of that building, down on that next block. Running in the other direction. I'm not sure, Officer, but the reason I called, I believe they had some kind of weapons on them."

The cop yelled his thanks and squealed away. By the time his car had squealed to a stop outside the building Teddy had pointed at, Teddy was on his way out of there—steering the Porsche around the corner onto the cross street while Davey followed in Teddy's Acura.

Teddy was thinking he could've stayed mad at Davey-Boy, but what was the point? A Porsche was a Porsche was a Porsche—even if it wasn't one that had been carefully selected for a transfer of ownership. He was going to take a lot of shit from Johnny D for allowing Davey to get involved. Probably take a fifty percent cut in pay for the complications. And he was going to have to ride Davey's ass to make sure it never happened again.

But as he had told Davey, it wasn't like he was going to leave the fucking thing sitting there.

THE SHERATON RITTENHOUSE was across the block from its major competitor, the Rittenhouse Hotel. The Sheraton had a nice view—you could look over City Hall and see the Delaware River, watch planes take off from Philly International if you wanted, or stare down at a thousand pedestrians as they bumped into each other every third step. The Sheraton had one hundred ninety-three rooms, was rated four stars, was two blocks from the biggest shopping district in the area and five blocks from the Theater District.

Donald Shaffer didn't give a shit about any of that. Shaffer was a runt—five-six, one hundred thirty-one pounds—with thinning hair that he touched, on average, every thirty seconds. He had suspenders, red, holding up Armani pants, fine Italian wool, a custom-made shirt, and a forty-five-caliber, big-assed automatic in a shoulder holster over it. His sleeves were rolled up. He was looking at his watch, a Rolex, turned so that the face was on the inside of his left wrist. The thing had run him seven grand and he was watching how it kept sliding down his arm. He could see a line of whiter skin from a tan he'd gotten down in the Bahamas two weeks previously, but he wasn't thinking about that. He was wondering, it was nine o'clock on the nose, where the fuck was he?

Dominic Scarlotti.

Shaffer was an assistant United States attorney, Federal Organized Crime Strike Force, Criminal Division, out of the United States Attorney's Office, Eastern District of Pennsylvania. He worked out of the Federal Building, 615 Chestnut Street, Philadelphia.

To him, the word *assistant* had a bad ring to it and was just a bullshit way to say that other people controlled what you did. Pissed on your ambitions. He was a thin man, clean-shaven and impeccably dressed, who pursued women with unbridled passion because he hadn't gone through puberty until he was nineteen and hated the fact that he was smaller than ninety-four percent of all the other men on the planet. He had taken some abuse about it growing up, and now he liked dating women one at a time, getting them to the point where they were expecting, what—a ring—and then telling them to go fuck themselves.

He'd been born and raised in an affluent suburb of Detroit, gone to private schools because his old man was a VP at Ford Motor Company and then graduated with honors from Villanova Law. He had juice inside the Justice Department, an uncle who was a federal appellate judge. It was an easy choice, the department had just expanded its Organized Crime program—ROC, the Russians nudging the Italians aside, and Asian criminal activity, AOC. Shaffer didn't know shit about Russians, couldn't tell one fucking Asian from another. He also believed there were enough Italians in America without worrying about what the ones in the old country were up to, the Sicilians and the 'Ndrangheta. So he stepped up to bat with a hard-on for the Philly mob.

Shaffer looked at his Rolex again, knowing that somebody was getting screwed. He was coming off a roll, spending the last six months prosecuting a Philadelphia city councilman—out of Kensington, Northeast Philly—who was tied in with a *capo* in the Scarlotti crime family *and* a prominent Philly attorney, all of whom were involved in a scheme to sell votes on zoning variances to two New Jersey land developers of more than questionable reputation. But this shit? Tonight? It could fuck it all up in a heartbeat.

He was staring out the window, not even seeing the view. People paid serious money to rent these rooms. What for? To watch the pigeons shit on William Penn? He knew who was behind him, two FBI agents, three guys from the Philly police's Organized Crime Task Force and two tough-looking guys, a black guy in his mid-twenties and a white guy in his forties. The guy in his forties stood out because he didn't know shit about how to dress. The two men were U.S. marshals. They were the only ones, especially the older one, who looked like they'd spent any time meeting criminals in their own element. Hell, turning, seeing acne scars on the older one's skin, a nose that'd been broken half a dozen times, boxer-looking ears, nothing in his eyes to say was he smart or not—but doubtful. Shaffer thought they both looked like they were looking to mug someone. The older one stupid with his off-the-rack Sears menswear.

When Dominic Scarlotti had entered the penthouse, Shaffer walked to the center of the room with a vicious smile on his face, glanced at his watch, waited, glanced again for effect and said, "Mis-ter Scar-lot-ti, you—are—fucking—*late*." He didn't say another word until the FBI tech, a little piss who didn't even have whiskers yet, had explained twice to Scarlotti how the gadget they were giving him worked. As soon as that was done Shaffer cleared his throat and timed it perfectly—knowing that everybody, even the leather-looking marshal, was watching. He stepped over to get face-to-face with Scarlotti. Stared into his eyes so the mobster couldn't miss the contempt and said, "Listen carefully, you greaseball pig. This agreement depends *entirely* on how much you fucking cooperate. That, and on whether *I* decide to let it happen." Shaffer pointed at the door. "You got your buddies, Anthony Bonica and Tommy Inzarella, they're waiting outside thinking you're getting fucked up here? Getting fucked is what'll happen if you *don't* do what you said you would."

Without wasting another second on Scarlotti, Shaffer turned to the FBI guys standing right there, the tech and another young one, mid-twenties, both wide-eyed at what they were seeing. What did they think, he was going to treat Scarlotti with respect? He said, without ever looking back at Scarlotti, "Get this piece of shit out of my sight."

Dominic Scarlotti controlled or had a hand in every single racket in Philadelphia and most of what went on out in the surrounding suburbs, let-

ting Anthony Bonica, his right hand, do most of the work. Dominic was getting to the point where he enjoyed his leisure time. He had a condo, top
floor, in a new high-rise overlooking the art museum in Center City. He had
a Bryn Mawr mansion, fifteen acres of prime real estate in the heart of the
Main Line, where his wife puttered around growing roses and didn't have a
clue—honest to God, he's a respected businessman—what Dominic did for a
living until she remembered that her father and two uncles were connected
and she had a cousin who was doing twenty-five to life in Atlanta Federal
Penitentiary for aggravated assault, involuntary manslaughter and robbery
while carrying a weapon. She thought her cousin was a nice guy who had
been railroaded by the system.

Mrs. Scarlotti saw her husband a couple of times a year, Christmas,
occasionally some wedding, or else—if she bitched enough—they'd meet
face-to-face so Dominic could give her large sums of money to buy more
rose fertilizer and keep her mouth shut for a while longer. She didn't have to
worry about putting out for any man anymore, which she enjoyed because it
had never been much fun to begin with.

Dominic also owned a beach house in New Jersey. A three-story Vic-
torian surrounded by a wide veranda and round white pillars. A miniature White House that dwarfed the other houses it neighbored that were
owned by respectable people: doctors, lawyers and high-ranking corporate
VPs who all thought the Jersey shore was the place to be, let their kids run
around at all hours and who went up to the casinos occasionally to gamble
but stayed the hell away from Wildwood because that's where the riffraff
hung out.

If Dominic Scarlotti wanted something done, it got done. Or if someone else did something and Dominic wanted a piece, he got it. Anything. A
sixteen-year-old kid wanted to buy half an ounce of pot at his high school
or a working-class mope wanted to place a bet on the Eagles game, maybe
somebody wanted to bang a prostitute or join a union—you paid the street tax
and Dominic got his cut. Period.

Dominic laundered his money in several quasi-legitimate businesses: a cement contracting company and a roofing company, waiting on sealed bids and bringing in a quote that was a hell of a lot lower. Afterward he used shit materials, union slowdowns and in-progress construction problems to skyrocket the budget. Paid the architects to get colds and miss work, paid off the city inspectors—fucking vultures, they wanted a raise every fucking year.

He had half ownership with his brother-in-law in a series of franchised retail shops that sold flowers, greeting cards, incense and every other kind of romantic bullshit conceivable. The flower-slash-incense shops were located in just about every mall within eighty miles of Philadelphia.

Donald Shaffer had watched Scarlotti walk back out the door of the Sheraton Rittenhouse three hours ago. A defeated old man. Fuck him. All Shaffer wanted was to put the whole bunch of them behind bars.

If the piece of shit ever came back.

GEORGE ABBOT thought that quite possibly Donald Shaffer, the federal prosecutor, was going to have a heart attack. He didn't give a shit if Shaffer did, except that George would have to help carry the body out.

George Abbot had eighteen and a half years' experience as a federal marshal—Witness Protection. He was due to retire on full pension in eighteen months. Meanwhile, he worked people like Dominic Scarlotti. Got them new identities, listened to them whine and made sure that they got to, and testified at, all the trials they were supposed to. Made sure they didn't disappear on their own or because some of their best friends found it insulting that they were going to jail because some motherfucker was going to rat *their* asses out to save their own. Dominic Scarlotti was just like all the others—a piece of shit, a small-time hoodlum turned big-time hoodlum who had risen through the ranks of Philadelphia's mob by whacking whoever he was told to whack and who was now in a position where he told other people who to kill. His feet were in the fire—the feds were coming down on him with a RICO indictment that was gonna fry him and he had made a deal, gonna dime out everybody else he'd ever met in order to keep his ass out of jail. Afterward he was going to live in some nondescript suburb just outside Nashville. George couldn't wait to see how *that* worked out.

George didn't care how it played out one way or another as long as none of it reflected on him. If Scarlotti made a run for it, or if someone came after him, he'd kill whoever was involved. Not lose a night's sleep because it would be the righteous thing to do.

He didn't care much for Donald Shaffer either. He didn't like prosecutors much to begin with, but Shaffer was a piece of work. He had taken his jacket off first thing—suspenders, for Christ's sake—and rolled up his sleeves so that each arm matched perfectly. He had a college ring on his right hand and was wearing a Colt .45 in a holster under his armpit. George wondered, Who the hell was he thinking of shooting, one of the bellboys?

Shaffer was pacing up and down between the front door of the penthouse and the wide window that overlooked the Schuylkill River, every once in a while stopping at the window and staring out. Making a production out of how pissed off he was. He stopped to stare out the window one last time and then turned to address everyone in the room simultaneously. "That son of a bitch—that fuck," glancing at his watch, "he thinks he can play games with me?" He went back to pacing, occasionally glancing at his watch and, every once in a while, reaching down to finger the butt of the pistol.

George watched Shaffer say the same words again, "Son of a bitch." Wondering, who the fuck, exactly, was he talking to? Shaffer stomped over to the middle of the room to glare at the FBI agents, who were standing as far away as possible, and said, "Who the fuck thought it would be okay to let that scumbag go out there without tracking him?"

The FBI agents were young, looking at most of their careers still in front of them, so they didn't answer. George was almost out of the gig so he walked over to Shaffer and said, quietly, "It was *your* idea, you simple prick. Quit trying to lay it off on anyone else." He pointed back at the FBI agents and said, "They're young and scared enough about their careers to sit here and take it. But I'm tired of your bullshit."

Shaffer's eyes opened wide. He looked for an instant as if he was going to go for his gun but George just stared hard at his eyes and Shaffer's hand went past his shoulder to land somewhere down around his waist, make it seem like Shaffer had meant to scratch his tummy all along. They both knew—and it probably pissed Shaffer off as much as what George had said—that if Shaffer *did* pull his gun, George would take it away and beat the son of a bitch to death with it.

He said, "You're walking back and forth, wondering, Is Scarlotti playing some kind of game?"

Shaffer's hand came off his stomach. He got some kind of flare to his nostrils, the WASP in him coming through fairly strongly.

George shrugged. "Instead of that—instead of walking back and forth, acting like this is some kind of movie—you're Alec Baldwin and Dominic Scarlotti is an upstart who got his lines wrong—why don't you do this? Why don't you figure out how we're gonna find Scarlotti's body and is that stupid fucking device you gave him going to be there when, and *if*, we do? 'Cause I guarantee you, the only reason he's not back by now is 'cause he is fucking *dead*."

2

TEDDY ORDERED an Absolut on ice from a cute-as-pie blond waitress in a skimpy outfit, told Davey that he was lucky he got two grand out of the Porsche deal, so why didn't he stop bitching and looked around the club. It was called Palisades and was referred to as a gentlemen's club, which meant it was nothing more than a glorified titty-bar.

Davey said, "Two grand. Jesus. Teddy, do you know how much that thing is—"

Teddy gave him a look, the same one he'd been giving him on and off for the last thirty or so years, and Davey shut his mouth. But it looked like he was grinding his teeth, the way his jaw was clamped. When his first drink came he gulped half of it down and told the waitress to bring him another before she even had a chance to give Teddy his.

The place was owned by Anthony Bonica. Teddy had grown up in the same neighborhood as Anthony, and they didn't like each other at all. Teddy had busted Anthony's nose when they were in grade school. When they were teenagers they'd gone at it again. It had been a nasty little street fight with biting, gouging and kicking at each other's crotches—anything to keep from going down. Teddy had ended it finally by hitting Anthony hard enough in the eye to fuck it up for life. Anthony Bonica hated Teddy in a way that a man hated another man who was banging a former girlfriend. It amused Teddy to go into the club, force Anthony to be polite to him when he knew what Anthony really wanted—minimum—was to have one of his bouncers throw him through the front door without bothering to open it first. Teddy knew all the bartenders well enough from being a good tipper that he could count on them pouring a better drink than Little Anthony would normally let them. The dancers were pros. You couldn't get them near a bed without paying for it, but most of them looked like they had just walked off the pages of *Playboy* and they danced their fannies off, so it wasn't hard to come in just to look at them.

TEDDY HAD DROPPED the Porsche with Johnny D, told him they'd discuss the whole thing tomorrow and that it wouldn't happen again, fronted Davey the two grand out of his own pocket and then driven over to the club. He pulled his Acura Legend into the back lot of Palisades, seeing that there was a space open near the rear entrance. Maneuvering his car into it just as Davey-Boy said, "Jesus!" because the driver's-side door of the car parked to his right was swinging open and Teddy's car was going to clip it.

Davey said "Jesus" again, but with a different tone in his voice now that Teddy had stopped the car. A leg—long, thin, but with good muscle definition— followed by an upper thigh and then a little bit of a skirt, was emerging from the Toyota. A moment later a woman was standing next to Teddy's right front fender. She was backlit, a movie star at a premiere, with a lot of contempt on her otherwise beautiful face, turning slowly to push her car door shut and then redoing the whole thing. Gazing back at the fender of Teddy's Acura with the look still on her face.

Teddy was wondering—why the extreme look? Everyone should just get out of their cars, smile and say, Hey, wasn't that a close one? You all right? Sure, I'm fine. You? And then they could all head into the club. Maybe have a drink together. Get married eventually.

But that wasn't going to happen. Not with the expression on the woman's face and not with the way she suddenly turned away from Teddy's car and sauntered—it was the only word that popped into Teddy's head as he watched her in the rearview mirror—toward the back entrance of the club and disappeared inside.

Davey-Boy let out a deep breath, "Jesus fucking Christ, you see the ass on her?" He turned to look at Teddy because Teddy was still looking in the rearview mirror, thinking, and wasn't paying attention.

Davey-Boy said, "C'mon, Teddy. Tell me. Am I fucking crazy or was that the nicest ass I've seen in a year?"

Teddy took his time about answering, trying to get a grip on something that was running across the back of his mind. He finally said, "Yeah, nice ass." Thinking a little more and adding, for his own benefit, "Personality, too."

Davey-Boy got out of the car and smoothed his jacket and the slacks he was wearing, checking his reflection in the window of Teddy's Acura. Teddy was *still* thinking about the woman. Coming up with it finally, what it was that had been bothering him ever since she had glared at his car. The interesting thing was, it had nothing to do with the fact that she had acted like a bitch.

What *was* bothering Teddy was that he knew for a fact that he had seen her before.

He just couldn't figure out where.

PALISADES WAS a nice place to go if you wanted to unwind, place a discreet bet or just stare at some good-looking girls who were wearing nothing more than thongs, four-inch hooker heels and, occasionally, long gloves or thigh-high boots. The place had a long dark bar, six wide-screen TVs, and forty tables set up around two dance stages, disco lighting above each one. The women took turns dancing to disco, rap and top forties and hardly anybody ever watched the televisions.

A half-hour after Teddy and Davey-Boy sat down Little Anthony Bonica swaggered into the club. Tommy Inzarella was a step behind him and Davey-Boy turned off of Teddy's expression to gaze at Anthony in awe. Every other person in the room who knew anything about the streets looked at the two men also. The crowd was half men who were in no real hurry to get home to the suburbs, a weekend of Little League, soccer practice and women who they'd been married to for a couple of decades. But bunched around the place were other types of guys, either mob-connected or on the fringe, hoping to get Little Anthony's attention—speak to him or at least get noticed by him. Take Davey-Boy. Straightening up in his seat as Anthony walked past the main dance stage where the girls moved in their sequined G-strings, heading toward the back of the club where there was always a section of four tables left permanently unoccupied.

Teddy thought it was a waste of time.

From fifteen feet away Anthony eyeballed Teddy. A little hate there, a quick flick of the eyelids which lasted just long enough for Davey-Boy to stand up and say, "Mr. Bonica, sir, ah, a pleasure to see you." Teddy and Tommy Inzarella looked at Davey. Teddy believed that he and Tommy were probably thinking the same thing—how fucking dumb could one person be?

Anthony left Davey-Boy with his right arm extended into thin air while Davey made it worse by saying, "Hey, Tony," which no one ever called Anthony, "that is a nice fucking jacket."

Anthony looked at Teddy but said to Davey, "Sit down, you stupid fuck." Davey sat down and looked hopelessly at the table like he couldn't remember where his drink had gone. Teddy made a point of taking a slow sip of his vodka, watching Anthony work a fake smile onto his face.

He said, "So, Teddy, if I asked you, could you replace my Cadillac for a brand-new model, is that something you could do? Seeing as how you're still boosting cars for a living like most people stopped doing when they were fifteen fucking years old."

Teddy grinned, everybody friends, "Anthony, you know me. I'm a stock-broker. I have an office out in Bala Cynwyd. I don't know what to tell you about your Cadillac, but you want to make some investments, build up a portfolio, why don't you give me a call?"

"Right, right—I forgot. You're a fucking stockbroker. All that other shit. Chopping up fancy cars. That's been over with for years. And Johnny D? He's just one of your broker buddies. Works for fucking Prudential. Absolutely. I fucking forgot. And you know what? I *am* gonna give you a call. Definitely." His expression went weird for an instant and then the smile was back in place. He rapped his knuckles on Teddy's table and said, "You have a good one, huh?"

"Hey, you too." Teddy took another sip of his Absolut and watched Anthony turn away. Tommy Inzarella took Anthony by the elbow, something Teddy had never seen him do, and guided him farther back into the club.

Teddy turned to Davey-Boy and asked, "Seriously, you're one for one in the fuck-up department already tonight, so you want to explain why you always do shit like that? That man's got nothing to offer you that you could handle and you do not—repeat, *not,* want to get mixed up with him in the first place."

"Hey, you never know. Maybe, what if, say he's got a bookmaking oper-ation. Somebody retires. They fucking die, I don't know. Maybe a small one—Anthony needs somebody to run it."

Teddy stared at him for a long moment and then said, "I just saved your ass from possibly screwing up a car theft and you're going to start *this* shit?" But he didn't get a chance to say anything else, because a shadow fell over their table and when he looked up, instead of seeing the nice-looking, sweet-as-pie blond waitress who had served them their first round of drinks, he was looking directly into the eyes of the woman with the Toyota who had given them a pretty good dirty look out in the back parking lot. Now she had a little heart-shaped name tag over her left breast that said "Valerie" on it and had put four-inch heels on her feet.

She had nice hair, highlighted brown, swept back around her shoulders in an expensive cut. She was dressed in the same tiny black skirt but had taken her jacket off, and was now wearing a nylon blouse, silky—the blouse playing tricks, one minute you could see her bra, a demi-cup, black, and the next minute it was hard to tell. Where did one end and the other begin? The light bouncing thinly off a gold necklace added a nice touch. A classy hooker's look, but nicely done. Was she or wasn't she? You could talk to her in a club, think you were in and at the last minute she'd lean forward, whisper in your ear how much it was going to be. But he didn't think so. Teddy saw her as a catalogue model. With a runway walk. Barrie Pace. Lew Magram. No, wait, Victoria's Secret. But not Frederick's. Staring into the lens with what? Desire. A woman guys dream about. Added to—the thong and garter belt on page thirty-two, the sheer skirt on page sixty, a chain-link gold belt. She puts the whole outfit on and then says, Where are we going? Guy ends up torn, looking at her and thinking, Huh? Because what he had in mind was for her to take the whole thing off, one bit at a time, and if he did go out the door with her he knew the first guy they ran into was gonna try to take her away.

She was working now, that was for sure. A plastic smile. Cheerful. "Hey, guys, Friday night, huh?" Looking at them like that incident out back had never taken place, maybe she really didn't remember, and asking, nicely, would they care for another.

It was right then that Teddy remembered where he had seen her before.

After she left, Teddy glanced at his watch, ten-fifteen, and told Davey-Boy to stay put, he had to take a leak. He wound his way through the closely packed tables, past the stage where a light-skinned black woman was dancing next to a blond with a chest so big it was hard to figure out how she stayed upright. Maybe the fact that she had glazed eyes and seemed lost in the music helped. He turned left just before the front door, walked by the service area, got a peek at Valerie-the-waitress waiting for the bartender to fill her drink order and then walked past the rest rooms and into the kitchen.

He ignored the looks he got from the cooks, the busboys and a couple of other waitresses and stepped through the employee's-only exit. By the back of his Acura he opened his trunk, checked once to make sure nobody was looking, walked ten feet, slim-jimmed the waitress's Toyota and took the coil wire off her distributor cap.

AT ELEVEN-TEN their waitress finally had enough of Davey-Boy's bullshit. He'd been jiving with her for the last hour, going out of his way not to hide the way he was peeking directly at her, commenting about her rear end like she was one of the dancers up on the stage and he had the right to reach right up her skirt and stick a five-dollar bill in the G-string. Somewhere along the line Teddy made a bet with himself that she was going to unload on him within the next thirty minutes. It didn't take half that long.

She was bringing them another round of drinks and some kind of salsa cheese dish with crackers when Davey reached up, touched one of her breasts with his index finger and tried out a half-drunk Southern drawl, "Seriously, sugar, these thangs, they'all real? They're small. I gotta say that, but still, they look perfect enough that I think y'all been to the doctor recently." He grinned like a lunatic and asked, "Am I right, sugar?"

Teddy admired the way she dealt with it. Some kind of poise that he didn't know she had because it wasn't the bitchiness he'd seen in the parking lot earlier. Coming from some other part of her, the part that had nothing to do with waiting tables dressed like a hooker or as a high-class catalogue model—stepping out of Davey's range, the drink tray going down hard on the table without her ever taking her eyes off of Davey, who didn't even know yet that he had gone too far.

Their waitress leaned over, grabbed his little finger, no expression on her face but boredom—Teddy knew guys who would've liked to be able to be that cool about it—and bent it backward. Hard. Davey said, "Whatthefuck—" once again, as far as he got, the good-looking waitress stopping him again, right there, leaning down—anyone at a nearby table would have thought she was being polite, trying to please—wouldn't've heard her hiss, "What's the matter, when you were younger, your mother, she didn't let you play with *hers* enough?"

Teddy thought that she might've thrown her tray at Davey-Boy. Called the bouncer over after. But this was better. He made a note to himself, she was a tough enough one. Looking at her right now, the vein in her neck standing out a little more than before Davey-Boy had touched her breast— maybe she was bending Davey's finger a little more—but other than that not giving up much of herself at all.

She dropped Davey's hand like it was contaminated. "You want to make a complaint?" pointing over to where Anthony Bonica and Tommy Inzarella were huddled at the back table. "I can go tell those two, have them stop by to ask you what the problem is."

Davey was shaking his head now, looking at the ceiling, the floor, back to the ceiling, "No. No. I waz kiddin', is all." The scotch in him talking, while the waitress made a point of looking up at the ceiling too, not willing to let Davey get away with anything. Bringing her gaze back to the table to say, "I didn't think so."

She looked at Teddy, the same sour expression on her face. What was he supposed to do, grab her other boob? She plunked Teddy's Absolut in front of him, locking eyes, "And how about you? You have anything you'd like to talk to me about? Maybe you want to see what color undies I have on?"

Teddy acted like a guy who had to think about it, let her think he might be horny and dumb enough to give it a try. He threw a little embarrassment in there, too. Frustration. Was he mad that Davey had done it because now he probably couldn't? Let her sort it out. Waiting. And then looking her right in the eye, catching her off guard by giving her what he knew was his most pleasant smile. Saying "Excuse me" pleasantly, a Boy Scout looking to do a good deed. "What I was wondering"—he pointed at his vodka—"do you think it would be possible to get another slice of lime here? Would that be a problem?"

Jay Leno started his monologue on one of the TVs over the bar, and Teddy told Davey-Boy to get a cab and call it a night. Davey looked at him in surprise, eyes glazed, not doing very well talking. Not even noticing Little Anthony and Tommy Inzarella breeze past their table headed toward the front entrance, because he was having trouble with the words "Waitamini—afucking waitaminute—whathafuckyou, shit, talking 'bout?"

Teddy said, "What?"

"Me—a cab? Thefuck—shit—thefuckyoutalkingabout?

"What does it sound like I'm talking about? Unless you want to walk home. You could do that, your head might feel better tomorrow. Otherwise I'm telling you to call a cab. I have some business to take care of."

Davey-Boy looked bewildered until he followed Teddy's gaze. Teddy was purposefully staring at one of the dancers on the stage, a brunette with beautiful legs and a cocaine smile. Davey-Boy squinted hard, saw legs moving, a bare ass. He tried smiling, looked ill, and said, "Allyouhadtodowastellme."

Teddy said, "Uh-huh?" He pulled out his cell phone. "You want to use this or you want to head outside, see if any taxis are waiting around?"

When Davey stumbled away, Teddy asked his waitress, nicely, would she mind getting him a change of drinks when she had a moment; he was done drinking vodka for the night. She gave him a look, maybe waiting for something else to come out of his mouth, but he just smiled and looked away. She came back a minute later and he acted like he didn't even know she was there, keeping his eyes on the dancers, but thinking, meanwhile, where was he going to go with this? It would come to him; he was fairly sure of that.

He settled down to wait. He had a mug of coffee now, which would perk him up. He had ice water, which felt good going down his throat because that's how hot it had been earlier. He didn't have anything else he had to accomplish tonight. So he could kill the next hour and forty-five minutes watching one woman after another get up onstage and take off everything but her underwear.

It sounded inspiring.

————

THEIR WAITRESS SAW Davey-Boy leave and thought that the other man was going to follow, but he didn't. Instead he caught her attention and asked her politely if he could get a cup of coffee and a glass of water—a weird combination for a place like Palisades. And then he sat there, not doing much of anything except sipping the coffee and his ice water and staring at the stage. Every once in a while, if she walked by his table, she *thought* he glanced at her. But there was no way in the world she was going to take the time to see if he really had.

She was glad when the first guy left. A warped little kid, physically all grown-up but, emotionally not knowing how to deal with women except to abuse them. She wanted to tell herself that she wished the other guy would leave—raising the glass of ice water right now, clean-cut, a golf shirt on with nice slacks, the end-of-the-day dark shadow of whiskers on his face. Nice eyes. But she couldn't quite do it, and that bothered the hell out of her.

She had been working here for two weeks, seen hundreds of guys come and go but there was something about the guy at table fourteen, sipping his coffee now, gazing at the stage while the music banged around the room, maybe lost in his own thoughts or maybe aware of everything going on around him, she couldn't tell. He hadn't said another word to her since he had asked for the coffee. But she had the feeling that if she went over and sat down he might start talking. She thought again back to when his friend had grabbed her breast. She had snapped, telling him to keep his hands off of her and making some remark about his mother. Bending his finger hard enough that he had been that close to crying. And then she had turned to the other guy, the one still at the table, ready for him to say something rude too. It was as if he hadn't seen what had just occurred with his buddy. Coming right back at her as if nothing had happened, asking her for a slice of lime as if they were in her apartment and she was fixing him dinner. Calm about it even though she was obviously pissed off. Could she get him another lime?

Unperturbed or just plain comfortable with himself.

She thought she might have to admit something else, too. She was stand-ing near the stage, putting drinks down in front of a bunch of kids who looked too young even to be in there and who couldn't seem to take their eyes off the dancers long enough to finish the drinks they had, let alone their new ones. So she took the opportunity to peek over at the guy at table fourteen.

There it was. What she didn't want to admit. If she brought any one of the other waitresses over to where she was standing and asked them, they'd tell her they thought the same thing she did.

He was good-looking. A guy, if you try to guess what he did for a living, you couldn't pin it down to fewer than three or four things. Handsome. A clean-cut, Ivy League look to him that was marred—if it even was—by a slightly hipper quality. Like he knew what it was like to scramble for a living but had gotten pretty good at it. She hadn't noticed it when he had walked in. Wasn't paying a lot of attention, though. And when he almost took her door off out in the parking lot she couldn't see anything but his shoulder and a shadowy image of his face. She thought he was a little more than average height. With wide shoulders and no belly.

He had a look like you'd see in the movies. Not Disney. More like, what? A John Grisham film. That was it. Sociable on the outside but something hidden behind the eyes. Something that made him seem to know something that you didn't.

It irritated the hell out of her because she didn't want to be interested in him at all. She had a job to do, which was going to take about another week, and all she wanted was to *do* it and then get out of this place and never come back. So it irritated her that some man could show up and—and what? Occupy her thoughts?

The other thing she noticed about him? He was sitting there, right this minute lifting the coffee cup to his mouth again, doing nothing but staring at the dancers in their G-strings up on the stage? Hell, it was what every other guy in the place was doing.

But *he* didn't seem to be paying the slightest bit of attention to what he was seeing.

AT A QUARTER of two Teddy watched her approach the table. She asked him if he wanted another ice water because it was last call, talking to him in a monotone, too tired to be polite anymore or else maybe a little of her own feelings simply pushing through. The shit starting to grind on her because she was counting the minutes until she could walk out of here. He told her he was fine, he would take the check instead.

Outside in the parking lot he unlocked his Acura and climbed in. But he didn't start the thing. He watched a steady stream of horny guys come out—some of them with women on their arms but most without—get in their cars and drive off. Then it was the employees' turn, walking in groups, laughing, still up, moving in that animated way that only people who worked nights could have at this hour—looking to find a place that was just like Palisades but was open all night long.

His waitress came out, by herself, looking around, used to being in a city where you had to check out an area before you went into it, was there a van with a couple of guys nearby, doing nothing but listening to their motor idling. Teddy wondered about that. Her being alone. She hadn't bothered to make any friends, even to walk to her car with her? He thought it was more likely that she didn't want to take the time.

He listened to her Toyota's engine turn over and over without starting and then the distinct sound of her saying "Shit," twice, before he got out of his car and wandered over.

By the time he got there she was standing next to the open door of her car, staring at the hood. He came up to her from behind and a little bit to the side and made a point of coughing softly so she wouldn't jump into the sky when she saw him. Still, she flinched when he got close, and for a moment Teddy thought this was the part where she might scream.

Instead, after looking him over, she said, "You're going to tell me you know how to fix cars. Is that what this is?"

Teddy smiled, "Tell you the truth, I don't know antifreeze from brake fluid. But if you want, I could give you a lift."

She shook her head. "I don't 'want.'"

Teddy shrugged. "Just offering. I guess, if you're lucky, you might be able to get a cab down here." He turned to walk away but then turned back. "'Course, it'd be a gypsy and it would take awhile for you to find one. Forty-five minutes to an hour. Who knows who'll be driving the thing?" He looked around. "But they don't have *too* many problems around here. Been a couple of days since I heard about anything on *Action News*."

He watched her think about it. She looked back at her own car as if she'd like to set it on fire, looked at the back side of the club and then finally met Teddy's eyes again. "A ride home. That's all this is?"

"Hey, I heard you try to start your car. Figured you could use some help. So, yeah, that's all this is. A ride home."

She looked back at her car one more time while biting her lip and then said, "Shit." Then she glanced back at Teddy and asked, "Which one is yours?"

He held the passenger door of his Acura for her, but he didn't get the feeling that she was particularly impressed.

In the car she told him she lived on Woodstock Street and he said, "I'm not sure which one that is."

"Over by Moore College of Art. Only a few blocks away from the Franklin Institute."

He nodded and took a right out of the parking lot, drove up to Walnut, took the left and told her he was going to get there by way of Twentieth Street. She didn't answer because she was busy trying to decide if she was going to have him drop her at the door of her apartment building or if she was just going to get out where Woodstock hit Cherry Street and walk the rest of the way. Her building had outdoor surveillance cameras and round-the-clock doormen, but she wasn't positive that she wanted him to know exactly where she lived even if there were Secret Service agents hanging out at the place.

He told her his name was Teddy. Then he held out a hand which she simply stared at for a moment before holding hers out. She almost told him her real name, had to catch herself in time, "I'm Valerie."

He said, "I know." And for a moment she forgot about the name tag she had worn earlier. Beyond that she didn't feel like talking much at all.

He was talking, though. Droning on about the city, the Eagles' chances to make the play-offs, other nightclubs besides Palisades. He said, pointing at an intersection, "You come down this way? To get to work? You could come over on the expressway, I guess. I'm wondering which has worse traffic. You know, the hours you go to work and all." She settled herself in her seat and made a point of staring out the window, telling him, "It depends," so that maybe he would get the idea that she didn't really want to have a conversation. But he kept at it.

He said, "You like it? Working at the club?" Christ, how many guys asked things like that. You take it a step further, ask a hooker, "How did a girl like you . . ." Men never figured it out, the possibility that it could be *their* fault.

She tried counting streetlights and when *that* didn't work she started to count how many pedestrians they passed. He was telling her, "I knew a girl once, this was a while back. A friend. Went to Moore College. She used to do these things. Paintings. They'd always, it didn't matter, was it a painting of a chair, a vase of flowers, there'd always be some kind of lingerie in there. A bra hanging over the arm of the chair. They were good, the paintings, I mean. But I couldn't figure it out. The thing about the bra. A woman's underpants sitting behind a vase of flowers. I used to wonder, why? I gave up on it after a while."

It made her look at him, check his face to see if he was trying to be funny. But he was driving, not doing much of anything else except watching traffic out the windshield. No grin to let her know if this was his line, talking about paintings with bras in them. He turned to look at her looking at him, surprise on his face, like he really had just been making conversation. A quick grin, making him appear younger now that they were in the darkness of the car, saying, "I lost track of the woman too, the painter. I wonder what she's doing. You know, did she do well?"

She looked away but his voice kept creeping into her thoughts. She was wondering how she was going to convince him that giving her a ride home was in no way connected with their ever spending time alone together and certainly didn't mean he was going to do *anything* more than drop her off exactly where she wanted and then drive away as if they had never met.

She made up her mind that she would have him take her all the way to her apartment building because—he could always find out where she lived if he really wanted to—and she liked the idea of the doorman being available. The doorman's name was Harry. Harry was a guy in his sixties, an ex-cop who was fat and out of shape but if things got out of hand with this guy, Teddy, she could always get Harry to bang nine-one-one into the phone. He'd be thrilled to. Every time she saw him he'd end up talking about all the friends he had who were still on the force. Hell, she herself knew a couple of Philly cops who would be more than happy to come to her rescue.

They were stuck at a red light at the intersection of Walnut and Sixteenth Street when she realized that he had lowered his voice, almost like he was talking to himself. He said, "The one about Main Line doctors abusing their own prescriptions, I liked that one. Like the cops, what do they call that, the blue wall, no cop'll ever dime out another cop. Same thing happens with the doctors apparently. That's one I didn't know." Still talking naturally, two friends discussing their work. Shooting the shit, except she felt the hairs on the back of her neck go up, turning slowly in his direction, knowing he was going to be looking at her before she even glanced at his face. He said, " Let's see, you did that thing about the narcotics, came up with the fact that one of our city councilmen, not only did he *himself* use cocaine, but he was selling it to a lot of his friends. What was it called? 'Council of Coke'? I liked that one, too. And the one about the nursing homes, I have to tell you, I think, not only did you nail it, but it truly was a subject that needed to be brought out into the open. The way some of those places treat senior citizens. I read it and got depressed." Was he putting her on?

She said, "What is this?"

Teddy said, "What else? Oh, yeah. 'The Run of Your Life: Inside a Mayoral Candidate's Camp.' I think you're the reason that guy lost the election because it was a hell of a nasty article. And the one you wrote about the Pro-Lifers. 'LIFE on the Inside'? I didn't like the title but I did wonder, did you really join that group or did you just take notes from the sidelines?

She was having trouble, the idea that he had known all along who she was and had waited this long to say anything. It occurred to her that maybe, somehow, he had set this whole thing up. Except, how did he know her car wouldn't start? She did know, all of a sudden, that Teddy was a lot sharper than she had given him credit for being.

Teddy said, politely, "You know, I read somewhere that people in this town would rather have Mike Wallace show up at their door than you. I guess that's a compliment. And also, you mind if I call you by your real name—Natalie—because 'Valerie'? It just doesn't fit."

Natalie closed her eyes and said, "You can call me anything you choose to. Just tell me what you want."

The light changed and Teddy hit the gas, going through the intersection and telling her at the same time, "Hell, Natalie, I'm not sure if I *want* anything. I just know that I *don't* want something."

That one got her. She opened her eyes. "What? What is it that you *don't* want?"

"I'll tell you—what I don't want is to pick up *The Philadelphia Inquirer* magazine anytime in the next month or so and see my face or read my name in print."

She laughed quickly, "Do you reall—"

"I know, I know. How conceited of me to even imagine that you would spend as much as a sentence about me when this article of yours comes out, whatever you're going to call, it—'Life in a Titty-Bar'—comes to mind. But I have to make *sure*. For reasons you don't need to know about but are pretty important to me. See, you see me in that place, Palisades, you're in there working undercover so that you can write one of your patented exposés. Well, that's all right. But I have a life, a business, I don't want to take the chance that my name is going to be seen in print." He grinned, showing her a little boyish charm again. "I mean, what would my clients think?"

She said, not bothering to hide the sarcasm, "I see. Your *clients*?" Wondering about it, what was it he did where he had clients? "And is that all? You happened to recognize me and now you're making sure I don't center my article on you?"

Teddy said, "That's it." She turned to peek at him again and the slow smile got a little bigger on his face, his gaze flicked halfway down her body and then came back up to her eyes. He said, "Hell, Natalie, that's all I can think of."

They drove another half a block in silence and then Teddy said, almost as if he were thinking out loud, "You know, I do have a piece of advice for you. You want to do a story about a topless place? A gentlemen's club? Well, if you're going to get in there, get a job as a waitress, you better learn how to be more polite. I don't mean to offend you and I am talking mostly about the incident out in the parking lot, before we met inside, but also, a little, toward the end of the night, the way you were serving drinks. A little cold. It'd be a hell of a shame to get fired before you finish all your research."

Natalie decided she'd heard enough. She pointed up the street and said, "You want to know something—giving me advice. Let me give you some. Go fuck yourself. Let me off at that corner and don't worry, I'll make absolutely sure I don't mention you in my article. As a matter of fact, I don't believe I ever need to talk to you again."

She kept her finger pointed toward the oncoming intersection while Teddy shrugged and started to say, "Hey, that's all right, you want to get out here—" but was interrupted by a loud bang from the left rear of the car as one of his tires blew out. The Acura swerved, Teddy grabbed the wheel with both hands and said, "Fuck," through gritted teeth while he fought to bring the car to the curb so he could change the tire and not get run over.

HE REALIZED that he had forgotten for a moment that Natalie was sitting next to him. And when he looked up at her she had a fuck-you smile on her face and he felt for an instant like smacking her. He could understand why some men did it, but knew he wouldn't because it wasn't the kind of thing he had ever done or would do so all he did was try to be cool about it, give a smile of his own and say, "This is making your night, isn't it?"

"What can I say? It beats what came before." She opened her door and stepped out.

When Teddy got out he was surprised to see that she was still standing next to the car. He'd expected her to be halfway down the block, either ready to walk the rest of the way to her apartment or else willing to head up to Market Street so that she could grab a cab.

He hit the button that opened his trunk and was heading for the back of the Acura so he could pull the bullshit miniature spare tire out, hearing her, happy for a change, "You want to know what I'm going to do? I'm going to stand here and watch you change the tire. See how dirty you get that nice set of clothes you have on."

Teddy paused by the trunk because the wind had changed and was moving from her to him and for the first time he noticed her perfume. It smelled expensive and a little bit like musky vanilla.

She said, "You're not going to get mad now, are you?" in a voice that, whether she knew it or not, could get her jaw broken in some circles.

"No. You want to stand here, watch me change the tire on my car? Get my hands dirty and maybe ruin my clothes. Be my guest." He pointed toward the trunk, looking for some way to top her even though he knew there wasn't a point; he was still going to end up changing the tire, "Hey, if you really want, *you* can change the thing."

She shook her head. "Not me. I want to see you do it." She smiled nastily.

Teddy watched her do it and wondered if she'd ever had surgery. Her face was that perfect. Even though she was gloating, he had the idea that he could spend all night out here, at least until he fell asleep, looking at her. The thing that bothered him even more than having to change the tire was that—most women—he would have no trouble looking away. So why was he staring now? But there it was, he having a lot of trouble looking away from her. Losing his carefully cultivated cool. She probably knew it, too. Had a lot of guys spend time staring at her. Knew how to look away at just the right time, like she was doing now, turning to pretend to check traffic on the next block while Teddy decided, for real, that their little game was probably over and it was time to change the fucking tire.

He reached to lift up the trunk lid, hoping to say something else to Natalie. Except anything he might have said suddenly went out of his head, like their little drive had never taken place, they weren't two adults jazzing each other, one of them looking to get to know the other and that one saying, "Fuck off." It was a different Natalie he was seeing than the one who had been there a moment ago. The one who was grinning about his having to change a tire and having a good time at his expense.

This Natalie didn't look like she was having a swell time at all. Matter of fact, she looked like she was either going to scream or throw up. Teddy was confused. He didn't know what the problem was. He thought he might even have something unpleasant on his face that hadn't shown until he got out here under the streetlamp, that was the kind of expression she had on her face, and he didn't find out differently until he looked down at the trunk.

Because who wouldn't want to puke or scream or decide not to have a good time or at least get a scared-child look on their face if Dominic Scarlotti, head of Philly's biggest crime family, was all bunched up, whiter than shit and dead as a fucking doornail in the trunk of your car?

3

ON MARCH 15, 1944, Adolf Hitler summoned Admiral Miklós Horthy, Regent of Hungary, and, in his usual diplomatic style, informed the admiral that he had one of two choices. He could face the idea of a German military occupation of Hungary or he could chose to accept a new, German-approved government. Hitler didn't mention any other alternatives, so when the conference was over, a very unhappy Admiral Horthy boarded a train back to Hungary and informed his existing government that things were going to change.

Saul Rubin had been a boy of nine, an identical twin to his brother Benjamin—when SS Obergruppenführer Dr. Otto Winkelmann arrived in Budapest to take over the Hungarian Jewish Problem and expedite a solution. Saul, along with Benjamin, his mother and father, arrived by cattle car in the sleepy little Polish town of Auschwitz on a bright sunny day. Saul's father was pushed away in one direction, where he disappeared into the sea of humanity, and Saul, Benjamin and their mother were shoved into another long line of crying, bleeding women and children.

An immaculate-looking German stood on the railway platform, a stark contrast to the thousands of half-dead Jews who had just gotten off of the train. Impeccably dressed, a white doctor's coat, shined boots, intelligent, gleaming eyes—other places he would have been a judge, a successful businessman. Watching carefully. Scanning the line as it went past, the Jews, the ones who could still think, scared out of their minds. The immaculate German, no expression yet, flicking a riding crop to the right or the left—*"Links"* or *"Rechts"* softly, but with the harshness of the German language. A man doing his job.

The German with the riding crop said something else too. Occasionally he would lose his detached attitude and his voice would rise—*"Zwillinge, heraus!"*—some excitement finally coming through.

When Saul, Benjamin and their mother got to the head of the line he took one look at Saul and his twin brother and smiled broadly. A father watching two boys play. He bent down—Saul was expecting a pat, a hand in his hair, a reassuring word, but it never came—and looked Saul square in the eyes and said with a terrifying tender satisfaction in his voice, *"Ach, mein Zwilling."* Now he did give Saul a gentle pat on the shoulder with his riding crop and said, in halting Hungarian, that everything was going to be okay, going to be wonderful, *mein Zwilling.*

The German stood up—Saul wanted to ask his mother how he could be that clean—still smiling, and barked out an order in that harsh-sounding German that could, by itself, send shivers up your spine, to an SS corporal who was standing nearby. The last thing Saul remembered from that day was the bang, the corporal pulling a pistol out of a holster on his belt, putting it to Saul's mother's head and pulling the trigger. Benjamin made it a few years more than his father or mother. He and Saul went through horrendous experiments at the hands of the white-coated doctor until Ben fell victim to typhus. Saul did everything he could to keep Ben alive, giving him more than half his own meager ration of bread and watered-down wormy soup and by the time the Allied guns could be plainly heard in the not-too-far distance, Saul let himself feel that their was some hope. But then a Jewish nurse, a vicious son of a bitch who was under the illusion that if he was cruel enough to his fellow Jews the Germans might look the other way about him going into the gas chamber, came into the hospital—Jesus, you could hear the American '88s pounding just a couple of miles distant, half the SS had already fled and it was only a matter of twenty-four or thirty-six hours before the camp was liberated—and without any apparent concern, injected every single patient with phenol, stopping their hearts instantly. It was the last significant thing the nurse did because Saul didn't even wait for the approaching Allies. He tracked the nurse down that night and, with a sharpened spoon, slit his throat from ear to ear. It didn't bring Benjamin back but it made the world safer by one less sadistic, cowardly son of a bitch.

IN THE SIXTY YEARS that followed, Saul Rubin had mellowed somewhat. He had heard all the rumors about Josef Mengele being alive and living in South America. Then he had read about the DNA tests confirming that Mengele *had* escaped, had lived like a free man and then had died at a ripe old age.

But Saul didn't particularly care. He didn't hate all Germans because it was a waste of time. Conversely, he didn't like all Jews, but that didn't mean anything either. Saul depended on no one but himself for everything from when to go to the bathroom to when, how and if someone who was bothering him should cease breathing.

Saul was a businessman, pure and simple. Some people might have told him, if they had dared, that he didn't have a conscience. But Saul had seen far too many people die and caused a number of them to die himself, so he didn't spend much time worrying about it one way or another. The world was a bitter, dangerous place, and it was best to be rich because it improved the odds of what little there was to enjoy.

Saul Rubin had emigrated to the U.S. in 1948, stepping off a steamer onto the New York harbor with nothing but the clothes on his back and eight medium-sized diamonds he had stolen from a German soldier just before the war ended. The diamonds were lodged carefully up his anus, and he watched over them during the entire voyage over. Overwhelmed by the immense throng of immigrants in New York and realizing that he was also going to compete with a million GIs who were also traumatized and looking for work, Saul had made his way down to Philadelphia. Using the proceeds from one of his diamonds he leased a street-front office in a run-down section of Philly and opened a pawnshop. Within five years he knew every single aspect of the import-export and retail end of the diamond business and one helluva lot of racketeers who either demanded protection money from him or came in to hock their watches when times got tough. Now, fifty-six years later, it was safe to say that Saul had branched out. Grown. Not only did he control every single diamond that came into the country; he owned large percentages in three of Hollywood's major studios—it was an easy way to launder money—and he bribed, seduced and blackmailed enough federal and state judges, civil servants, career diplomats, spies, police, federal and international agencies that it would take the United States Supreme Court, backed by the army, to put him behind bars.

By now the main bulk of his income involved running sophisticated schemes involving foreign governments. Particularly in the Middle East. He wasn't afraid to deal with the ruthless men of the newly burgeoning Russian Mafia, he had connections in Chinatown, the Tongs, in Philadelphia, New York and in Hong Kong. He knew how to get along with the dead-souled children of the Vietnam War—the born-to-kill gang of sociopathic young refugees fleeing from the Vietcong and the Cambodian Khmer Rouge, who had settled on Canal Street, Manhattan, and quickly taken revenge against their predicament on anything that breathed. Saul was also a master at dealing with the CIA, the FBI, the NSA and the State Department. He kept them tripping over each other, blaming each other but thanking him profoundly for his help—and made millions by exploiting their inability to maintain any semblance of a realistic foreign policy. While President Bill Clinton was scrambling to redefine the meaning of the words *sexual encounter*, Saul was dealing arms to six different Middle Eastern "freedom fighters"—all of whom thought they had exclusionary rights to their products. He also imported high-grade heroin out of a ravaged Afghanistan while selling Yemeni goat herders as slaves to rich Kuwaiti clients who believed strongly that the very idea of manual labor for themselves was expressly forbidden by the Koran.

In short, Saul never pondered the good or evil of what he did. What was the use? What the Germans had done to him was being repeated—albeit on a somewhat smaller scale—in all corners of the earth and didn't seem likely to stop any time soon. In this day and age in particular, what was the difference between an autocratic ruler of a country and the top-level management of a company like Enron? Either way, someone was getting screwed. And, in fact, his dealings, because he worked both ways of the street, tended to even everything out in the long run.

Even though Saul Rubin knew it was true, it had been a long time since he had pondered how ridiculously easy it was to make large quantities of money if you were only willing to put forth a little hard work and some imagination.

The only two things Saul did care about besides a comfortable living were his dog, Benji, and the thirty-eight-year-old Jew who stayed in the house with him, Itzhak Feldman. Izzy. Itzhak fed the dog, the dog watched Saul and Saul paid for the dog food. Itzhak also ran a few errands, kept the house going, and was willing to murder anyone who had thoughts about getting at Saul.

Itzhak was the son of an Israeli whom Saul had admired who had died along with his attractive wife in a Palestinian-engineered car bombing eighteen years before. Saul had spent some time tracking down the persons responsible for the bombing, made arrangements to see that they never bombed anyone else and had taken Itzhak into his house because where else was the boy going to go? He sent Itzhak to Friends Central School out on City Line Avenue, a Quaker school that was seventy percent Jewish, and then to the University of Pennsylvania, Wharton after, where Itzhak winged his way through his undergraduate classes and then breezed his way to a master's.

Saul pulled a few State Department strings and sent Izzy back to Israel so he could serve in the army over there. When Izzy asked him why, if Saul had gone to all the expense of bringing him to the States after the murder of his parents, putting him through college and grad school after, he was now going to have him go fight in an army for another country, Saul said, "This is where you get a *different* kind of education, my boy."

IZZY HAD LEARNED THINGS, all right. He learned that Islam was like any other religion; a lot of times it was used to control people and make them do things—often bizarre things—that they would never think to try if they were lucky enough to be left alone. He'd also learned that the Jews had worked on their image since they'd gone down without much of a fight in World War II and now there were a lot of them that were nasty sons of bitches, ready to kill in retaliation or else over a dusty little plot of land on the Gaza Strip or on the West Bank. Another thing that was driven home to him was that there always had to be *someone* at the bottom of the heap. The Jews had been there for thousands of years and the Palestinians had been there too, first under the British and now under the Jews.

Izzy knew what Saul had been through during the Second World War and if he could've gotten his hands on Adolf Eichmann before the Mossad did, or Josef Mengele before he died, he would have torn them in two. But every once in a while Izzy would see some poor shlemiel of a Palestinian who was only trying to keep on living and maybe protect his wife and children. A man who couldn't read or write and only knew what some twisted sheikh or maulana wanted him to know about the Koran. A man who knelt down fives times a day to face Mecca and chant, "*Allahu akbar,*" "*Subhan Allah,*" and "*Hamile-u-lilch.*" and spent the rest of his time inside the barbed wire of one of the refugee camps that didn't look that different from Auschwitz, Dachau—maybe there weren't any gas chambers, but still—and reminded Izzy of what a vicious thing life was.

At the time Izzy had decided that maybe it was exactly what Saul had *wanted* him to learn.

Saul Rubin lived in a four-story brownstone on St. James Place in Society Hill in Philadelphia. He'd had the place completely renovated after he'd bought it in October 1957, and now it resembled a museum. The works of art on the wall, by themselves, were worth more than the house.

Izzy had his own kitchen, two full bathrooms and an office on the third floor. The office had DSL, two computers on a long countertop along one wall that jutted up against a large safe. The wall opposite had a bank of TV monitors, each one of which showed a different portion of the exterior of the house so that Izzy could tell what was happening at a glance, twenty-four hours a day. In the corner was a false-fronted bureau that had, if you knew where to look, a lever that flipped the whole side open and exposed an Uzi, another Jericho nine-millimeter and three stun grenades.

When Izzy entered the study, Saul was sitting on the couch, watching CNN News.

Itzhak said, "I have a bit of news for you, Mr. Rubin."

Saul said, "Yes." And immediately began to wheeze. Izzy had an inhaler out of his pocket in under a second, a little yellow, L-shaped container. Saul took it, put it into his mouth and pressed the top.

Izzy waited politely for Saul to get his breath back and then asked, "You okay, Mr. Rubin?" Izzy had never in his life called Saul anything but Mister Rubin.

"I'm fine, Ithzak. Thank you. What did you have on your mind?"

The room was dark except for the bluish light coming from the TV in the far corner, but Izzy could see Saul start to smile. There was a desk behind the couch Saul Rubin was sitting on and a German shepherd lying with deceptive laziness in the middle of the room.

Izzy took a step forward. CNN was going to commercial. Saul muted the TV and Izzy said, "That gentleman, Mr. Bonica, everyone calls him Little Anthony? The thing he proposed to us a couple of weeks ago?"

Saul nodded, "Yes."

"Well, that's where I was. Taking care of the matter."

Saul nodded. "And everything went okay?"

Izzy said, "Sure, except that Mr. Bonica, I think, when he was growing up, no one ever bothered to tell him that silence was golden."

Izzy reached into his pocket and brought out a miniature tape recorder. He placed it on the coffee table and pressed the Play button. There was some rustling noise and then a squealing sound.

Izzy said, "That's the door opening."

Saul nodded.

On the tape, Anthony's voice came through, tinny, but recognizable, "What the fuck? Okay, *okay* already." Some more rustling and then Anthony's voice again, you could almost hear the smirk in it, "You wanna look down there, Izzy?"

With the recorder still running Izzy told Saul, "I've already done an initial edit, the time sequence is speeded up."

Saul nodded, "That's fine. If we need to use it no one's going to care about that, Itzhak."

Izzy said, "Right." Nodding at the recorder. "This'll be Mr. Scarlotti himself. Asking me, can he have a smoke? I think he knew it was his last."

Scarlotti's voice was also recognizable, "You mind if I keep this, or are you afraid I'm gonna beat you to death with it?"

Izzy leaned forward and turned the recorder off. "The rest is all there. If need be we let Mr. Bonica know we have it. Bonica's in a terrible bind, but he doesn't know it yet."

Saul said, "He may never find out. I can't see Mr. Bonica being a problem with this thing we're trying to do. Not like Dominic Scarlotti was."

"No. Anthony Bonica—I can't see him figuring our business out." Izzy paused and then shrugged. "But, even if he does"—he picked the tiny recorder up—"he's powerless to do anything"—and put it back into his pocket. "No, I don't think Little Anthony Bonica is smart enough for us to even worry at all."

Saul nodded. "Anthony Bonica's a *bulvan*. Dominic Scarlotti was more—civilized. Certainly he tried to move on us. Extort us. I have to say, I was surprised. Everybody knows he controls the piers. The longshoreman. Did we think it possible he would find out what we were doing? Of course. But would he *act* on it? No. He and I had a long history of minding our own business. Why he would *want* to plague us? He must have known it would be trouble."

Izzy said, "I don't know, maybe he was ill. He seemed to be resigned. I'm talking about when I shot him. I got the impression that—I'm not sure—it was *almost* as if I was doing him a favor. Or, at the very least, he wasn't going to fuss. At the time I thought it was his sense of dignity."

Saul said, "It's a thing we'll never know, Dominic's motivations after all these years. I've known him for a long time. He came from good people. I remember a few occasions, before your time, a few conversations with him. One thing I'll say about Mr. Scarlotti. He tried to lean on me just two weeks ago once he got information of what we have planned with the ship. But still, even that was business. Perhaps stupid on his part. But still, nothing personal. And he could listen. Didn't have a foul mouth."

Saul turned to the TV just as CNN was coming back but didn't rehit the Mute button. He was thinking while Izzy waited patiently. Saul finally said, "Izzy, why is it that those people—remember, they are *adults*—why is it that most of them have these childish nicknames? Little this. Fat that. It's not something I understand."

"Maybe I'll ask Mr. Bonica next time we meet."

Saul smiled, "No. It's not that important. It doesn't have anything to do with our own business. The important thing is Dominic Scarlotti is out of the way. And I'll bet you this house that Anthony couldn't catch wind of what we're doing—let alone try to take advantage of it—even if we wrote him an anonymous note. But I'll tell you what might be important. That man, Mister Bonica? Little Anthony? You understand? He's going to assume he's running the show now. It's all going to go to his head."

Izzy said, "I know it is. But I don't believe it matters what he assumes for now. We're patient people and I believe he'll figure it all out eventually."

Saul nodded. "I believe you're right." Saul settled back in his seat. "Now tell me about your progress."

Izzy stepped closer. "The ship is ready. Tongan registered, through a shell corporation. The paper trail will be *just* hard enough to unravel so that it'll seem realistic. Lead to a man who calls himself Khattab. It's actually the name of one of Mohammed's successors. He's from Al Khobar. Northern Saudi Arabia. Family name of al Suwailem. He fought the Russians in Afghanistan and now keeps in close contact with Hamas. Al Qaeda. Helps blow up buses occasionally. He's going to be as surprised as anyone else when his name comes out concerning the ship—which it will; the Mossad is already on top of that. But, the irony is, Mr. Rubin, knowing what I do about Mr. Khattab, he may even do us a favor and take credit for the whole thing. The captain is a Palestinian named Hamza Khalid. No political associations whatsoever. A nice enough guy who thinks he's taking wheat, electrical transformers and canned goods to Israel. He's going to have to take a fall—be put in the hands of the Mossad. But they will cut him a break if he agrees to say what they want, point the finger at Iran. In a way it's a shame, the captain, but we can't all be lucky."

"No, we can't. Especially if you want to make good propaganda." Saul said, "It sounds fine, Izzy. Excellent."

"Good. It sails within the week." Izzy smiled. "I'm waiting on a few odds and ends. A load of surface-to-air missiles, Strellas, that's the Russian equivalent of the Stinger, a nasty piece of equipment. Don't worry, they're guaranteed to arrive and if something goes wrong there's no trail back to us."

Izzy looked at his watch. "Today's the twentieth. The ship sails, say, by the thirtieth. Headed ostensibly to the port of Eliat."

"The Red Sea."

"Exactly. A week after that, helped with an anonymous tip-off, the Mossad stops her, searches her and finds thirty million dollars' worth of armaments instead of wheat, transformers and canned goods? Enough fire-power to start a full-scale war. The Likud Party gets to point the finger at the Palestinians. And who's going to blame them? The Iranians will be con-fused as hell because they're actually going to be in the unique position of telling the *truth* when they deny involvement—not that anyone will waste their time believing it. And while the international news has a field day with it, the Israeli army will go in there and stop the PLO, Hamas and Hezbollah—probably for good this time. The only thing we have to do is make sure the Mossad comes through on our end. Five million up front, which I've been notified has already been deposited in your account. And an additional seven million when they seize the ship. But the Mossad won't play any games. They know we'll somehow go public if they do."

By the time he was finished, Saul was smiling and the corners of his eyes were crinkled with humor.

Izzy said, "What's wrong, Mr. Rubin. Did I say something wrong?"

"Hell no, my boy." Saul smiled again. "You just make it sound so easy."

Now Izzy smiled too. He squatted down so that his eyes were even with Saul's and said, "Mr. Rubin, the reason I make it sound easy is because you taught me how to do it. That's all there is to that."

The smiled disappeared from Saul's face to be replaced by a look of pride. "It's not just a matter of what I tried to teach you, Itzhak, it's how well you learned it."

TEDDY STARED at Dominic Scarlotti's corpse, thinking, oh shit, was he ever in a predicament. Two seconds later he slammed the trunk because he was hearing a low murmur coming from Natalie's throat and knew it was going to turn into a scream any second. He took two steps, saw that her face was a shade whiter than it had been when she was burning him in the car and had his hand wrapped around her biceps before the murmur got any louder.

He didn't know what else to do, so he just started walking her down the street. Her legs were stiff, like she'd played sports hard the day before and it hurt to walk. She kept turning her neck, her mouth an O, looking back at the car and then turning to Teddy.

He said, "Just walk. Don't even *think* about what's back there. Just keep walking."

"I can't." She sounded like a little kid. All the edge to her personality that she'd shown earlier, waiting their table at Palisades, and after, was gone.

"Yes you can. One foot in front of the other. I've got your arm, so nobody here is gonna fall down. All *you* have to do is concentrate on your feet."

As soon as he said it she tried to pull away. He thought about letting go but didn't want to risk it, somebody seeing her fall would come running or call the cops. He just tightened his grip and kept walking.

She stopped trying to pull away from him but moved stiffly, her shoulders hunched up and her head held rigid. He said, "You have to listen to me. Right now, you and I, regardless of how we are going to get out of this mess, right now we have to act like everything is okay. You understand? Like everything is *perfect*. I know there's not much chance of it, but if a cop car *does* drive by, thinks we're fighting, or maybe I'm trying to drag you into a back alley, he's going to stop. And I don't think you're ready for that just yet." He looked at her. "Can you work on it? I know, I know, after what we just saw, but can you *try* for some nonchalance?"

"How?" Her teeth were chattering.

"I don't know. Do what I'm doing. Instead of thinking about what's in my trunk, try thinking about what we're going to do about it."

For the first time she looked angry. Teddy thought it was a good sign. She said, "That's it? Think of a plan while we walk down the street like we're dating?" Either she had forgotten that he had her arm or she was done arguing about it.

"It's the best thing I can think of right off the top of my head. So, yes, you and I, we try to look like we're on a date." He pointed down the street. "Maybe we just drove down from the Academy of Music, listened to some Beethoven—something—and now all that's on our minds is can we find some-place to eat."

He stopped walking long enough to turn and face her, gaze directly into her eyes. At some point during the ride or else after they had found the body, her coat had opened and the third button of her blouse had come undone. He could see the top of the black bra—there it was, no mistaking it now from the sheer material of her blouse—and a small line of freckles over her breasts. He made himself look away, gazed back into her eyes and asked, "Can you do that?"

She was getting her voice back, a little color too. "But"—looking behind her—"what *are* we going to do?"

"Listen, we go somewhere, sit down and have a drink. Nobody's going to touch the car. If they do, I report it stolen. We relax, let some people see us having a nice time. Maybe I'll spill a drink so they'll remember us. And then I'm going to figure out a way to deal with this. Try to keep you from getting caught up in all this."

THEY FOUND A RESTAURANT on Arch Street that was still open and was jam-packed with people. Natalie saw Teddy slip the maître d' a hundred-dollar bill and the maître d' went from snotty to nice in a nanosecond and suddenly remembered a small spot just outside the kitchen that they were most welcome to have. Within a minute Teddy and Natalie were sitting at a table that was, indeed, too close to the kitchen, but one that hadn't been there when they walked in.

A waiter came over and handed them menus but Teddy told him, "Never mind the food. Could we just get a couple of cocktails?" Natalie watched him as he ordered for both of them, thinking about the last thing he had said to her: "We're going to try to keep you from getting caught up in all this." She was picturing his face when he had said it. What was it that had been in his expression? Jesus—sincerity. That was what it was. And then she thought about what wasn't there. Nervousness.

She knew that she already *was* caught up in it. You drive somewhere with someone, it didn't matter if you had never met him before, if you found a dead person in his trunk, how the hell could you *keep* from being caught up in it?

But still, there was something about the way Teddy had said those words. As if he truly meant them and was going to try like hell to live up to his statement. Or else it was just the fact that it had been the first thought to cross his mind.

Teddy had said it would be all right? Okay. But she was a little curious to find out how he was going to accomplish that.

Teddy said, "I'm trying to remember back. Did anyone at Palisades see us together? I mean, it's possible they saw you arguing with Davey, the other guy at my table, But did they see you do more then bring us a couple of drinks? I don't think so. I think that might be the key."

Their drinks came and Natalie gulped at hers without knowing better because she never drank hard liquor. Her eyes got teary and she had a coughing fit. To make matters worse, she thought about the body inside of Teddy's trunk and was sure, for a moment, that she was going to throw up right then and there.

Teddy—she was startled to already be thinking of him by his first name— simply reached across the table and took her hand. They must've seemed like half the other patrons in the restaurant, including the two men at a small table ten feet behind Teddy's back, starry-eyed and holding hands. Lovers. Except Natalie was certain that neither Teddy nor she had what you would call a starry-eyed look in their faces. Manic maybe. She did bet that they were the only ones who had a corpse in the trunk of their car.

Teddy said, pointing at her drink, "It's vodka. It's not something you want to pour down your throat." He took a sip of his own and then said, "Or would you like me to get them to put something in it. A little tonic? Or wait, do you want a glass of wine? Something else?"

She shook her head. "No. I'm okay."

She took another sip of her drink, a smaller one, and it seemed to go down easier than the first. She felt a little warmth spread through her body. His hand was dry, which surprised her because she knew that hers wasn't. She could feel a thin sheen of sweat all along her back next to her spine, and there was a droplet forming on her temple next to her right ear. She picked up her napkin, wiped it off and then realized that Teddy was still holding her hand. Watching her intently. She said, "What?" Fifteen minutes before, she would have yanked her hand away if he had so much as looked at it for too long. But right now she didn't have the energy to care. "I'm going to be okay, if that's the look you're giving me."

"I didn't know I was giving you any kind of look. But now that you mention it, I believe you. You're going to be okay. That's good." Now he did take his hand out of hers. He leaned back, still studying her, and said, "No, what I'm wondering now, this has got to be the limit in surprises for you. That's what I would think. But maybe I'm wrong. Maybe, in your line of work, investigative journalism, you get this kind of shock more often than people realize."

"Not this kind of shock."

"Well, still, you're handling it. A lot of people wouldn't be able to. But maybe it's because you—what you do—like what you're doing at Palisades. You go undercover. There's pressure there I would assume. For how long usually?"

"How long what?"

"You're working at Little Anthony's club. I assume you're going to write some sort of exposé. How long until you have enough to write an article about it?"

"A couple of weeks, whatever it takes to get the whole story. I do research before. Write the story as I go along."

Teddy was finished with his drink already and signaling their waiter. Without looking at her he said, "You want another?"

She said, "Yes. Thank you."

He said, "You're welcome." He paused and then said, "That's what I would have thought. Go in as a waitress, put up with shit like what my brother gave you. By the way, he's like that sometimes. What can you do?"

"I didn't know he's your brother. There's not much—"

"Physical resemblance? I've heard that one before. Anyway, ah—right— you work a place for a while and then you're out of there." He stared at her for a moment. "I can't see you getting up on the stage and dancing in a tiny pair of underwear." He smiled—there he was again, the nice guy, your neighbor who took your trash out on a snowy day—and said, "Believe me, I'm not saying you don't have the figure for it because you do. The looks. No, definitely, you have them."

She didn't know how to respond because it was a compliment, but he said it as if he'd mentioned it a hundred times before. He was looking past her, staring off into space, thinking, and she took the opportunity to study his face. The first real opportunity she'd had to see *his* features clearly. It had been dark in the parking lot when he had almost hit her, and she had tried not to bother in Palisades. The only other times, the interior of his Acura, or even the street while Teddy was opening his trunk, were dimmer than this place.

He was saying, "I imagine you've been in some sticky situations."

She had narrowed it down; he was a lawyer or maybe a VP in some middle to large corporation. The shirt he was wearing was a Tommy Hilfiger, and she knew that the slacks he had on hadn't come from the Gap. He wasn't wearing any jewelry except his watch. She took a closer look and realized it was a Bulgari Sport Gold. Two years back the publisher of the *Inquirer* had retired, and everyone had been asked to chip in fifty bucks to buy the exact same watch. Natalie had counted up the number of employees at the *Inquirer*, made a phone call to a jeweler she knew and found out that the thing retailed for just under twenty thousand dollars. She forgot about Teddy being a lawyer or a middle-management VP. She was beginning to think a little higher. A CEO. Of a *large* corporation.

He startled her by leaning a little bit farther across the table. "I got it for a lot less than retail. Friend of mine is in the business and owed me a favor. Money actually. He couldn't come up with his end, so we settled for the watch."

"How'd you know I was thinking that?"

"Because we're both doing the same thing."

"And what's that?"

"Thinking about everything—anything—except for what's back in my car." He shrugged. "I don't want to make a big deal out of it, but we're checking each other out. Who wouldn't, given the . . . the . . ." He waved his hand in the air in the vague direction of his car. "Situation."

"I don't want to think about it. I don't want to think about *any* of it. Do you?"

"I think maybe I'll have one more drink first. But, the thing is, we have to give it some thought eventually. Come up with some way to deal with what's happened."

She said, "Well, first of all, let me ask you a question."

"Sure."

"It's not an easy thing to ask. That—that man. Did, ah, did—"

"Did I kill him? I think you just hurt my feelings. No. I opened that trunk and what I was expecting to see was some dry cleaning I had picked up earlier and also my spare tire. I know you don't know me, but you have to ask yourself, if I knew he was there, would I have let you see him?"

"That's what I thought. So, since that's the case, I know exactly what we do."

"And that is?

"We go to the police."

"Aha."

"What's that supposed to mean? You say 'Aha,' and I get the feeling you're making fun of me. What's wrong with going to the police? We didn't do anything. I can swear you were in the club for hours. You're the victim of a horrible coincidence. So, yes, absolutely, we go to the police."

Teddy shook his head slowly. "You wanna know something? I think you're over the shock. I think you're starting to see something else in this besides a dead guy in my car."

"What are you talking about?" she snapped.

"What I'm talking about is your job. You're an investigative journalist. I already told you I've read a lot of your pieces. And now, here you are, a week or two into working undercover in a titty-bar so you can write about it. You meet me and we go for a ride, never mind the fact that at the time you couldn't stand me."

She said, "I never said—"

"It's okay. Really. Halfway through the ride we get a flat tire, I pop open my trunk and there's a stiff in there. You get a quick peek at him and then we come here because we could both use a drink. Now, I have to tell you, I'm impressed. A lot of people would go screaming off to the police immediately, which brings us to what you're talking about. I'm getting the impression that you're not looking at the situation the same way you were when it first happened."

A little bit of it was coming back, the irritation. She thought that it might be because she still hadn't managed to get a handle on him. How to deal with him. Every time she tried one way he seemed to change into something else. Never acted like anything was bothering him. She said, "And how *am* I looking at it? You're doing so well up to now—reading my mind when I'm looking at your watch, telling me I have a good figure. That was nicely done, by the way. Why don't you tell me what I'm thinking again? I'm dying to know."

"All right, I will. What you're doing is, suddenly, you're looking at this as a story. A Pulitzer Prize."

She shook her head. "Bullshit." But then she shrugged. "You have to admit, though, it'd make a good ending to the piece on the topless club."

Teddy straightened up. "Listen to me. You don't quite understand how *much* trouble we're in, do you?"

"What are you talking about? We didn't do anything."

"I didn't realize."

"Didn't realize what?"

Teddy seemed confused for a moment, as if he didn't believe something he had just thought of. He leaned close to her and without thinking she leaned forward also. She got enough of a whiff of his cologne to decide that she liked it and then he was telling her, "I thought you *knew*."

"For Christ sake, knew *what*? Are you getting some kind of kick out of this?"

"No. I'm not trying to be funny, either. But listen, what's back in my car, the dead guy, it's a mob hit. I think—maybe you already have—you would've figured that much out."

"Okay." She nodded. "I see. A normal murder, why go to all the trouble of putting it in someone else's trunk?"

"Right. But the thing you have to understand, why we can't just go waltz- ing into the local police precinct is this: What we're dealing with is not just your run-of-the-mill mob hit. That's Dominic Scarlotti in my Acura. A woman like you, in your profession, I would've thought you knew who he is."

"Hey, it isn't like I took a long look. I saw his shoulders and the back of his head." She made a face. "What was left of it. But, if you're asking do I know who Dominic Scarlotti is? Then yes, I do."

"*Was*. Then you see what my point is. Only three, maybe four, perhaps even five people know where he is right *now*. And I'm talking dead in my trunk. You, me and the guys who killed him. I believe I actually might even know who did it, but it's gonna take me a little time to find out and I don't even know if the information is worth anything or not. Maybe the whole thing'll blow over. But if it doesn't—" He let the sentence dangle in the air for an instant and then said, "Meanwhile—instead of running to the cops—what you have to keep in mind is this, if somebody's got the balls to take out the number-one mobster in the city—then it's a serious decision. So if we *do* go to the cops and it gets out that we know anything about this, you won't have to worry about writing any story. You'll be too busy trying to stay alive."

HE WATCHED her think about it, working it through her head until he could tell by her expression that she agreed with him. But then another look came over her face. Confusion. Maybe a little anger.

She said, "Wait a minute."

"What?"

"You!" She pointed a finger at him and said it again, "Wait a goddamn minute. Let me ask you something. What do you do for a living?" Still pointing, "You say you got your watch for less than retail because somebody owed you money? How much money did they owe you and, more to the point, why'd they owe it?"

"Right now I can't remember."

"Well, do you remember me asking you a question a few seconds ago?"

"What do I do for a living. I'm a stockbroker."

"I was going to say lawyer. Or head of some company that made little gadgets that no one ever thought about but that were used for a million different things."

"Nope. I'm just a stockbroker. Try to make my clients money so that I make money too."

"You must be pretty good at it."

He shrugged. "I do all right."

"That's good. I'm glad. But let me ask you something else. You say you're a stockbroker? But when you find someone dead in your car, what do you do? Why were we worried about my reaction but not yours? You see what I'm getting at?"

"Not really."

She said, "I guess, when I first saw it, what was in your trunk, I freaked a little. You had to help me down the street. I keep getting an image of *you* freaking out. But you didn't. Why is that?"

"I don't know. Maybe it'll hit me later."

"Sure." Now she reached across the table and touched *his* hand. Made a production out of stroking his fingers. But there was a look in her eye that he didn't like.

She said, "Or maybe, since you're sooo used to dealing with the pressures of the market—the ups and downs of the Dow Jones and Nasdaq—maybe *that's* why you've been so calm about this whole thing. Able to comfort and advise me and, at the same time, have no trouble with your own thoughts."

He said, "You might be right."

"Cause you're a—"

"—stockbroker."

There was still a little bit of vodka in her glass, watered down because most of the ice cubes had melted. She picked it up, finished what was left and then set it carefully on the table between them.

She lifted her hand off his, stared straight at him and smiled. "My ass you are."

NATALIE SAID, "I definitely am *not* drunk," and then tripped on a ridge where two sections of the sidewalk came together. Teddy reached out and caught her. He inadvertently slid his hand halfway around her waist and immediately wondered what she would be like in bed. She brushed his hand away quickly, smoothed her blouse and said, "A little tipsy maybe. But can you tell me there's something wrong with that?"

"No. You had a couple of drinks. That's all. So did I."

She gave him a dirty look. "Yeah, but I don't see you falling down. Teddy Clyde, ah—Mr. Cool, Calm and Collected. You never do *anything* that's going to make you lose that edge. Right?"

"I think maybe you better give it a little while. Maybe if we see each other a half a dozen times or so, *that* might be the time to sum up my entire personality in a single sentence."

"Are you making fun of me?"

"Not that I know of."

She picked up her pace. He watched her rear end for a couple of seconds. Admired the way her muscles moved every time she took a step and then caught up to her right as they were approaching the double doors to her apartment complex.

She hadn't wanted to see the body in the trunk again so Teddy had worked the spare tire out from under Dominic's dead body—happy for a change that the spares were so small—while Natalie stood fifty feet down the street and watched nervously. There was no room for the flat tire to go back into the trunk, so Teddy rolled it over to the curb and left it there. He dropped Natalie down the street from her apartment because she insisted on it. There was a doorman on duty and he nodded his head at Natalie just before she stumbled, and then he seemed to turn to stone, letting both of them know it was none of his business whether Teddy and Natalie were fighting or were headed upstairs to fuck.

At the front door, just out of earshot of the doorman, Teddy said, "Look, I'm not trying to make any kind of huge point here, but, just to be safe? Don't answer your door for the time being unless it's someone you know or else me."

She looked at him for a long time and then said, only slurring the words a tiny bit, "Who the hell says I'm going to open it if it *is* you?"

4

TEDDY HAD TO WAIT for the phone to ring eight times before he heard a groggy voice on the other end. Davey-Boy kept asking him exactly what was going on, but Teddy would only say, "All you need to do, you need to be outside your apartment in fifteen minutes and you'll find out." He thought for a moment and then said, "One other thing. Bring a shovel."

Davey-Boy said, "A *what*?"

"You heard me."

"Teddy, where the fuck am I supposed to get a shovel at this time of night?"

Teddy said, "I don't know. Just bring one."

Davey was waiting outside his apartment building with a small gardening spade in his left hand. He got in the car and Teddy looked from the shovel to Davey's face and said, "The fuck is that?"

"It's a goddamn shovel. What do you think it is?" Davey held up the shovel. "Hey, you didn't say what *kind*. And you definitely didn't say what for, which I still haven't heard word one about."

They took the Schuylkill Expressway, west, all the way out to the City Line Avenue exit and then turned right around and came back toward the city.

Davey said, "You woke me up at two-thirty in the morning to go for a drive?"

"No. I woke you up at two-thirty in the morning to change a tire. Why don't you do this; pretend this is reality TV, prepare yourself for a little bit of a surprise and be patient."

Davey-Boy said, "It's what, three o'clock in the morning now? Ten after? And you want me to be *patient*?"

Teddy said, "All right. Dominic Scarlotti got whacked tonight, I believe by Little Anthony Bonica. I also believe Anthony thought it would be funnier than hell to put Dominic in my trunk so right now I'm looking for a good place to bury him."

Davey stared at Teddy for a full ten seconds before he burst out laughing. "You're funny. You're a fucking riot, Teddy. But I got an idea, unless you're driving me to some Overbrook whorehouse I haven't heard about yet, I'd just as soon you take me home. You can keep the shovel."

Teddy got in the right lane and then pulled off to the shoulder of the expressway just before it split. He could either go right, past the Thirtieth Street Amtrak station to the airport—the Walt Whitman Bridge—or he could go left and on into Center City. Teddy looked past Davey's head and out the window to his right. There was some scrub and then, farther on and down a small slope, the top of a wall, beyond which a whole series of railroad tracks converged toward the large station another half a mile on. It was where the commuter trains and the Amtrak lines all came together in order to get into the Thirtieth Street Station. Teddy had driven by this spot a thousand times without paying attention. But now he studied it carefully.

The tracks farther away looked relatively new. And he knew from experience that those were the ones that the trains actually ran on. Brought the commuters in from the suburbs and the Metroliner up from D.C. But the tracks closest to the highway were older. Much older. Some of them were just short spurs that ran for a few hundred yards and then stopped either by design or else because they were ancient enough that the ties had rotted and the tracks themselves had disappeared, probably to be used elsewhere. Some of the short spurs held the repair equipment, the cranes on flat-backed railway cars that the SEPTA—Southeastern Pennsylvania Transportation Authority—workers rode on wherever there was a problem with a track on one of the dozens of lines that ran into Philadelphia from its surrounding communities.

A little farther on, a few, very old, commuter cars sat in a hodgepodge manner on the tracks as if they'd been there since the signing of the Declaration of Independence. They were brick red colored, wooden, with tiny windows and no air-conditioning. Teddy remembered riding them as a kid. Now they were too rotted out even to be carted away for scrap.

He figured, not only was it a good place to put a body; he probably wasn't the first person to do so.

HE PULLED OFF to the very far side of the shoulder of the highway, popped his trunk and then had to wait while Davey-Boy vomited up something that looked like rotted fish and didn't smell much better. Davey-Boy stood up long enough to point at Teddy's Acura, trying to talk and puke at the same time, "Jesusareyou—shit—areyououtofyourfuckingmind?" Teddy could barely make out what he was saying.

Finally Davey quit puking and pointed at the Acura again. He said, scared, "What the fuck happened? Do you know who that is? Do you fucking *know*? Jesus fucking Christ, Teddy, that is Dominic-fucking-Scarlotti."

Teddy said, "Just because you didn't believe me doesn't mean it wasn't true."

Davey said, "I as*sumed* you were fucking with me." He stomped thirty feet away, moaning and rubbing his head with both hands hard enough to pull some hair out, stomped back and, from three feet away, yelled, "What did you do? What the fuck did you do? Did you to go to the library and look up the word *suicide* in the dictionary and then go out and do this? Wait—wait—I know. You're terminally fucking ill. You didn't tell me, you've got every kind of cancer there is, you don't have the guts to off yourself and Pennsylvania doesn't have—whatever the fuck they are—assisted fucking suicide. You're afraid of suffering so you what? You're looking for an easy way out?"

Teddy said, "Davey, look at me."

" 'Look at you'? Fuck that. I don't wannna look at you. I don't want to *know* you." He stomped away again and turned, yelling from twenty feet, "Listen, you're my brother, that counts for I don't know what. Yeah, Mom died and you looked out for me. Well, fuck you. I don't want any part of this. All I wanna know is why the fuck you killed him and then I want you to take me home. Maybe drop me off at a church so I can go to confession, cover my ass."

Teddy said it again, quietly, "Davey, look at me." Waiting until Davey calmed down just long enough to meet his gaze. "I didn't kill the son of a bitch and, yes, I know who he is. Why do you think I called you?"

"You didn't kill him?"

"I think you know I'm not that dumb."

"Absolutely. So, it's silly of me, fucking ridiculous, to wonder—if you didn't whack the motherfucker—how come he's in your car?"

Teddy moved over until he was standing next to the trunk. He had covered Dominic's body as best he could with an old, shredded bedsheet and now he gazed down at what he could see of the corpse. He was trying to remember what he'd read about rigor mortis. He knew it happened and then went away and maybe came back, but he couldn't remember anything about the time frame.

He said, "The reason he's in my car is because I beat the shit out of Little Anthony Bonica twice in his life. I know you remember *that* because both times it was because of you. I humiliated him and he couldn't come back at me after, get Dominic Scarlotti's or whoever's permission he had to have, to do anything about it. So this is his idea of payback. Plus now he gets to play boss of all the Philadelphia rackets."

Teddy turned away to hide his face from an oncoming car and then he asked Davey if he was up to helping him lift the dead guy out of the trunk or did he have to vomit some more?

———

THEY WAITED for a break in traffic and then carried Dominic Scarlotti's body as quickly as they could across the shoulder of the road and through the underbrush. When they got to the top of the cinder block wall that separated the highway from the railroad yard below them they looked at each other. Teddy thought that any second a better idea might come to mind. But, in the end, they just heaved the body over. When it hit the ground, eight feet below them, it sounded like a watermelon being hit by a sledge hammer. Teddy looked over the wall and tried to figure out if it was okay to jump over himself or was he going to break a leg doing so? Out of the corner of his eye Teddy saw Davey bend down to the ground and pick something up, heard a slight metallic scraping noise. By the time he turned Davey-Boy was putting his hand in his pocket and staring in the direction Dominic Scarlotti had just gone with a stupid look on his face.

Teddy said, "What are you doing?"

"Nothing."

Teddy studied him for a moment and then said, "Well, go on back to the car and jack it up. Act like you're changing a tire. But don't actually take a tire off in case we have to get out of here in a hurry. You understand? Just keep doing it. Anybody—especially a cop—drives by, all you are is an innocent motorist with a car problem? Right? It gets bad enough, go ahead and actually take the spare off and put it right back on. Whatever you do, make it look realistic. Then drive on away. I'll find my car later on."

"What do I say to the cop when he asks me whose car it is? You wanna tell me that?"

Teddy said, "If a cop does stop, I'll hear it from down there. I'll stop making any noise and, meanwhile, you simply show him your license and explain that you're my brother."

"And then, tomorrow, when they find the body here. What do I do then?"

"Davey, think it through. They aren't going to find the body. That's the whole point."

THE WHOLE MESS—beginning to end—took over an hour because Teddy had to dig three different graves and the shovel was about useless. The first two holes he started didn't work because, on the first one, scrambling like a badger, he ran into a block of concrete one minute after starting. The second time he hit an old railroad spur that must have been built by Andrew Carnegie's U.S. Steel Corporation in conjunction with the Pennsylvania Railroad around the turn of the century. There was nothing left but the rails themselves. Even the spikes were gone.

Teddy's biggest worry was that Davey-Boy was going to panic for no reason and tear out of there leaving him to walk the half mile to Thirtieth Street Station looking like a street bum who had rolled in the mud for added effect. But he finally scraped a hole that was about five feet long, three feet wide and three feet deep. Davey helped out by leaning over from the edge of the expressway every ten minutes to ask what the problem was. Finally Teddy told him, "Hey, I understand you're my brother and all that—I'm supposed to be nice to you—but if I see your face one more time before I get back up there, I'm gonna bury *you* too."

Davey got a hurt look on his face. But he stopped leaning over the edge and let Teddy work in peace.

Getting Dominic into the grave was not as big a problem as Teddy had anticipated because by then Teddy was pissed off enough that his adrenaline kicked in and he simply crammed the son of a bitch into the hole. Fifteen minutes after that Teddy had filled the hole up. As an afterthought he walked over to a nearby thicket of bushes and yanked a few leafy branches out and jammed them into the top of the grave. Then he scuffed old dirt and a bunch of trash around until, to his eye at least, and in this light, the grave site didn't look any different than the surrounding area.

He didn't say one word to Davey the whole ride back except to tell him, one time, "Nobody. I don't care if Mom comes back from the grave. Nobody knows about this. You understand?"

Davey-Boy said, "Teddy, c'mon, man, what do I look like?"

"Why do you think I'm telling you?"

"DO I *LOOK* like I'm not busy here?" It was the next morning and Anthony Bonica was on his cell phone but speaking right then to one of his dancers, Vicki, who was bringing him a cup of coffee. Vicki had a chiseled face, classic, but marred by a nose just that much too long. She was wearing tight Levi's and a halter top with the word "Guess" printed across it that, later on, she'd take off so she could get up on the stage and dance while a bunch of drunken guys shoved bills into the waistband of her undies. She had a coke habit and had been twice before accused of stealing by the other girls, but nothing ever came of it. Tommy Inzarella shook his head. He didn't think it was any of his business, but he did figure that the only reason she still worked there was because she was fucking Anthony.

Now Anthony was back on the phone, saying, "No, not you, asshole. I was talking to one of my em-ploy-ees." That got a frown out of Vicki, but Anthony either didn't notice or didn't give a fuck. He said, into the phone, "Sure, I *hear* you say it, you telling me how much you *know* I'm a busy fucking man. But *hearing* it is bullshit. What you better do is come up with a way to convince me that you fucking *realize* it. Sing it or bring it, and I'm not a fucking opera fan. Which is why I originally asked the question which, so far, you haven't fucking answered, you prick. How much fucking money you got on the street? And yes, so you don't even have to ask, I mean right this fucking minute."

Anthony frowned and yelled into the phone, "You fuck! You miserable fuck. I'm sitting here and you think you can bullshit me with that? A hundred large? My fucking grandmother has a hundred grand on the street and she's in a fucking hole in the ground. That's how much fucking change you got in your *pockets*, a hundred fucking large." Anthony paused for a second, his face getting redder and then he yelled, "No, no—*you* listen to me. My cut—Mr. Scarlotti's cut—just went up by five percent. You understand? And I don't mean drop by the club sometime next month. I want it in my fucking hands tomorrow."

Anthony hung up the phone and looked at Tommy. "A bunch of fucking crooks. Jesus. That's who I got working for me. Fucking criminals. Dominic gets old and tired and these fucks think they can walk all over the place." Anthony picked up the phone and started dialing again, and Tommy got up to get a cup of coffee for himself, because it didn't look like Vicki was going to wait on *him*.

Anthony was moving way too fast. Dominic had been dead for what, less than twenty-four hours? And here Anthony was, the very next morning, calling everybody who worked for him, raising the street tax. He was right about one thing: He did have a bunch of crooks working for him. He pushed it *too* hard he'd have someone coming to put him where Dominic was.

Tommy got his coffee, a little sugar but no cream, and stood by the bar. Anthony was still on the phone, talking with his hands. Jabbing his index finger down on the table. If Tommy were in Anthony's position he would sit tight, wait for Dominic's body to turn up and then make his move. But Anthony had already explained his thinking, telling Tommy on the ride over, "Hey, I got to consolidate my position," sounding like some kind of corporate fuck. "What we did, you and I both know it wasn't a sanctioned hit. The pricks up in New York? They find out—it's none of their fucking business but they're gonna make it like it is—they're gonna be asking a lot of questions. So what I got to do, I got to make sure I'm already on top. Let the fucking Gambinos, whoever wants to know, think that it's not worth the effort to send somebody down here to make a fucking commotion."

Anthony had already taken to riding in the backseat of the Caddy, first day, just as Dominic always did, and Tommy had looked at him in the rearview mirror without commenting. A "commotion"? They were both dead men if somebody in New York got mad enough about Dominic. It wasn't like Tommy was gonna run around worrying about it. But there it was.

Anthony said, "Bottom line? Those fucks in New York, the five families? All they really care about is whether things are running smoothly or not. Are they getting money out of some things I have going on here and also, some joint situations we got running down in Atlantic fucking City? Which, by the way, maybe it's time I change the percentages on *that*. Maybe take it away from those pricks altogether. All in all, I'm gonna deserve it because, sure as shit, I'm going to make sure things run smoother than they did under fucking Dominic."

Tommy didn't know how beating everybody up on the street tax the very first day was gonna make things run smoother. He also thought that, if Anthony was that worried about the New York Families, he should've done what they had originally planned. Spent the weekend in Miami and come on back just in time for Dominic's funeral. But, no, at the last second, Anthony had changed his mind, saying, "There's no way. That Jew? Izzy whatever-the-fuck-his-last-name-is? He's not even gonna get close to Dominic unless I'm there to fucking arrange it. No"—shaking his head—"I gotta bring Dominic to *him*."

Tommy knew Izzy casually. He had seen him around town often enough, spoken to him a couple of times and heard some stories from reliable sources. He was fairly certain Izzy was capable of doing the piece of work without any help from Anthony. So not getting out of town had been a dumb move on Anthony's part. Why create trouble? Go down to Miami and read about it in the *Herald* instead. Tommy had the feeling that what it was, was, at the last minute, Anthony had decided to stay because he wanted to *see* Dominic get whacked. Whether it was out of some kind of perverse sense of power or just because Anthony wanted to make absolutely certain that it actually happened, Tommy didn't know. All he did know was that they should've gone to Miami, gotten some sun, picked up some broads, gone deep-sea fishing and maybe caught a marlin. Made enough of a commotion so that anybody, the New York Families, the feds, PPD, fuck, *anybody*, who had an interest in their alibi would have no trouble believing it.

He finished his cup of coffee and began to make his way back to the table. Anthony was talking slowly now. He had a fake, nice sound to his voice, asking a Girl Scout how much her cookies cost. But it was a setup because all of a sudden he started to yell again. Tommy could tell who he was talking to, "Fat Jimmy," Jimmy Decaro, a bookmaker and loan shark who was getting old and worked out of a small club on Forty-first Street on the other side of the University of Pennsylvania, just above Woodland Cemetery—a nice view if you didn't look at the headstones.

Fat Jimmy was small-time. Dominic Scarlotti had always left him alone, let him eat like a pig and skim off the top as long as he didn't get carried away. It was stupid to call him up this early in the morning just to give him a hard time.

But it was Anthony's choice. Little Anthony wanted to let everybody know he was in charge, give them a bullshit line about how all this had Dominic's blessing? It was his decision.

Tommy hadn't forgotten what it had been like when Angelo Bruno got blown to bits by a bomb that had been planted on the front porch of his row home in South Philly. Phillip Testa took over the reins until Little Nicky Scarfo came out of exile down in Atlantic City, and proceeded to kill anything that moved. The Scarfo/Riccobene war alone had been something to see. Tommy could recite the victims of the overall war by heart. There was Michael "Mickey Coco" Cifelli, whacked, not because he dealt drugs, fuck, everybody did, but because he'd been too obvious about it. There was "Tony Bananas" Caponigro, Angelo Bruno's *consigliere*, found dead, in the Bronx, of all fucking places. There was Frank "Frankie Flowers" D'Alfonso; first he gets the shit kicked out of him in 1981 by a couple of Scarfo's crew and then gets whacked four years later. There was Dominick "Mickey Diamond" DeVito, who Scarfo hated but had waited twenty years to kill. There was Vincent Falcone, an Atlantic City cement contractor who died for no more reason than that he had insulted Little Nicky Scarfo and Scarfo's nephew, Philip Leonetti. And, naturally, there was Phillip Testa, the one who'd first tried to take control after Angelo Bruno got exploded. Hell, there was *Salvi* Testa, Phillip's kid and one-time good buddy of Scarfo's—his main executioner—who died because Nicky's paranoia was getting the better of him. There was, there was . . . shit—forget about it. Tommy Inzarella felt tired just thinking about it.

Walking back to the table, watching Anthony dial yet another number, Tommy Inzarella had to wonder about it. What kind of boss was Anthony going to be? And how was he, Tommy, gonna watch his ass if the shit hit the fan like it did the last time?

TEDDY WOKE UP at nine o'clock with a slight hangover and thoughts of how, for a long time to come, Dominic Scarlotti would be listening to the commuter trains running back and forth over his head. He took a couple of aspirins and tried to think about Natalie Prentice instead of Scarlotti. It was easier and more pleasant at first, but it also made him grab the phone as soon as he realized that Natalie just might have had a change of heart about what had happened the night before.

As soon as she answered, he said, "Hey, it's me. Teddy. I was thinking we ought to talk."

The silence on the other end made Teddy think they might have been disconnected. He said, "Hello? You there?"

"I'm thinking." She said, "I guess the best thing— I'm going to take a quick shower. Meet me in the garden"—she paused again, and Teddy pictured her looking at her watch—"in an hour."

"The garden?"

"You'll see, it's right inside the building. First floor."

Teddy put a casual outfit on to go with the nervousness in his stomach and then drove over to Natalie's apartment building. He parked in an empty spot on the cross street a quarter of a block down from her front door and spent a minute wondering if he was being set up. What if Natalie had had a change of heart?

Teddy watched the doorman in front of Natalie's building carefully. He looked like an ex-cop. Not encouraging. A black woman in a postal worker's outfit pulled a cartful of mail along the opposite curb, stopping at every doorway to stick envelopes in the mailboxes. A hundred yards farther down, and on the same side of the street as the doorman, a priest was hailing a cab. Besides those two, and the cars driving by, no one else was in sight. There weren't any patrol cars on the street, no four-door sedans or bogus power-company vans. No bums pushing shopping carts and talking into their hands and looking everywhere but at Teddy as he sat in his Acura.

He got a quick image of the priest flinging off his collar, the doorman pulling out a .38 special and the postal woman grabbing a Glock from her shoulder bag. More cops would come running out of the building, and before Teddy could say "I didn't do it," he'd be up against the wall, legs spread and somebody's hands checking his crotch and ankles for concealed weapons.

Finally he thought, fuck it, if it was going to happen there was nothing he could do about it. He could take off from here, but they'd be waiting for him back at his apartment.

Besides, it felt better to hope that Natalie hadn't done anything except get a reasonably good night's sleep. Not had too many nightmares about dead mobsters in automobile trunks.

THE GARDEN turned out to be a small café in the back part of the first floor of Natalie's apartment building. It seemed out of place, a health-food-salad-bar-slash-luncheonette that was decorated to excess with tropical plants. Each table had a silly gold-painted wicker container for the salt, pepper, horseradish and Parmesan cheese. A middle-aged waitress showed Teddy to a table and handed him a plastic menu.

An elderly woman was sitting at a table to his right, drinking what looked to be tea and working on a crossword puzzle. A young couple near the back fussed over a toddler who looked like he was pissed off at the world. Besides that the place was empty. Teddy watched the father for a moment. The guy alternated between eating, wiping his kid's face and scanning the room. While Teddy watched, the father sat suddenly upright and seemed to forget all about his kid. Teddy knew, without even turning yet, that Natalie had just walked in.

She looked like something you'd see in the pages of *Elle* magazine. Designer jeans, nicely tight but not overdone. Black platform shoes with a conservative, two-inch heel. A bright yellow buttoned-down cardigan, half open over a man's style white T-shirt. Her hair looked like she had just washed and blow-dried it and Teddy couldn't tell whether she'd put makeup on expertly or simply didn't need any.

When she saw Teddy, she waved and walked over as if they'd done this a dozen times before. Teddy stood up and watched her approach, realizing that, since she had entered, he had completely forgotten about the Philadelphia Police Department. He let his gaze travel the length of her body, taking her all in one last quick time. When he looked back at her face he realized he'd been caught.

She said, with just a hint of a sardonic smile on her face, "You all right?"

"Sure." It came out sounding phony even to his own ears. He cleared his throat, tried for cool, calm and collected and said, "I woke up this morning, thought things over and decided you and I definitely need to talk some more."

She said, "Do we, now?" Natalie disappeared into her own thoughts for what seemed like a full minute before she glanced back at him and nodded slightly. "I was headed down here to have breakfast anyway. Now we can do both."

Apparently breakfast for Natalie consisted of a cup of coffee, so Teddy told their waitress that he'd have the same. When it came he took one sip, made a face and put the cup back on the table.

Natalie said, "I know, it's terrible, but usually I'm in a rush and it's better than the stuff at work or at Palisades." She put her own cup down, looked directly at him and let her voice drop to a near whisper. "So—you want to talk. Fine. Why don't you begin by telling me what you did with the—the—"

"The body?" He shrugged. "You can look at it like it never happened."

"Absolutely." She rolled her eyes. "Of course we both know that it did."

"Sure, it actually took place. But as far as you're concerned there's no way anyone could look at it and say you had any involvement in it whatsoever."

"You're telling me you buried him. Something like that?"

"What I'm actually telling you is I don't know what you're talking about and neither do you, no matter what happens or who you talk to. I don't want to be rude, but I do want you to take that very seriously."

"And suppose I were a police detective?" Natalie said, "What would happen if I wanted to examine your car?"

He allowed himself a smile. "I forgot to mention that. I had an accident. Spilled a whole quart of oil in my trunk. It's being steam-cleaned as we speak."

"So what you're saying, that's it? It's as if Scarlotti never existed. What are you going to do?"

"What do you mean?"

"Let me ask you a question. What do you do for a living? And I mean, really."

Teddy paused for half a second and then said, simply, "I'm a car thief."

"I see. A car thief." She put her elbow on the table and propped her chin on her hand. "Let me ask you something else. How long have you been going to Palisades?"

He shrugged. "I don't know. A half dozen years. Maybe longer."

"Um-hum. I bet longer. And other places? Restaurants? That whole neighborhood? That whole—how can I put it? That whole circle? Atmosphere?

Your, ah, contacts. Which, by the way—from everything I've learned from working in this city and dealing with, with various people on both sides of the law—means, if you steal cars, somewhere, even indirectly, you have to deal with people like Anthony Bonica. Am I correct?"

"He gets his cut. Not from me. But, yes, somewhere along the line. It's the way the mob works."

"Right. So what are you going to do now? You say you buried the body or whatever. But what are you going to do tonight? Stop by Palisades, ask Anthony Bonica what's new? Because I thought about it last night. The only person who could've put Dominic Scarlotti in your trunk *is* Anthony."

He said, "You're right. And you also have a point. I'm not going to tell you I haven't thought about it. What Anthony Bonica did, you know, and what I am going to do about it."

"That's exactly what I'm worried about. What you might do in *return*."

He said, "I like that part. You being worried."

"You're cute, you know that?" she said. "But back to real life? What are your other choices? You could always move."

He pushed his coffee away and sat back. "You know what a multiple personality is?"

"Sure."

"Well, I'm not one. But—and this is the truth, I don't care how silly it sounds—right now, part of me *feels* like one. A multiple personality. Part of my brain, here I am, I'm telling you that everything's over and nothing can ever tie either one of us into what happened to Dominic Scarlotti, except Anthony could try to parade a bunch of his crew members through court, swear the last time they saw Dominic he was with me."

The toddler over in the corner started to cry. Both Natalie and Teddy looked over. The kid had slipped getting out of his booster seat and clunked his head on the table. Within seconds his shrieks were all they could hear.

Teddy turned back to Natalie. "Where was I?"

She said, "What?"

He said, "Where was—" He stopped because he couldn't even hear himself now. The kid was wailing.

Natalie frowned, shook her head and then said something to Teddy that he couldn't catch. She must've realized it because she simply dug in her purse, put a ten-dollar bill on the table and stood up. Teddy joined her as she pointed at the door of the café.

They made for the elevator, and while they waited for it she nodded her head back at The Garden and said, "Jesus, we think *we* have problems." And then broke into a smile.

Teddy was amazed because it added a whole new dimension, softened her features. Made her go from high-fashion classic gorgeousness to farm-girl beauty in just that instant.

5

HER APARTMENT was neat in the sense that it looked like it was vacu-
umed and cleaned on a regular basis. But it was messy, with books, newspapers and a few items of clothing strewn in every direction—a coat and a
scarf thrown haphazardly on the sofa; her Palisades waitress getup in a heap
in the living room; dry cleaning still in the plastic wrap hanging from the top
of the kitchen door; and a grocery bag with a loaf of French bread protrud-
ing from the top. An empty yogurt carton was in the sink, a spoon in it. In
the corner of the living room was an area that had been made into an office
cubicle. A computer sat on a desk, an opened copy of *The New York Times* next
to it, and a filing cabinet behind so that the whole thing formed an L.

Natalie said, "If you want, I can probably make coffee better than they do
downstairs."

"That would be nice," Teddy said. "Thank you." He sat at the table while
she got the pot going, trying not to look at her rear end even though he was
finding it harder and harder not to. He was also hyperaware that he had
made it into her apartment. He didn't know what it meant, but he did know
that twice, last night and this morning—meeting at the café—she had made
an attempt, seemingly, not to let it happen. Finally, so he could stop think-

ing about it, he walked over and picked up the *Times,* brought it back to the table and pretended to read it until she joined him at the table.

"All right," she said, surprising him by picking up the conversation right where they had left it off. "You were saying, what if Anthony tries somehow to pin the murder on you. Maybe that's the whole idea. He could kill you—for, you know, what'd you do, punch him in the eye? You said something about that last night, in the restaurant or else driving back here. I forget which."

"He was coming at me with a broken beer bottle at the time. But yeah."

She gave him a look. "I'm making coffee for a guy who fights people with broken beer bottles?"

"It was him, not me."

"Still."

Teddy leaned forward. "You want to know the truth. I'll tell you. My brother made a pain in the ass out of himself—he does it a lot. I think you probably gathered that last night. Anthony was in the process of getting ready to kill him. Davey, my brother, I mean. So I—stopped it." Teddy spread his hands as if to say, What would anyone have done but the same thing I did under those circumstances?

But it did seem to relax Natalie. She said, "Okay, okay, so you're not a thug. You're just a simple car thief. And now Anthony's coming after you. Maybe trying to frame you."

Teddy nodded. "Right. I don't believe a jury would *believe* them—any witnesses Anthony could produce—even if Anthony *was* crazy enough to give it a try. But it would be a huge pain in my ass. And, I have to admit, you're right. A part of me, excuse my language, is thinking, Who the fuck does Anthony Bonica think he is, pulling shit like that? Because, number one, once more you're right, it *had* to be him. He's the only one who would let it happen. Plus which he and I do go back. And number two, you're right again, this *is* where I live. And I can't, it's not right, I can't just let him get away with it. He can't go around treating honest citizens like this."

She made a production out of looking past him. "Somebody I don't know just come in the room?"

He said, "Hey, I'm trying to make a point, is all. I boost cars. I don't kill people."

"Uh-huh. But, you do realize that he's the head of a major crime family. Hell, I take that back, he is head of Philadelphia, period." She stood up, poured two cups of coffee and brought them back.

Teddy said, "Sure. But he's still the same dumb son of a bitch who I beat the hell out of twice."

She put cream and sugar down on the table and then sat down. "Twice?"

Teddy shrugged. "First time was in the third grade. I don't even know if Anthony remembers that one."

"I'm sure he does. Your brother again?"

"More or less. I've been watching out for him—well, you know."

She studied him over the rim of her coffee cup and suddenly her voice softened. "You're a nice guy, Teddy, you know that?"

"Thank you." It surprised him, how good it made him feel, hearing her say it.

But then the softness left her face. She said, "What I'd like to know is how you managed to stay alive after? After you—did whatever—to Anthony's eye."

Teddy smiled. "I'm quick on my feet."

"I said you were a nice guy. I didn't say you were funny."

He shrugged. "Put it this way. Anthony probably couldn't do anything about it while Dominic Scarlotti was around. Not without Scarlotti's say-so. And Scarlotti wasn't like Nicky Scarfo. Didn't let things get personal. Now? I don't know. I assume, Anthony putting the body in my car, is just the beginning of payback."

"And you're not worried? If I were you, I'd be long gone."

He said, "I'll be careful. That's for sure. But you have to understand. Little Anthony? Sure, he wears those custom suits, what do they run him these days? A lot. And he walks around surrounded by members of his crew.

But to me he's still the same mope who cried when I busted his nose in elementary school. Wanted to get permission to kill me a decade later when I hurt his eye, but Scarlotti wouldn't let him."

Natalie said, "Are you listening to yourself? You're talking about a guy—you yourself just said so—who walks around surrounded by 'members of his crew.' Guys with guns. You're right about one thing—this *isn't* elementary school anymore. I'm going to be truthful with you here. You don't have to act macho if you don't want to."

"I didn't realize I was. But I'll give it a shot." Teddy said, "But seriously, I work here. Philadelphia. I can't just pack up and go to some other city. Chicago, Detroit. Someplace like that. I don't have any contacts there." He smiled. "Besides, I don't like their football teams except for the Lions, and that's only on Thanksgiving Day because I've watched them since I was four years old."

Natalie said, "See, this is where I remind you we've been thrown together by circumstances. We're in a predicament. I believe I can tell you to quit bullshitting. Quit trying to change the subject."

Teddy said, "Hey, don't worry about it. All I'm going to do, if I even bother, is talk to Anthony. Nobody's going to get too excited."

She stared at him for five full seconds. "Nobody's going to get too *excited*?"

"Sure." He said, "Why should they?"

"Uh-huh? Maybe, instead of that, maybe your first priority should be to make sure no one kills you." She shook her head. "Christ, am I glad I met you."

Teddy smiled and spread his hands. "Me too."

She looked past him and suddenly her expression went sour. She said, "Oh, shit."

"What?" He turned around and saw that she was looking at the clock on the kitchen wall. Eleven-fifteen. He said it again, "What?"

"I've got a meeting with my editor." She said, "The son of a bitch likes to keep tabs on me." She made a face. "I think he worries that with me doing this Palisades gig, I'll suddenly get an overwhelming desire to become an exotic dancer." Looking at the clock again. "Christ, I'm late already."

"What are you going to do? Blow it off?"

She sounded like she was thinking out loud. "I'd like to blow him off. I've heard his speech a hundred times." She made a face and lowered her voice. "'You have to remember, Nat, your loyalty has to be with the paper.' Jesus, what am I, a subversive element? But it's not that easy because he is my boss and he can screw up my day without even half trying. Sometimes I wish he'd get hit by a bus, or else get it through his thick skull that I work better when I don't have someone watching every move I make." She looked at Teddy and smiled. "God, listen to me." Pointing at his coffee. "Listen, you finish up. I just have to change and then I'll walk you out."

Before he could say anything else she had hurried from the room. Her voice came floating back in, "So, I'm curious. A car thief. What's it like?"

He said, loudly, "What, are you thinking of maybe writing a piece about it someday?"

She yelled back, "You never know."

He said, "I don't know. It's a job."

A moment went by and then she leaned back into the kitchen doorway. "A *job*?"

"A career. It might not be something you want to have your kid strive for. Although, and I'm not going to brag, I live a comfortable life."

She gave him a funny look. "Seriously, you look at it just like it's a job? Honestly? You *are* aware that it's against the law, right?"

"Sure, but so are a lot of things. And, seriously, I steal cars. I don't bash people over the head."

"I suppose, in a way, you're right." She disappeared back into the rear of the apartment where there was a sudden noisy flurry of activities, drawers being opened and closed. Her voice came floating back out. "So what do you do? You just go out, find a car, break the window, whatever, and drive off?"

He stood up and walked to the kitchen doorway so that he could hear her better and said, "That's what everyone thinks. I suppose it's one way to do it. Maybe it's even how I got started, but I'm old enough that I have trouble remembering. But to tell you the truth, people watch too many movies."

"In what way?"

"They think all you do is connect a couple of wires together under the dash, the red one to the red one and the black one with the red stripe to something else, and off you go. Let me tell you something, dashboards on cars these days are built like the Space Shuttle—you can't get behind or underneath or above them or around them without a lot of time or else a couple of sticks of dynamite. Maybe that other stuff would work if all you were in the market for was a 1969 Volkswagen Bug. What people don't take into consideration is this: Automobile manufacturers have gotten a lot more sophisticated in the last ten years."

Her head appeared around the door again. If she was surprised to see that he had moved closer, she didn't show it. He could see her face and a tiny bit of her shoulder and had the distinct idea that she had taken her sweater and T-shirt off. What else she was wearing he could only imagine.

She smiled and said, "Just think, they must've had people like you in mind. How flattering." Just before she disappeared down the hallway she said, "Seriously, how do you do it?" then she disappeared once again.

He yelled, "What's the easiest way to start a car?"

"You mean, my own, or if I was planning a career as a car thief."

"Doesn't matter."

"A key. It's kind of a stupid question."

"Right. Absolutely. But I don't know if you realize it or not, automobile makers, it's not like they have a different key for every single car they make. I mean, where would they keep them? Most companies, for each model they make, they have a dozen, maybe fifteen different keys. Maybe they don't want people to know that, I'm not sure. But it's true."

"So?"

"So, I'm a businessman, I make investments. Call it overhead if you want. I find guys, go to different dealerships, I act like I want to buy a new car but, sooner or later I find the right guy. I take him out to lunch or meet him at a bar and we have a few beers. More often than not, I take him to Palisades. Introduce him to a couple of the dancers whose names I happen to know just from being there a number of times. What he does about *that* on his own time is up to him. He wants to invest a hundred bucks to find out some things his wife doesn't even know exist? That's up to him. All I want to do is talk to him."

She came back out to stare at him as if he were in the zoo and were some kind of animal she had never even heard of. She had a baggy sweatshirt on, but it looked like she'd just grabbed it so that she could come out and talk to him for a moment.

He shrugged. "He and I reach an agreement and I give him an envelope full of hundred-dollar bills. He gives me copies of every key made for whatever specific vehicle I'm interested in. As a bonus, I ask him to throw in all the alarm codes, program them into the little beeper things you can by at Pep Boys."

She shook her head and said, "I don't want to be impolite, but they do have things called real jobs."

"Sure they do. But I forgot to go to college. It slipped my mind at the time because, well, never mind. But I *have* been reading a lot ever since. Also, I did a couple of crossword puzzles. What I'm saying is this: You know what I'm qualified at? You don't have to guess 'cause I'm going to tell you. Cars. That's about it. I can guess at the stock market well enough to please four people that I'm aware of. But mostly what I know is automobiles. By the way, you ever meet anyone who does repossessions?"

She had turned to walk back down the hallway and without pausing she shouted, "No."

"Well, that might be something worth writing about because, to be honest, it's scary shit. You're out there, dealing with people who're both poor *and* pissed off. And, unlike what I do, they *know* you're coming for their car and they are definitely not happy about it."

He heard the sound of a door opening, the sound of hangers sliding inside a closet and then the door slammed shut. And then another door opened, sounding like it came from farther away. He also heard the distinct sound of her swearing. Teddy leaned around the corner of the kitchen door and looked in the direction she had gone. There was what appeared to be a bathroom halfway down the hallway on the right, and past that, straight ahead another fifteen feet, Natalie's bedroom. Natalie was wrapped from just above her chest to her mid-thighs in a bright blue towel, looking through a big closet, growing more frantic with each passing second.

She said, "Shit," and then looked up and caught him staring. "What are you doing? I thought you were in the kitchen."

"I was just trying to hear you better."

For a second she looked as if she was going to get mad. But then she shrugged and said, "Listen, can you do me a favor? There's dry cleaning hanging in the kitchen. Can you get it for me? A lavender blouse. You'll see it."

Teddy had no trouble finding the blouse. But then he didn't know, was he supposed to march right back into her bedroom and hand it to her. He didn't even know if he could pull it off with any kind of dignity because already, the sight of her in nothing but the towel had gotten to him. He could feel it through every muscle in his body.

She solved his dilemma by appearing in the kitchen doorway, a trace of nervousness in her voice that he'd never heard before. "Yes, that one. Thank you."

Teddy watched her take a tentative step in his direction. She reached out as if he would simply hand the blouse to her, leave and she could finish dressing. He wondered if a part of her regretted inviting him up. He certainly didn't feel like going anywhere.

She took another step in his direction and he held the blouse out. But he did it slowly, saying, "I don't know if I should even tell you this, but seeing you, like this. Hell, just plain seeing you. It's—"

She shook her head and interrupted him. "Look, I don't have time and now's definitely not the time to go down this road. Maybe—I don't know—before we leave, maybe, if you want to, you can ask me out on a date. For, say, six months from now. We can split the check and see if it works out at all. For now, though, just give me the blouse. Please?"

But she didn't reach for it. Didn't even look at it. She seemed frozen in place, watching Teddy watch her. Teddy had the distinct idea that if ever she was going to let it happen it was now, that he was looking at a very small window of opportunity because if she took even a little more time to think about it she might change her mind.

He stepped over to her and touched his fingertips to her check. He knew that if she did get the blouse she would probably scramble back into her bedroom and the next time he saw her she would be fully dressed—the successful reporter masquerading as a waitress at a topless club. Maybe it was the other way around. The successful waitress masquerading as a reporter. He was getting confused because all the rational thoughts that had been in his brain five minutes ago were suddenly at war with his hormones.

Still touching her cheek he said, "Hey . . ."

Her expression changed immediately. She pushed his hand away. Gently, but still, she was pretty firm about it. She said, "Listen, don't get the idea that there's anything—anything going on here that—that—"

He said it again. "Hey." This time reaching much more slowly. His hand moved down to brush her lightly on the shoulder.

She flinched and then reached up and took his hand off her shoulder. There was a little color in her cheeks now. Anger. She said, "What'd you do, call me up this morning because you were what? Horny?"

"You know I didn't. And you know this doesn't have anything to do with being horny."

"What is it, then? I let you in, made you some coffee. Maybe I made a mistake. At the least I should've shown you out before I changed my clothes."

"You look fine in a towel."

"Don't make me mad. You're pushing it already." She took three steps away from him and then turned back, her eyes flashing. "Do you hear yourself? 'You look fine in a towel.' Did somebody write that for you?"

"I didn't mean it in—" He paused and then said, "You're a very attractive woman."

"Yeah, I know. You keep telling me." She gave him a flat look, no expression, maybe having fun at his expense. "And *you*—you're a crook. A car thief. A guy who has dead mobsters wind up in the trunk of his car."

"I didn't put him there."

"It doesn't matter." Her face brightened. "I know what. Maybe I should call the police. This isn't my problem. All that happened, I was in the wrong place at the wrong time. With the wrong person." Pointing her finger. "You!"

Teddy walked slowly over to where she was standing. He faced her, moved slightly when she turned her head so that she had no choice but to look him in the eyes.

"You going to do it?"

"Do what?"

"Call the cops." He wondered what she would do if he mentioned the fact that her being angry—right this second was a good example—was only making her seem more attractive. Maybe she'd hit him. Instead of finding out he nodded at the phone. "You want to call the cops. I take back what I said last night. Go ahead. Call them. The phone is right in the kitchen."

She stalked past him. He followed her into the kitchen, where she grabbed the phone and started dialing. Halfway through she disconnected, stared at the floor and said, "God damn it." She looked up at him and said, "God damn *you*. Yesterday all I had to worry about was if I was going to finish

my article on time. Now"—she waved her hand to indicate her kitchen—
"I have you here, telling me about dead mobsters and then, Jesus, like that
wasn't enough, coming on to me."

Teddy said softly, "You want me to stop?"

"I want you to get out of my life."

He reached up again and touched her ear so softly that at first he wasn't
sure she could even feel it. But then he felt her shoulder muscles tense. She
seemed to think deeply for a moment before saying, "Look—"

"I *am* looking."

"Let me finish. First of all—no matter what, whether I think you're
attractive or not—"

"Do you?"

"It—Christ—that's not the point. It's not even a big deal."

"If it's not a big deal, then why don't you answer my question."

"I don't even remember what your goddamn question was."

"Yes you do."

"No I don't. And this whole thing is a mistake." She touched his shoulder. "Listen to me. I—I'm a journalist."

"I know that."

"Yeah, well, the whole idea—the point is—you don't get involved. I don't
get involved with—with—"

"What are you talking about?"

"You *don't* sleep with someone who's part of a story. You just don't *do* it. *I*
don't do it."

"What?" Now he was a little angry. "Wait a minute." He took his hand off
her. "I'm not some goddamn story."

"I didn't mean that you were. I mean—" She sighed. "I don't know what I
mean. All right?"

Teddy took a deep breath and counted to five. Then he said, as calmly as
possible considering the speeded-up way his brain seemed to be working
and the way he could feel just being near her all the way through his body.

"Yes, hell yes, it's all right. I didn't come over here to—to put you—to push you. It's just—"

"I know. 'It's just'—a lot of things. Dead people in cars. You being a crook." She shook her head and said, very slowly, "It's a *lot* of things."

Still not touching her, Teddy said, "You're a beautiful woman, Natalie."

She said, "Thank you." And then it was as if her hand moved with a mind of its own. She brought it up slowly, both of them watching it, and put it flat against his chest. "I don't want to make a huge mistake here."

"Neither do I. But it feels right. It feels better than—than a lot of times before. I know that much." Teddy carefully reached up and touched her hand where it was resting on his chest. She flinched again but didn't move away from his touch and then she slowly closed her eyes and leaned toward him. He cupped her chin and said, "Because you are—this isn't a line, I swear—my god you are *beautiful*. And I swear, coming over here today, I wasn't thinking about—about this." She gave him a look and he grinned slightly. "Okay, maybe a little. But first I wanted to make sure you were, you know, all right. After last night."

She put her head against his chest now, looked up into his eyes. "Jesus, why do I believe you when you say things like that. You're supposed to— I don't know—how do criminals act? But you're supposed to act like a bad guy. I'm supposed to be afraid to leave my purse around without keeping an eye on you."

He took a breath, bringing her head up and leaning forward until they were inches apart. Locking eyes with her and feeling a wave of excitement go through his body just because it felt so good—being this close to her. He brought his other arm up to put his hand on the lower part of her back.

She ran her tongue slowly along her lower lip. She was probably unaware of it but it sent another jolt through Teddy. He could feel himself getting aroused now. He slid his arm around her back and then he kissed her. He held back on purpose—just enough so that it didn't reach full passion on his part. She herself didn't do anything for a full two seconds, didn't put her lips together to kiss him back but didn't push him away either. But then, slowly, after what seemed an eternity to Teddy, she began to kiss him too. Moving farther into his arms and starting to murmur something softly—encouragingly—into his ear.

He reached down and pulled at the towel. She had knotted it across her chest in that way that women seemingly were born knowing how to do. When he got it undone he reached up slowly and tugged it off of her shoulders. The thing fell to the floor and he stopped what he was doing just so he could stare at her.

He said, "Jesus." And stared long enough that she finally smiled.

"You all right?"

He looked back at her face, not even hearing any of the streets' sounds from outside her apartment anymore. "I don't know. Really."

He started to unbutton his shirt and she reached out to unbuckle his belt. They were moving faster now. Making the decision had done something to them, speeded them up and increased the desire so that soon both of them were tearing at Teddy's clothes, stopping when he still had his boxer shorts on so that he could grab her and kiss her again, no holding back this time. Both of them excited. He touched her left breast and then touched the other one, running his hands back and forth softly over both of them, seeing her close her eyes and tilt her head back in pleasure. And then he felt her touch him—Jesus Christ—the coolness of her hand on his penis making him seem like his skin was on fire.

She came back into his arms. Wrapped them around him and kissed him. Kissed him again and whispered "Couch" into his ear. They shuffle-danced out of the kitchen door, moving in a clumsy, groping way, trying not to let go of the kiss, turning slightly when they got into the living room and then both bumping into the arm of the couch to fall down and get tangled up in the throw pillows. Teddy heaved them off, rolled off of Natalie just long enough to look at her one more time and then she was reaching up to him even as he was starting to ease back on top of her. He kissed her breasts, put his hand between her legs and felt the wetness of it as she gasped and said, "Jesus, just now. *Now*." Reaching down one more time to guide himself inside her.

He pushed once, hard, went all the way into her because he was lost in it, saying "Jesus, Jesus" in rhythm to their movements, in and out of her, while she grabbed at him with her right hand and reached down to push off the floor with her left because they were in that much danger of falling off.

They did end up on the floor but only because, somewhere in the middle of it, with Natalie starting to say his name, "Teddy, Ted-*dy*," louder and more quickly with each passing second, he picked her up bodily, lowered her to the carpet and started to move back and forth with his hips as fast as he possibly could. He had a vague sense that he was burning his elbows on the carpet but didn't give a shit—a feeling that things were happening fast, he wasn't going to last very long and then she arched her back, dug her nails into his biceps and along the base of his spine and he forgot all about time. Didn't remember anything else except the physical rush of coming and the surprise he felt when it was all done and he looked up to see that they were a good ten feet away from the couch, almost over on the other side of the room where there was a small, natural-gas fireplace with fake logs on a grate.

He had no idea how they'd made it there.

6

JOSEPH CARNIGLIONE said into the phone, "I wouldn't be calling you if I didn't think it was important. I know your time is valuable."

Carniglione was a *capo*—a captain—in the Gambino crime family in New York City. He had previously worked for John Gotti. He had also worked for Paul Castellano until the night of December 16, 1985, when John Gotti had Big Paulie and Tommy Bilotti gunned down in the street just outside Sparks restaurant. Carniglione had always wondered what exactly had gone through Paulie's mind the moment he saw John Gotti's brother Gene, along with Anthony Rampino, and Bobby Boriello, all of them wearing ridiculous yet effective disguises, identical overcoats and Russian-looking fur hats, waiting for him just outside the restaurant entrance and realized he had only a couple of seconds to live. Tommy Bilotti was Paulie Castellano's driver and also Paulie's only complete confidant. Tommy went everywhere with Big Paulie and talked about everything with him; from whacking that fucking drug-dealing upstart John Gotti before he whacked *them*, to how much better Paulie's dick was working now that he'd had a penile insert put in so he could bang his uglier-than-hell Colombian housekeeper, Gloria Olarte. But Tommy Bilotti was soft, out of the killing business and spending most of his days up at Paulie's big mansion—the FBI had planted a bug in the kitchen months before and Big Paulie never found out until it was too late—and he proved to be as capable of defending Castellano as a Cub Scout when John Gotti finally made his move.

Carniglione had been a personal friend of Sammy "the Bull" Gravano. He thought he understood why Sammy had done what he did, gone into the Witness Protection Program to dime Gotti out. Sammy had nineteen hits under his belt and it took a lot to shake him. But he knew it was either do that or be killed. It was a thing Joseph could see. But he also knew that if he saw Sammy today he'd whack him in a fucking heartbeat because it was treachery. A made member of the mob, no matter how good of a guy he was to be around, didn't do that kind of shit.

Carniglione was fifty-seven years old, a man with a distinctive look to him, having lost part of his ear at the age of eighteen in a bar brawl so vicious that Carniglione, even having just lost some of his hearing, had emerged as the winner. He spent the next few decades—and five years in Attica—working his way up the mob ladder until he was now in the position to answer to no one but his boss, the man who now ran the entire Gambino Family.

Carniglione had his driver take him a half a mile away from his social club in the heart of Queens and then told him to pull into a McDonald's on Lexington Avenue for the simple fact that, in this day and age, it still had an outdoor pay phone.

Carniglione exited the car after telling his driver to stay put, scanning the street out of habit, a uniformed cop giving somebody a ticket across the street and down a hundred feet, same side, a mother walking a kid in a stroller, across, with a cigarette stuck in her mouth, a hooker turning to check both directions, trolling, looking for Johns but, also, close enough to a bus stop so that maybe she could talk her way out of things if an undercover vice squad guy came along. She was starting early, paying no attention whatsoever to the uniform cop, as comfortable on the street as if she'd been born there. Two black guys were just this second walking into a liquor store a hundred feet down, the opposite direction from the hooker, both of them wearing woolen caps, gonna maybe pull them over their faces and yank out a couple of handguns. Rob the place if they hadn't noticed the cop giving the ticket. Carniglione saw the cop look up, sweep his gaze past Carniglione's car and spot the spades. He turned to speak to the motorist, talking quickly, a ticket turning into a warning because maybe those two guys were going in to buy a pint or maybe they thought it was a savings-and-loan, gonna try to make a withdrawal. The cop got back into his patrol car and Carniglione saw him reach for the radio. A moment later he was back out again, walking this way, his hand on the butt of his holstered gun, but not hurrying. You wouldn't hear any sirens but give it a couple of minutes and there'd be two, maybe three more squad cars in the immediate vicinity. Guys working robbery out of the Six-Two would be coming by a minute after that. Next to the outdoor pay phone was the door of the McDonald's. If things got ugly Carniglione could always go in there, take a leak, shake every last drop out of his pee-pee until the cops figured out what to do with the two black gentlemen. They could take care of his driver, too—Carniglione didn't give a shit—because ever since John Gotti had gone down to the feds via Sammy the Bull, Carniglione didn't trust anyone—never mind the fact that his driver was his brother.

LATE THAT AFTERNOON Saul Rubin heard the phone ring but didn't answer it at first because he was watching a show about sharks on the Discovery Channel. Itzhak had asked Saul did he need anything before he cleaned up and Saul had said he was fine. Izzy told him, in that case, he was heading upstairs to take a shower. Saul thought sharks were fascinating creatures but when he remembered where Izzy was, he got up, muted the television and picked up the phone.

The guy on the other end kept calling him Mr. Rubin. Saul told him if he was looking for a Mr. Rubin he had the wrong number, but if he felt like talking sensibly he could keep chatting. Joseph Carniglione was an okay guy, but you had to be direct with him, explain that it didn't pay for anyone to be using *anyone's* name on a line, never mind the fact that Izzy had the place electronically swept each week, including the phones.

Joseph Carniglione apologized but then almost said Saul's name again. Finally he got it right. He said, "To start with, I want to let you know that I'm calling from a Mickey D's that isn't anywhere near where I usually am."

Saul said, "A Mickey D's? I might be getting old, but what is a Mickey D's?"

"Shit, it's a hamburger place. You know, they have one on every corner."

"A McDonald's?"

"Yeah, that's what I said. Where I'm calling from, so I just wanted to let you know, you know? That, that no one is, ah, listening in."

"Ah."

"But see, we have a fucking situation, ah, a thing that we're concerned with up here. I told a friend of mine. A very important friend, I know you know who I'm talking about. The man I work for. He requested, and I told him I would, that I'd make a call, I'm talking about this one right here and that I would, ah, try to get to the bottom of it."

"This situation you're talking about?"

"Yeah, sure. That's why I'm calling."

"Well, can you tell me what it is?" Saul glanced at the TV. A crew on a research boat was lowering a huge piece of fish, it looked like grouper, into the ocean just off the side of the boat. There was a little shakiness to the camera, either nervousness or because the boat was rocking, and then a shark, Saul thought it was a great white, rocketed out of the water, grabbed hold of the grouper and started to twist. The water thrashed and then the shark was gone. Half the fish was missing too.

On the phone, Joseph Carniglione was saying, "What it is, all day, this friend of mine, he's been trying to get hold of a certain person lives down your way. On the phone. This person is someone that both you and I know. The reason, the problem is, we keep calling and no one is picking up the other end. The phone just keeps ringing if you know what I'm getting at. And, this person down there, where you are, they were expecting—at least we *thought* they were expecting this call. So this friend of mine, my boss, he asked me, he wanted me to call you because—as, ah, as, I guess, a neutral party—we were hoping you could shed some light on the situation."

Saul had a good idea of what was coming next and he knew that, as soon as he hung up the phone, he was going to go back to the desk in the corner of the study and press a buzzer that would bring Izzy on the run from upstairs whether he was finished his shower or not. But he had to ask, "Are you, by any chance, getting through to a fellow whose last name begins with the letter B? His first name starts with the letter A? Are you having success getting that person to answer *his* phone?"

"See, I told my friend that you would know exactly what the problem was without my even having to go into details. Yes. That's it exactly. We *are* getting through to that person. That second gentlemen. The one you describe as having the last name begins with B and the first begins with A. But, ah, frankly, my friend up here is concerned with the responses we're getting from that exact fellow."

Saul felt himself nodding even though he was alone in the room. He said, "Well, perhaps—perhaps you can do me a favor. Perhaps you can tell our mutual friend up in New York that I'll be in touch. I'll be in touch very soon. Tell him it might take a day or two. But tell him that when I do call I'll have a satisfactory answer." Saul took a quick breath, wondered whether his asthma was going to flare up, and then said, "But one more thing?"

"Yes?"

"Tell him—your friend—that there is a possibility, just explain that, if he hears anything, and I want to emphasize this, tell him if he hears anything, rumors, anything of that sort, ask him to please wait until he speaks with me directly. I'm afraid that there might have been a misunderstanding. This might turn out to be a thing where some of the parties were doing things only because they were assured that someone had given a specific okay to have them done. Is that something that you understand or is it necessary for me to go into greater detail?"

To Saul's relief, Joseph Carniglione said, "I understand perfectly. I think I know exactly what you're talking about, and what I'll do is this, I'll make sure our mutual friend up here gets that exact information you want him to have, and I'm positive, absolutely positive, that he'll wait until he hears from you no matter what he hears otherwise."

When Saul hung up he did walk over to the desk and press the button he had had an electrician install some years back, just under the front drawer. He heard the sound of water being shut off and then, a few seconds after, the sound of Itzhak's bare feet pounding down the stairs.

IZZY CAME through the door, holding a towel in his left hand and his pistol in his right but otherwise naked. No sign of panic on his face, though. Saul told him to relax and then said that life was full of little ironies.

Izzy wrapped the towel around his waist and sat down while Saul said, "I remember, this was back in 1946. *After* the war. Himmler, Hitler and Goebbels were dead. Goering, Speer, Dönitz and the rest were on trial at Nuremberg—I can still picture the look Goering had on his face, he came *that* close to taking over the proceedings. Ended up cheating the hangman along the way. And still, the Poles, you know what some of them did?"

Saul shook his head, remembering back to that time. "The Jews who had managed to survive the camps, obviously they were in no shape to make decisions. So what a lot of them did, they went right back to where they had been living before the war. It was a very sad state of affairs because you had to wonder, what were they expecting? To see family? To even see friends? No, there was no one left. But they went back anyway, some of them did. The thing that was the most heartbreaking, and this is *including* the camps, the Jews that went back? A lot of them, you want to know what happened?"

Izzy said, "They were murdered."

"I forget, Itzhak, I've told you of these things before. But every once in a while, and it happened just now, something in life reminds me of it. Those poor fools back in 1946, they thought, and I can't blame them, they were so hoping that if they just went back to their homeland, their old neighborhoods and villages, that everything might suddenly turn out okay. I can't say for certain, but perhaps they even thought somehow that their families that they knew—*knew*—had been reduced to smoke and ashes would be there to greet them. No one can hazard a guess as to what was in their minds."

Saul took his inhaler out of his pocket, put it in his mouth, pushed the button and said, "But, in reality, who did they think helped send them to the camps in the first place? Who was it that pointed the fingers and told the Germans where the few Jews who had escaped the ghettos were hiding? And who looted their houses, down to the last possession, as soon as they were gone? I'm not going to say that all Poles were involved. No, I won't say that. Far from it. But enough were. It wasn't just the SS or the Einsatzgruppen. It was the Jews' own neighbors. Their friends who would have them over for dinner and shop in their stores before the war broke out. And some of those neighbors, even though the Jews had managed to survive everything—or perhaps because they *had* managed to survive—it's hard to understand, but some of those same people, quite a few of them good Catholics, murdered the returning Jews. I'm talking about mostly isolated incidents. But still, the war was over. It's difficult to fathom."

"Almost impossible. But sadly, not quite. Not in this world."

"Yes." Saul sighed. "As I said, life's little ironies. Fascinating in a morbid way. And it seems we have one on our hands today. Obviously on a much, much smaller scale."

"In what way, Mr. Rubin?"

Saul said, "Well, it's exactly what we expected, Itzhak. I didn't mean to upset you by buzzing you. I knew you were in the shower. But the situation we predicted has, indeed, arisen. So now we're going to have to act as if we're completely surprised."

"The hit wasn't sanctioned?"

"No, it wasn't." Saul shook his head. He thought the situation was mildly amusing. He said, "Why don't you do this. Go on back upstairs, get dressed. Do whatever you have to do. And then, if you could, I'd like for you to run down to that club that Mr. Anthony Bonica has. I forget what it's called."

"Palisades."

Saul nodded. "That's it. Palisades. I can never remember. That's what I want you to do, though. Go on down there—and I'm afraid you're going to have to put on quite an act—and ask Mr. Bonica a question for me."

Izzy said, "And the question is?"

"Ask him, why was it he told me that the Gambino Family up in New York—who we all knew had to approve of Mr. Bonica's actions last night—ask him why he went to the trouble of telling us that the Gambino Family had sanctioned the—the thing you did—on Mr. Scarlotti? You can tell him that the reason I'm curious is, that, just now, I got a call from our friend, Joseph Carniglione, and he's wondering where in the world Dominic Scarlotti is. Make it seem like we are really worried, Izzy."

"You think Little Anthony lied to us?" Izzy smiled in amusement.

Saul said, slowly, "I have to tell you, Izzy, considering that it would be Joseph Carniglione himself who would be in the position to give the go-ahead to do something as significant as what we did, then, yes, I do believe Mr. Bonica misled us. Having said *that*, let me add that I certainly am curious to hear what Mr. Bonica tells you."

Izzy said, "I bet, whatever it is, it's a lie too."

Saul smiled. "Izzy, I'm not going to take a bet like that." Then he frowned. "Oh, yes, if Anthony gives you any problems, play your little recording for him. Let him know *exactly* where he stands."

LEAVING NATALIE'S APARTMENT Teddy remembered that life wasn't completely about sex and that he *was* going to have to have some kind of discussion with Little Anthony Bonica. He could do that or he could stop going to Palisades, begin working in areas that lessened the chances that he would ever come into contact with Anthony or any of his associates, especially Tommy Inzarella who Teddy knew to be a quiet but dangerous man. He could also ask around town, find out where Lorena Bobbitt lived.

The end result would be the same.

Leaving town might seem to be the prudent thing to do. But Teddy wasn't sure prudence had anything to do with it. If he moved he'd have to start from scratch and deal with people whose ambitions might not prove to be his own and might therefore be far from trustworthy. The other problem with that was if he moved his operation elsewhere it didn't negate the insulting fact that Little Anthony Bonica had stuck a body in Teddy's car, which could have, and still might, cause Teddy a serious amount of trouble with people who worked on *both* sides of the law.

He knew people who would've had no trouble at all coming up with a solution to the problem. Men who—it didn't matter *who* Anthony Bonica was, mob boss or not—would walk into Palisades, stick a pistol under Anthony's nose and pull the trigger. Wouldn't think twice about it. Teddy could see their point, too. The Mafia had a field day with the word *respect*. They certainly talked about it enough. But what happened when it was their turn to put the meaning into the word? Teddy thought about it, and the term *Witness Protection Program* came into his head.

Johnny D might shortchange him if, just like last night, Davey went out and played around with a game that wasn't a game at all. Johnny D would take the car off Teddy's hands, out of respect. But he wouldn't want the same thing to happen again. But Teddy knew that Johnny D wouldn't say a bad word about him behind his back and probably wouldn't let anyone else say one either.

That was because Teddy had earned his respect.

Shit, Johnny D certainly would never leave a dead man in Teddy's car.

So that's what Teddy decided to do. Go talk to Anthony and see if they couldn't come to some kind of agreement about their ongoing feud, if that was what you wanted to call it. He wasn't going to bother sticking a gun under Anthony's nose. After all, he didn't even own a gun.

But he thought, just for the hell of it, he might get one.

DAVEY-BOY SAID, "It's a—"

"A Beretta, yeah I know. A nine-millimeter."

Davey said, "Where all of a sudden did you hear about guns?"

Teddy said, "The old man had one. You were too young to remember. He was always playing with it. I think, after he came back from that stretch for B-and-E, maybe a year before, ah, before, you know, he left. I think he got violated for having one on his possession, had to go back to jail for another six months or something."

Davey's apartment was a pigsty, roaches all over old food in the sink, a line of ants from a crack in the woodwork to the top of a Kmart table and back. Dirty clothes everywhere. Teddy didn't usually like to step inside of the place; you never knew what you'd sit on. But Davey had been a gun nut all his life, in the process right now of explaining how the Beretta worked, a little deflated that Teddy already seemed to know. Davey always had at least a couple of firearms that he was fond of bringing out and showing off to Teddy or whoever else had the stomach to spend any time in Davey's apartment. Teddy had one time watched Davey take a pistol apart, it might even be this Beretta, disassemble it with the precision of a well-schooled Marine, and have it back together inside of ninety seconds while staring fixedly at a spot somewhere on the wall behind Teddy. It had been impressive as hell, but Teddy thought Davey ought to use some of that energy and focus on keeping his apartment neat.

Davey brought out another gun. A two-shot derringer that fit between the palms of his hands. He grinned and said, "Cute, huh? A forty-five, if you can believe that shit."

Teddy thought the thing looked pointless, so he turned his attention back to the Beretta while Davey put the derringer on the coffee table.

Teddy popped the clip out of the Beretta, popped the bullet out of the chamber and then took a good look at the thing. Davey said, still with that teacher-to-pupil sound to his voice, "See, that's why it's called an automatic. You fire the fucking thing and, right away, you're ready to fire again. You don't have to cock anything. It's ready. Bam!" He shrugged. "They jam sometimes. But the Berettas are pretty good—you can usually depend on the thing if, say, you have to shoot something or someone a bunch of times and you're in a hurry to do it."

Teddy heard a different tone creeping into his brother's voice. A little excitement there.

Davey pointed and started to say, "That's the—"

Teddy said, "Clip. Yeah, I know."

Davey smiled, superior. "Well," as Teddy jacked the slide a couple of times, "did you know, unless you do that, rack that thing one last time, you stand a good chance of blowing the back of your head off accidentally. A lot of mopes, they take the clip out and forget that there's still that last bullet in there. They go to clean it and *blam*, there's blood all over the wall behind them and they ain't ever going to play golf again."

Teddy had the idea that Davey-Boy liked the image and liked talking tough. It was possible he was pretending he had actually seen a wall with blood all over it. But he stayed silent while Davey-Boy picked the clip up off the table and took each individual bullet out of it. He handed it back and Teddy practiced the same thing—loading the clip, sliding the clip into the gun butt and then emptying the pistol one bullet at a time by jacking the slide again and again. When he was done with that he dry-fired the thing, trying to get used to the weight and feel of the pistol.

Davey said, as soon as Teddy was done, "Let me ask you something. You want a gun, why don't you just go get one? Nowadays—at least in PA—they have that instant waiting period, you walk into a gun shop, pick out what you want, show 'em your license and wait ten minutes. Cost you ten bucks for the state background check, but all you got to do is stand there. If you're clean, that is, and we're not talking speeding tickets here, you walk right back out with a new firearm, bingo, you're ready to go."

Teddy shrugged. "You think I ever needed a gun before? You get caught stealing a car—that's one thing. If you have a piece while you're doing it—forget about it."

Before Teddy left, he reloaded the Beretta and tried to decide how best to carry it. He absolutely didn't want to get caught by the cops with it, and it felt wrong when he stuck it inside the waistband of his trousers just in front of his hip. Every time he took a step he could feel the thing dig into his thigh. Plus which, he suddenly got afraid that if by any chance the pistol went off on its own, the first thing the bullet would encounter was his testicles. He ended up putting it behind his back. It was more comfortable and you couldn't tell it was there as long as he kept his sport coat on.

Davey watched for a moment, his eyes getting a gleam back in them and then said, "Hey, you didn't say you were just gonna *take* the thing. I thought you were gonna buy it from me. It cost me seven bills. And besides, you come here and ask me do I have a gun that you can have. What am *I* supposed to do? What if Little Anthony finds out that I had anything—*anything*, man—to do with whatever we did with his boss?" Davey picked the derringer up off the table. "What am I supposed to do, carry this? Sure, it's a forty-five caliber. Take your fucking head off. And then knock down the wall behind you. But that don't negate the fact that it only carries two bullets and you can't hit the side of a fucking barn from more than ten feet away. The barrel—unlike say, on a rifle—"

"Davey, be quiet."

"Huh?"

"All you have to do is listen to me. *You* don't have to carry any kind of gun, I don't care whether or not it'll kill a fucking elephant. I'll tell you why in a minute."

"I bet it would."

Teddy said, confused, "You bet *what* would?"

Davey held the derringer up. "This. I bet it *would* kill an elephant. You get close enough."

"Davey, can we keep on track here?"

Davey gave him what he probably assumed was a sneer. "Sure, tell me you're gonna pay me for the pistol." He nodded at the Beretta in Teddy's hands.

"I'm not going to pay you for the pistol."

"She-it."

"The *reason* I'm not going pay you for it is because, one way or another, you're gonna get it back. Either I'll decide in a week or two that I don't need it any more. Or else, Anthony Bonica is not going to listen to reason and I might wind up dead or in jail. I promise, whichever happens, I'll make sure you get the goddamn thing back. Worst-case scenario, if it's registered, you go to the cops and *ask* for it. Besides"—Teddy pulled an envelope from his inside jacket pocket—"it's not like you're hurting for money." He tossed it to Davey.

"The fuck is that?"

Teddy said, "I'll tell you what it is. Five grand."

"You shittin' me?"

"No. Five thousand dollars. It's yours. But *only* if you do one thing."

Now Davey looked suspicious. "And what's that?"

"You said it yourself. Asked yourself, 'What should you do'?" Teddy pointed at the derringer. "Should you use that little two-shot piece of crap to protect you if—and I do mean, *if*—Anthony Bonica or Tommy Inzarella pays you a call? No. That's a stupid idea. But I *am* going to tell you a good one. I'm going to *tell* you what to do. What you have to do—as a matter of fact—to keep that five large."

Davey kept looking at the bulging envelope, wanting, Teddy knew, to tear the thing open. Find out whether or not Teddy was playing with his head.

He waited until he had Davey's full attention and then said, "You remember, I don't know, we were like eight and five years old. Mom had her cousin—her second cousin, I think—come up to visit us from Florida. Miami Beach rings a bell, but I don't believe it's that's important. What *is* important is this. Claude? That was his name. We had to call him Uncle Claude, but we didn't like him because he wore dentures and his breath stank. You remember?"

Davey said, "I don't know. I guess. Maybe."

"Good, 'cause here's what you're going to do. Last I heard, I think it was two years ago, Uncle Claude was still alive. He's down in Miami somewhere. In a rest home. I think he's senile. But what would be nice is this: I find out exactly where he is. Then you pack a few things, go down there for a week and see how he's doing. Tell him I miss him more than words can convey, but I got tied up. Once you've been there for a week, give me a call. I'll let you know how things are back here. Whether or not I think it's a good idea for you to come back. Meanwhile, that five grand? That's for expenses. A nice hotel. Whatever. Just don't blow it on something stupid."

"You're gonna send me down to see some old fart, doesn't even know his own name—let alone mine?"

"I'm going to send you down with a nice chunk of change. Unless, do you want to give me that envelope back? And also, unless you want to take the chance that Tommy Inzarella is gonna come knocking on your door." Teddy held the Beretta up in the air. "I don't think it matters how many of these things you have—no offense—but Tommy'll take it out of your hands and eat it. Then he'll slit your throat if that's what Anthony Bonica wants him to do. So go down to Florida. Get a beachfront room, my expense. Enjoy the view and maybe try to get laid when you're not visiting Uncle Claude. Maybe get him laid too. It might cure his senility and surely wouldn't have any detrimental side effects."

"But what about—"

Teddy said, "Davey!" loudly enough to shut his brother up.

"What?"

"You have to understand, I'm not asking you. I'm *telling* you. I want you to look me in the eye and promise me, this time tomorrow morning? You'll be in Florida. Promise me."

It took awhile, but Davey finally looked him in the eye and promised.

Teddy said, "Yeah? Well, listen, I'm gonna call this number—your apartment—tomorrow night. And I *don't* want to hear you answering the phone, okay."

"I already promised."

Walking down the hallway he heard Davey yell something, so he went back and peered in the still-open door of the apartment. "What now?"

Davey said, "The fuck am I supposed to do if this goddamned Uncle Claude guy is dead?"

Teddy shook his head. "Davey, you have no imagination, you know that? If Uncle Claude is dead, you go to the nursing home regardless. Find some other poor son of a bitch who doesn't know what year it is. Pretend you're *his* nephew and make *him* happy for a few days."

ANTHONY WAS STILL on the phone, and Tommy Inzarella had stopped watching the girls arrive for work, walking in bunches, laughing, getting ready to put their asses on the line more or less. Now he was paying attention to Anthony because there was something creeping into his voice that Tommy hadn't heard all day. It took Tommy a moment to come up with it, and when he did he took another moment to try to remember if he had *ever* heard it in Anthony's voice before. He didn't think he had.

From where he sat, he could look past the two stages, past the bar and see where a shaft of skewed sunlight came through the front stained-glass window. He couldn't actually see the entrance to the club. *That* was around the short corner to the right and another fifteen feet on. But someone coming into the building, unless he broke into the employees' exit in the kitchen, which was locked from the inside, either had to come in that exact way—the front—or he had to come in to Tommy's right, the back exit. The back was open now to air the place out but was locked every night when the place was packed. It was kept that way to keep any deadbeat—and there were a lot of them—who thought he could have a few drinks, stare at the girls and get out without picking up the tab. All Tommy had to do to see everything in that direction was turn his head forty-five degrees to his left, look in the big mirror over the nearest wall, and he'd be able to see exactly who was coming toward him before they had a chance to figure out what *they* were seeing.

Anthony always had at least two of his guys hanging around. It was Tommy's job to make sure of that. Right now Nicky Migliaro and Frankie Morelli were talking to three of the dancers while making a half-assed effort at keeping their eye on the door. Twice in the last half hour Tommy had caught them walking as far away from the front entrance as the door on the opposite side of the club where the girls went to take off their clothes and put on makeup. He knew he was gonna have to speak to them again soon. Explain to them that their job was to watch the *door* and not the poontang— they could look at *that* all they wanted on their time off. Maybe he'd tell them, hey, they liked hanging with the women so much? No problem. They could drop their slacks tonight, get up there and dance in their underwear just like the broads. See how they liked that.

But he suddenly realized what the tone was in Anthony's voice.

It was fear.

Tommy took his eyes off Frankie and Nicky just in time to see Anthony hang up the phone. There it was, a look in Anthony's eyes that Tommy hadn't ever seen before, like he wasn't paying attention to any of his surroundings, he was still back there talking to whoever had called him and wasn't even aware that the phone was back on the hook.

Tommy saw movement out of the corner of his eye, Nicky or Frankie moving back around the front entrance—was it possible that they had read his mind and were actually going back to work? He decided he'd wait for Anthony to come back from where he was before he said anything. But Anthony was still gone, still deep in thought about something, and the sound in his voice—fear—had somehow transferred itself to the expression around Anthony's mouth. His lips were tight together and he was grinding his teeth. Tommy thought, here we go, watching Anthony work his way past fear toward a thing that was much more familiar to Tommy.

Rage.

Tommy was relieved, more used to seeing this expression on Anthony's face. Almost uncontrollable anger. Jesus, Anthony made Nicky Scarfo look like a reasonable guy sometimes. Rage, fury, whatever you wanted to call it, was Anthony's normal expression, unless he was banging a broad, even then sometimes not if the broad didn't fake an orgasm convincingly enough.

Tommy waited another three seconds, watching Anthony's face go through a range of expressions and come right back to fury and then finally he leaned forward to say, "Anthony, whatever it is, somebody told you something on the phone, it's bothering you? Let me ask you a question," waving behind him at Nicky, Frankie and the dancers. "You got something on your mind that someone just told you, it's causing you anxiety, who the fuck are you going to talk about it with besides me? Vicki? Nicky or Frankie? You see anyone here at the club besides me that you tell your troubles to?"

Anthony came back to earth finally and looked up, about to tell Tommy what was happening. But then Anthony's gaze kept on moving, up past Tommy's face to land somewhere above Tommy's head. Close. Anthony's eyes locked on something that Tommy knew he would see if he turned his head, looked behind him toward the front entrance. And it wasn't going to be Vicki or one of the other girls, wasn't going to be Frankie Morelli or Nicky Migliaro, not from the look on Anthony's face. Tommy knew, too, that he wasn't going to like what he saw because he heard Nicky Migliaro shout, "Hey, the fuck you doing?" at somebody headed this way, causing Anthony to stare over Tommy's left shoulder. Tommy's hand snaked into his jacket to feel the butt of the Glock that he had under his armpit even as he felt someone step so that they were directly behind him.

A voice said, "Mr. Inzarella, did you forget to put on deodorant this morning? Is that hand going to come out holding onto one of those little roll-ons or are you planning to keep it inside your jacket until I leave?"

Tommy froze, recognizing the voice and realizing that even if he had needed to bring his Glock out it was already way too late. He glanced across the table, expecting to see concern in Anthony's face to go along with the fear that had been there a moment before. Seeing Anthony smiling instead, any trace of fear gone, looking up and winking, Jesus, he was a schizophrenic, a chameleon, and saying, lightly, "Izzy—Itzhak—how the fuck are you? You come by to have a drink, maybe play with one of my dancers? Either one and it's on the house."

Tommy watched Izzy grab a nearby chair and bring it over. Izzy didn't have anything in his hands. No gun in sight anywhere.

Nicky Migliaro came up to the table and nodded at Izzy. "You want I should throw this fuck outta here, Anthony?"

Tommy said, "I don't think you could, Nicky. You want to do something useful, why don't you go check on Frankie, make sure he isn't getting raped by the girls."

Nicky said, "What?" and Tommy told him it meant get the fuck away from them.

Izzy sat down, turned around and surveyed the club. And then slowly turned back to look at Anthony.

When he spoke there seemed to be an almost painful expression on his face, like he was about to deliver bad news, somebody had died, something like that, and it hurt him almost as much as it was about to hurt Anthony.

"Mr. Rubin had an interesting conversation today. A fellow we both know, Mr. Joseph Carniglione called him and was a bit perturbed—"

Anthony said "perturbed" not like he didn't know the word, but more as if he didn't quite believe Izzy had used it.

Izzy continued his sentence as if he had never stopped, "—by the fact that he couldn't get in touch with Dominic Scarlotti." And here Izzy spread his hands and said, mildly, "I'm certain I wouldn't know, but apparently Mr. Scarlotti and Mr. Carniglione keep in regular touch. Spoke on the phone and occasionally met. Whether it was every day or not, you would be in a position to know better than Mr. Rubin or I would."

Tommy wanted to lean over and whisper into Anthony's ear that now was the time to take it easy. This wasn't Nicky Migliaro or Frankie Morelli sitting here, complaining that the girls weren't putting out for free, or some asshole union rep moaning about the size of his kickbacks. But he knew the look in Anthony's eyes and knew that whispering in his ear, or hitting him with a baseball bat for that matter, wasn't going to change whatever it was he had in mind to say.

Anthony said, "You talked to Joey, huh?"

Izzy shook his head. "Not personally. I'm just doing a favor for Mr. Rubin."

"Yeah, right. Saul talked to Joey Carniglione. Or you talked to fucking Joey. I don't see that it makes any fucking difference. Let me tell you a little something about Joey Carniglione. He's an old fuck that's gonna drop dead of a heart attack—" Anthony made a point of looking at his wristwatch and then said, "—any fucking second now. Are you telling me, sending a message through your boss, that Joey Carniglione is of *any* fucking significance to me? Well, Izz-zzy, why don't you do this. Why don't you go back to Mr. Rubin, 'cause I know what you're gonna say and I don't got time to fucking discuss it, go on back and tell him. Yeah, I fucking lied. I told a fucking fib when I hired you through your boss to do a hit on my ex-boss. Ask him *this* though, now that's it's done: Scarlotti is gone. What the fuck difference does it make *what* Joseph-fucking-Carniglione from New York fucking City thinks about it? They want to come down here, to *my* fucking city, tell me they don't approve? Why don't you call them up and tell them to bring some pine boxes with them? We can put them on Amtrak. When they hit New York they'll be ready for their own funerals."

"Excuse me," Izzy said, dead calm, "Mr. Bonica, but why do you use that word so much?"

For the first time Anthony looked off guard. "What fucking word?"

"That one. 'Fuck,' 'fucking.' I meant to ask you before. I was listening to you last night, talking to Mr. Inzarella." Izzy nodded at Tommy, "And just now. I think you use it in virtually every sentence that comes out of your mouth."

Anthony stared at Izzy for a second and then burst out laughing. "Fuck, tell me you're not fucking serious."

Tommy watched him say it and had to wonder, was Anthony out of—he thought of Izzy's question for a second but couldn't help himself—his fucking mind? Why create headaches with Izzy? It was the same thing as saying you wanted to piss off Saul Rubin. What would be the point?

Anthony had turned to Tommy by then and he said, like he still couldn't quite believe it, "Tommy, get this Jew—" Turning to Izzy, "How old are you?"

Izzy said, mildly, "I'll be thirty-nine. October nineteenth."

Anthony nodded, turning back to Tommy, still grinning, and said, "This Jew," pointing his thumb back at Izzy, "he's thirty-nine. Almost. Maybe we should throw a party for him in a coupla weeks. He comes into my fucking place like I owe him a big favor or else it's his fucking Bar Mitzvah and, first, he calls me a liar and then he questions my use of, what are they? Adverbs, some shit?"

Izzy said, "Interjections. Adjectives. It was only a question."

"Now I'm getting *another* fucking grammar lesson here."

Tommy said, "Anthony, maybe we should listen—"

But it was as far as he got. Anthony smashed his fist hard enough down on the table that Anthony's Diet Coke spilled over and Tommy had to grab a couple of napkins to keep it from running onto his trousers.

"Izzy, what you got to remember"—Anthony stuck his index finger out so that it was pointed at Tommy—"my associate here, he's a compassionate man. I don't know. Sometimes, I wish I were more like him. Able to see some of the—the what? The subtleties of life." He hit the table again but not nearly as hard and said, "But, what the fuck, I can't. I am what I am. So when you come in here, my fucking place, to tell me maybe I fibbed to you and maybe the New York crime families—who're they to me anyway?—are pissed off because they think this is the old days and I forgot to go to them to get permission to do what I did? I say, fuck 'em. You relay *that* message to your boss. And while you're at it, explain to Saul Rubin how it was that you missed Dominic wearing a fucking wire even though you went through the fucking motions of searching us all. Had Dominic's pants around his ankles and you *still* didn't see it. You wanna go explain that one, Izzy?"

For the very first time, Izzy looked startled. Tommy watched his face, a bit of color, a blink, a quick breath—if you didn't know him, you wouldn't even notice. But he sat forward, staring at Anthony. "What are you talking about?" Forgetting to call Anthony Mister Bonica for once.

Anthony pointed at the phone like it was a living object. "I just this minute, before you walked in, got a call. A guy, he's a detective with the Philly cops, got a loser fucking gambling habit. He can't pay me off, his teams lose? Which is every time this guy bets, that's how bad he is. I let him slide 'cause I'm a generous motherfucking guy." Anthony grinned. "Plus which, in return, he passes along any information he thinks I oughtta know about."

Tommy turned to look directly at Anthony. John Freeman, a cop out of the Twelfth Precinct, a degenerate gambler—but a guy who would never fuck with Anthony. If Detective Freeman had called to say there was a wire on

Dominic, they were fucked. Anthony didn't act like they were, though. He was still talking okay, with an even tone to his voice. He and Izzy could be discussing food for all the emotion he was showing now.

Now he told Izzy, "One thing, this guy, he never—he wouldn't even think about it—he never passes me shit. You understand?"

Izzy said, "Mr. Scarlotti was *not* wearing a recording device."

Anthony turned to Tommy, jerking a thumb at Izzy, "This guy, you notice. Never unsure of himself." Turning back to Izzy. "Listen to me, you schmuck, I am not jerking anybody off. You understand? This fucking cop, he knows better than to jerk me off, you understand *that?* So, you wanna go back and ask your boss which he thinks is more important, some guinea fuck up in New York who stopped being a wise guy ever since they flew those fucking airplanes into the World Trade Center? Or maybe we should believe—instead—my guy who informs me that, all of a sudden, a tape exists of us—you actually—whacking Dominic Scarlotti?"

IZZY TOOK a deep breath, and wondered how he was going to handle this? He had, right this second, the edited recording of Dominic Scarlotti's murder. But he had to know whether Anthony was bullshitting him or if it was possible that Scarlotti really—somehow—had had a device on him. Izzy didn't believe it was possible because he had searched Scarlotti himself. Watched him drop his pants and—

Hell, there it was, right there. An amateurish mistake. Izzy had been so busy doing things according to Anthony's plan—*pretending* to search for a wire—that he had let Scarlotti drop his own pants. Hadn't really checked him out except as a way of relieving any suspicion on Dominic's part. So, yes, the possibility did exist that Anthony was telling the truth. Then again, the possibility also existed that Anthony was just trying to put one over on him. Create some leverage of his own. But could Izzy afford to bank on that? Un-un. Not until he found out positively one way or the other.

And he had to put any plans he had for showing his own hand—the fact that he had his own recording—on the back burner until he figured his way out of this.

He got his emotions under check and then said, looking deadpan right back at Anthony, "I guess, between everything that has happened since last night—I guess we do have a *fucking* problem on our hands."

Anthony sat back—Izzy could see how satisfied he was with himself. He had a problem, sure, they all did, but he was ahead of Izzy for once—and folded his own hands on the table in front of him. He seemed to time it, like a good comedian would with his punch line, looking at his hands, and then up to Izzy, grinning from ear to ear, to say, "No, no, no, Izzy. We don't have a problem. *You* have a fucking problem. 'Cause, me? I know ex-act-ly where the body is."

Izzy said, "And where is that?"

"You know a guy name of Teddy Clyde?"

Izzy cocked his head, thinking, and then shook it. "No, I can't say I do."

"Well, that don't matter. All you need to know is Teddy Clyde's a bullshit car thief and an asshole at the same time. He's also driving around, I'm talking, right this fucking second, with Dominic's body in the trunk of his car. He don't know it, but he gets pulled over for a traffic violation he's gonna spend the rest of his days in Gratersford fucking Penitentiary.

Izzy sat up straight, stared across the table and said, slowly, having a hard time not shouting at Anthony or reaching across the table and snapping his neck. "You mean to tell me"—stopping because he still couldn't believe it— "that you put Mr. Scarlotti's body in some *car thief's* automobile?"

"Izzy," Anthony said, grinning, "you sound like you're gonna have a fucking coronary."

"Mr. Bonica, whatever I sound like is of no importance. But what is important, is this: You say *I* have a problem, something about maybe the fact is I was the one who pulled the trigger. If there is a tape, whatever it might be, then I'm sure you know, we *all* have a problem." It crossed his mind, Was it possible that Dominic Scarlotti had discussed his knowledge of Saul Rubin's arms deal with Anthony? Was this where this was headed?

He needed to talk to Saul.

Anthony was talking again, shaking his head, grinning. "No. I still don't have a problem. Tommy here, he don't have a problem. 'Cause all I have to do, I send Nicky and Frankie over there"—pointing toward the front of the club—"over this guy's place. We pick him up. B-a-bing, I solve *your* problem like that." Anthony sat back. "And then, after? Well, I feel like being a good guy, I call you up, tell you it's been taken care of. Course, if I'm in a bad mood, anybody does anything to piss me off, maybe I forget your phone number." Anthony leaned forward to stick an index finger under Izzy's nose. "The point being, everything works out okay maybe you won't ever make the mistake of coming into *my* club with some kind of hard-on again, you Jew fuck. You know what I'm saying, Izz?"

7

THE MOMENT he stepped out of the bright sunlight and entered the dimness of the building, Teddy Clyde decided that it was the stupidest idea he had ever come up with. What the hell did he hope to accomplish? Maybe he should've followed his own advice and gone down to Miami with his brother. Rent a car instead of stealing one for a change and cruise the beaches. Take the time to make some connections and start up his business down there. Become a Miami Dolphins' fan and not worry about what his reputation in Philadelphia was or wasn't.

Instead, here he was, going into a place that he couldn't ever remember being in before it was dark outside. Seeing it as it was getting ready to open, a few girls over to the side, a couple of them eyeing him, maybe even recognizing him, but none of them smiling or acting like they were glad to see him, which they would have done automatically if the place was open for business. Teddy had seen the women before but was having trouble coming up with names because they were fully dressed and he was used to seeing them dance naked.

He had the idea in his head that he might never come out of the place again.

But it was too late to turn around because two guys were talking to the women. He didn't have trouble recognizing *them.* He'd seen them dozens of times. A couple of guys on Anthony Bonica's crew. Frank—Frankie something. Frankie Morelli. Yeah. The other guy was Nicky Migliaro. Both looking back at him now. Recognition on their faces, but surprise too. Like either they knew what had been put in the trunk of Teddy's Acura or they just weren't used to anyone coming in at this hour—one thirty-five in the afternoon. Most of the guys who came here on a regular basis were either still asleep at this hour or worked legitimate jobs.

Frankie Morelli was headed his way, raising his hand and pointing at the door. He was saying the words, "Hey, Teddy," recognizing Teddy right back, "you got to fucking know, business hours—" but stopping right there because a voice came from the back, Little Anthony's, who only now Teddy realized was visible in a large mirror that hung along one wall just past the bar.

Teddy put a smile on his face, getting used to the dimness in the back here, walking toward the table while saying to Frankie Morelli, "Hey, I'm expected," because it seemed to be partially true and it also didn't look like Anthony, or Tommy Inzarella, for that matter, sitting next to Anthony with a cold expression on his face, was about to shoot anyone without at least talking about it first. Nobody pulling pistols and playing John Wayne. Maybe they were all going to have a drink while they were waiting to see what came next.

A third man sat there too. Facing away. Big shoulders inside a black jacket over a black turtleneck. Way too hot for the kind of weather they were having outside. Teddy assumed he was another one of Anthony's crew. Or a business associate. A loan shark or a union rep—except for the outfit—here to pay Anthony money and shoot the shit with him afterward. Possibly wait until the girls got into costume.

The carpet was a cliché wine-burgundy with dark slashes every two feet, inch-thick zigzags that all seemed to point in the direction of the stage. Teddy made himself keep walking across it, one step at a time, while he thought about two things: What was going to happen next, and did Anthony buy that exact carpet on purpose? Did he think that somebody actually needed to follow the zigzag pattern to figure out where the good-looking women all danced?

It wasn't until he got up to the table that he saw that the third guy was Itzhak Feldman. Izzy. Teddy had seen him a few times before. He hadn't ever seen him in Palisades, though. Izzy's hands were folded in front of him and it wasn't until Anthony smiled and said, "Teddy, man, how the fuck are you?" like they were old war buddies, that Izzy took his first real look at Teddy.

Teddy wasn't sure, but he thought that he had actually spoken to Izzy in the past. He'd seen him with Saul Rubin, who everybody knew was an honest jeweler, but who everybody *also* knew was a fucking deadly mobster behind the gentle-looking expression on his face. Teddy had heard the gossip; Saul Rubin was bigger than a lot of governments. He had the capability to make or break more than a few dictators' grip on their countries. He was an arms dealer who didn't care if the Palestinians shot at Israelis and the Israelis shot back—all using arms brokered by Saul.

Teddy had heard that Saul had played a part in the breakup of the former Soviet Union and, while it was a stretch, Teddy wouldn't waste his time arguing the fact with anyone. It wasn't worth it and it might just be true.

Teddy could remember one night, a few years back, when he and Izzy had arrived at a coat-check counter in some Center City restaurant at the same time. Izzy was getting his and Mr. Rubin's coats and Teddy was getting his date's coat. He thought they might've talked about the weather. It had snowed or something and they had bullshitted about that. Both of them being polite because why not and because they both knew that they had something in common. Beyond that Teddy had no idea why Izzy would be in Little Anthony's topless club on this particular day.

He hoped it didn't have anything to do with anybody putting bodies in other people's trunks.

It took a lot of effort just to sit down. There was one more chair at the table, and Tommy Inzarella hooked his foot around the leg and slid it out. Anthony said, smiling, "Teddy, my man, have a seat," pointing at Izzy, "you know Itzhak here, I bet. We were just talking about you. And fuck, can you believe it, you walk into my club like you can read my mind. You're something else, you know that?"

Teddy said, "Coincidences, huh?" smiling because it worried the hell out of him, the way Anthony was acting. Left him with nothing to do but act like he didn't care.

Teddy sat down and looked at Izzy. Izzy said, "Now I have it. You're the guy, someone wants a relatively new car, they come see you? Am I correct?"

Teddy thought it was a nice way to put it. Relatively new. Maybe used-car dealerships should use that slogan instead of preowned. He said, "Some people have that idea. I'm not sure, except, maybe they remember back to when I was much younger. Right now, what I do is sell securities. Stocks and bonds. You want one of my cards?"

"No, that's all right. If I want to find you I can always ask Mr. Bonica here."

That reminded Teddy of something he'd been struck by when he'd stood with Izzy at the coat check in that restaurant a couple of years back. Izzy had referred to everyone by their last names. Or he'd put a Mister or Miss in front of their first names if he didn't seem to be sure of their last names.

Teddy felt like he was being stared at, so he turned to see what Tommy Inzarella was doing. Tommy was staring at him just as Izzy had been.

He said, "Tommy, hey, how're you doing?"

Tommy shrugged. "What can I say? I was down in Atlantic City last week, my wife's busy spendin' every fucking nickel I got in the fucking slot machines but she has time to bitch that it's too hot to go down to the beach. I bring her back here, she starts bitchin' that it's too hot to go out to the fucking King of Prussia Mall. The Court, she calls it. What am I supposed to do, turn down the fucking outside thermostat? Call up God and complain?"

Teddy smiled. "You could always go up to the Poconos. I always heard, if it's ninety-five here, it'll be ten degrees cooler up there. You got the Delaware Water Gap—all that water, a lot of trees—and, I guess, a different elevation. Gives you more of a breeze." Teddy was thinking, Keep talking until he could figure out why nobody was asking what the fuck he was doing here yet.

Tommy said, "Yeah, hey, that's not a bad idea. What I should do, you know that place, they got that big lake? Shit—Lake . . . Lake Wallenpaupack or some bullshit name. I read about that somewhere."

Teddy tried smiling and said, "I know it."

Anthony had been looking at the two men like he was watching a tennis match. "You guys done? You want to go over to the fucking bar and pour a couple of beers? Keep fucking chatting? Or do you want to cut the shit."

Tommy Inzarella turned back to Anthony and said, relaxed, "It's okay, Anthony, we all know Teddy here in varying degrees. I'm saying hello. Having a conversation. But if you want, if that's what you're saying, it can be over right now." He looked back at Teddy. "Unless, you got anything else you want to chat about?"

There was something in Tommy's expression that Teddy couldn't figure out. He glanced to his right and saw that Izzy was watching Tommy too. Something different in Izzy's face all of a sudden, like he was filing something away so he wouldn't forget it. Teddy realized that, except for Izzy, who hadn't shown a flicker of emotion, Tommy, of all of them, seemed the most calm. Teddy wondered why that was.

He said, to Anthony, "I can listen if you want. Somebody else has something to say."

Anthony stared at him and then said, "You wanna listen? Listen to this. What we have here, Ted-*dy*, is a fucking situation. You look in the trunk of your car any time recently?"

Teddy said, "If you're asking me, did I find something inside my trunk yesterday that I didn't expect, then yes, I did. I was looking for my golf clubs, but I had trouble finding them."

Anthony grunted. "Golf clubs. You wanna know what? You grew up in my neighborhood but every time I see you, you look more and more like one of those yuppie faggots I see when I take a drive out in the suburbs which I try to do as little as fucking possible." He put his hands on the table, palms down hard against the top. "I sit here, this close to you? I'm ready to puke. I hear Tommy talking to you like you deserve some kinda fucking respect, I'm ready to puke again. You say you found something in your trunk? *I* say we cut the crap. What you found? I want it back."

Teddy said, "My golf clubs?" and saw out of the corner of his eye a quick smile cross Tommy Inzarella's face. Even Izzy seemed to think it was a tiny bit funny, because he looked down at his hands and then back up at Teddy, and when he did, there was a softer look on his face. Teddy had the uncomfortable idea that, while Izzy might admire his guts, he also had some inner knowledge of how close Teddy was to pissing his pants.

Anthony half stood, turned to Tommy Inzarella and said, loudly, "Hey, Tommy, you're the one, all the time, I want to do something and you? You're telling, me, 'Anthony, be patient.'" He pointed at Teddy. "Is that what I'm supposed to do right now?" Jabbing his finger. "I'm supposed to be patient with this fuck?" Now he looked at Teddy and said, "I shoulda whacked your ass a long time ago."

Tommy started to say something but Izzy held up a hand and said, "Mr. Bonica"—talking to Anthony but watching Tommy at the same time—"if you don't mind, perhaps I could speak to Mr. Clyde. Explain our view of the situation. I'm only saying this because it appears to me that perhaps there's some—some bad *feelings*—between the two of you."

It took a moment, Anthony still standing half out of his chair and leaning over the table with his anger so plain that Teddy could feel it. But finally he sat back down. He even smiled, a brief flicker that had nothing to do with humor. "You know what, Izzy? You're starting to sound just like Tommy here. He spends half his life saying that exact kinda shit to me. 'Why don't we settle down.' Hey, I know what, maybe, something ever happens to Tommy you could stop by every once in a while, tell me to take a couple of deep breaths."

He turned and stared at Teddy, still talking to Izzy. "*You* want to explain things to this fuck? Tell him how close he is to being carried out of my club on a fucking stretcher I hear any more cracks about golf clubs? Be my fucking guest."

Teddy was listening closely to Anthony's voice. Getting past how red he was in the face because anyone who knew anything about Anthony knew he was always pissed off about something. But this was different, what he was listening to, the tone, the anxiety. It suddenly occurred to him that there was a reason that Izzy was trying to calm Anthony down. Tommy Inzarella, too, reaching out and touching Anthony right now, and saying, "Hey, Anthony, c'mon, we're talking to Teddy. That's all we're doing. Talking." There was a mood hanging over the table that Teddy hadn't expected.

Teddy leaned back in his chair as Izzy looked over at him—ready to present some situation in which all three men had made a mistake, businessmen overestimating a market for their product and now scrambling, but politely, to minimize the damage. Teddy looked carefully at all of them and knew, Jesus, Teddy had been worried, coming in here? These guys were *scared.*

Only thing Teddy had to figure out for sure was, What was in it for him?

IZZY THOUGHT Teddy Clyde made a habit of getting by in life by relying on his smile, the charm there. Nice teeth and a good-guy look to his face. It turned out he did remember Mr. Clyde. He recalled a restaurant, talking to Teddy about a snowstorm, knowing Teddy was some kind of criminal but thinking, back then, that he was an individual who stole art. Fine paintings out of museums or rich people's houses.

It took the same mind-set though—stealing art or automobiles—expensive ones because Izzy could tell with one look that Teddy Clyde wasn't into hot-wiring Honda Civics. Teddy seemed to have managed to stay out of prison, so Izzy assumed he had to be fairly good at his work.

He was a little smart-mouthed, though, asking Anthony did he mean golf clubs when he knew damn well Anthony was talking about his boss's body. But that wasn't a reason to form a judgment about him yet. All that might be was a form of protection, a defense mechanism so that Teddy could hide the fact that he was afraid.

Izzy cleared his throat and waited for Teddy to glance in his direction. There was a look on Teddy's face as if he knew more about what was happening here than he was letting on. Izzy wasn't surprised. He was sharp, that was clear enough. Surely a lot sharper than Anthony Bonica seemed to give him credit for.

Izzy said, "Mr. Clyde, apparently a thing has happened which, in effect, involved you in a situation that was none of your business and, ah, put you in an awkward situation." Izzy glanced at Anthony Bonica. "What we're here to say is, that, number one, we're very sorry if what occurred caused you even the slightest inconvenience."

Anthony said, "Jesus fucking Christ." Izzy ignored it, and Teddy Clyde seemed to get a quick, ironic smile on his face that was gone a second later. Izzy wondered whether, under different circumstances, he and Teddy Clyde might find that they had some common interests. Maybe. But maybe not.

Izzy said to Teddy, softly, "All we're trying to do is rectify what has been an unfortunate misunderstanding."

TEDDY SAID, "Okay. Let me see if I have this straight. One of you, maybe all of you, you put a very compromising item—fuck it—you put a dead god-damned body in the car I drive. Trying, at the least, to make my life miserable. And now you're saying it's a mistake?"

Tommy Inzarella said, sounding quiet and sincere enough that it was hard to tell where Izzy left off and Tommy began, "That's it, exactly, Teddy.

There was some confusion. Mr. Scarlotti had, ah—had a heart attack. Very sudden. Try to understand, we were worried, as I'm sure you can imagine, that if the wrong people found out before we were in a position to, ah, consolidate our—our business interests—that those same people might try do something drastic."

Teddy turned to Izzy. "And now, what *you* are saying is—wait a minute," looking around, "are we being overheard here? The feds?"

Anthony said, "The fuck you think I am? An idiot."

"Good." Teddy said, looking around at the other three. It was at that moment that he made up his mind, figured how he'd play this one. "Soon as I saw who was in my trunk, I figured it had to be some kind of mistake. Thought, come on over here, you know, you guys would say what to do." Looking over in Izzy's direction. "I didn't know you would be here, but hey."

Izzy took a long look at Teddy and then turned slowly to Anthony. "See that, you were worried. And now, just like we were hoping, Mr. Clyde here is going to help us out." Teddy was watching the way Izzy could go from talking, animated a little bit, to being absolutely still in just that couple of seconds it took to finish a sentence. He thought of a predator, some kind of lizard, the analogy not being that Izzy *looked* like a lizard, just that he had that sleepy-looking patience, a stone until it was time to talk, or move. Do whatever.

Teddy said, "You bet. Only thing is, since, at the time, I didn't think it would be a good idea to keep Mr. Bonica in my car—well—I moved him."

Tommy said, quickly, "Where to?"

Teddy took a deep breath, knowing that he could simply go dig Dominic Scarlotti up, hand him back over and then watch to make sure that Anthony didn't come after him.

Or he could play it this way.

He decided, fuck it, Anthony was going to come after him regardless. He frowned, hey, look at me, I'm truly puzzled here, and said, "That's the funny part, I can't seem to remember right this second."

Izzy and Tommy were motionless. Behind them, if Teddy wanted to, he could see Nicky Migliaro and Frankie Morelli peeking sideways at the table, nearby if they were wanted. He said, "Why don't you do this—all of you, or else just you, Tommy, since you're the one brought it up? Why don't you come up with the name of exactly what type of heart attack it is that involves a man having a neat little hole between his eyes and half his brains blown out of the back of his head. I don't believe I've heard of that one before."

No one spoke and Teddy filled the silence. "And while you're taking care of that, what I'll do is try like heck to remember where I put Mr. Scarlotti. I'm thinking it'll come to me in a day or two. Another thing—the extra time? It'll give me an idea of why you might want him back and how much it might be worth to you. 'Cause I'm sure none of us would be having this nice luncheon if there wasn't something dreadfully wrong with what happened Tuesday night."

Anthony rocketed out of his chair again, his face red with fury, fists clenched. Izzy and Tommy Inzarella put their arms up to restrain him. When Anthony finally sat back down—breathing loudly enough that a couple of the dancers actually got up the nerve to look in his direction—Izzy looked at Teddy carefully and asked, "You sure? I mean, you seem like an intelligent man. Are you sure this is what you prefer to do?"

Teddy shrugged. "You look at it from my point of view, there's no reason not to." Teddy turned so that he could see Anthony clearly and said, "I'm thinking, what the hell, I give you Dominic Scarlotti and you give me— I know, how does a million dollars sound? Cash. Call it for my emotional trauma, post-traumatic stress disorder. Whatever you want."

"You're signing your own death warrant," Tommy said calmly. "You gotta know that."

"Maybe. But maybe it's already been signed. But—and this is what I'm hoping—you guys fucked up. How? I don't know. Why? I'm not sure that's even important right now. But I don't believe I've seen any three guys trying so hard *not* to act nervous. So maybe you'll be smart, I give you what you want, you give me some compensation. Then you stay out of my hair, and we're all happy. It's all I can hope for." He turned to Izzy. "What about you?"

Izzy said, "Maybe you should listen to Mr. Inzarella. He seems to have your best interests at heart. But then again, maybe you have a point."

Teddy made a big deal out of leaning back in his chair to scratch his back. When he settled back down he had Davey's Beretta in his hand and he slid it under the table far enough so that the barrel rested on Tommy Inzarella's leg. Tommy got a quick look of shock on his face—stared at Teddy like he was seeing him in a new light—but managed to get his cool back before either Anthony or Izzy picked up on what was happening.

Anthony said, "The fuck—" but Tommy quieted him down with a hand on his arm.

Tommy said, "Anthony?"

"What?"

"I think we should listen to Teddy. As long as the body—as Dominic—hasn't turned up, it's what we should do. We should listen to him. Consider his proposal carefully."

"See that?" Teddy said. "That's what I always liked about you, Tommy. You think before you act."

Then he stood up, let them all see the gun. Anthony went bug-eyed, but Izzy didn't seem to have much of a reaction except mild curiosity.

Teddy said, as jauntily as he could, "I'll tell you what, gentlemen. Maybe, we all give our various roles in this some thought. Hey, I know, maybe we can do lunch again."

WALKING OUT OF PALISADES, Teddy got in his Acura and drove down Sansom Street. He drove around the same block three times to make sure he wasn't being followed and then he took a right on Broad Street, headed north, past City Hall, past Vine and found a parking place on Noble. He left the Beretta under the front seat of his Acura and walked the two blocks to 400 North Broad Street—the *Inquirer/Daily News* building. When he entered he had to go through a metal detector and show ID to a security guard who carried a pistol on his belt and looked like he wanted to use it.

He got on the elevator and realized that his fists were clenched, the veins in his arms were standing out and had been the whole drive over. When he got out on the fourth floor the first thing he did was go to the men's room and splash some water on his face. Drying off with a paper towel, he took a long look in the mirror and heard Tommy Inzarella's words run through his head one more time: "You're signing your own death warrant."

Was he? He didn't *feel* dead.

But he didn't feel too bright either.

THE NEWSROOM where they put together the *Inquirer* Sunday magazine was like something you'd see in the movies. A lot of glass and noise with a main walkway past rows of cubicles in the middle of the room, and a dozen or so open desks along both sides. People typed and talked at the same speed. Lightning fast.

Teddy took a moment to scan the room, and when he caught sight of Natalie he took his time studying her—the intensity in her face, half turned away from him, her profile close to her computer screen. She sat hunched over the keyboard, absorbed enough in what she was writing that her eyes were open wide and her fingers were a blur. She was at one of the open desks and had a window right next to her. There were a couple of houseplants on the sill next to her, and it was probably a good view.

He got that strange feeling he'd had the night before, comparing her now—the dedicated reporter in designer jeans and silk blouse—to the snotty waitress he'd first seen in the parking lot outside Palisades. It was still hard to equate the two.

He walked to her desk, leaning over her carefully and saying in a deep voice, as if he were reading what was on the computer screen, " 'Local car thief turns hero, saves Philadelphia from imminent peril.' I like that."

She turned around and smiled. "You always do that? Sneak up on people? Almost run them over in parking lots? Give them rides home and tell them you know who they really are when they're trying to work in a place without being recognized?" Glad to see him, which made him feel good, until she caught something in his face. She asked, "You all right?"

"Sure. I'm fine."

She looked down at his hands. "You're fine? You want to unclench your fists and try that again?"

He said, "I have a better idea. I know"—he pointed at her computer— "you have work to do. But I was wondering, can I buy you lunch? Maybe a drink?"

She stood up and touched his elbow, either not worrying about or not noticing that a couple of other reporters were watching them closely, their investigative instincts taking over. Seeing a new man in her life maybe. Teddy found himself hoping that was the case, what he and Natalie had, hoping it was going to work out so that it kept on going.

She said, still holding his arm, "Why don't we do this? You can buy me lunch and I'll buy *you* a drink. Maybe a couple. I can tell you how my day went, and you can reassure me that the reason you look so grim has nothing to do with us sleeping together."

That got a look from a few more reporters.

8

NATALIE ORDERED some kind of pasta dish and kept sticking her fork into it and coming up with individual noodles that were curlicued and had tomato sauce on them. He had told her about going into Anthony's place, Izzy sitting there. How it had changed midstream when he realized that they were nervous about the body. She was talking and eating at the same time but somehow making it seem okay. Teddy had a club sandwich in front of him to go with his drink, but he'd only taken a couple of bites.

Natalie ate another curlicue and said, "You know what I've always liked about our relationship? Why I think it's lasted as long as it has without us getting bogged down in arguments the way other couples do?" She was being funny but Teddy knew that, behind the smile on her face, she was serious. She stopped jabbing at her plate and pointed at him with a fork that had a noodle on the end. "As long as we've known each other, I've admired the fact that you seem to be a bright, serious individual." She popped the noodle into her mouth, swallowed and said, "So, can you tell me, explain it again, why in the goddamn world you decided to try to extort—I'm going to have trouble even saying this—a *million* dollars from Anthony Bonica?"

"Well, it just kind of popped in my head. You ever see that movie, *Austin Powers*? The first one? He's threatening the world with total destruction and he says, 'I want a million dollars.' His advisors, I think Robert Wagner played one of them, have to explain inflation to him because he's been frozen for twenty years or whatever. It was how I felt. Not knowing exactly what was going on but seeing a chance to make some money."

She shook her head. "*Some* money? What are you going to spend it on, a coffin?" She shook her head again. "And the third guy—the guy who you said wasn't part of Anthony Bonica's crew. The one you didn't expect to be there. What did you say his name was again?"

"Izzy. Itzhak Feldman."

"Right. First Anthony Bonica. And if you say that it means you're also saying Tommy Inzarella." She frowned. "Actually, first Dominic Scarlotti in your car—and now this Jewish guy. Izzy. Itzhak. I assume he's some kind of mobster also?"

"You're good at this, you know that?" He took a sip of his drink and shrugged. "Izzy works for a guy named Saul Rubin. An old guy. A deceptively tough guy. If he had a big belly and a white beard he could be Santa Claus at the local mall. And yes, they are mobsters. Izzy's weird, though. I've seen him twice in my life, counting today, and both times he looked like a movie producer, something like that. All dressed in black."

"Hey, I know what," Natalie said. "I did a piece, I think it was two years ago. 'Black Gangs in Philadelphia.' It scared the hell out of me, but I could probably introduce you to a couple of nasty people. You could call them niggers. That way you make sure *everybody* in the city is pissed off at you."

"You want to tell me what choice I had? I'm in Palisades with the three of them. Whether I give them the body or come up with some bullshit number—a million dollars, a *trillion*—Anthony made up his mind a long time ago, and now Tommy and this Izzy Feldman are looking to kill me too because I know too much. But now I think that they can't kill me until they're absolutely certain of where Dominic Scarlotti's body is."

"Well, what *are* you going to do?"

"Hell, why do you think I came over to see you? Let you buy me this drink? I thought maybe *you* might have an idea."

She gave him a look and went back to eating her pasta.

IN HER CAR driving down Spring Garden Street, Natalie said, "You must've thought about it."

"Why they want the body back? Sure."

"And?"

"The simple reason is that they changed their minds. They want to bury Dominic themselves so they know exactly where he is. Possibly Anthony changed his mind about me, his little idea of revenge for me busting him in the face." He paused and then said, "Or mybe they're afraid I can somehow turn it back on them. Plant the body on the doorstep of Anthony's topless club. But I'm thinking it might be more complicated than that."

"Complicated in what way?"

"I said I was thinking about it. I didn't say I had any answers yet."

Natalie took her eye off the road long enough to look at him and say, "Do you have *any* clue what you're doing?"

"It'll come to me. Eventually."

"Terrific."

IT HIT HIM LATER, after bothering him through most of the next few hours except for thirty minutes in which he and Natalie had a pretty good time in bed. That's where they were now, channel surfing. Feeling a nice afterglow.

Natalie had the remote, and she stopped on CNBC to watch a videotape of the president talking to the press corps. Close-captioned at the bottom of the screen were the words "Recorded earlier." Natalie began to say something, some comment about how, in her opinion—and in the opinion of a lot of her colleagues—the president had made it to the White House almost exclusively on charm and good looks. Not a lot else.

She said, "The man should've been an actor. Another Ronald Reagan."

But Teddy wasn't paying any attention to her *or* the president. He was staring at the screen, at the words running at the bottom—and he was thinking of Dominic Scarlotti at the same time. Coming up with an idea and deciding—he didn't know how or why—that it was definitely possible.

Prerecorded.

Jesus, maybe that was it.

Natalie must've sensed something because she muted the TV and said, "What are you doing?"

"I don't know. I don't have it all figured out yet. But let me run it by you."

"Okay."

"My thinking is this. If Anthony Bonica is running scared about whacking Dominic Scarlotti—which, by the way, he is—I saw it in his face just a few hours ago—then maybe the key isn't *where* Dominic Scarlotti's body is. You know, my trunk. Maybe it's what's *on* the body."

"You're guessing."

"Sure. I'm guessing. But two things: One, it's all I have, a guess." He was quiet for a moment and then said, "Number two, what else could it be? I mean, how many times have you heard—I'm not talking sickos like Ted Bundy, who want to revisit the body for sexual reasons—"

"That's disgusting."

"It's also not the point here."

"What is the point?"

Teddy pointed at the television. "That."

Natalie looked at the screen for a moment and then smiled thinly. "Anthony Bonica want a Sony? You going to give him one with a built-in VCR? Jesus, Teddy, you all right?"

"Not the TV. What are we watching?" When she didn't answer, he said, "A recording."

He let it sink in, saw her expression go from where she was looking at him with mock pity to where she believed it.

He said, slowly, "You go from A, to B, to C, where else is it going to lead you?"

She got a different look on her face. Faraway. He waved a hand in front of her face and said, "Hey, you mind telling me what planet you're on?"

She shook her head slightly, seemed to come back from whatever she'd been thinking about and said, "Well, first of all, you have to realize, in my job?"

"Yes?"

"I meet all kinds of people. And there's this prosecutor I know. Federal. I don't believe I've ever met someone who's more of a jerk. Egotistical doesn't begin to describe it."

"This guy have a name?"

"Donald Shaffer."

Teddy thought about it and nodded. "I've seen the guy. TV maybe. His picture in the paper."

"Believe me, with this guy it's probably both. Listen, I've gotten information from him before." She smiled. "Unlike a lot of people who work for the federal government—who all want to remain anonymous—Donald Shaffer likes nothing better than to see his name in print or his face on TV. Preferably both."

"He wants to be the next mayor of Philly?"

"More like president. Teddy, this guy is something else. He's been all over the mob for years. A Rudy Giuliani, but without the class. Making a name for himself while other people do his dirty work."

"What's your point?"

"My point is this: Usually when I see him, I can't get him to shut up. He's locking this bad guy up on a RICO case, sending this other bad guy to the gas chamber on a capital murder, and on and on. Now I'm thinking, this wannabe Eliot Ness—all-around crime buster who's completely full of himself?"

"Yeah?"

"Well, here's where it does get interesting. Maybe means you're right. Usually he goes on and on about how he's making the streets of Philadelphia safe. But last time? I mean, I didn't make much of it then, but looking back, he didn't have a lot to say. For him that's way out of character."

Teddy said, "See, that just goes to show I'm right. The feds *were* after Dominic. That's what it is. At least it's as good a idea as I can think of."

"You don't know that," Natalie said. But then she nodded. "It wouldn't surprise me, though. The way Shaffer operates? He doesn't open his mouth until he's sure that he's got a high-profile arrest that'll stand up in court. Then he calls a press conference, waits till every reporter in the city is there. Spells his name a couple of times so no one will screw it up."

"There you go. Maybe this Shaffer—the feds—they somehow turned Dominic."

"Got him to wear a wire?"

"I can't think of anything else that fits. So all I have to do is get it."

She sighed, possibly a little exasperated because he couldn't see something she was getting at. "Teddy, what are you talking about? If the feds had a wire on Dominic Scarlotti?—"

"Yes?"

"Why don't we simply let *them* handle it. You let them know—anonymously, of course—where the body is and your problems will end like that." She snapped her fingers. "The FBI, whoever it is, pick up Anthony Bonica, Tommy Inzarella. That Izzy guy, too. Hell, maybe they're already looking to do it. Suddenly you don't have to worry about anything. You can go back to work without ever having to worry—at least, no more than you normally would."

"I can't."

"What? Of course you can. You'd be an idiot not to."

He let his eyes look past her, thinking about it. Finally he said, "No, I have to do it myself."

She shook her head. "No you don't. You let the feds handle it and—"

"And my life changes just as certainly as if I let Anthony Bonica tell me when to go to the bathroom from here on out."

"What are you talking about?"

"I'm talking about the fact that you're forgetting one important thing."

"And what," she said angrily, "is that?"

"Natalie," he said, "I'm a car thief. Remember?"

She blanched. "Oh shit."

" 'Oh shit' is right. I've worked on it. Have it set up so that it'll stand up to a *fair* amount of scrutiny. Maybe fool a local Philly detective long enough for me to get out of town if it gets that bad. But the murder of a major mobster? Hell, the feds would be all over me. Lock me up as a material witness for starters."

She was shaking her head. "No, wait. They're not going to care what *you* do. You think they'd rather arrest a car thief or nail Anthony Bonica?"

"Yeah? How about this. I get picked up, say as a material witness—which is the least that will happen—then every two-bit mobster in the city'll be looking to ace me, just to get in the good graces of Anthony Bonica. Let alone I don't want to spend any time in jail. My only other alternative. Well, ask yourself this—you know me well enough by now—How well do you think I'd do in the Witness Protection Program?"

The look on her face told him all he needed to know.

He reached out and put his hand on the back of her head. Pulled her close and kissed her softly on the mouth. "Listen to me. I don't have a choice. Not one I can live with. I'm stuck. But it's my *own* doing. More or less. But you? You don't have to deal with this. I want—I like being with you. But not if it's going to put you in danger."

"Don't start down that road. I appreciate what you're saying but—"

"Natalie, come *on.* You have to give it some thought. As of right now, no one knows anything about you."

She smiled at him, but he could tell it was taking some effort. "How do you know I'm not just hanging around because I smell the story of my life?"

"It's not a story that's worth your life."

"Listen, if I'm going to go along with your theory"—she kissed him quickly—"then you have to let me decide that one. Okay?"

"Okay." He took the remote out of her hand and flicked the TV off.

"What are you doing?"

He grinned. "I read somewhere that there's too much sex and violence on TV."

"So?"

He reached for her, slid his hand underneath the sheet and touched one of her breasts with the back of his fingers. "You know me. I'm not a violent man."

She said, "Jesus." But she reached up and took his other hand in hers. Guided it toward her other breast and smiled at him.

She said, "Don't get carried away. You're not the sexiest man, either."

He made a show of looking around. "You see anyone else in the room?"

DONALD SHAFFER WAS FURIOUS. No, fuck that. He was pissed off beyond human belief. He had it in his head that it was fine for him to use any means he could: Philly cops, the FBI, federal marshals, informants— *any*thing—to take full and entire credit every time they managed to bring even a mid-level wise guy to justice. But he was goddamned if he was ever going to take the rap for somebody else's fuck up.

He had the morning paper in front of him, spread out on the desk—the *Inquirer,* front page up—and could see a close-up picture of the right half of his own face, the other part hidden in the fold of the paper. He kept looking from the picture to the group of men in the room. A bunch of fucking traitors all trying hard not to meet his gaze. Wasting his time because he had to come down hard on this kind of shit, spend time in his office in the U.S. Attorney's building at 615 Chestnut Street, chewing these idiots out instead of heading out to talk to reporters or getting something to eat.

The same two FBI agents, the two members of the Philadelphia Police's Organized Crime Task Force and the hick-looking federal marshal—all of whom were to blame, in varying degrees, for losing track of Dominic Scarlotti just forty-eight hours before.

He picked out the snotty federal marshal among the group. The marshal who had spoken up the day before. Abbot. George Abbot. A rawboned man with a gut that looked like it hid some muscle and leather-looking skin on his face. Abbot had told him that Dominic Scarlotti was dead? Who the fuck didn't know that? But, no, this asshole had to come out and say it to Shaffer in front of everybody else.

Plus Abbot looked like the kind of guy who would think it was a fucking hoot to create the mess they now had going on in the papers. Make sure they call him a high-level member of the U.S. Attorney's Strike Force but be too chickenshit to give them his name.

Shaffer cleared his throat and said, "It's Abbot, right?" Everybody in the room stopped dead and turned to look at George Abbot. Abbot was staring at Shaffer, and Shaffer let a moment go by quietly, giving the other people—and maybe even Abbot himself—the idea that things were going to proceed relatively smoothly.

Abbot said, "Yes." He had a midwestern drawl, Arkansas, some shit hole like that.

"I believe you have another eighteen months to go? Something along those lines?"

Abbot said, "Something like that," with a little wariness creeping into his voice. Shaffer could picture what was going through Abbot's head, his retirement suddenly not sounding so secure. Good. "I'll tell you what, Mister Mar-shal, you want to keep any fucking hope of collecting your pension, you better listen to what I have to say." He swung his gaze over all the men in the room and said, "All of you. You want to stay in your careers? Move ahead? Then don't even think of fucking this one up more than you already have."

Now he held the paper up, the banner headline stretching across the page, the picture of himself just under, no way not to connect the two. A thing that was going to be hard to fight because, how the fuck do you fight public perception? Walking over to stick it close to the marshal's face and giving him ten seconds to read the thing.

FEDERAL PROS. LETS ONE GET AWAY

And underneath, starting with bold print, an article that mentioned Shaffer's name twice in the first five lines, went to smaller type and ran on to ask the general question: How could the U.S. Attorney's Office with all its technological expertise, its trained agents, in cooperation with the Philadelphia Police Department, and under the direction of—a third fucking time—Assistant U.S. Attorney Donald Shaffer, lose a key suspect—at *least* the papers didn't refer to him as a witness—Dominic Scarlotti, before they'd even really had time to mount a case against anybody?

So, yes, Shaffer did feel like shooting someone. But he couldn't because that would cause even more adverse publicity.

He pulled the paper back away from the marshal's face, seeing nothing there, no grin, no worry. Fuck him. He looked the guy in the eye and, just as though George Abbot could read what his thoughts had just been, said, "I'll tell you what, you think you're going to coast from here on out? Collect your fucking pension with no problem? I'm here to tell you that's not going to happen. Not even in your wildest fucking dreams—unless you do *everything* in your power to make me forget what a piece of shit you are. So, starting right now, you grab a fucking car and you drive down to Anthony Bonica's place. That titty-bar. And you sit on it until I personally tell you not to. If Bonica steps outside to fart, I want to know about it. If he drives down the street to get his fucking hair cut, I want to know how short it is." Shaffer took a half a step closer to Abbot; they were nose to nose now. "You got a problem with that, Abbot?"

Abbot didn't do anything but stare right back for long enough that Shaffer wondered briefly if he was going to take a swing at him. Then he exhaled loudly and said, "No. No problem."

Shaffer turned to the other marshal, the younger black guy, who now had a worried look on his face, and said, "You"—jerking his thumb at Abbot—"go with him. Make sure he doesn't fuck anything up. And make sure he doesn't talk to any goddamn reporters."

He turned to the rest of the room. "That goes for all you pricks. Only one who ever—repeat *ever*—holds a press conference around here is me."

ANTHONY BONICA said, "Let's walk."

Tommy Inzarella said, "Where to?" and Anthony looked at him like he was crazy.

"Where *to*? Fuck, Tommy, I don't give a shit 'where to.' I want to get some air. Clear my head."

Outside, Anthony said, "What I want you to do, you tell me everything about this motherfucker. This Teddy Clyde."

Tommy said, "Shit, Anthony, you know him as well as I do. He grew up in the neighborhood, we used to play ball together. He—" Tommy stopped suddenly.

Anthony said, "You about to tell me the man kicked my ass? Is that what you were about to say? Teddy Clyde fucked up my eye fifteen years ago? What, you losing your fucking balls suddenly? You can't tell me something like that without fucking stopping in the middle of a sentence? You think I *forgot* the asshole and I had a couple of fights? *That* I know. What I want you to do now is do me a favor. Can you do that? Can you do me a fucking favor, Tommy?"

"Anthony, c'mon."

"Well, quit jerking me off and realize I'm a busy fucking man. You think I go around all day long thinking about this cocksucker, Teddy Clyde? Well, the fucking news flash is this—I don't. So, if you don't fucking mind, I want you to tell me about him—remind me about things I mighta forgot—so I can see if there's anything I can use against him. This piece of shit wants to extort me—*me*—for a million fucking dollars? I wanna know what his weak spots are. Because I know, sure as shit, I ain't paying him any fucking money."

"What if he does come up with—with whatever Freeman told you Dominic was wearing? *If* he was wearing anything at all."

"You think this fuck—this Detective Freeman, this guy who's into me for sixty-eight grand—you know how long it would take him to pay that off on a fucking detective's pay—you think he's gonna call me up for, what, a joke?" Anthony spat on the sidewalk. "I make a couple of phone calls, once we make sure one way or another about this fucking recording device"—Anthony suddenly smiled—"and instead of whacking Teddy Clyde, I set it up so he gets sent away for life. Gratersford Penitentiary, or Holmesburg Prison, both of which are about ninety percent spades. He can keep them all happy. Become somebody's girlfriend. All I have to do is let the U.S. attorney know that Dominic spent some time in the asshole's car. Their forensic shit? I don't care what Teddy does, how hard he tries to cover up. There's gonna be traces of Dominic all over his fucking trunk."

Tommy was nodding. "Maybe. You do that, you solve two problems. You let the people in New York—"

Anthony was shaking his head, so Tommy said, "Hey, I know, I know, those people should mind their own fucking business. I agree. This is *your* city. But still, it eliminates a headache if they think Teddy Clyde took Dominic out. We tell them Teddy was out of his mind, maybe get one of the girls, Vicki—yeah—to say that Teddy was under the misapprehension that she was his and his alone. We explain to them that Teddy found out that Dominic was also dipping his candle in there and Teddy went fucking crazy."

Anthony stopped walking. "See, that's what I need. Now you're startin' to think along with me." He took a deep breath and then strolled a few steps away to exhale loudly. Without looking back at Tommy, he said, "I love this motherfucking city. Nowhere else in the world do you get that smell. I swear to fucking God, Tommy, you take me anywhere, a dozen places, blindfolded—I don't give a shit—and I'll *tell* you when we get back to Philadelphia." He took another breath and then started walking. Tommy followed, catching up to him in time to hear Anthony say, "So, go on, tell me about this scumbag. I wanna hear anything. Anything you think of."

By the time they reached the corner, Tommy had reminded Anthony that Teddy Clyde's father was a drunk and small-time burglar who took off with a semipro hooker when all of them were around ten or eleven. He said, "You remember, Teddy's mom, she worked at Chicki Dimaro's club for a while. Wore that little outfit almost like the *Playboy* bunnies wore. Chicki always thought that was the slickest thing he ever did, copying those fucking playmates. Teddy's old lady worked as a waitress until her tits started to sag too much and Chicki had to put her up front, behind the cash register."

Anthony nodded. "Sure. I remember. Not a bad-looking broad."

"Word was that Chicki was banging her, although I never knew whether that was a fact or not."

"What else?"

"Well, he's got that brother. Everybody calls him Davey-Boy. The one you pushed around inside that bar and Teddy came over to rescue him and he busted—busted up your eye."

Anthony shook his head. "Why didn't I whack both their asses a long time ago?"

"Hey, you were smart not to. It wasn't a business thing. Look at Little Nicky Scarfo. He was a fucking maniac. We all saw what happened. He let everything get personal. To the point where, right now, he's spending twenty-three and a half hours a day in a little cell for the rest of his fucking life. Marion, Illinois."

They stopped so Anthony could buy a soft pretzel from a street vendor. The vendor knew exactly who Anthony was and said, "No, no, Mr. Bonica, c'mon, I can't take your money," giving him the biggest pretzel he had.

Anthony acted like the vendor hadn't even spoken. He took the pretzel and walked away while Tommy threw a buck on the vendor's cart. He said, "Mr. Bonica don't like to be recognized, you understand?" and then he hustled up to Anthony.

Anthony had a smear of mustard on his upper lip. Tommy handed him a napkin and pointed at it. When he was finished wiping, Anthony took another bite and said, through a wad of pretzel, "Tell me more about this brother of his. He's a fucking retard or something, right?"

THEIR SEX DIDN'T WORK magic the way they both had thought it would. Teddy was reminded of the old Woody Allen joke—there's no such thing as bad sex—but he didn't think Natalie would appreciate it. He *tried* pretty hard, thought of some tricks he hadn't considered in quite a while and even a few things he'd read in magazines. He and Natalie squirmed around and changed positions and procedures at least ten times. But it all came up to zero for Natalie.

Natalie said, "Hey, I can't concentrate. That's all that's happening. Besides, *you* seem to be having a good time."

Teddy was on top of her, running his right hand through her hair and staring at her left breast. He said, "Well, to tell you the truth, you're right. *I'm* not having any trouble concentrating. So—"

She said, "Jesus," and acted like she was about to punch him. But she reached up and grabbed his head instead, pulling it down to kiss him and then whispered, "It's all I am to you anyway, a body."

He kissed her back and said, "That's true enough." Looking down at her while they started to move again. "But *what* a body."

"You know what?" Natalie said. "There're a few times when you're not as funny as you think you are."

"Well maybe, we give it a little while, and we can try again."

"Oh no you don't." She looked at her watch. "Besides, I'm working Palisades tonight." She leaned over and kissed him. "Is there anything you want me to do while I'm there? Check up on Anthony? See if he's acting even more crazy than usual?"

"No. But maybe I'll stop by, let him know he's in my thoughts."

She went somber for an instant. "Look, I understand. You have to do what you have to do."

"Yes."

"But, for God's sakes, don't push it. How about this, you pick me up. Ten after two. We can talk then. But"—she touched his forearm—"you're already taking a lot of risks. Don't take ones you don't have to. Promise?"

He looked her squarely in the eye. "I promise."

TEDDY GOT TO PALISADES a few minutes early and sat in his car so he could watch Natalie walk out. He let a few seconds go by, watching her, and then he tooted the horn. She saw him and hurried over. When she slid into her seat she leaned over to kiss him like they'd been doing this for a long time and then settled back into her seat. Neither one of them mentioned Anthony Bonica or dead bodies the whole ride back to her apartment.

He had packed a light bag and as soon as they were inside her apartment he said, "Well, listen," glancing at his watch, "if I'm going to do this thing, it's now or never." He pulled a pair of jeans and a dark, hooded sweatshirt out of the bag and started to pull them on.

Natalie popped into her bedroom and came out wearing jeans herself. She had taken her silky work shirt off and was holding a sweatshirt in her hands that said "University of Pennsylvania" on it. Teddy stopped dressing—

his own pants were at his waist, but he hadn't buttoned them or pulled the zipper up yet. Natalie sat on the sofa.

He said, "Let me guess, you have another boyfriend and when I leave you're going to sneak over to his place. Hopefully he can do for you what I couldn't do this afternoon."

She didn't even look up from what she was doing. "No. I'm going to take a ride with you. Dig up a body."

Teddy zipped his pants up, sat on the couch too and said, "Hey." When she finally looked at him he said, "I made a mistake here."

"What?"

He pointed at her. "I'm thinking one thing. Keeping you out of it. I told you that I like you—which is very true—but that doesn't mean that I want you to get yourself caught up in all this. And now look what you're doing. I have to go dig up Dominic Scarlotti and try to get out of a jam that I didn't even create. Right now, I have to tell you, instead of keeping out of it, it looks like you *want* to come along."

She shrugged. "I do."

"Well, you can't."

"Look, I know that's what you're doing—watching out for me. And I appreciate it."

He said, "Yeah? Right now, if you don't mind, we're talking about what *you're* doing. Maybe more importantly, why? In other words, how are you seeing this thing?"

She had taken off her Palisades blouse but still hadn't put on the U. of P. sweatshirt.

He said, "You're looking at this—Jesus—still, as a story. A continuation of your Palisades thing."

"That's crap."

"It's crap, huh? You want to go ahead and put your sweatshirt on so I can take it right back off—strip-search you? See where you're carrying your laptop?"

He knelt in front of her. "Look at me."

She made a face. "Oh, Christ, 'Look at me.' Who're you, Chilli Palmer? 'Look at me'? What am I supposed to do, then . . . melt? Get goose bumps?"

"No, we're not talking about anything you might've seen in a movie or read in a book. What we *are* talking about is, are you going to go out tonight— this isn't a date—and dig up the body of one mobster so we can try to sell something to another and still keep on breathing?" He shook his head. " 'Cause I have to tell you something. Tell it to you again, actually. No matter how this thing ends up, Little Anthony—believe me, I've known him a long time—he's going to try to kill me. So it's going to be hard enough, me figuring out how not to let that happen without worrying if he's going to kill *you* too."

She stood up and stood there, silhouetted against the hallway light. "You remember, I said that I knew some people from a piece I did on black gangs in Philadelphia?"

"Sure, you suggested I should go call them some names. See how I'd look gutted like some kind of fish."

"Well, about that, I was only kidding. But I'm going to tell you a story."

He shook his head. "Natalie, any kind of story, no matter what it is, you're still not going with me tonight."

"You going to shut up and listen?"

"I'm listening."

"Good. This article? The one on the gangs? It was about five years ago. One of the first pieces I did where the paper let me go out on my own. I'd stop by work every once in a while, but mostly it was me out on the streets. I approached several different gangs through ah, intermediaries—"

"Intermediaries?"

"You're going to make me lose my train of thought." She cleared her throat. "Anyway, most of them thought it was pretty cool. The gangs, I mean. Maybe they didn't like me too much, white woman coming onto their turf. But they thought that the idea of being written about—maybe get their pictures in the Sunday magazine—was hard to put down."

She came over and sat next to him. "You have to understand, I do about three pieces a year. I get paid pretty well, but the reason I don't do more is because they each take awhile. Months sometimes. You have to spend time getting everything right. Researching things. Like what I'm doing at Palisades. If you want to know what a topless club is like, you have two choices: You can go to one every night or you can work at one. Since I'm not a man, I'd pretty much get noticed by my third evening if all I did was watch. I don't know, maybe five years ago, I would've taken my clothes off and got up on the stage. Written about it from that angle. But this time I decided, hey, be a waitress, you can learn everything without having to deal with even *more* jerks every night."

"Are we getting to a point any time soon?"

"Yes. I started doing research. Meeting with guys in these gangs. They're all pretty cool about it. Treating me nicely. Except there's this one group. They're talking to me, but I can tell, they're not really *saying* anything. Finally I put it to them, either they want to be part of the article or they don't. I get word back from this guy, Jameel. He's their leader of sorts. I think he changed his name himself. From what I learned he was Larry or something until he got the idea of Jameel in his head. Anyway, he tells me, 'Hey, we're sorry, we were screwing with you, we'll get serious now.'"

She scooted closer and lowered her voice. "I didn't know *how* serious until I got a call at home. Jameel's girlfriend, Shauna? She's pretty much of a hard case, too, but I guess she had some sympathy for me. She tells me, when Jameel and his boys have me over again, they're planning to have a party. Shauna tells me, *I'm* going to be the party."

Teddy was interested now, trying to picture her five years before. Getting a message like that. "What'd you do? Call the cops."

"No, see, I think that would have ruined the article. What I did do, though, I went up to see my father. He lives in Massachusetts. Same house where I was born. My mother passed away ten years ago, and my father recently retired. But he still likes to go duck hunting every fall. I drove up there and had a nice visit, and when I left I don't think he even noticed that he was missing one of his favorite shotguns."

"What?"

"I have to tell you, I got blisters on my hands cutting down the barrel and trimming the stock. But it was worth it to see the expression on Jameel's face when I stuck the thing under his nose. To this day I believe Jameel peed himself, thinking this dumb white girl was beating him at his own game." She stood up. "Now, do you want to go dig up Mr. Scarlotti or do you want to patronize me a little bit more?"

Teddy stood up, too. He looked at her for a long time, getting a glimpse of the hardness underneath her beauty. The tough girl who would have the nerve to walk into a place—sawed-off twelve-gauge or not—and feel like she was going to be in control of the situation.

He said, bringing out his car keys, "Tell you what. You drive and I'll dig."

9

IT WAS TEN OF FOUR, almost dawn, when Natalie said, "Jesus, I think I'm gonna vomit." She was looking around at the surrounding bushes, trying to find a suitable location, but she stopped long enough to look at Teddy. "If I do puke, I don't want to hear an 'I told you so.'"

Teddy was over by the makeshift grave he'd dug the night before. The stink was all around them because the last few shovelfuls had uncovered a bit of Dominic's chest and most of his face. It was god-awful work, and Teddy stopped long enough to look back at Natalie. He said, "Hey, you find a good place let me know, because I'm right behind you." He looked back down at the body and said, "I'm a goddamned car thief, not a grave digger."

He scooped a little more dirt off the body while gritting his teeth and then walked over to where Natalie was standing. She didn't look so good—pale and a little smaller in the dim light that was getting to them from the moon. Teddy had bought a pocket flashlight to go with the shovel, but he didn't want to turn it on until the last moment.

"Seriously, you think you're going to be okay?"

She shuddered. "I had no idea. I mean, how long has he been dead? Twenty-four hours? A little longer? God, I can smell him from here."

"Well, I heard on the news it went up to almost ninety today. So, what with the heat, I guess, human flesh, it becomes unhuman fairly quickly."

"Real quickly."

Teddy said, "Uh-huh," and then walked around so that he was looking directly into her face. He had the distinct feeling that even though he hadn't actually touched Dominic—yet—he smelled as if he had. The odor seemed to be inside his nose or else a part of him. He didn't want to get too close to Natalie.

"Nat, unfortunately, it's something we have to decide. Are we both okay to go through with this? If you're not—if *I'm* not—that's one thing. We throw some dirt on him and head out of here. But that means I have to leave town. My brother, who already is out of town, won't be able to come back. And I don't want that to happen without at least making an effort." He pointed back at the body. "I know it smells like hell or whatever over there. And if we do it—dig him all the way up—the smell's only going to get worse. But I'm also thinking I'm going to have to search the corpse, get his clothes off. And Natalie—are you listening to me?"

She nodded her head quickly.

"I can't do it alone. I already did it once with this son of a bitch, and I don't think I have it in me to do it again."

She looked up at him, glanced at the shovel and then finally turned so that she was facing the exposed portion of Dominic's body. "I'll do it. But when we get back, I'm going to take a shower until tomorrow morning." She pulled at her sweatshirt. "I'm going to throw these goddamn clothes out first, though."

HALF AN HOUR LATER Natalie did get sick. Teddy watched her run to some bushes and felt that he probably shouldn't have told her what he was about to do. He could have sent her up to the car and then just gone ahead and done it. Hidden it from her. But they'd been sharing so much during the last hour it had just popped out of his mouth.

She looked at him like she'd never seen him before. "You're going to do *what*?"

All he could come up with was "Do you see a wire anywhere? A tape recorder? Anything? I have to do *something*."

He was looking down at Dominic's corpse which was now naked and didn't have anything on it except for a tattoo on the right biceps that appeared to be at least forty years old. They had found a wad of cash in Dominic's right front pants pocket that neither Teddy nor Natalie could bring themselves to count, let alone take. They also found a silk handkerchief in Dominic's left rear pocket. But that was it. No wire. No tape recorder.

No nothing.

But Teddy wasn't about to walk away from all this work and not continue to try to make something of it. The way he figured, you didn't just dig up putrefying bodies for the fuck of it.

So he told Natalie, "Look, one thing we're going to need—if any of this works at all—is something that'll identify Dominic. Identify him beyond any doubt. Maybe it won't even come up." He bent down to point closely at Dominic and said, "A wad of cash won't do it. But *that* will. We'll figure out the logistics after."

It was at that point that Natalie ran for the bushes. Teddy listened to her for a moment but then forced himself to focus. He reached down and grabbed the corpse. It took him almost a minute but finally he had the body positioned just the way he wanted it.

He picked up the shovel and was just raising it over his head when Natalie emerged from the bushes, wiped her mouth and said, "I'm not sure, do I even *know* you?"

Teddy didn't answer because he was too busy positioning the shovel directly over Scarlotti. He remained poised like that, getting his aim perfect. And then he brought the shovel straight down as hard as he could—concentrating on not missing by even an inch. To finish it off he had to put a foot on the top of the shovel blade and put his whole weight in a final downward thrust.

As soon as he was done he went running for Natalie's spot in the under-brush.

THERE WAS a three-car collision on the Vine Street entrance to the Schuyl-kill Expressway at three-fifteen in the morning. A guy driving a U-Haul rental truck took a right on red and didn't see a sleek little BMW coming until it was two late. The car behind the BMW—some kind of SUV—plowed into the BMW and pushed it and the truck even farther into the intersection. There was nothing that Izzy Feldman could do but sit in the black Lincoln Town Car he was driving and watch Natalie Prentice and Teddy Clyde dis-appear up onto the expressway in Teddy's Legend.

Izzy couldn't believe the dumb luck of it because he'd been sitting on Teddy Clyde the whole evening, following him to his apartment, to Palisades to pick up the woman—interesting, that, was she a dancer there? And then he'd followed them back to the woman's apartment where he had waited until Teddy and Natalie reappeared, dressed as if they were going to break into the art museum or dig up a body. Izzy thought it was going to be the lat-ter, but he hadn't planned on getting involved in a three-way accident and now there was no way he'd be able to catch up to them.

He sat in his car for a minute and decided that the best thing to do was to get some food and head back to the woman's apartment.

More than likely they would go back there. And if they didn't, Izzy could always head crosstown to where Teddy lived. One way or another he'd catch up to Teddy.

The woman was a mystery. Earlier Izzy had watched Teddy Clyde park on Noble Street, waited a bit and then strolled along the opposite sidewalk a hundred fifty feet behind Teddy until Teddy had entered the *Inquirer/Daily News* building at 400 Broad Street. *That* made Izzy wonder, because see-ing Teddy pick her up later, what was a dancer from Palisades doing in the building that housed the two largest city papers? By the time Teddy had reappeared with the woman, Izzy was back in his car and was in a position to watch as Teddy Clyde appeared with the woman. They were talking animatedly and walked a half a block down the street to a small restaurant. A half an hour later they came out, got in Teddy's Acura and Izzy followed them back to what seemed to be the woman's apartment. The woman had left, presumably to go to Palisades. And then later, after Teddy picked her up, Izzy had followed the two of them as they headed toward the expressway, only to lose sight of them when the accident happened.

Now Izzy drove back the way he had come and parked down and on the opposite side of the street so that he had a clear view of the front entrance of the woman's apartment building. He knew which one was hers because he'd watched which lights flicked on a minute after she and Teddy had entered the building before they had reemerged to drive to the Vine Street entrance of the expressway. Izzy had a bottle of water and some pretzels on the passenger seat, a can to urinate in if necessary and a large black coffee from 7–Eleven. Once Teddy did show up Izzy would figure out what his next move was going to be.

And as soon as he got a legitimate chance, he'd break into the apartment and find out exactly who the woman was.

NATALIE SAID, "Are these real?" She'd been pacing back and forth in the living room of Teddy's apartment. Now, for the first time, she noticed the three Picasso prints on the wall opposite the sofa Teddy was sitting on.

Teddy said, "You want to talk about art or do you want to discuss what we're going to do next?"

"Hey, I was only asking."

Teddy shrugged his shoulders and nodded. "Yes. They're real. They cost a little bit of money but not as much as you'd expect. The man did a lot of sketching in his lifetime."

Natalie glanced at Teddy, and he took the opportunity to stare at her face, seeing it from all different angles as she turned to take in a couple of other pieces of art that he'd hung on the walls when he first moved in. The light from the table lamp was making her face change every few seconds. Go from hollow-cheeked model to healthy farm girl in just a moment or two. Either way, Teddy still thought she was something to see.

She caught him finally. She looked down at her body and then back at him again and said, "Hey, seriously, tomorrow maybe. But for now, you want to cut that out?"

Teddy smiled to show he knew he was lying and said, "Cut what out?"

Natalie said, "Never mind." And went back to pacing again.

An hour before, Teddy had stood in the center of Natalie's apartment—feeling more filthy than he ever had before in his life—and tried to stay motionless for the entire thirty-six minutes it took Natalie to take a shower and throw some clean clothes on. He had no desire to sit down, and every time he took a breath he could smell decaying flesh. He kept track of exactly how long Natalie was taking so he wouldn't have to dwell too much on what they'd just done.

When she came out she gave him a weak smile. "I was thinking, back there in the shower. The good news is we're not the ones still over by the railroad tracks."

Teddy smiled back at her and said, "Hey, you got that right."

Natalie's smile got a little bigger but when she came over to kiss him she stopped five feet away and made a face, sniffing and saying, "I'm sorry. Really."

Teddy said, "I'm not going to take offense, I can smell it myself."

Natalie said, "How about this: When we get to your place—as soon as you shower—we give each other a hug and a kiss and then you can explain to me again how it is that everything's going to be okay."

"Sure. We go to my place. I get cleaned up. Then we come up with a plan."

"Meaning you still don't have one?"

"I have a loose idea of things. You look at it the right way, and that's only a step away from having a plan."

"What happens if you look at it the wrong way?"

Teddy said, "I'm working on that, too," and then he walked her out to his car where the first thing she did was ask him to open all the windows *and* the sunroof.

NOW, IN *HIS* APARTMENT, watching her pace, Teddy said, "Why don't you do this, find someplace to sit down."

She stopped walking but didn't make any kind of move toward the sofa. "If I sit down are you going to tell me you have more than a loose idea of what we're doing?"

"I'll tell you what. You sit down and I'll tell you my plan. I can't explain how absolutely foolproof it is if you keep wearing out my carpet."

She went on over to the sofa and sat next to him. A moment later she snuggled closer and said, "Okay, tell me what you have in mind."

"Well, the first thing you have to think of, I come up with a plan, what's the best thing to keep in mind?"

"I don't know."

He smiled. "Well, I do."

"You going to tell me?"

"Sure—" He held his hand out and smiled wider when she put hers into his. "The best thing? You keep it simple. The first thing we do—tomorrow morning—we go shopping. After that we call Anthony Bonica. Tell him we're ready to do business."

She looked at him as if he had no brain.

He said, "I'm serious. You'll see."

"That's what I'm afraid of."

"Hey," Teddy said, "all I'm looking for is a way out. But a little respect wouldn't hurt."

———

WHEN IZZY SAW TEDDY and the woman come back to the woman's apartment at five-thirty in the morning and then leave thirty-some minutes later, he took the risk that they were headed to Teddy's apartment. It was close enough to dawn that it was probably too late for them to visit wherever Dominic was buried—if that *wasn't* what they had just done. If it was—well, there was nothing Izzy could do about it now. Plus which, he figured, if they were just going out to get a very early breakfast, they wouldn't have needed a car. There were two diners and a deli that Izzy could think of—open all night—within easy walking distance.

Already traffic was picking up. Delivery trucks and earlier morning commuters trying to get a head start on the day. He locked his car, went over to one of those metal stands and bought a copy of yesterday's paper so he would look like he had other things on his mind and then he skirted around to the back entrance of the apartment building.

He had to climb a six-foot wire fence to get onto the back lot of the apartment building. There were a dozen cars parked in lined spaces and he took his own keys out and walked toward the one closest to the back of the building as if he owned it but then veered off at the last second and walked to the back door of the building. The lock on the door wasn't anything special, and he didn't care if someone noticed that it had been broken into. The cops would put it down to junkies and stop their investigation before it started. He had brought a crowbar with him and now he pulled it out from his belt, put the blade against the lip of the door next to the lock and yanked hard. The wood split like cheap cork and made a sound like someone sneezing loudly. Izzy didn't even bother looking around to see if anyone was leaning out a window watching. He'd seen people with keys have more trouble opening a door.

The woman's door was more of a challenge because he didn't want her to know that she'd been burglarized. He put on a pair of latex gloves but didn't even bother with trying to pick the lock. He just leaned his weight against the door—slowly—and kept pushing until the inside trim splintered and the door opened. Once inside, he waited for any unusual sounds or activity from the hallway or the street outside. When none occurred he took a tube of Super Glue and—having made an assumption based on percentages—a tiny glass jar of white touch-up paint from his jacket pocket and spent two minutes making it look like the door, the inside locks and the trim had never been touched. After that he swept up what few splinters remained on the floor and stuck them in his pocket.

There were some pictures along one wall of the living room, a reproduction of Rembrandt's *Man in a Golden Helmet*, a van Gogh, and a generic seascape next to that. Farther along was a wooden bookcase. He read some of the titles: *One Hundred Years of Solitude*, which Izzy had read and enjoyed. Next to that was a book about interpreting dreams, a big book that looked like a college text, *Journalism in Today's Society*, which told Izzy that not only did she work at the *Inquirer*, but also it wasn't in some secretarial position. She wasn't an accountant or someone who worked the business end of the paper, finance, something like that.

No. She *wrote* for the paper. Izzy admired that.

He hit the Play button on her answering machine and listened to someone named Carol ask the woman why she didn't return her calls and were they or were they *not* going down to the Jersey shore in two weeks. Somebody else, a man, whom Izzy gathered the woman worked for, asked her could she please get off her high horse and let him know how the story was going. "Check in with me occasionally, huh? I heard you were in the building yesterday. What happened, you forget where my office is? Jesus, you *do* still work for the paper—which means you work for me." Another message seemed to be from the woman's father. He asked when she was going to come up to see him and, "This time, for real, honey, could you *please* bring back that goddamn thing you took? You know what I'm talking about."

The machine beeped when there were no more messages, and five minutes later Izzy found what he was looking for.

It was in the top drawer of an ornate-looking but assembly-line-built
desk that had a Macintosh computer on it, an old fashioned Rolodex next to a
phone that had a headset attached and a two-day-old copy of *The New York
Times* spread across the top. Izzy had to pull some junk out of the desk, but in
the end he found what he wanted. An expired driver's license in the name of
Natalie Prentice, five-foot-seven, and one hundred eighteen pounds, blue
eyes, Social Security number 184-33-9845. He took a long look at her photo.
One, because he wanted to implant her appearance in his memory. Number
two, the other reason, was that he was surprised. He hadn't gotten a good
look at her in person and—even though she was a journalist and worked at a
large paper in a large city—he had it in his mind that somehow there would
be something sleazy, cheap-looking, about her. He had the idea that Teddy
Clyde had seemed to be on familiar territory yesterday in that topless club,
Palisades. Maybe that was influencing his thoughts. But, looking at the picture of Natalie Prentice, he remembered that there was a difference between
someone like, say, a Mr. Anthony Bonica and a Teddy Clyde.

The woman in the photo on the driver's license was staring directly
into the camera. She had a smile on her face that made Izzy come to two,
simultaneous conclusions. She had a natural beauty that even a license
photo couldn't screw up. And she also had some kind of dignity about her
that Izzy could sense just by being in her apartment and taking a quick peek
at a photo of her.

When he let himself out he was thinking that if Anthony Bonica hadn't
been dumb enough to put Dominic Scarlotti in Teddy Clyde's trunk, then
Teddy Clyde could consider himself a very lucky man.

He also realized *why* the woman might be spending so much time at
Anthony Bonica's topless club. More than likely it had nothing to do with
augmenting her income from her day job.

———————

DAVEY-BOY DIDN'T REALIZE how hot it still was until he got kicked out of the second cocktail lounge in a row. He wore a sport coat when he left his hotel because that was what he'd been used to back in Philly. Back there it warmed up enough in the afternoon but was still chilly in the morning or after the sun went down. But here? Shit, within minutes he took his coat off and slung it over his shoulder. Tried to be hip about it—not like he'd guessed wrong about how much to wear. More like he was a snappy dresser and was setting some kind of fashion trend.

But, still, it was humid as hell. Hotter than hell. To top it off—walking down the street to the first club—it looked like rain with huge dark clouds on the horizon that, back home, say, in July, would've guaranteed a thunderstorm. It hadn't rained yet, but Christ, he couldn't believe how heavy the air felt. Maybe he should've paid more attention to the weather guy on TV, although it was hard to believe there was *this* much difference between here and back home. It had to be—minimum—ten degrees cooler back in Philly. All he could figure was that it must be some kind of freak of nature. Or something to do with being closer to the ocean. Maybe *that* was it. It had to be something because Davey never sweated. Period. It was a matter of pride—of principle. But right now he could feel his shirt sticking to his back.

He remembered the look on Teddy's face when Teddy had told him to go to Miami. Davey wanted to call him up and say, Hey, it's steaming outside, fucking humid as shit, a goddamn sauna—you crazy?

The first bar that he'd been asked to leave was a place he didn't really care about. A bullshit cocktail lounge that was so dark you knew they were hiding the fact that the dishes weren't clean. There was a chubby white woman playing the piano—she had to be fifty years old—banging out show tunes and half-assed blues like she was asleep at the wheel. Davey had ordered his third Chivas Regal because—after all—everything was on Teddy's dime. But then he caught the bartender turning away like he was going to sneak a pour from the cheap shit they kept underneath the bar. Davey knew he was right too because, five minutes later, when he said, "You wanna do that again? Only, this time, pour what I fucking ordered, you thieving prick," the bartender gave him one look, picked up the phone and told Davey he was dialing nine-one-one if Davey was still there three seconds from now. Davey told the guy to go fuck himself, but he also walked out because if the cops *did* show up they'd hassle him just because they'd be pissed off about having to drive on over for such a bullshit complaint. Give him an extra dose of shit because he was from out of state.

The second place was different. The air conditioner actually worked, so that walking inside it felt like dipping your toes into a cold lake. There was a long bar out front, mahogany or some kind of dark wood, and an area farther in where people were sitting down and eating dinner. As Davey-Boy entered, a black-haired waitress, drop-dead good-looking, came out from the dining room carrying a tray and started to give her drink order to the bartender. Davey didn't even waste a second thinking about it; there was a stool next to where she stood and he beelined over in time to exchange a look with her and say, "Hey, is it me or is it always this hot out?"

She gave him a smile and said, "Maybe it's you." Which could have meant a lot of things but which Davey took as an encouraging sign. He ordered a Chivas, for real this time, from a bartender who wore his hair in a ponytail and then he turned around in time to see the waitress saunter back into the dining area. Goddamn, she had a walk too. Nice legs. A gorgeous ass. Tan all over. God almighty.

He took a sip of his Chivas when the bartender put it down, handing the guy a twenty and telling him to keep the change and then feeling the reassuring warmth of the liquor flowing into his stomach. He was feeling good. Thinking, fuck that first place. Bunch of crooks pouring rotgut liquor into a dirty glass and trying to fool him.

The waitress came back and Davey said, "What is this, you always on the job? I was in here last week and you were working days." It was a lie, but

Davey-Boy thought it was a pretty good one. Let the woman think he was a regular so maybe she'd try to remember him even though he never had been there before. He had the feeling she was thinking about him already.

The bartender gave him a funny look and watched the waitress say, "Last week, huh? I don't know about that because tonight is only my third night."

Davey had to do a little quick thinking, but he came up with "Yeah, but you could have been here last week, you know what I mean?" He wasn't quite sure himself what it meant, but he liked the reaction it got. The waitress had been getting ready to walk away, her tray full of drinks, but now she turned and stared at him. Said, "Ex-*cuse* me?" with enough emphasis that Davey knew she was seeing him as some kind of mystery man. A guy who walks in off the street, makes himself right at home by ordering the most expensive drink at the bar—let's not forget the tip, hold that twenty—and then comes up with conversation that makes the woman feel that she should hurry back with more drink orders as often as possible.

He kept it up, ordering one drink after another and chatting with the waitress for the next hour and a half. At one point the bartender told him to take it easy, but Davey didn't know what the fuck he was talking about. He said back, "Take it easy? Me?" pointing at his drink. "I think you're the one been taking it easy. You got to learn to loosen up your elbow, put a little effort into pouring these drinks, my man. You're way too fucking young to have arthritis. You know what I'm saying?"

He scooched his stool just that much closer to where the waitress was going to have to stand and started to think of the next snappy thing he was going to say.

He didn't get the chance, though, because the next thing he knew a big guy with a tan you could only get at a salon, wearing a sport coat over a white T-shirt, was standing by his side. Davey-Boy had to think back to it, where had he seen the guy before? He came up with the memory of walking past him at the front door. The guy was the bouncer. Big, four or five inches taller than Davey, and looking like he'd run, two-fifty, two-sixty minimum. Davey wanted to ask him whether he'd ever played college ball. Hell, maybe even pro. Middle linebacker someplace. Detroit. The Atlanta Falcons. Maybe even back in Philly although *that* Davey probably would've remembered.

The guy had a funny voice. A Mike Tyson, steroid squeak in it that almost made Davey laugh. The bouncer said, "What I'm gonna do, sport, I'm gonna ask you—politely—if you could go on home now. Maybe come by and see us when you're in a little bit of a better mood."

Davey was thinking what he'd do if he had a baseball bat with him. Hit this big motherfucker with the stupid-looking shirt and the girlie voice in the knee and then order another Chivas. But he didn't have anything bigger then the glass his Chivas was in and the bouncer had a look on his face like he could eat that without having to swallow any Pepto-Bismol, so Davey had to act as if he didn't understand what the guy was all about.

He said, "I don't know, you must have me confused with someone else." Making a big deal of looking around the place and getting a little embarrassed because all of a sudden he realized that everyone—including the hot-looking waitress—was staring in his direction.

He took a deep breath and looked back at the bouncer, wishing even more now that he had something to hit the cocksucker with. He said, "What, a guy can't come in, have a drink and not be hassled? Have a nice time? That's the kind of place you're running?" He could hear the nervousness in his own voice, and it bothered the hell out of him.

The bouncer said, still quietly and nodding slightly in the direction of the bartender, "Listen to me. Timmy here says you've had nine drinks, not *a* drink. I'm getting an urge—a real strong one"—lowering his voice so that Davey realized that only the two of them could hear—"to pick your silly little ass up and throw you out the fucking window. You understand me, asshole? But I don't want to upset our regular clientele who're here to have—as you put it, a nice time—by causing a commotion with a fucking pervert who won't stop bothering one of our waitresses."

"What?" For the first time it occurred to Davey that maybe the guy did have the wrong man. *Bothering* her? Jesus, he was this close to *fucking* her. He said, "The fuck you mean?—"

And that's when the guy reached out and grabbed Davey's elbow. Shit, second time in two days someone had caused him that much pain, the bitch at Palisades being the first. It didn't seem like much at first. Maybe even something that—if the diners in the room didn't know what was happening— they'd think was a friendly gesture. One guy helping another guy off a bar stool. Or else just a funky way of shaking hands. But God *damn,* it shot a fucking bolt of pain up through Davey's shoulder and all the way into his brain. He couldn't move for a couple of seconds. Couldn't do more than stare at the bouncer's face and realize that the guy wasn't even breathing hard at all.

Davey tried like hell not to yell out in pain as the bouncer eased him off the stool and headed him toward the door like two friends leaving together.

The worst part of all—worse maybe even than the fucking pain in his arm—was that Davey had to walk right past the hot-looking waitress. She was staring at him, and he had to put a lot of effort into looking back at her. Let her know that the only reason he wasn't kicking some ass here was that the guy would probably not fight fair and also, Davey-Boy was too fucking civilized to cause that kind of commotion.

He did manage to say, "Hey," nodding his head at the bouncer, "you believe this shit?"

The girl had a strange look on her face. She didn't say anything for a moment but when she did open her mouth, all that came out was a soft "Jesus." And then she shook her head.

The bouncer walked him out of the club, across the street and then let go of his arm. He wiped his hands on his trousers with an expression on his face like he'd stepped on a dog turd. Then he turned around as if Davey didn't even exist and headed back across the street toward the entrance to the club. Davey tried hard not to grab his elbow and concentrated instead on timing it perfectly—letting the bouncer get within six feet of the front door before he yelled, "Hey?"

The bouncer turned around. Davey wasn't sure from this distance, but he thought the guy still didn't have much of an expression on his face. Davey didn't give a shit. He screamed as loud as he could, "I'll be back, you fucking faggot."

It wasn't until he was absolutely positive that the guy wasn't headed back that he wrapped his left hand around his right elbow and groaned loudly. A minute after that—walking along trying to figure out where the fuck he could get a cab at this time of night—he began to feel the heat again. Jesus, sweat popping out on his forehead. Everywhere. A lousy fucking night and now he had to deal with some kind of freaking weather phenomenon.

Not only that, he couldn't for the life of him remember where he'd left his sport coat.

HE HAD TROUBLE with the lock on the door of his hotel room. It was one of those credit card kind of keys, and Davey kept sliding the thing in upside down, waiting for the tiny light to turn green and saying "Fuck" every time it didn't. Finally he turned the key card around and got in. But when he did he realized that he must've left the Do Not Disturb sign on the outside of the door because the place was still a colossal mess. It stank of cigarette smoke, there was trash everywhere, food wrappers, a couple of empty beer cans and an open *Hustler* magazine lying in the exact center of the bed, propped up by wrinkled sheets. To top it off, it was even hotter than the outside.

He tried opening the window but then realized that not only was it locked permanently shut, but if he *did* get it open it would only let in more heat. Then he had to fuck around with the air-conditioning unit, bang it with his fist a couple of times and twiddle the knobs until finally he felt cooler air coming in. He figured out how to set the fan on High and then walked over and sank down onto the bed.

He shut his eyes and instantly the room started to swim. He moaned, got up off the bed and went into the bathroom. He took a wobbly piss and then splashed cold water onto his face until he felt a little bit more awake. Then he went in, turned the TV on, channel surfed until he found what station here was VH1. Some eighteen-year-old black bimbo, showing a lot of cleavage, was jouncing around a pure white bed to a rap beat. Davey swallowed hard, sat back to watch and thought about what Teddy had told him.

Go to Miami.

He counted his money. Jesus, nine hundred some dollars left out of the original five grand Teddy had given him. In twenty-four hours? Jesus-fucking-Christ. He remembered back to when he'd first gotten to the hotel, slipping a hundred-dollar bill into the doorman's hand 'cause he called a fucking bellboy to carry Davey's one suitcase? Shit. And then, giving the fucking *bellboy* another C note. For what? So he could feel like a big shot? Jesus. He'd like to go find them both and demand his money back. But it wasn't like they'd be around this late.

That morning he had gone to a casino. Played craps. Not paid too much attention to how much money he'd lost because a hot-looking waitress kept bringing him Bloody Marys and the dealer was talking to him nonstop, complimenting the way he was throwing the dice. But now he realized that it must have been a helluva lot—the money he had burned through. He'd had a couple of drinks—no, wait, thinking about it, the casino waitress, blue eyes against brown hair, an awesome combination, showing up at the table every twenty minutes without even being asked—it had to be at least four, maybe five drinks. Before noon. Let's see, some other woman, not as good-looking as the casino waitress, had begun to pay a lot of attention to him. Betting on every roll of Davey's dice. At the time Davey had thought it was great. He could win a pile of money—put an extra zero in the five grand that Teddy had given him and then talk the woman into going back to his hotel room. But shit, now he realized that she must've been employed by the casino too. Not a hooker. No. Just paid to flash Davey some leg, let him cop some elbow tit and laugh with him until the casino had taken most of his fucking cash.

Then, if he remembered correctly—he was a little hazy about it—but it seemed like all of a sudden, bingo, the broad was wandering over to some other fucking guy at some other fucking table, schmoozing him so that he couldn't fucking concentrate either.

It had all been a setup.

How many times had he told himself in the past, shooting craps was for fucking losers? They send in the broads to distract you, plus which they feed you booze, *plus* which they probably fixed the dice. Wouldn't put that past them either because, hey, Davey didn't usually lose *that* much money in one night—never mind the fact that he didn't usually *have* that much money to lose. Besides, rethinking it, there wasn't a broad alive could make him lose his concentration when it came to a bet. But again, that didn't matter, because—just like the doorman—there was no way he could get *that* money back either. Especially not from a casino, for Christ's sake.

Teddy had wanted him to go to Miami? Get out of town because, what, it wasn't safe? Anthony Bonica was pissed and Dominic Scarlotti was dead? So what?

So *fuck* Miami.

Davey-Boy had made it as far as Atlantic City, New Jersey. It was hotter than hell here and his luck had turned to shit. Was it supposed to be cooler and luckier two thousand motherfucking miles *south*?

Bullshit.

He wasn't going to Miami. Wasn't going anywhere near Florida. In fact, first thing he *was* going to do—tomorrow morning—he was gonna hop on a bus. Go back to Philadelphia.

Where the weather was better.

And where people knew enough not to fuck around with him.

10

NATALIE SAID, "You really think this is going to fool them?"

Teddy shrugged. "If you're asking, they take it home, or over to Palisades, listen to it over and over again? Then, no, I don't think it'll work out. But if I play it for them, or part of it, where, say, the *acoustics* aren't that good, are they going to be able to take the chance that's it's *not* the real McCoy? In that case, I think they're going to want to believe in the thing."

Twenty minutes earlier, Teddy had run out to the nearest Radio Shack. It was three quarters of a mile down Spring Garden Street, near the Community College of Philadelphia and he had bought the smallest mini-cassette recorder they had in stock. The recorder was about the size of a pack of cigarettes, maybe a little longer, but only half as thick.

By the time Natalie had finished taking her second shower in seven hours Teddy was sitting at the dining room table, putting batteries in the thing and trying to figure out exactly how it worked.

He walked into the living room and turned the TV on. He opened the living room window, telling her, "Street sounds. I'm not sure, you know, where and when they did this thing. But I guess it had to be in Philly. In the city itself." After looking around for a minute he decided that the sound of running water might be a good idea too. He turned the kitchen sink on and said,

"I read somewhere that when people thought their place was bugged, or wanted to hide a conversation, they turned the tap water on."

Natalie rolled her eyes. "Did you, now?"

Teddy stood with his back to the TV, facing her, and said, "Look, the idea is to produce a tape—one where Anthony Bonica can't be sure *what* he's hearing. But hopefully one that Anthony—and Izzy Feldman too—hear what they're *expecting* to hear."

When he walked back into the dining room, Natalie was pointing at the TV. "Well, maybe you're right," she said, "especially since, any minute now, we're going to see Ginger star in a play that Mr. Howell is producing because Ginger misses Hollywood so much. Mary Ann is in it too, along with the Skipper. I think the Professor is going to be the leading man. Gilligan's working the stage curtain—which, incidentally, they somehow managed to make out of what looks to be a hundred square feet of cotton. Where'd they get that on a deserted island? I think, if I remember correctly, Gilligan screws it up and the whole thing falls down on Ginger. Do you want me to tell you how it ends or do you just want to tape it and let Anthony Bonica find out?"

Teddy said, "Let me guess. Someone told you—probably a long, long time ago—that you were funny?"

"I think it was last week."

Teddy turned the VCR on and then switched channels until the screen was snowy and the television was putting out that static-fuzzy noise that was normally irritating as hell. He turned the volume down until it was just a hiss and walked over to Natalie. "Hey, I think we're ready." Getting a look in return and telling her, "If you have a better idea, you're welcome to clue me in anytime."

She shook her head. "No. I think you have it covered. All we can do now is see how it turns out."

It turned out to be a lot harder than they expected. After the third attempt, Teddy said, "You know those movie people? Producers, directors, sound people? Especially the ones that are at the end credits of every movie? The ones you never pay any attention to? I'm getting some new respect for them here."

They ended up holding paper towels over their mouths, speaking so that almost every other word was purposefully unintelligible and every third word was foul. Finally Teddy slammed one of Natalie's shoes down onto the dining room table as hard as he could. It produced a surprisingly credible imitation of a gunshot but it also made Natalie frown because you could see an indentation on the table where the shoe had hit.

An hour after they started they listened to their eighth attempt and decided that it was probably as good as they were going to do.

Teddy said, "Well, you have to admit, if you listen to it with the right attitude, it does sound like it *could* be somebody *trying* to commit a homicide."

Natalie opened her eyes wide, looking at him from where she was hunched over the mini-recorder, and said, "And if you listen with the wrong attitude?"

Teddy shrugged, walked over to where she was, leaned down and kissed her. "I'm an optimist. I go to the track? I bet on the horse with three legs if I like the look of its tail."

HE WAS HELPING HER look for her purse when he was hit hard with just how much he had become used to the way they were doing everything together. A team. He stopped looking and sat on the sofa to think it through—the idea that he hadn't even discussed any of it except to plan out a way that she could back him up when he met with Anthony. Looking back on the last hour he realized that she had been nothing but optimistic and enthusiastic.

She hadn't once questioned him when he told her what his plan was. Hadn't once brought up how dangerous it was. The bad thing was—neither had he.

What had he been thinking?

"Nat?" he said.

She was pulling a cushion away from the couch, muttering, "Damnit," because her purse wasn't there, and she didn't seem to really be paying much attention to him.

He said it again. "Nat. Sit down a second." She turned to look at him and he added, "Please."

Maybe she saw something in his face, because she dropped the pillow and lowered herself onto the couch. "What's the matter?"

"What's the matter is *me*."

"What's wrong?" she leaned forward. "Are you all right?"

"I'm fine. But—" He couldn't find the right words yet.

"But what?"

He walked to the middle of the room, watching her the whole time, and then finally said, "I can't ask you to do this. It's crazy. I don't know what I was thinking."

"I want to do it."

"No. Think it through. This is something—it's dangerous. I got myself into it somehow. But—"

"But you can't ask me to get involved. Right?" Now she stood up. She came over and put her hands on his shoulders. "That's sweet. Really. I mean it. It is very, very sweet. Gallant."

"I'm not saying you couldn't do it. I'm not"—he almost smiled—"saying, you know, that you're not capable. I know, the thing you did with that guy. Your father's shotgun?"

"Jameel."

"Right. So, I'm not, in any way, implying—it's just, Christ, Anthony Bonica. We both know he doesn't want this to work out. Sure, if there's a huge problem with the murder of Dominic Scarlotti and if we can get Anthony out of a jam, he'll go for it."

"But he's going to try to kill you anyway."

Teddy nodded. "There's no fooling around with that. And anybody he sees connected with me? Same thing. It's why I sent my brother out of town. I can't let him know about you."

She looked at him for a moment and then, without saying anything, she walked back to the couch. After a moment of staring into space she turned to look at Teddy. Her voice sounded serene when she spoke. "I was engaged once. The guy broke it off at the last minute and I was devastated. In retrospect, though—well, hell, if that was his level of commitment, how long would we have lasted anyway? I could go on and on, tell you about other relationships I've had since and how they all seemed to lack something. But that's not going to help us now."

She stood up again and made her way back to Teddy. She leaned up and kissed him. "But I could also do this—at the risk of sounding, I don't know, corny—I like the way we are. I like the way—we *feel*."

"I do too."

"Well, that's nice. Except you're in a situation that's bad." She smiled. "You haven't met him yet, but you will. My father. When you do you'll find out that he did not—that's right, I said, *not*—raise me to run away from trouble."

"But this is not *your* trouble. I gave you a lift home, got a flat tire—and now look at where you are."

"Oh Christ, Teddy, you're going to drive yourself crazy like that. What if I hadn't gone into journalism? What if I had called in sick to Palisades that night? We could do 'what-ifs' for hours. But it doesn't change the fact that we're here now. Dealing with something that neither one of us really wants to deal with but have to." She touched his cheek, put a finger on his earlobe and stroked it. "But think about it, if you were in my shoes, what would you do? You don't have to answer because I think, by now, I know. You'd do everything you could to help me."

Teddy started to speak, but she put her finger gently over his lips. "I *know* you would. And I also know this: I couldn't live with the idea that something might happen to you and I had chosen to walk away. Is that fair enough?"

Teddy had no idea what to say. He had never been in a situation where, not only was he accepting help from someone but he also was beginning to like her more than he had ever liked another human being in his life.

He didn't get a chance to speak in any case because she said, "You know what occurs to *me*? We've been talking this thing through since last night. All we keep coming back to is 'Is it going to work out?' You know—how dangerous it is. What are our chances?"

"Yeah?"

"And now you're being gracious. Making sure I know I don't have to do anything more. Don't have to feel guilty if I bow out quietly. I already told you it's sweet and it is. But what about this—what if it *does* work out? What if—I'm not sure I even think it's likely—but, what if you actually *do* walk away from this with, say, a suitcaseful of hundred-dollar bills? What do—ah—what do *we*—do next? That's what occurs to me. The *we* part. Because that's how I'm starting to think. You and me. I don't want to put any pressure on you." She held her hands, palms up, in front of her chest as if to say she didn't know the answer to any of her own questions. "But that is the way it is in my head."

Teddy spent the next ten seconds staring at her and trying to come up with the right kind of response. But it was difficult because she had a point. They had talked to death about the possibilities of the thing not working. But they hadn't actually considered where they would be if they did succeed in snookering Anthony Bonica and Izzy Feldman.

Finally Teddy said, "I think—what you're getting at—is, where do you and I—I mean, *personally*—go from that point? We have a bag with a million dollars in it—what does that mean? There could be a lot of possible situations. Can I stay in the city? Can you? If the answer's is no for *both* of us, then I imagine—for, ah, want of any other solution—we hightail it out of here together. But let's say—maybe it gets a little hot around here for me but you can stay?"

"Exactly. I was being funny before—kidding around—yesterday. Talking about how we've managed to keep our relationship together for so long. I guess I thought it was cute. But where are we really?"

Teddy tried grinning. "You've got your body and your face. That's a good start. Being with you?" He was thinking hard and realizing, shit, this wasn't as easy as he wished, knowing that because he was beginning to joke around about it.

He exhaled slowly. "Nat—Natalie—I can't remember the last time—I'm not sure there *was* one—when I looked forward to seeing someone as much—as much." He paused and then said, "Shit, Natalie, I'm not very good at this."

She was watching carefully. "You're doing fine." She held her hand out.

He took it, and together they walked back to the sofa and sat down. He took a deep breath, looked her squarely in the eye and said, "I've never met anyone like you. I've been on my own for I don't know how long. All my life. My father—shit, I wouldn't recognize him if I saw him. I've been watching out for my brother all *his* life. I—I don't know how to accept help. I always thought—with Davey, my mother before she died—that it was all on me. And then you come along, act like it's so natural to help. You do it and half the time I don't even know you are. Helping me, I mean. I think I took it for granted."

"But you need the help now. Don't you?"

He nodded. "Yeah—I do."

She leaned forward and kissed him and then said, from six inches away, "Well, here I am. I want to help. I *want* to. All right?"

"Even the idea of the stadium? What we talked about? The pistol? The window?"

"All of it, Teddy. *All* of it. I want—to be with you."

"What am I supposed to say?" Teddy ran his hand through his hair. " 'Thank you' sounds—sounds lame."

"Nothing." She put her hand in his. "You don't have to say another word about it. We can talk about the plan. Go through it one more time—make sure we know exactly what we're supposed to do, each of us—and then we go out and do it. Besides that, there's nothing more either of us has to say." She smiled. "Not yet. There's no hurry for anything else."

TEDDY DROVE NATALIE back to her apartment. When he pulled up to the curb outside the building he said, "What are you supposed to do today?"

"I should stop by work. I mean, real work—the *Inquirer*. Then I'm supposed to show up for the lunch shift at Palisades. They open early on Saturdays. But I only work until two."

"Do it. Both of them." Teddy said, "Do everything that's expected of you. It's important that you act like you're having a normal day."

"What about you?"

"I'm going to do the same thing. Try not to attract any attention to myself."

"Except that, unlike a normal day, you're going to call Little Anthony Bonica and Izzy Feldman."

"To tell you the truth, I don't believe I will call Izzy today. I think—all around—it would be easier if we just deal with Anthony. He's a guy I can relate to. I know him. Grew up with him. Him and Tommy Inzarella. I feel more comfortable dealing with Anthony because I can pretty much predict what his next move is going to be. He may want to shoot me, but at least I won't be surprised by it. But Izzy? He's in a whole different league. The stories I've heard about him—I don't know how many are true, but I've heard enough of them to make me want to stay as far away from him as possible." Teddy glanced at his watch. "I'll give it a couple of hours and then make the phone call."

Natalie said, "And"—raising her eyebrows—"you *are* going to remember to call me. Right? Let me know when and where the big date is going to be."

Teddy shook his head. "You think I'm going to hold out on you? Jesus. What'd we just argue about? You're my backup."

DRIVING HOME he tried to decide whether or not he wanted to call Anthony Bonica directly or if he wanted to go through Tommy Inzarella. Things would definitely go more smoothly if he talked with Inzarella. But he decided he probably would have to talk to Anthony in person. Anthony would demand it so he could give Teddy a piece of his mind. Hopefully afterward Anthony would have the sense to put Tommy Inzarella on the line so that he and Teddy could talk more sensibly. Figure out a good time and place to swap the recorder for the million dollars.

He almost stopped at the Rite Aid pharmacy a few blocks from his apartment to invest a couple of bucks in earplugs. It would save him from getting a headache—listening to Anthony. Then he changed his mind because it occurred to him, maybe this one time it would be a *good* idea to listen carefully to every word Anthony said. Even if it did mean his ears were going to ring for a half an hour afterward.

The door to his apartment was wide open. The Beretta Davey-Boy had given him was down in the Acura, so Teddy reached behind the door for the Ping nine iron he had left there the night he had gone out to save Davey's ass. Only the golf club wasn't there.

It was in Izzy Feldman's hands and Izzy was sitting on the couch as if he owned the place, holding the handle of the club and bouncing the head lightly on the carpet. When he saw Teddy step in, he nodded at the door. "It was open. You ought to be more careful about that. I rang the bell and then figured you wouldn't mind if I made myself at home."

"Why not? Only I could've sworn I locked it when I left."

Izzy shrugged. "Perhaps you did. Perhaps I missed a burglar by just a couple of minutes. Or else possibly the door is broken. I don't know if you own or rent, but if you rent, you should call maintenance."

Teddy walked past Izzy to sit in the armchair. "Maybe I will."

Izzy lifted the nine iron and read the word on the head of the club. "Ping. From what I know, these are supposed to be very good clubs."

Teddy was looking past and slightly to the right of Izzy. At the dining room table where the mini-cassette was almost in plain sight. You had to look past a box of Wheaties and maybe pick up a portion of the paper Natalie had read while Teddy took his own shower. But still, if he remembered correctly, at least a part of the recorder was sticking out. Plus there was the package of six little mini-cassette tapes. Teddy knew for a fact that those weren't hidden by anything. He hadn't even thought to put them away. Then again, he hadn't been expecting company.

He looked back at Izzy—seeing that Izzy was studying him, almost as if he knew what Teddy was looking at. Teddy had to ask himself, How long had Izzy been here? Teddy had driven Natalie home. That was, say, round-trip, thirty-five minutes. Had Izzy been waiting outside? Seen them leave? Or had he just stopped by three minutes ago, rung the doorbell and broken in? Made himself at home right away on the sofa so he could get the feel of Teddy's nine iron? Not bothered to wander around and look at anything else? Or had he poked around, gone through Teddy's mail, maybe his underwear drawer while he was at it? *Had* Izzy noticed the tape recorder? Known exactly what it was? Maybe even listened to it and had himself a good laugh? But if *had* listened to it and it sounded anything like what had actually happened, why hadn't he just taken it? Why was he sitting on the sofa, admiring Teddy's latest piece of athletic equipment? Teddy found himself hoping that Izzy wasn't here just to mop up a messy situation. If he was, that meant that Teddy himself was the situation.

He said, hoping none of his thoughts were showing up in the sound of his voice, "Ping. Yeah. They're the best."

"To tell you the truth, I can't understand golf. All that fuss, you hit a little white ball a couple of hundred yards. If you're any good, that is. Try like crazy to get it into that little hole in the ground. And what happens when you do? You have to start all over again."

"Yeah, well, some people can't seem to get enough of it."

Izzy nodded and studied Teddy carefully. Finally he smiled slightly— Teddy thought it was the first time he'd ever seen him do it—and shook his head a tiny bit. "Not you, though."

It crossed Teddy's mind that if Izzy wanted to, he could start hitting Teddy with the nine iron any time he felt like it. It was hard to sit here with that knowledge in his head, but it wasn't like there were any more golf clubs lying around for him to use in defense. He said, "Pardon me?"

"What I mean is this: You don't actually play, do you?" Izzy lifted the golf club a foot off the ground and said, "No. What you do, you carry this around so that folks will think a nice-looking gentleman such as yourself, a gentile, actually *owns* the car he's driving away in." He looked Teddy up and down. "It probably works."

Teddy made himself smile. "So far. But I will tell you this. I did play golf one time. At the Merion Country Club. A friend of mine took me. I don't remember exactly what happened, but I believe I shot a one twenty-nine— something in that neighborhood. And I might've even cheated. Afterwards the guy who invited me wouldn't talk to me for a month. He had invited his lawyer and I believe his doctor to complete the foursome. I think they all hit just a little over par and spent a lot of time helping me look for my ball and a fair amount of time giving me dirty looks. I know I never got invited back. I didn't really care, though. All that time I trudged up and down those hills, got sand in my shoes—I agree with you—chasing after a little white ball that I didn't know where in the hell it'd gone? I can find other ways to kill an afternoon."

Izzy suddenly handed the nine iron to Teddy. It surprised him but he tried to be as nonchalant as possible, even saying thank you, which sounded dumb to his ears.

"You have to know that Mr. Bonica—aside from something of a personal vendetta I understand he has against you—can't let you get away with this."

"Bad for his reputation and all that?"

Izzy shrugged. "He's a businessman. And in his business he can't afford to look soft."

"He *is* soft."

Izzy gave Teddy a sharp look but then nodded. "Perhaps he is. He certainly is too emotional. All that anger, I don't want to go into Anthony's psyche—but perhaps his rages are a defense mechanism."

Teddy said, very seriously, "Per*haps* he just has a very small penis."

Izzy smiled again. Teddy had enough time to see that he had perfect teeth. But then the smile was gone and Izzy said, "I'm not sure I care to know."

Teddy said, "Well, maybe you want know something else then. When I went into Palisades—and I mean the very moment I entered—I was asking myself, what was I doing? I could've let it go. Bury Dominic Scarlotti and then forget about it. Not only would no one ever be able to prove I had been involved after the fact—but why would they even think to try? I've had people not care for me before. Maybe some people hate me. But I don't believe anyone would think I was crazy enough to murder the head of the Philadelphia mob."

"I can understand that."

"Uh-huh. So, at the last minute—walking into Palisades—I almost changed my mind. But then, when I saw how nervous you guys were, especially how upset Anthony was, instead of walking out, I decided to stick around. I have to admit, I don't know where I came up with that number. One million dollars. But I noticed that nobody fell out of their chairs laughing when I said it. And I've repeated it enough times in my head that I'm getting comfortable with the sound of it. It's easy to say. 'One—million—dollars.' "

"But you have to ask yourself, how easy is it going to be to collect?"

Teddy shrugged. "There's only one way to find out."

"I suppose you're right. As long as you're willing to risk the consequences." Izzy seemed to think about something for a moment. And then, Teddy realized, he came to the real reason he had picked Teddy's lock. "My employer—"

Teddy said, "Saul Rubin."

Izzy nodded. "That's right. Mr. Rubin. Well, I explained the situation to him. Told him—" Izzy paused for a moment and then said, "Actually, Mr. Clyde—"

"Call me Teddy."

Izzy shrugged. "Teddy, before I proceed, I'd like it if this bit of information was kept between you, Mr. Rubin and myself. I'm saying that Mr. Anthony Bonica doesn't necessarily have to be privy to our discussion."

"Sure."

Izzy said, "Thank you." And Teddy wondered how he did it. Sound so polite and intelligent but also seem so dangerous at the same time. Did he practice it or did it come naturally?

Izzy said, "As I said, Mr. Rubin and I—what we would like, what we would truly appreciate—is this: Suppose you *do* have knowledge"—pointing at Teddy with his right index finger "—about something that a certain party, who is no longer with us, might have had on his person. Apparently you are the only one who would. At least the only one even remotely inclined to discuss the subject with me because even Mr. Rubin can't reach out to any federal authorities on something as delicate as this. Do you see what I mean?"

"I'm still with you."

"Fine. Well, if you did come across an—an item—even if you're not sure what it is. If you could let *us* know. Let *us* see it. I'm talking about either Mr. Rubin or myself. Ah, before—"

"Before I let Anthony Bonica see it."

Izzy spread his hands wide and nodded. "I told Mr. Rubin about you. I said, 'This is an intelligent man who minds his own business. A careful man.'" Izzy frowned for an instant. It looked to Teddy as if he was deciding whether or not he wanted to say anything else.

Izzy nodded to himself and then said, "Actually, Teddy, Mr. Rubin and I—you have to understand—the business we have with Anthony Bonica is, how shall I put it—so remote from what some of our other concerns are."

"You have better things to do with your time."

"Exactly." Izzy smiled. "And, while I wouldn't want to begin to bother you with the details, it is true, we have, ah, ongoing projects which require more of our attention. As I said, you needn't concern yourself with what they are. Just be assured, anything you can do to help us out, put this unfortunate mess behind us? Well, it certainly would be appreciated." Izzy stood up and carefully smoothed his slacks. "And, as I told Mr. Rubin, you certainly do seem to be a man who could understand our concerns. Help us out. You are, after all, a professional. A man who's able to pursue a career with apparently little risk when others who do the same thing seem to be constantly in and out of jail."

"You told Saul that? I'll be damned." Teddy acted like he was thinking hard. He turned halfway around, still holding the nine iron and said, "Hmmmm."

Then he whipped around, used the head of the nine iron like a sword, and jammed it into Izzy's throat, dead center into his Adam's apple, pushing him back against the wall right next to the sofa. He held Izzy there, but it wasn't easy.

Teddy said, "Did you also tell your Mister Rubin that—if I get prodded long enough—I have a temper? I didn't ask for any of this bullshit, but now I have people telling me I'm a walking dead man. People breaking into the place I live. People putting dead bodies into my car."

Teddy let up on the pressure and stepped back. But he stayed close enough so that if Izzy had a gun he could plunk him onto the ninth green before he had time to get it out. He said, "I gotta admire your balls, Izzy. Coming into—hell, *breaking* into the place I live. Talking politely. Calmly. Hell, you don't even look mad now, and what I just did was pretty goddamn rude."

Izzy touched his throat but didn't say anything. He was studying Teddy carefully. Teddy wondered if he'd made a mistake. Perhaps Izzy's reaction was *too* calm. Teddy hefted the club in the air and had the satisfaction of seeing Izzy blink twice and almost take a step backward. It made him feel better. Izzy showing caution—some actual fear.

"Why don't you do this?" he said, "Go back and tell *Mister* Rubin I'll consider his proposal. Because I will. But first, I want to know something. You can act pissed off because of what just happened if you want to, or you can answer my question because maybe it's a situation that, if you tell me, it'll help me help you."

Izzy sounded like he had a cold when he finally did speak. "What's your question?"

Teddy said, "Why is everybody so concerned with Dominic? He was wearing a wire, wasn't he?"

A startled look flicked across Izzy's face as if he couldn't control it in time. A moment later, looking purposefully nonchalant, he simply nodded his head.

"I thought so." Teddy realized that there *was* no way Izzy had seen the tape recorder on the dining room table. Teddy must have arrived only seconds after Izzy broke in because Izzy definitely would've taken the recorder and, quite possibly, taken out Teddy the second Teddy walked through the door.

Teddy had a sudden hunch. "Izzy, you didn't kill Scarlotti just as a favor to Anthony, did you?"

Izzy stepped away from the wall. Teddy got ready to whack him with the nine iron if the need arose, but all Izzy did was shake his head slowly. "Mr. Clyde—Teddy—I'm not going to comment on that last remark. Not in any way, except, possibly to say, perhaps I owe you an apology."

"What?"

"I've become accustomed"—Izzy waved a hand through the air—"because of my recent dealings with Anthony Bonica—who is not an intelligent human being—to dealing at a certain level. Mr. Inzarella? I think he's a different story. He's quiet, you don't even know he's listening sometimes. But he is." Izzy touched his throat again and then dropped his hand to his side. "But to my point, perhaps I've forgotten what it's like to deal with a person such as yourself. An intelligent man."

"I'm flattered, Izzy."

"Are you? That's nice." Izzy lowered his voice and it somehow came out sounding much more menacing than it had a moment earlier. "But please, flattered or not, Teddy, don't go speculating—poking your head into business that doesn't concern you at all. It can only lead to—to difficulties."

"Difficulties? I like that, Izzy." Teddy thought about the situation for a moment and then told Izzy, "All right, two—no, *three* things. First, possibly I will take your advice, mind my own business. And, second, the price hasn't changed the slightest bit. Hell, it might even go up. Number three, I don't care who pays me, you *or* Little Anthony. But somebody has to. You say you'd like to get your hands on the wire—or whatever it is I'm going to find"—Teddy acted like he had to think about it—"*if* and when I even decide to go dig the motherfucker up. Which brings me to another point. Tell your boss and Anthony Bonica too that there's no way for any of you to know whether or not I've told someone who'll tell the cops if I wind up unavailable for more than a normal amount of time. You understand what I'm saying?"

Izzy said, "I do." There was still some scratchiness to his voice.

Teddy nodded. "Good. I suppose that, if you want to guess—take that chance that you can figure out where I put the body on your own—then there's nothing I can do about it. Sooner or later I'll make a mistake. Then again, why bother? A million dollars. Yeah, it's a lot of money. To *some* people. To you guys? No. It's a business expense. That's all."

Izzy shrugged. "It's not something that we can write off on our taxes, but I see what you're getting at. And the other thing, the possibility that—if we don't deal, ah, fairly, with you—you might have already made arrangements to let others in on something we'd rather remain a secret? Mr. Rubin and I have already discussed that possibility. I told him you would cover yourself."

"Bet your ass I am." Teddy took a step closer to Izzy, staring at the hard brown eyes in Izzy's face but not blinking himself. He figured, what the hell, he'd already pushed a golf club into his throat so expressing an opinion wasn't going to make matters worse. "The last thing? This one's personal for you, Izzy. Don't ever fucking break into my place again."

The second Izzy closed the door behind him, Teddy hid the cassette recorder, ran out of his apartment door and down the six flights of stairs to the parking garage. He got there in time to see Izzy getting into a black Lincoln Town Car and was inside his own Acura before Izzy had cleared the gate to the street entrance of the garage.

Once on the street it was easy enough for Teddy to hang back, keep the Lincoln in sight and follow it down Callowhill Street to where it dead-ended into Columbus Boulevard. Teddy hadn't tailed too many people in his lifetime, but he was smart enough not to worry too much if Izzy caught a light and Teddy didn't. It happened twice and each time Teddy managed to catch up to the Town Car without losing it.

Izzy took a left onto Columbus Boulevard, headed north and drove along the Delaware River past two piers that jutted like huge, robotic limbs out into the water. There didn't seem to be much activity at the first two piers, but there was a freighter docked at the third. Izzy pulled in and stopped his Lincoln a few feet from the gangplank.

The ship looked to be about fifty years old, something out of an old World War II movie. It was painted a lighter version of battleship gray with a wide, dark-green band running the length of the vessel a few feet below the main deck. The paint itself was apparently new but had simply been slapped on over huge rust spots so that the ship had a pockmarked look to it, a teenager suffering from a terrible case of acne and caking on makeup in a desperate effort to hide it. A bright green, yellow and orange flag fluttered in the wind above the wheelhouse.

By the time Izzy stepped out of his car Teddy had pulled off onto the shoulder of the boulevard. Below him a man with a patchy beard, dressed in a half-assed captain's uniform, walked down the gangplank and shook Izzy's hand.

The captain and Izzy watched as a huge cargo container was loaded aboard by a huge crane, and then they walked up the gangplank and disappeared inside the ship. Teddy waited until he saw both men reappear inside the bridge and then he started his Acura, U-turned onto Columbus Boulevard and headed back to his apartment.

He didn't know what to make of what he had just seen. But he was fairly certain that Izzy wasn't a member of the United Sates Navy. On the way out, just for the hell of it, and because he had no idea what else to do, he pulled a pen and an old envelope out of the glove compartment and wrote down, "Pier 25N."

When he was finished that he stuck the envelope back into the glove compartment, took the right to get back onto Callowhill Street and started to think about what he was going to say when he called Anthony Bonica.

TEDDY FINALLY GOT HOLD of Little Anthony and had to wait for a full thirty seconds until Anthony quit telling him what was going to happen if Teddy fucked around with him anymore. Teddy finally said, "Anthony—" He waited another few seconds and said it again. "Anthony. Nobody's going to do anything *but* fuck around, you don't manage to control your temper long enough to have a reasonable conversation with me."

Anthony calmed down and said, "Whatta you got in mind?"

Teddy said, "Veterans Stadium."

"What?"

Teddy said, "Jesus, Anthony, you run most of the bookmaking in this city. You going to tell me you don't know what the 'Vet' is?"

"I know what the Vet is. The fuck you got in mind? You and me, we should take in a motherfucking *Phillies* game?"

"The Phillies are in Cincinnati playing the Reds. And I don't care that they don't play football there anymore. The Eagles. The *parking* lot is still there. So, you and I meet—we've got a transaction we need to complete, and there's no place in that parking lot for anybody to get cute."

"Asshole, *I* decide where we meet."

"Hey, Anthony, you mind if I hang up now? I gotta call the cops."

There was a long silence before, "What time?"

Teddy looked at his watch. "I got eleven-thirty now. Why don't we say, three o'clock. It shouldn't be hard to find each other because I'm thinking the only two cars that better be there are going to be yours and mine."

"Hey, I can't get the money together by then. The fuck you thinking?"

"What do you have to do, Anthony, go to a goddamn bank? If you're not at Veterans Stadium parking lot by three o'clock the cops'll have what you're looking for by four."

11

TEDDY CALLED NATALIE and told her things were set. "I'm going to swing by Palisades at about two o'clock. What I want you to do is tell a couple of people—make a point of it—that you're going to lunch. Don't tell them where but maybe hint that—hey, I know—you're going to meet your new boyfriend who happens to be a wealthy, brilliant, handsome stockbroker."

She said, "And that would be you?"

"Exactly. One other thing?"

"What?"

"I just want to make sure. You still have time to back out of this thing. We both do."

"What, and miss lunch with my new boyfriend?"

"You're sure?"

"Christ, Teddy, are you going to pick me up or not?"

"I'll see you at two. No. Wait a minute. Make it quarter after. Can you do that? I have an errand to run."

"Sure. What is it?"

"It's a surprise."

———

IZZY STOPPED BY Anthony Bonica's club just long enough to listen to Anthony tell him that he hadn't heard from Teddy Clyde. Izzy was fairly certain that Anthony was lying, but he figured the best way to find out was to see what Teddy himself was up to. Plus which he wanted Anthony to believe that he respected his opinion. He left Palisades, drove to Teddy's apartment and didn't have to wait at all because there was Teddy's Acura pulling out of the exit of the apartment's parking garage. Izzy was in position to follow him without having to even slow down with traffic.

Izzy followed the Acura as Teddy pulled down Spring Garden Street headed toward the Benjamin Franklin Parkway. Teddy wasn't doing what a lot of other motorists were, gunning the engine every block to try to beat the next light. He was driving at a steady speed, apparently doing nothing more than cruising around the city. Izzy couldn't make up his mind whether or not Teddy was up to anything more than a bagel run.

Izzy had to admit, for a guy who had a noose around his neck and *had* to know it was tightening, Teddy was acting pretty cool. Izzy still didn't know what he was going to do about the golf club incident. Was he going to take it personally or not? He could see Teddy's point, a guy breaks into your house, your apartment, whatever, if you let it go without doing something then you were saying something about yourself. Giving something up to whoever it was that broke in. And it wasn't as if Teddy Clyde had actually hurt him. He could have taken Izzy's head off with the nine iron. But he hadn't. Anthony Bonica certainly would've tried. He wouldn't have succeeded, but that wasn't the point.

He watched the turn signal on Teddy Clyde's Acura. He was taking a left onto Broad Street and Izzy realized that he was headed toward Palisades, probably on his way to see his new girlfriend again. Ms. Natalie Prentice. Now it really made Izzy start to wonder. Was Teddy *that* cool or was he being stupid. He had to know that people were scrambling to find out what he knew and that those same people would just as soon see him dead the moment they got what they wanted from him.

And here he was, picking up his lady friend—at Anthony Bonica's own club—for what? A quick bite before he went out and took care of business? Maybe even a quickie, a short hour in bed because they couldn't keep their hands off each other no matter *what* else was going on? It made Izzy wonder about his original estimation of Mr. Clyde, thinking he was an intelligent man. Maybe not. Not if he was risking getting his head blown off just to have, what, a date?

Izzy pulled to a curb and left the engine running. Teddy stayed in his car, too, and a minute later Ms. Prentice came out of the back of the club. She walked to his car carrying a white cardboard box. Three feet long but only six by six for the other dimensions, the kind of thing that flowers came in.

Izzy almost grinned now, seeing the humor in it and thinking the woman must be special. Teddy, he could lose his life at any second, and he takes the time to send her flowers? Now that was admirable. Stupid. But still . . .

It was when Izzy was pulling out that he saw the car behind his own. He thought he might even have noticed it before but wasn't positive. Seen it in the rearview mirror without giving it too much thought because traffic was heavy and there wasn't a lot of reason to be suspicious.

Now he took a good look at it. A brown Ford sedan, four door, that'd been on the city streets long enough to get dinged up a bit, its front left fender dented so that the plastic lens over the turn signal bulb was broken, a small hole there that showed up every time the car took a turn. Izzy couldn't believe it, the shape the car was in. How in the world were the Philly cops supposed to fight crime like that? Didn't they ever hear about asset forfeiture? Grab a drug dealer off the street, those guys drove BMWs, Benzes, hell, six-figure SUVs. He thought, when he got the chance, he might call them and anonymously suggest that they rethink their vehicular strategy. They could blend a little better. Of course, it didn't *have* to be the Philly cops. It could be the feds. But it wasn't as if it could be anything else but *some* sort of law-enforcement vehicle.

Izzy was tempted to lose the thing. Zip through traffic up ahead like he used to do in a jeep on the Gaza Strip, the West Bank, the .50 caliber machine gun mounted on a swing tripod behind and above so nobody shot a friend's head off if things got exciting. Running Palestinian outlaws to the ground on dust-packed roads, not worrying whether the jeep was going to flip over because there were worse things that could happen.

He could do that. Disappear from the cops. Leave them with nothing more then a desire for doughnuts. It would take about a minute. Or else, and this might be amusing, work it so that the cops ended up at an intersection at the same time as he did. Wait for a light to go yellow, change lanes at the last second so that whoever was driving the Ford behind him would have no choice but to pull up next to him. Izzy could roll his own window down while the cops looked at everything but him, get their attention somehow and then give them the name of a good body shop. Get a good look at the cops' faces while he did it.

He looked at Teddy Clyde's Acura up ahead. By now they were all headed toward the oil refineries a few miles past the Thirtieth Street train station just before you got to the international airport. What was Teddy up to? Driving as if he didn't have a care in the world. Izzy took a chance—he didn't think that Teddy Clyde was about to hop on an international flight. No, Izzy was thinking about the picture he'd seen on Natalie Prentice's driver's license and what he would do if he were in Mr. Clyde's shoes. The roses? Sure, have them delivered first and then show up to take the woman to lunch. Izzy knew, the direction they were all driving, there were two of Philadelphia's finer restaurants less than four blocks ahead—just after you went past the auto mall—the rows of dealerships that crowded both sides of the highway. Mr. Clyde might've called one of those exact restaurants up this morning, last night, gotten reservations, a table for two. Intimate.

It was what Izzy would do.

So he made up his mind. Since Teddy Clyde seemed to be doing nothing more than going on a date, he'd take the trouble to find out who was driving the Ford behind him.

TEDDY SAID, "How was work?"

"You mean at the *Inquirer*? Or Palisades?" Teddy was driving with one hand on the wheel and his arm draped out of the window because that's how nice it was out. Natalie had scooted over in her seat, half turned to face him, and now she was waiting for him to answer.

He said, "Palisades."

"It was its usual pain in the ass. The lunch shift is three hours and feels like twelve."

"Uh-huh." Teddy pointed at the flower box. "Tell me that's not a dozen roses."

"It's not. It's what you asked for."

"Good." He reached behind the passenger seat and grabbed a brown grocery store bag, pulled it up and put it in Natalie's lap.

She rummaged through it and then looked at him. "This is where you tell me you're kidding."

"I'm not."

She began to take things out of the bag, talking as she did. "A sweatshirt. You hear a weather report? Something about us having a cold spell today?"

Teddy shook his head. "Keep looking. And remember, now is not the time to cop an attitude."

She reached into the bag and came out with a baseball cap that said "John Deere." "Good Lord." She went back to the bag and burst out laughing. "Now I *know* you're kidding me."

"I'm not kidding about anything."

"Where'd you get this?" she brought her hand back out of the bag. She was holding a fake beard. It had two wires on each side of it so that you could hook it around your ears.

Teddy said, "At one of those funky costume shops on South Street. Don't ask me what other kind of stuff they had in there. I think some of it was for sex, but I'm not even sure. Lots of leather." There was a black Lincoln behind them. A Town Car that was three cars back, behind a cab and a beat-up pickup truck that had two aluminum ladders on a rack that extended over the cab. Teddy changed from the left lane into the right, and a moment later the Lincoln did too.

Natalie shook her head. "There is no way I'm—"

Teddy said, "Listen to me. What we're going to do—and I apologize if this makes me a chauvinist pig—but, you have to understand, if Anthony Bonica sees you the way"—he looked over at her—"the way you look now. I mean—"

"You want me to put a beard on? Seriously?"

"It'd be doing me a favor. They see you, as you are now, one, they might be able to ID you later. Plus, I want them to be thinking, who—"

"Who was that bearded man?" She was shaking her head again. Almost laughing.

"That's not what I was going to say. But you have to understand, these guys, they have a certain mentality. They see some other guy in my car—and you won't be close enough for them to get a good look at you—and they're gonna wonder, Do I"—Teddy pointed at himself—"meaning me—have even *more* people backing me up? Maybe I put a sniper on the roof."

She put the beard back in the bag. "No way. I'm not going to wear it."

He let it go. Concentrated instead on traffic. But by the time he had gone two blocks he made up his mind that he was going to quit right now. It didn't matter. He could move. How many times—in the dead of winter or the heat of July—had he told himself he'd be having a better life somewhere else?

They stopped at a red light and he looked at Natalie. Didn't say anything, just stared, getting the words right in his head so that he could come up with something like, Hey, forget it. We don't know each other and this whole thing is crazy.

She stared right back at him and just as he was opening his mouth to tell her what was on his mind, she must have seen something in his face. Realized how serious he was, because she nodded and said, "All right, all right—

I see your point." She pulled the sweatshirt on, put the John Deere cap on with her hair tucked up into the cap and then used the rearview mirror to hook the beard over her ears and get it straight. Then she readjusted the mirror as best she could and turned to him. "I don't want to hear—"

"Nothing. You won't hear a thing." He hit the gas because the light had turned green and then looked up to readjust the rearview mirror. The black Lincoln was still there. Only two cars back now. The pickup truck had turned off but the cab was still behind them, blocking Teddy's view of whoever was driving the Lincoln.

Teddy put his left turn signal on and moved into the left-hand lane of Broad Street as soon as it was clear. A moment later the Lincoln did the same thing. But he still couldn't see the driver's face.

He turned to see what Natalie was doing. She had taken off the beard, but from the expression she gave him he knew she would put it on when the time came. He wanted to tell her something special, but all he could come up with was "Thank you, I appreciate it."

She held his gaze for a moment and then nodded solemnly. "It's okay. Just don't you dare call me Moe, Larry or Curly."

"I won't."

A moment later he felt her hand touch the outer part of his thigh. He reached down and took it into his own. Gave it a soft squeeze and got one back in return.

The next time he looked into the rearview mirror, the black Lincoln was gone.

GEORGE ABBOT HAD LISTENED to the little cocksucker federal prosecutor Donald Shaffer tell him off in front of everybody, holding the newspaper no more than six inches from his face, as if Abbot had written the fucking thing himself, and decided that, one way or another, when they were all finished with the Dominic Scarlotti mess, he was going to take Shaffer up to the roof of the goddamn building and throw him off. See if the little piece of shit could fly, because nobody was going to threaten *his* pension.

He was driving one of the beat-up cars the federal government had issued him, and every third traffic light the thing seemed about to stall. Next to him was the other federal marshal, James Lacombe, a black guy in his early thirties who Abbot thought might have watched *Shaft* one too many times. Abbot had seen Lacombe around a couple of times in recent years, but he'd never had the opportunity to work with him. He could've waited for that treat for a while longer because Lacombe was giving him a hard time.

Lacombe said, for what was probably the third time, "I'm telling you, we should be back at Palisades, watching Little Anthony."

Abbot said, "I didn't realize he was a friend of yours."

Lacombe looked confused. "Who?"

"Anthony Bonica. You say his name like you go to the track with him or something. Place bets with him personally on the Eagles. If you want, in a little bit, we can stop back at his club. You can go on in and have lunch with the prick, count how many tits are in the place."

"Fuck you."

"Not right now." Abbot was watching a black Lincoln Town Car ahead of him. They were headed toward the airport, and Abbot thought he might be seeing a pattern here. Thought, actually, that while *he* was tailing the black Lincoln, *it* might actually be tailing somebody else. An Acura that unfortunately Abbot couldn't get close enough to yet to see its plates. There was a pair of binoculars in the glove compartment but Abbot was going to wait because, for one thing, he wanted to make sure of what he was seeing. And, another thing, he was goddamned if he was going to ask James Lacombe to reach in there and get them.

A minute later he got his chance. Traffic backed up near the University of Pennsylvania, and Abbot had to slow to a stop. It was a surveillance nightmare, but there wasn't a lot Abbot could do about it. He had to keep *some* distance between his car and the black Town Car, but he didn't want some ass-hole behind him blowing his horn. He was fairly sure the driver of the Town Car wasn't paying him any attention because he could see the back of the driver's head and it didn't seem to be moving, looking into the rearview or turning around to peek at Abbot's beat-up Ford. But he could also see the Acura too. A lone man driving and another man, smaller, wearing a baseball cap in the passenger seat. It could be anyone, but Abbot memorized the plates for the hell of it. Pennsylvania tags. W/R1351H.

It was habit. A learned trait—memorizing license plates or mug shots from just a quick glimpse. He knew, from past experience, if he needed to come up with the plates later, he could go into his memory and pull them out, no trouble at all.

Traffic started to move again, and Abbot turned his car off and on a couple of times deliberately. Anyone watching would assume he was having car trouble. James Lacombe was rolling his eyes and making a big deal out of sighing audibly, but who gave a shit about that. When the Town Car was a hundred feet ahead of them Abbot started his car for real, gunned it in front of an approaching cab and began to keep pace with the Lincoln again. They were in a parade, the Town Car, a beat-up cab, now a roofer's pickup with ladders on top and then Abbot in the Ford. The pickup turned off, and now it was just the three cars.

He knew full well who was driving the Lincoln. And because of that—because he'd been so surprised to see the driver walk out of Anthony Bon-ica's club while he and Lacombe were staking the place out—he had a hunch that somehow the driver of the Lincoln might know a little bit about what had happened to Dominic Scarlotti.

Except now he noticed that, just as he was doing with the Lincoln, the driver of the Town Car kept making the same turns, changed lanes at the same time and kept the same speed, as the driver of the Acura.

Abbot had to fight the urge to check his mirror to see if anyone was fol-lowing *him*.

Suddenly Lacombe said, "Look, enough is fucking enough. Get me back to Bonica's club. I'm not fucking around with my career just because you got a personal hard-on for Shaffer."

Abbot made sure he caught the next light before he turned to Lacombe and said, "Look, I understand you can't help how ignorant you are."

"What?"

"You heard me. But just so you don't have a coronary, that guy"—Abbot pointed at the Town Car—"is a man named Izzy Feldman. Works for another guy named Saul Rubin. Rubin's a guy who—even if I *felt* like telling you how high his connections go—you wouldn't believe me. But I will tell you this. I see Izzy up there walk into and out of Palisades a half hour ago? I aim to find out why. You can either hang in there or jump out the fucking window. Don't make no never mind to me."

Lacombe glared at Abbot. Then he made a production out of sitting back and staring out of his own window.

Abbot didn't care. He was too busy keeping the right distance between his and Izzy Feldman's car. The Philly Mob were fucking amateurs compared to Izzy Feldman and Saul Rubin, and Abbot wanted to try to make sense out of the fact that Izzy had stopped by Anthony Bonica's main hangout.

There had to be some kind of connection.

A minute later Abbot realized he was wrong about one thing. Izzy Feldman wasn't tailing anybody. Maybe he was running an errand for Saul, going out to get kosher food. Because Izzy suddenly stopped following the Acura Legend, put his turn signal on and took a right off the highway. Up ahead was Franklin Field, where the Penn Quakers played and a little farther, the Palestra—where some of the better college ball in the country had ever been played.

Izzy had picked a tiny street that was little more than a wide alley and only ran until it dead-ended into Thirty-fourth Street. At first Abbot was confused. What the fuck was Izzy doing? Why get off Route 76 just to head down here?

He figured—only thing to do was follow and find out.

A trash truck was pulling onto the street from out of an alley a half a block in front of the Town Car. One of the big ones the city used to empty commercial dumpsters. Izzy's brake lights came on as the truck moved slowly backwards, blocking the entire street. When Izzy's car was completely stopped—with Abbot stuck in no-man's-land fifty feet behind—Izzy's door suddenly opened and he stepped out onto the pavement.

Abbot looked around, wondering, where the fuck was Izzy going? Abbot hurriedly checked out the buildings on both sides of the street, run-down apartments and the back entrances to a couple of small retail shops—a small shot between the buildings to part of Drexel's campus. But Abbot wasn't recognizing anything and was getting slightly puzzled until he turned back once more to see what Izzy was doing.

It went through Abbot's head that fast, the word *fuck*, because Izzy wasn't going into any building. He was walking toward Abbot's car, a quick yet subtle grace to the way he moved, his eyes glued on Abbot's face.

Abbot thought it again. *Fuck.* Rolling down his window because what the hell else was he supposed to do, shoot the guy? Watching Izzy lean down, cool, his face kind-looking in this instance, and say, "I think I know you." He got a different expression on his face now, thinking hard and then nodding. "Abbot. Mr. George Abbot? Am I right?"

Lacombe gave a short laugh. Abbot wanted to put his elbow through his face. Instead, he made himself look Izzy in the eyes and said, "Yeah. That's my name. But if we ever met, I don't remember it."

Izzy shook his head. "No, I don't think we actually met. I think I just saw you once. A courtroom or something. You're a federal marshal, correct? Witness protection?"

"It's a possibility."

Izzy said, "Sure." And then he squatted next to the driver's door of the Ford so that he and Abbot were face-to-face. "What I was wondering is this. Why don't I just *tell* you where I'm going? That way you can meet me there."

TEDDY MADE NATALIE CRAWL into the backseat of the Acura a block and a half before they got to the stadium complex. The old Spectrum was on the left. The newer First Union Center was to the right and behind and past both structures the brand new Lincoln Financial Stadium rose into the sky like some kind of bad Hollywood imitation of a spaceship.

Driving closer, Teddy told Natalie that now was the time to put the beard on. He also told her to keep a low profile until she was sure no one was paying attention to the car. "Give me a minute to get out and talk to Anthony to see how he's gonna play this thing. *Then* you sit up."

She said, "And I'm going to be able to tell that *how*? I use my X-ray vision and look through the back door of the car, sit up just before you touch your head?"

"No, you give me a minute and then you let your journalistic instincts take over. Hey, I have an idea, pretend that black dude, what was his name, Jameel? Pretend *he's* the one we're meeting and just let your gut tell you when to peek over at us, see how things are going. I'm going to leave the key in the ignition, the car turned on but not running so the power windows'll work. Lower it and for God's sake don't rush things."

They pulled into the huge parking lot on the south side of Veterans Stadium that on any given Sunday—when Teddy was younger and when the Eagles were still playing at the Vet—would be jammed with twenty to thirty thousand cars. For a moment he thought about the Eagles—the ones who were playing when he was a teenager, maybe early twenties—Dick Vermeil coaching them all the way to the Super Bowl only to lose out to the wild-card Oakland Raiders. Shit, he'd gone down to see the game and come away with a sour feeling because back then, just starting as a small businessman, a dealer in warm cars with shaky pedigrees—he'd thought a football game was something of serious significance.

He'd come a long way since then and didn't particularly care who won what football game unless—as he occasionally did—he put money down on the point spread.

Christ, he had to stop his mind from wandering and come back to the business at hand. The stadium parking lot was empty, and right now Teddy liked it that way. He stopped the Acura just before the main entrance to the lot, got out and went around to the trunk of the Acura where he had put a pair of bolt cutters. Then he snipped a link on the chain like it was made of silly putty, opened the gate, climbed back into the car and drove onto the huge expanse of the lot.

It was weird to see it this empty, looking like a huge ghost town or some vast area where a low-level nuclear disaster had happened and everyone had fled, waiting for their impending cancers and leaving nothing but an occasional bit of trash blowing in the breeze.

A service warehouse stood a quarter of a mile away from the main entranceway—to the south. To the north, a little closer, was what looked to be where the parking receipts were collected and counted. A low, flat building maybe a hundred feet long and twenty feet wide that had a small mobile home—looking office next to it. Both of them seemed deserted. Teddy wondered, why hadn't anyone ever held the place up, gone in with an automatic rifle, a couple of AK-47s, and knocked the place off? Score a couple of hundred grand minimum because the parking authority went out of their way to charge as much as they could get away with—if Teddy remembered correctly it was ten bucks a car. All cash, too. It wasn't something Teddy would do, go in with a gun, but if he thought about it for ten seconds he could come up with the names of some acquaintances of his who would do the job in a heartbeat. Wind up killing people and not care too much because they'd be thinking about what they were going to spend their hard-earned money on.

Teddy put the thought out of his head and drove to the very far edge of the parking lot and swung his Acura in a slow U-turn so that he could eyeball all the entrances to the place simultaneously. He set his mirrors so that he didn't have any kind of blind spot behind him. To the left, behind him, he could see the back edge of the Philly airport a half a mile away and the beginnings of a huge, low-income housing project even farther away than that on the right. Between them and his car was nothing but polluted-looking marshland. It wasn't likely that anyone would be coming up through there, unless Anthony had enlisted the aid of some Special Forces commandos. But, still, you never knew. When he was satisfied with his position, he put the car in Park but didn't turn off the ignition.

Now, three or four hundred yards in front of him, was Lincoln Financial Stadium, where the Eagles played. The other two structures, the First Union Spectrum and the Union Center, were no longer that easy to see. He was thinking of leaving the parking lot—driving one time around the big block to see if there was evidence of Anthony Bonica setting him up—when behind him Natalie said, "Is it all right if I get some air before they get here?"

Teddy thought about it and was about to say, Sure. Tell her she could sit up, they could chat about the what-ifs while they waited for Anthony Bonica and whoever he was bringing with him to show up. But before he could a black Caddy appeared near the main entrance, slowed, and then turned into the parking lot. It was three hundred yards away. But Teddy didn't have to wait for it to get closer to know that it was the vehicle he'd been waiting for.

He took off his sport coat and belt, grabbed the flower box Natalie had brought out of Palisades, ripped it open and tied his belt around the thick end of what was inside. Then he slung the belt over his shoulder, pulled his jacket back on and stepped out of the car, trying to get everything as comfortable as he could, so he wouldn't walk around as if he had something sticking him in the back.

LITTLE ANTHONY SAID, "Did you bring the fucking thing?"

The smirk on his face worried Teddy. Anthony should be nervous—at least a little—worrying that Teddy might not play this straight up. He should be wondering what was in Teddy's mind. But he didn't seem to be. Maybe the fact that Tommy Inzarella was on his right and Frankie Morelli was on his left made him feel more confident.

Teddy said, "I brought it. The question is, did you bring the money?"

Anthony said, "Tommy?" and Tommy Inzarella stepped back to the Caddy, grabbed a gym bag and walked back, leaving the back door of the car open. Tommy unzipped the bag far enough to reach in and pull out what looked to be a rubber-banded stack of hundred-dollar bills and then he rezipped the bag. Then he stood there, holding the bag calmly, waiting for whatever was going to happen next.

Teddy's Acura was sixty feet behind him. The Caddy was fifteen feet behind Anthony, and all four men were facing off in what Teddy was beginning to think of as no-man's-land. He was hoping that Natalie could hear what was happening but he wasn't sure because a breeze had kicked up, blowing from behind him, maybe taking the sounds of their voices away from her.

Frankie Morelli was checking his left side, as if he'd like to start moving in that direction soon but hadn't decided exactly when yet. He was wearing slacks and a sports shirt and jacket. But no tie. Teddy decided that if Frankie Morelli did take a step in that direction, or if Tommy Inzarella moved to his right, the two of them looking to circle around, Teddy was going to open his coat, show them what was inside and tell them to freeze right where they were.

Anthony was talking, getting a little mad because he had to repeat himself until Teddy came back from his thoughts to listen. "So which is it, asshole? You say you brought your end, but I don't see it anywhere."

Teddy made a production out of bringing the mini-cassette recorder out of his jacket pocket. He held it up in the air so that all three men could see it.

Anthony said, "Fuck you. A thing like that. *Fuck* you. Scarlotti took his clothes off. You think we wouldn't've seen that. You scamming fucking prick."

Teddy saw the opening right there. How he was going to make it work. He looked at the arrogant confidence on Anthony's face and said into the relative quiet—timing it, "Yeah. You saw him naked? His clothes were what,

piled on the floor?"—seeing that Anthony was paying closer attention—
"Scarlotti's standing bare-ass. I imagine, what, you all went through the
charade, had Izzy search all of you. Well, I guess Izzy's slipping. Because
while you were looking at Dominic's butt, ask yourself this, did anybody—
Izzy, you, even Tommy—any of you bother to check what was in his *clothes*?
Did you happen to do that?" A big guess here but one that looked like it was
paying off because it wiped the smile off of Anthony's face.

Tommy said, "Shit." Disgusted.

Anthony looked at Tommy like somehow it was his fault.

"Look at it." Teddy held the cassette player up. "It's what, half the size of
a pack of smokes? You want me to tell you where it was? It was sewn into his
pants. You don't believe me? I'll walk away with it. But if you want it, then
quit fucking around and let me have the money."

Tommy took a step toward Teddy, but Anthony grabbed his arm. He
looked at Teddy and said to Tommy, "Fuck this guy. I want to know what I'm
dealing with."

Teddy said, "I'm outta here in five seconds. Four, three, two—"

"Yeah? You think so? You think you can just show up here, leave when
you want?" Little Anthony nodded his head in the direction of the Caddy and
Frankie Morelli walked back to the still-open rear door.

Anthony said to Teddy, "You want to pull tough-guy bullshit with me?"
jerking a thumb back at the Caddy. "How 'bout this, you motherfucker. How
'bout we ask *him* what's what?"

Teddy watched it as if he'd watch TV. Confused because what he was seeing couldn't be taking place. Like he was there but he wasn't. Thinking, shit,
no, because he was a dead man, and his brother, Davey-Boy, getting out of
the back of Anthony's Caddy like he owned the thing and saying, Hey, to
Frankie Morelli like they were gonna be best men at each other's wedding,
was a dead man too.

Davey walked right over to Anthony and Tommy, still grinning, punched
Anthony lightly on the arm and then looked over at Teddy. He said, "Sur-

prise, surprise, huh?" Still clueless about what a monumental fuckup he had just committed.

Anthony clapped his hands together—enjoying himself immensely. "The whole family's here. I think I'm gonna fucking cry."

Teddy locked his gaze on Davey and concentrated on keeping his voice even. "Davey?" He had to say it again because Davey was still too busy enjoying the idea of hanging with Anthony Bonica. Teddy said, louder, "Davey."

"Yeah?"

"Listen to me. What I'm going to do"—looking up at Anthony to make sure Bonica knew he was really talking to *him*—"I'm going to just give this thing to Mr. Bonica. Just *give* it to him. Meanwhile, I want you to walk over here." Teddy now looked at Tommy Inzarella, held up the mini-cassette and said, "Really, Tommy, talk to your boss. I'm gonna put this thing down on the ground. I don't have any copies, nothing like that—so there's no sense in anyone taking this matter any further." Still looking at Tommy, he said, "You get to keep your gym bag too. I hope we're clear on that matter."

Davey said, "Teddy, what are you doing?"

"Just come on over here, Davey." Teddy was wondering what Natalie was doing. He hoped she was paying attention, because if this got hairy in the next few seconds he was going to wave his hand in the air like a terrorist trying to stop an airplane from landing at Philly International.

Davey was shaking his head, grinning, turning to Anthony and saying, "Can you believe him? He doesn't get it." Still thinking that they were playing by the Geneva Convention.

Davey turned to Teddy and said, "Anthony here"—turning to smile at Anthony once again, for Christ's sake—"told me what the problem was."

Teddy wanted to get Davey away from the car so he could signal Natalie, never mind waiting around for things to get hairy—they were already there. He said, "Did he?" motioning Davey over, fighting to keep his voice even. "Come on over here, Davey—really—and tell me exactly how he put it."

Davey said, "It's simple. A misunderstanding." He started to take a step toward Teddy to explain, but Anthony put a hand on his elbow and held him in place.

Davey shrugged. "Anthony told me, when we buried the body, there was something he needed back from it." Davey shrugged again. "I told him you'd bring it."

Teddy said, "Anthony, why don't you let go of my brother? Let him come on over here and explain things? I'm having trouble hearing him."

"You can hear him fine, you prick."

And then, suddenly, there was Davey, slipping out of Anthony's grasp. Acting like some kind of marriage counselor. "Hey, c'mon, you guys. Anthony"— turning to look at Bonica—"I told you he'd come. He picked it up and here he is. I don't see a problem." He turned back to Teddy. "I knew you would remember, me picking it up when we were lifting Dominic over the fence."

Teddy didn't want to confuse anything by hurting Davey's feelings. But he had to do it. He said, "Davey, shut the fuck up," thinking over the night they had buried Dominic by the railroad tracks in his head. Davey had picked something up? What? What was there to pick up and what was Davey babbling about now? He didn't remember Davey picking up anything. Hell, all he remembered was the sound of Dominic's body hitting the ground when they tossed him over the wall.

It was turning Teddy's insides to mush, the idea that he didn't have a clue what Davey was talking about but knowing that the more his brother talked the less likely they were to get out of this.

Davey said, "Hey, Anthony's going to give us our own book." He grinned. "Didn't I tell you? Huh?"

Teddy said, carefully, "Yeah, Davey, you told me."

"Un-huh. Get this, he's already got a place picked out. We're talking—am I right, Anthony—serious money."

Teddy said, "Oh shit, Davey." He was thinking of all the should'ves. He should've put Davey on a plane himself, should've walked him to the gate— maybe held that Beretta against his head to make sure he boarded the goddamn jet. Because he should've known Davey would think about going to Miami and decide not to. He should've known that Davey would be taken in by whatever Anthony Bonica promised him.

Jesus Christ, another one—all these years—he should've just been nicer to Davey. Should *not* have given him whatever shit he had during their lives, yelling at him for trying to steal a Porsche when all he was doing was trying to impress his older brother and would never be bright enough to realize it was a stupid thing to do.

Davey was talking fast, not paying attention to anything but the speed and sound of his own voice. "All we have to do—and I told Anthony you would agree—we pick up that thing I grabbed. From Dominic." He pointed at Teddy. "Actually, you have to pick it up because Anthony here wants me to stay by his side, figure how we're gonna turn that bookmaking around so we can make some nice money for a change. I told Anthony I had some ideas, starting with the deadbeats." Davey grinned proudly but then frowned. "But hey, if you already went and got it"—he shrugged—"fuck, we're halfway there." He was nodding now. "I shoulda known you'd figure out where it was. From when we were kids. Where we used to hide—"

Davey stopped in midsentence because he got his first good look at the mini-cassette recorder that Teddy had in his hands. He cocked his head. "Teddy? What the *fuck* is that?!"

Teddy took two quick steps toward Anthony and spoke to both him and Tommy Inzarella. "Listen to me. I'm serious. I got the message. Absolutely. I'm fucking around with the wrong people and shame on me for doing it. I understand now. Definitely." He held the tape player up so that it was even with his shoulder. "This? It's fake. Davey's right. I was scamming you. It was a big—no, no, *huge*—mistake. But it was one I made myself. Just me. Davey didn't have anything to do with it. Okay? What I'm gonna do now, though, I'm gonna go get the real thing, I know just what Davey's talking about. I remember now, him taking it off of Dominic when we were—were burying him." There was nothing in Anthony's face to even indicate that he was listening. But Teddy, desperate, kept going, "Anthony, what I'm going to do, you give me two hours, I'm gonna bring it to you this afternoon. No later than that. The whole thing. I swear to fucking God." He looked Anthony squarely in the eyes. "You got a grudge against me, that's one thing. I'm gonna bring you the real tape, or whatever it is that Davey palmed from Dominic before I put him underground. You decide you don't want me to walk away from that, I'm a headache and you've finally had enough of me? Okay." He pointed at Davey. "But, I swear to Christ, Anthony—please—Davey doesn't know what he's doing. He doesn't have a *clue*. You *gotta* know that. Let him be."

"But he knows where the real one is." Anthony was now grinning. "I saw it in your eyes. You didn't know until he just said it. But you sure as shit know it now."

"Christ, Anthony, it's not code. It's just Davey telling me where it is. A stupid thing from when we were kids growing up in the neighborhood, what, three doors down from you? A thing when we wanted to hide shit from the old man, my mother—you remember her from Chicki Dimaro's place. Pot, anything like that. We shared a hiding place. Davey still has one, I guess, so now I'll go get whatever's there. And I'll go get it. I swear to fucking God. You can come with me. Or Tommy can if you want. Just let Davey go. This is between you and me. Davey never did a fucking thing to you."

Anthony smiled. "No, the retard never did anything."

From behind them, Davey said, "Hey, nobody calls me a retard."

Teddy said, "Davey, seriously, this isn't your fault. But for now if Anthony says you're something, that's what you are." Looking at Anthony, willing him to think a certain way. A way he almost never thought.

Anthony said, "Davey?"

"Yeah?" Christ, Teddy could still hear it, the excitement in his brother's voice.

Anthony said, "Davey, this place, when you were kids," pointing at Teddy, "he gonna know where it's at?"

Davey said, enthusiastically, "Sure."

Anthony pushed Davey away from him and told Teddy, chuckling, "Then," the chuckle turning into a full laugh now, "the fuck do I need him for?"

And in the nanosecond that followed, Teddy told himself he should have seen it coming. Anthony turning to nod at Frankie Morelli, grinning sideways at Teddy, who was still fifteen feet away, way too far to do anything to stop it.

He watched Frankie Morelli reach inside his jacket and come up with a pistol that had a silencer on it. Without thinking Teddy slipped the mini-cassette into the outside pocket of his jacket. Then he reached inside the jacket, to where Natalie's sawed-off shotgun hung from his right shoulder with his belt looped around the stock. He screamed at Davey to run even as he was struggling to get the shotgun out from the folds of his jacket, thinking, why the fuck had he bothered to hide the thing?

He heard a flat crack and one of the windows in the Caddy disintegrated. Anthony, Tommy and Frankie Morelli froze for a second, trying to figure this new development out. A second later another window in the Caddy disappeared but Teddy didn't hear the shot because Anthony screamed, "You set me up. You *fuck*." Like he was some kind of innocent bystander, moving to the cover of the other side of the Caddy even as Teddy had worked the shotgun out, pumping it and looking up to see that Davey still didn't know what the fuck was happening. He had an expression on his face like Teddy was some kind of madman.

Davey opened his mouth like he was about to say something but all Teddy did was shout, *"Down!"* at the top of his lungs and swing the shotgun toward Frankie Morelli. Anthony and Tommy were moving quickly toward the Cadillac.

There was a popping sound, right in front of Teddy. The pistol in Frankie Morelli's hand jerked upward and Davey's head exploded, his left eye leaped out of his skull like it had a mind of its own. Davey jumped and then plopped down onto the ground like a headless mannequin. Teddy pulled the trigger, felt the shotgun kick more then he expected, saw Frankie Morelli do an airborne dance of his own, and watched him land like a rag doll so that his feet were almost touching Davey's.

Something whizzed by Teddy's head, a fast-flying hornet, and Tommy Inzarella clutched his sleeve but seemed unhurt. Tommy grabbed Anthony and hustled him to the car while Teddy stared at his brother's body. Davey was supposed to be in Miami. He was supposed to be fucking Cuban girls, for Christ's sake. Visiting senile people.

What the fuck had happened?

He could hear a loud, steady wailing noise and at first he thought it was the police. He didn't give a damn. He just stood where he was while Anthony's Caddy screeched away and the wailing noise got closer. Any minute a cop was going to jump out of a patrol car and slam him up against the fender.

Instead Natalie appeared seemingly out of nowhere. He had forgotten all about her but now she screeched up in the Acura, got out, looked at Davey and said, "Fuck," and then she was pulling at Teddy's arm. Walking him backward and around to the passenger side of the car, saying, "I know. I know. He's dead. I'm sorry. But we have to get out of here. We *have* to." She kept it up the whole time, talking him into sitting down in the passenger seat of the Acura, fastening his seat belt for him, running around to hop in the driver's seat and then gunning the thing out of there. Leaving a god-awful fuckup behind them.

It was all he heard, her saying, "I know, I know." Over and over again as he turned to watch Davey-Boy's lifeless body get smaller and smaller in the middle of the parking lot.

12

THEY SPENT THE NIGHT in Natalie's bed. Natalie knew that there could be all kinds of repercussions. Anthony Bonica could be headed over to Teddy's apartment right now—the main reason she had insisted they come here—looking to force the issue with Teddy. Get the tape and then kill him. Also, as soon as the cops put a name to Davey, which might or might not take awhile—she had seen what little was left of his face—they would want to talk to Teddy. She was thinking furiously, first thing tomorrow, when he could talk, they'd have to discuss going over to his apartment—Davey's too—and removing anything that could trace Davey's murder back to them. But she didn't mention any of that to Teddy because he was in no shape to deal with it. Instead she held him close and stroked his stomach, his arms and his face, but didn't do anything else except lean up occasionally and kiss his cheek. At one point she got him to agree to her taking his temperature; he was sweating through the sheets. But it came out at ninety-eight point six and both of them realized that his state had nothing to with maybe catching a quick fever. It wasn't something antibiotics were going to do any good against.

Occasionally he would groan, but otherwise he remained silent. Sometimes she could feel all his muscles tense up at once, feel a hardness to his body, solid with rage, that she had underestimated. She had lost her mother ten years before and knew what grief was all about. But she also knew that she couldn't possibly understand what Teddy was going through. Couldn't visualize what it was like to see your own brother gunned down before your eyes, even though she had seen the whole incident from beginning to end.

But your *brother*?

No.

She remembered back to when she had waited on their table at Palisades, before Teddy had told her he knew who she really was. She'd been rude to Davey-Boy because she thought he had been just like all the other creeps who gave her a hard time. In a way he had been, but maybe that wasn't something he could help. Lord knew, Teddy wasn't like that. She thought about genetics. It was hard to figure out sometimes. What was passed down and what was learned. Teddy had mentioned that his father had left when both he and Davey were young. Maybe Teddy had been old enough that it didn't affect him as badly as it had Davey. Because, from the few sentences Teddy had managed to say since the murder, and from what she had seen of Davey-Boy's actions, she realized that he wasn't a creep. He was just a simple-minded soul who wanted to be a tough guy. A guy like his own brother. Except he wasn't, and his efforts had gotten him killed.

Around dawn, with the first pink rays of the sun filtering into her apartment window, she felt Teddy slip into sleep. She kept her arms around him and held him close. Letting him sleep and wishing she could do more.

When he finally woke up, she had already been awake for about an hour and a half. She showered, dried her hair and puttered around quietly so she wouldn't wake him. She peeked in twice, seeing his hair mashed against the pillow, the way he was breathing gently, no concerns because he was asleep and wasn't dreaming—right now at least—about what had happened the day before. When she heard noises finally, him beginning to wake up, she knocked softly and entered, carrying a cup of coffee and a glass of orange juice to the bed. She sat quietly on the edge while he drank them and then, finally, asked, "How are you feeling? Are you all right?"

He said, "No," and she nodded. He stared at her and she moved closer. Let him put the coffee cup and the glass of orange juice on the floor and then, suddenly, he was all over her. Using her body as some kind of therapy. Becoming an animal, lifting her completely off the bed, a wild expression in his eyes and then crashing down on top of her. She wasn't sure what was in his mind while he was doing it, knew that it wasn't something that had anything to do with her being satisfied, but also realized—she was almost crying now—that it was the best, the only thing, right now, that she could do for him. Feeling him rage against her—inside of her—she realized that it had been a long time, maybe never before, that she had felt even remotely protective of a man.

A minute later, as they were lying next to each other, trying to catch their breath, she asked him again . . . gently, "Are you any better, now?"

He turned to look past her. Some of the haunted expression was gone. He said, "No," staring off into space as if he were thinking hard, lost somewhere between the ugly stadiums surrounding them and memories of growing up with his brother. Then he said, sounding like he believed it, "But I'm going to be. " He leaned over and kissed her.

A minute later he was asleep again.

WHEN GEORGE ABBOT HEARD of the mob murder in the parking lot at Veterans Stadium the previous day, he didn't go out to the crime scene. Instead he dialed Philadelphia police detective John Drummond, who worked Major Crimes out of Thirty-ninth Street and Lancaster Avenue. Drummond had worked Organized Crime for six years out of the Frankford Arsenal, Building 110, third floor, over on Tacony Street before transferring over to Major Crimes. Abbot had worked with him previously on mob cases and, a month after his transfer, Drummond had told Abbot that he couldn't tell the difference between working the mob or working Major Crimes. He said, "Either way, people carve each other up all over this fucking city."

Drummond viewed life the same way that Abbot did. They agreed that most of it was crap, but they did enjoy a few things in common. Over the years they had slipped each other little bits of information so that they wouldn't have to deal with the bureaucratic bullshit that went hand in hand every time two different law-enforcement agencies tried to work together. When Abbot was in town, he and Drummond went out to a few clubs, had more than a few drinks and occasionally got laid.

Drummond told Abbot that, yes, he'd heard of the murders but no one was quite sure what had happened or what to make of it. "From what I understand, the one mope that got dead, Frankie Morelli? *He's* one of Anthony Bonica's crew."

"What about the other guy?"

Drummond laughed over the phone. "We got a make on him, too. At least according to his driver's license—because, to tell you the truth, there wasn't much left of his head. But that's where the problem is."

"Why's that?"

"Because it doesn't make any fucking sense. We have a name, David C. Clyde. If he's the David C. Clyde who showed up on the computer when we ran a check, then he's a petty crook. A candy thief compared to Bonica. Guy buys pills over the Internet and sells them to suburban teenagers, he has one auto theft and a bullshit B-and-E a while back—he broke into an abandoned warehouse, God only knows what he was hoping to find—that was dropped because no one had the energy to prosecute. Some judge gave him probation and probably couldn't have come up with his name two minutes after. This guy is a fucking sparrow compared to anyone in Bonica's crew. He's got a brother who's got a slightly heavier rep than him. But, otherwise, no way."

Abbot said, "So what *was* he doing there?"

"What do you think everybody over here is asking themselves? Whatever he did to Bonica there's no way they're gonna take him out to the stadium complex and blow his head off. Lose Frankie Morelli in the process? No fucking way."

"What about this brother you mentioned?"

"Officially?"

"You can start with that."

"He's a stockbroker. Has an office in Bala Cynwyd. But off the record, I know a guy over in Auto Theft, Henry Simpson. You know him?"

"I think I've heard you mention him before."

"Yeah, well, Simpson's a good cop. He told me, this Teddy Clyde? He's been stealing cars for a living since he was fifteen. He's turned into a high-class auto thief. You want a Ferrari, a nice Jag, you reach out to Teddy Clyde. But there's still no connection to the murder at the Vet."

Abbot told Drummond they had to get drunk together soon and then hung up the phone. He sat deep in thought for a few minutes and then dialed the number of a guy he knew who worked out of the Department of Motor Vehicles in Harrisburg and said, "Hey, I got a plate number for you."

He was getting it straight in his head, the Acura he'd seen Izzy Feldman following yesterday, before Izzy had blown Abbot's and James Lacombe's cover by stopping in the middle of the street to say hi. Getting a feeling in his gut that had nothing to do with straight facts.

His contact at the DMV was asking him would it be okay if he got back to him tomorrow because he was busy as hell, bringing Abbot back to the here and now. Abbot told him, "Hey, you busy? Is that what you're saying? Well, fuck whether you're busy or not. It's not okay. I want a plate run. W/R1351H. And if I don't have the owner's name in five minutes, I'm gonna put a call into your supervisor, tell him how *busy* you've been selling me all this information over the years. See if we can't get you an unemployment check. You understand what I'm saying?"

Two and a half minutes later Abbot had the information he wanted. Teddy Clyde. The only living relative of a guy who just got killed at the same time that one of Anthony Bonica's crew members did.

Abbot thought it was worth introducing himself to this Teddy Clyde. Pay his respects for Mr. Clyde's recent loss.

Maybe have a chat while they were at it.

IZZY PUT ON a clean turtleneck and a jacket over it and then he walked downstairs to the first floor. Saul was on the couch in his study watching CNN's Business Report. Izzy knew Saul was aware that he was there, but he sat quietly and carefully on an antique chair until CNN went to commercial.

Saul muted the TV. "So?"

"It was about what you'd expect. Mr. Bonica, he couldn't even wait a day or two to find out if there is a reasonable way to settle this matter. Even when there's a feasible option already in place. No, he's got to grab Teddy Clyde's brother, hold him hostage—I'm not aware of all the details—and then kill him. And from what I understand, Mr. Bonica lost one of his own men in the process. One Frank Morelli. I assume that was Mr. Clyde's doing, which I can't blame him for. So now we have a negative/negative situation. Everybody comes out on the downside."

"Anthony Bonica had to go ahead and complicate things."

Izzy nodded. "It's what he does. He throws these fits. Temper tantrums. The first time you see one it's a novelty—why is he so emotional about things? But after that you get a sense that Mr. Bonica can't control it. It's what appears to drive him. Rage. Even what we're dealing with. Yes, it could be a problem if the wrong person got their hands on the feds' recording of what happened to Mr. Scarlotti. By the way, I did a little checking. Seems a U.S. attorney by the name of Donald Shaffer was behind that end of the affair. But as I say, it, the recording, shouldn't be that big of a problem. Certainly not something to get as—as excited as Mr. Bonica got. After all, it's why we made one ourselves. But why not try, at least initially, to handle the matter discreetly?"

"It sounds like Anthony Bonica can't handle anything discreetly."

"I agree with you. But it's not going to be a problem. Our own affairs are in order. Captain Khalid called earlier to tell me the crates of trans-formers"—Izzy smiled—"the Strella missiles—have arrived and are being loaded onboard ship. That means we've speeded up the whole process by what looks to be at least forty-eight hours."

"Good, good. It'll be nice to have that all taken care of." Saul said, "And you think this Mr. Clyde—what'd you say his first name was?"

"Teddy."

"Right. Teddy. You say he's a car thief?"

"He steals high-end—expensive automobiles. Porsches, Mercedeses, cars of that nature. Apparently, if you're as good as he is, there can be some substantial money in it."

Saul said, "I see. And you think *he* was the one who took Anthony's man out? This Frank Morelli? I mean, there's no conceivable way it could be tied to the shipment, is there?"

"No. Teddy Clyde had to be the one. It's a low-level affair. I've asked around and his brother—Mr. Clyde's that is—was a guy named David. Everyone seems to refer to him as 'Davey-Boy.' Word is he's not at all the kind of person to get the better of someone like Frank Morelli, no matter what the circumstances were. I think what happened is that Teddy Clyde met with Anthony, perhaps trying to complete the, ah, transaction without involving us. Things went sour. Maybe his brother was there to back him up. I don't know. Either way, Teddy's brother is dead and Teddy—well, he's got to be upset."

"And Teddy Clyde, you think he is capable of something like that?"

"I think, having now met Mr. Clyde, and having heard about him off and on over the past several years, that yes, he would be capable of it. It's not the kind of thing he would *want* to do, in my opinion. But hypothetically? Pushed far enough?" Izzy touched his throat. "Mr. Rubin, Teddy Clyde comes across as mild-mannered. And I think, under normal circumstances, he is. But I told you what he did to me with that golf club. Could I have saved myself if he really wanted to hurt me? I think so, but he could have hurt me a lot more than he did. He chose not to. *That's* the difference between Mr. Clyde and Mr. Bonica."

Saul took a moment to think. "I believe you're right. If you think it through, Mr. Clyde's an automobile thief. Why is it that all of a sudden he's killing people? You're right, it is because he got pushed too far."

"Well, I don't believe he went out to the stadium with it in his mind. He doesn't appear to be that type. I'm sure he wanted to protect himself. I believe he went there to sell Anthony Bonica that recording we're all concerned about. And things went completely haywire."

Saul Rubin stood up and went to the window and opened the drapes. Izzy put a hand on his shoulder and guided him away from the window, pulling the drapes shut quickly.

"Mr. Rubin, seriously, listen to me. Please. How many times have I told you—when you're on the first floor—you don't go near any windows. Can you bear that in mind please?"

Saul smiled. "I'll try to, Izzy. Really."

"Thank you."

Saul sank back down on the couch and Izzy waited while he appeared to run the whole scenario over in is head. Finally Saul said, "What worries me is that this Teddy Clyde, if what you say is true, he saw his own brother shot to death, he's got to be sore. Grief-stricken. I feel badly for him, but at the same time I don't want him to get it in his head that *we* are the people he should be looking to for revenge.

"I was thinking the same thing myself, Mr. Rubin. Running the possibilities over in my mind as to how we can communicate to Mr. Clyde that we're—we are appalled—at what happened. And more important, we are still very interested in getting whatever type of device Mr. Scarlotti had on him when he died. At the very least, find out—truly—what potential threat it poses."

Saul smiled thinly. "Well, there's one thing we could do, Itzhak."

"What's that, Mr. Rubin?"

"Well, Itzhak, we can always invite him over. Offer him our condolences, and then see what he has to say for himself."

———

TEDDY HAD HEADED BACK to his own apartment after leaving Natalie's and spent ten minutes driving around the block, looking for anyone or any vehicle that looked out of place. He had some things he wanted to accomplish, but he was damned if he was going to rush anything and run the risk that Anthony might've staked out the place.

Sure enough, Nicky Migliaro was standing outside the subway entrance a half block down the street. He had a newspaper in his hands, held open in front of him so he could act as if he was reading it, but keep an eye on Teddy's apartment at the same time.

Teddy drove past Nicky while looking out the window in the opposite direction and then pulled his Acura over to the curb another half block down. He dialed nine-one-one, described Nicky and told the dispatcher there was a rape in progress right where Nicky was standing. Teddy had to wait a full five minutes—a real rapist would've been long gone—but then he got the satisfaction of seeing two squad cars, followed closely by a third, screech to a halt in front of a startled Nicky. Nicky must've been sore as hell, used to cops recognizing him and giving him a free ride because he ended up yelling at the cops and then—from where Teddy sat at least—he seemed to take a swing at one of them. After that it was over in seconds. The cops wrestled Nicky to the ground, cuffed him, threw him into the back of a squad car and had him out of there in a matter of moments.

He spent an hour in his apartment looking for a key that Davey had given him a couple of years back when he had a cat and wanted Teddy to take care of it while Davey went on one of those Club Med cruises, where everyone but Davey got laid. The cat didn't like Davey or anyone else, was white, with black splotches on it, never purred and had run and hidden every time Teddy went over to feed it. Davey hadn't housebroken the thing, hell, he was barely housebroken himself, and, even Davey, slob that he was, booted the thing out when it pissed on Davey's ankle the day after he got back from the cruise.

Later, telling Teddy about it, he had said, "You know, the whole cruise? That cat was as close to seeing pussy as I got."

There was a spiderweb of yellow police crime-scene tape stapled to the front door of Davey's apartment, which told Teddy that the cops had already identified his brother and come here to see if there was anything to indicate why Davey might have been involved with—let alone killed by—a made-member of Anthony Bonica's crew.

He pulled Davey's Beretta out from the back of his waistband, stepped through the yellow police tape and entered his little brother's apartment. If anyone else was in there, Teddy planned to ask him if he was a cop. If he was, Teddy would put the gun away, maybe run like hell, maybe not. If he wasn't a cop, Teddy planned on shooting him.

But the place was empty.

He walked in, stepping over a colossal mess that was due partly to his brother's housecleaning and—Teddy could tell this because of the way the drawers in a bureau were pulled out and dumped—partly to the fact that the police or somebody had searched the place. In the middle of the living room he realized he was breathing as if he had just run a race and that his hands were shaking. Maybe from the tension of watching out for Anthony or maybe from the idea of being in his dead brother's apartment. Probably a little of both.

He made his way to the couch and sat down.

13

ALMOST IMMEDIATELY Teddy was overcome by memories. Davey crying—while Teddy absolutely *refused* to—the night their father said good-bye to them that last time, sneaking out the front door with a woman named Wanda who had trouble with her high heels on the outside stairs and was mad as hell because their father was telling her to hurry it up, for God's sake, let's get out of here before the bitch gets home. The woman had had some kind of terrible perfume on—way too much of it—that, at the time, had reminded Teddy of bug spray.

He could remember, Davey, blood dripping from his nose, coming home from the playground without his new Christmas basketball, crying again. Teddy had trudged down to the playground. Gotten there ten minutes later only to see a bigger kid playing with Davey's brand-new Spalding, grinning at Teddy until Teddy knocked him flat on his ass, took the ball and asked any of the half dozen bystanders whether they wanted to take a stab at it. No one had volunteered.

A lot of memories. A lot of things you took for granted.

He could see it as if it were being played out in front of his face right now; Davey, with a brand-new toy pistol, pointing it at Teddy and going Bang, Bang, Bang, until Teddy got tired of it and told Davey why didn't he go shoot

                                                                          ᴢ that
                                                                    . him that
                                                               ᴀtlantic City.
                                                          ᴢ comped casino
                                                     ᴡrge." He had said,
                                                 ᴀ motherfucking dollar
                                             ᴀt money in his hands.
                                        ening—Davey had stopped by
                                     ᴀace, telling Teddy, "Man, those
                                 ᴏw that? Let you win a little money
bu.   ᴀn honest guy, trying to make an honest
buck. bᵥ   ᴛake it all back. Steal it out of my pockets
when I won ıᵥ

    Teddy had looᵥ   ᴀvey and said, "It didn't occur to you, you had the
twelve grand in you poᴄket, and it didn't occur to you to quit? Or wait, maybe
I'm missing something. You're about to tell me the part where the pit boss
held a gun to your head, made you keep gambling."

    Davey had looked at Teddy like he had sawdust in his head and said,
indignant, "Whatta you talking about? Jesus Christ, Teddy, I was on a fucking winning streak." In the same sentence asking Teddy could he have five
hundred bucks because he'd borrowed his original stake from Louie DiCaro
and he didn't want to go have to tell Louie—who was waiting the very next day
for his big payment—what had happened. Davey said, "Hey, talk about
people with bad tempers, you wanna know what Louie should do? He should
get a scrip for fucking Prozac is what he should do. Put himself in a better
mood so that maybe he can understand how it is. You play the casinos,
they're gonna rob you."

    Teddy had given him the five hundred bucks to keep Louie DiCaro happy
plus three hundred to get him back on his feet. But he didn't waste his time
telling Davey to stay away from the casinos because it was like handing an
alcoholic a bottle of booze and telling him to sip it slowly.

He realized that he'd been sitting on Davey's couch for a long time, not moving, still stupidly holding the Beretta in his hands. He stood up, put the pistol behind his back again, and made his way into Davey's bedroom. He had the idea that he wasn't going to have to look very hard if what Davey had said the day before was true.

Jesus, here it came again, the image of Davey, standing in the middle of a gun battle that was about to happen, not having a clue what was about to go down, telling Teddy, smiling, to remember back to when they were kids. Not even *suspecting* that by passing that information along he was a dead man. Expendable. A simple and direct opportunity for Anthony Bonica to begin to pay Teddy back for a fistfight, a fucked-up eye that Anthony either should've gotten fixed or should've forgotten about a long time ago.

He found Davey's hiding place in one minute. The floorboards of the bedroom closet had been sawed, pulled up, fastened together and then put back to form a trapdoor, the edges sanded carefully and restained so that if you weren't looking for it you wouldn't find it. There was an unobtrusive hook to pull the whole thing out. Teddy thought, Christ, Davey had been right, it was *exactly* what they had done when they were, what, ten and twelve years old? His little brother, an adult but with parts of him still going through puberty, stuck in a time when he and Teddy used to hide a little dope, a couple of cheap commando knives and some *Hustler* magazines, some *Penthouses*, from their mom so she wouldn't throw them out—and from their dad, while he was still around, so he wouldn't *steal* the fucking things.

There was a shoe box in the tiny cubbyhole below the trapdoor. Payless Shoes. Teddy lifted it out and then took the lid off. The derringer that Davey had shown him when Teddy had borrowed the Beretta was inside it. To Teddy it still looked like a toy. But then he cracked the thing open where the barrel met the grip and saw, not only that it was loaded, but that the two bullets that sat one over another inside the twin barrels were bigger than the bullets in the Beretta Davey had lent him. He didn't know what else to do, so he slid the thing into his jacket pocket and started to rummage through the box again.

There was a smudged, business-sized, white envelope inside the shoe box. Inside it were a half dozen Polaroids taken someplace where the light was terrible and the flash hadn't worked very well. It sure as hell wasn't Palisades because the place was a dump. Davey was sitting in a chair, grinning, while junkie whores in G-strings, or nothing at all, took turns lap-dancing on him. By the second picture, Davey's eyes were squinted shut, and he looked on the verge of an orgasm.

There was box of condoms, Ultra Thins, eleven left out of a pack of a dozen. Teddy hoped Davey had gotten a chance to use that twelfth one at least. Maybe it had come in handy when Davey had gone wherever it was he ended up instead of going to Miami like he had promised Teddy.

There were also two joints and a little Baggie of pot in the shoe box. And eight pill bottles. Teddy held them up one by one and read the labels. Painkillers. Most of them empty.

The only other things in the shoe box were a loaded, spare clip for the Beretta and a fancy gold cigarette case. No tape recorder. No tape. It figured. Teddy put the clip in the same pocket he had the derringer in and then looked at the cigarette case. Jesus. What was this, the Roaring Twenties? Teddy could picture Davey, say, at a singles bar, flashing the case around, not even realizing that most people didn't smoke.

Teddy walked over to the bed a moment later, still holding the gold cigarette case, trying to get his thoughts together because now his options were severely limited. He could walk into Palisades and hand Anthony the box of condoms. He could give Anthony Davey's girlie pictures. Or he could waltz in without a word and start blasting away with the Beretta that Davey had given him and Natalie's dad's shotgun, now underneath the front seat of his Acura. Or he could flee. Wait a month or two, send Natalie a postcard from some beach down south and see if he could convince her to join him. But before he chose any of those options, he had to make sure Natalie knew what was going on. Make sure she was all right even if it meant getting her out of town, too or—shit—going to the cops with what he knew. Explain the whole thing to them and hope he didn't get some hard-on of a prosecutor who would settle for just putting Teddy behind bars. Natalie could back him up, but then he'd drag her name through the courts.

Teddy hadn't smoked for years, but he didn't see much point in worrying about cancer right now—in all likelihood it took more time to develop than he probably had. He opened the gold cigarette case, took out a cigarette and was in the process of putting it between his lips when he realized he didn't have a match. Goddamn but it had been one of those days.

He found a little plastic lighter in the second drawer down from the top in a bureau where Davey kept the few actual clean clothes he had. The clothes were all wrinkled, stuffed in there like Davey didn't give a shit what they looked like when they came out, but at least they smelled okay.

The lighter was red, a plastic Zippo jammed into the corner of the bureau drawer and as Teddy reached for it, his other hand knocked into the far side of the bureau and he dropped the cigarette case.

A voice said, "Enough is enough." And then there was a startling, metallic bang.

Teddy forgot all about the lighter because he was too busy reaching back toward the small of his back, bringing the Beretta out and whirling toward the door of the bedroom at the same time. Hearing the voice again, maybe a different one, right behind him—something wrong with it—but still, sounding mean and authoritative. Somebody talking loudly, but sounding far away, "Holy fuck, you didn't even want to talk to him first?"

The hell was it coming from?

Teddy took a step backward and had his finger whitening on the trigger before he realized there wasn't anybody in the doorway. But he was still hearing sounds. He whirled toward the bed. Jesus, nothing. Nothing anywhere in the apartment. But there were still noises coming from somewhere. The sound of something falling. Someone grunting.

Teddy stepped to the window and peeked out. Nothing. He stepped to the front door and listened hard, only to realize that the noises that he was hearing, as faint as they were, were definitely coming from Davey's bedroom.

There it was again, garbled enough so Teddy missed the first part of it, "About what—enough talking—both of us."

Teddy thought for a minute that he might have inadvertently turned the TV on. Maybe the remote was buried in Davey's sheets and Teddy had sat on it or something. But the TV screen was blank.

It was only when he relaxed, put the gun back inside his pants that he realized—Christ—the sound was coming from the cigarette case.

He squatted, picked up the case and fiddled with it for a while. Realized what it was. Realized *who* it was. And finally—Jesus fucking Christ—

Realized how the fucking thing worked.

TEDDY CAME OUT of Davey's apartment with a lot of bright ideas in his head but got a sinking feeling in his stomach because there was a plain-clothes cop leaning against the fender of his Acura. The guy looked like he'd been there for years. Eyes perpetually tired, a face that had been beaten on by the sun forever, wearing such a cheap suit that Teddy couldn't figure out if he dressed that way on purpose or if he simply didn't give a shit. There was something in his appearance that Teddy couldn't quite get a handle on. Either way, he certainly didn't look like anything except a cop.

It was too late to run. The cop had already seen him, so Teddy did the only thing he could think of—kept on walking toward his Acura as if he had never done a single thing wrong in his life.

When Teddy was ten feet away the cop said, "Hey"—jerking his thumb behind him at Teddy's car—"these things? Acuras? I heard they ride pretty nice. I bet they ride better than the piece of shit Ford I drive."

Teddy shrugged, very aware that the Beretta was digging into the skin of his back and the cigarette case/recorder of Dominic Scarlotti breathing his last was jammed into the inside pocket of his jacket. If the cop searched him maybe he could throw a cigarette into the air, pull the Beretta and shoot the smoke in half just the way they did in those old westerns. Tell the cop to get out of town by noon tomorrow. The other possibility was that the cop could throw *him* up against the wall. Slap some cuffs on him and Teddy would wind up down in the Tombs, the huge Philly holding jail, spend the first half hour trying to explain to a lot of muscular guys who wouldn't listen really well when he said, No, he didn't really want to be anyone's piece of ass so why didn't they go fight over somebody else.

Or else he could just wait on the whole thing, see how the cop decided to play it.

"They ride all right. This one's"—Teddy pointed—"got sixty-four thousand miles on it and I'm thinking it needs new tires. Maybe shocks all around."

The cop got up off the fender but moved so that he was between Teddy and the front door of the Acura. He looked up at the sun, seemed to check what the weather was even though it was obviously nice as hell out. The sun was directly over their heads, it was in the low seventies and there didn't seem to be a cloud in the sky.

The cop said, "I listened to the news this morning—the weather—those pricks, you know what they said? They said it was going to rain. Usually I would ignore them but today, no, I hadda listen to what they say." He held his hand out, disgusted. "I go into work today and I'm carrying an umbrella. You have any idea what kind of idiot I felt like?"

Teddy said, "You could tell yourself, better safe than sorry."

"Uh-huh. I could." The cop looked Teddy right in the face now, smiling a little. Teddy had figured out what it was about him that had bothered him before. It wasn't his clothing. Or lack of style. It was his general attitude. The fact that he truly seemed tired. Not sleepy. Just worn-out. Like he'd put in a fairly decent career at whatever he did—and Teddy was starting to smell federal here, not city cop—and now all he wanted to do, at the most, was talk about solving crimes, the weather or automobiles. It was okay with Teddy.

The guy even stuck out a hand. It took Teddy by surprise but he figured, the hell with it, why not, and shook his hand. Listened to him say, "George Abbot. Federal marshal. Don't worry about introducing yourself, I already know who you are."

"You do, huh?"

"Sure. Theodore Clyde. How's the stock market going? Should I be worrying about my portfolio?"

"I was just about to drive to my office. Find out. I can call you when I get there."

"Nah, really. I was kidding. What would an old fuck like me be doing playing the stock market? If I wanna gamble, I go down to Atlantic City. Maybe Vegas if I can cop a promotional flight, stay at one of the hotels for free or half price."

Teddy pulled his keys out of his pocket and jingled them loudly on the off chance Abbot would take the hint. "Well, good luck with it."

"Sure," Abbot said, but didn't make any kind of move to get far enough away from the car so that Teddy could climb in.

"There *was* one thing I wanted to ask, Teddy. You mind if I call you Teddy, or do you prefer Theodore?"

"Teddy's good."

Abbot pointed at the Acura again. "You say it needs tires. Maybe shocks? You have to know—*especially* you—you take it someplace, they're gonna mark you up. A dealership especially. Tell you your vehicle needs brake pads. New rotors. Maybe a tune-up. Transmission service. You thought you were bringing it in for an oil change; it ends up costing you two grand." Abbot laughed. "Some of these places'll sell you *three* wiper blades—one to put in the glove compartment as a spare. Believe me, I deal with crooks on a daily basis, but some of the shit I've had done to my own car legally? Well, I *wish* I could take the bastards to court."

Teddy said mildly, "I believe I'll be all right."

"Sure you will. After all, you have a background in—you know a fair bit about cars. They won't be able to pull any scams on you." Abbot stepped farther away from the Acura, looked hard at Teddy. "Except—and here's where, from your point of view, I mean, from what I know about you—why hassle with the possibility that they might scam you? Which is what brings me to my point. What I wanted to know. A man with your exper*tise*." Abbot took one more step closer. He was almost in Teddy's face and any other time Teddy might've objected. But right now he let Abbot get away with it. Watched as Abbot got a wide grin on his face and said, slowly, "Hey, Teddy—your Acura needs some work? I say, fuck it. Why don't you just go out and steal another one? You know what I'm saying?"

Teddy stared back at Abbot, admiring the lazy way he had come around to the subject. Tired or not, he was good at his job. "If I tell you I don't know what you're talking about, is it going to make any difference?"

"Not really." Abbot took a step sideways so that there was a clear path to Teddy's car. Teddy thought he was letting Teddy know he could leave if he wanted to. But Teddy didn't. The cop was interesting. Teddy might be wrong. But he thought Abbot wanted to say something specifically but was taking a hell of a long time getting around to it.

Finally Abbot cleared his throat. "Here's a question for you. If I told you that I knew your brother did, in fact, get himself killed yesterday by Anthony Bonica—would that make any difference to you?"

Teddy gritted his teeth but forced himself to look puzzled. "Now I *really* don't know what you're talking about, ah, George. See, last I heard—and bear in mind we don't, my brother and I, don't keep in touch as often as we should—last I heard my brother's in Miami. I got a postcard from him. I believe I threw it out but I can tell you what it said. He's got a Cuban girlfriend I believe, lives near the water. A houseboat or else a condo. I forget. Still, right on the water. I never met her, the Cuban woman, but I hear she's something else. My brother spends as much time as he can with her."

"Tan all over, huh? Those Cuban women, they're like some of the Puerto Ricans up here, some of them, you think they're white women who sat out in the sun all day long until they take their panties off. You realize it's natural and your eyes want to pop outta your head. I seen other woman try to do it. They step into those tanning booths in their birthday suits—they're willing to fry themselves like a good Carolina chicken—where I'm from, incidentally. Beaufort, South Carolina, home to good cooking and way too fucking many Marines. But nobody comes—I don't care *how* hard they try, and they do, believe me, they try their asses off if you'll excuse the pun. But *nobody* comes close to someone who's light brown all over to begin with."

"Like I said, I never met her, my brother's girlfriend."

"And your brother—I believe his name is David—you *sure* you didn't hear anything on the news about him?"

"I don't watch the news. Don't read the papers. But is there really something I *should* have heard? You say Davey got himself killed by Anthony Bonica yesterday. I think you're wrong. I think you have my brother—and me too, for that matter—confused with a couple of other guys happen to have the same last name. You ever look up 'Clyde' in the white pages? There're a lot of us."

"Yeah, I imagine so. But I also couldn't help but noticing. Most folks, I say the name 'Anthony Bonica' and they're walking around, asking me, Anthony who? You didn't do that. You notice that? I did."

Teddy made himself laugh. "Hey, we *were* having an intelligent conversation. I may say I don't watch TV, don't read the papers. But I grew up in South Philly. I know who Little Anthony Bonica is. Everybody around here does. I know who Dominic Scarlotti is too. Tommy Inzarella. I knew who Nicky Scarfo was. Shit, I hardly ever go up there, New York, but I knew who John Gotti is too." Teddy's laughter had died away, but he still had a smile on his face. But it was fake because all he really wanted was to get out of there. Get that cigarette case out of his jacket pocket before it ate a hole through to his skin. He said, "If you think it's a bad sign that I happen to know there's organized crime in Philly, maybe we should end this conversation now."

Abbot said, "No, you're right. That was stupid of me. I apologize. It was silly, me asking do you know who Anthony Bonica is? Of course you do. You're just like thousands of other people in the neighborhood. To you, he's a fact of life."

Teddy took his time. "Okay, look, you're telling me things—personal things concerning my brother. Do I believe you when you tell me my brother Davey got himself hurt—you said, killed—by Anthony Bonica? No, I don't. To be honest with you, I believe that my brother *has* broken a few laws in his life. If you won't tell anyone else I'll admit to you that he's guilty of smoking an occasional joint, maybe selling a Baggie or two of pretty bad pot. Hell, maybe he's even boosted a couple of car radios in his time. I've tried to talk him out of it. But him—Davey, I mean—him doing something that would even get the *attention* of a person like Anthony Bonica? You and I know that's an impossibility."

Abbot pulled a pack of cigarettes out of his pocket, lit one, and offered the pack to Teddy. Teddy said, "No thanks, I just quit." Abbot squinted past the smoke at Teddy. "I'm just making conversation. I think you *know* what happened to your brother. Maybe even why. But I don't believe now is the time to bust your balls over it. I'm only out here because of simple curiosity and because I have a partner and a boss I don't like. And right now, my partner's back at the office waiting to complain to my boss so that they can agree how much more they don't like me. Form a club maybe."

Teddy said, "People don't like you? Seems hard to figure."

"Yeah, I know. My partner is one thing. I tried talking to him about it, come up with a solution, but he told me to go fuck myself."

Teddy shook his head sympathetically. "Harsh words from a man supposed to be your partner. Back you up and all that."

"Don't I know it? I'm thinking of suggesting that we go to a therapist together. But that's only if he doesn't shoot me first. But what is worse is my boss. I gotta tell you, the asshole's less than half my age, thinks his dick is bigger than a fucking elephant's and I'm seriously thinking of throwing him off the roof one of these days."

Teddy laughed in spite of himself. "Your partner's going to shoot you and you want to *throw* your boss off the roof? And you call the people *I* know crooks?"

Abbot took a step closer to Teddy and lowered his voice. "Listen, we both know what we're doing. Chatting. Meeting each other. Maybe we can have a beer sometime. And—*maybe*—you *don't* know anything about Anthony Bonica. Beyond what any mope on the streets would know, I mean. But, I gotta tell you, I have serious doubts about that. I think you know why your brother was hit. And you got my sympathies cause I understand Anthony Bonica's a prick right up there with Nicky Scarfo." Abbot snapped his fingers suddenly. "Or wait, maybe you know a guy name of Itzhak Feldman?"

Teddy felt himself flinch at the mention of Izzy's name and knew that Abbot saw it because Abbot said, "Yeah, see, right there—I said, 'Itzhak Feldman'—I look at you, I believe I struck a nerve."

Abbot reached out, took Teddy's car keys out of his hands, opened the door and stood there like a valet parking attendant. "Listen, all this is— seriously—I stopped by to check you out. Now, if anyone asks, I can say I did it and not have to lie. I got eighteen more months and then I'm thinking of becoming a crook. Beat some of the assholes I worked with for so long at their own games. I think I could do it, too." He flashed a smile and continued to hold the door open for Teddy. "Hey, I'm kidding, although it would be interesting. But I'm *not* kidding about Anthony Bonica, and you don't have to even listen to me. But I feel like saying it because you didn't give me any shit while we were talking just now. I think you know about your brother and from what I understand, from what I know, I think it was a shame what happened to him. I hear he was a—a simple soul. Kinda guy didn't really mean anybody any harm."

Teddy climbed into the car, shut the door and rolled the window down because Abbot had leaned down and looked like he might have more to say. When the window was down, Abbot stuck his face close enough to Teddy's so that Teddy could smell stale smoke and whiskey masked only slightly by some cheap aftershave.

Abbot studied Teddy for a moment and then patted the top of the Acura twice loudly. "Listen to me. Forget I'm a cop for just an instant. I'm not my boss, some hard-on federal prosecutor. If you were Anthony Bonica—or if I even thought you were directly connected to him of your own volition—I'd be dragging you behind this building, beating the shit out of you on general principles, not because I gave a fuck about any kind of confession. But you? You seem to be minding your own business. So, here it comes, I feel like I have to say this. I were you, I'd stay the fuck away from both of them. Izzy Feldman *and* Anthony Bonica."

"Is that a warning?"

"Fuck no, it's advice." Abbot handed Teddy his keys back and stepped away from the door.

Teddy looked up at the sun just as Abbot had earlier. When he looked down, George was still staring at him. Teddy said, "I guess I'm supposed to thank you."

"No, you don't have to do that."

Teddy stuck the key in the ignition and started the Acura up, knowing George Abbot was watching his every move. He reached down, put the car in drive and then looked back up. Sure enough, Abbot's eyes were glued to his head.

Teddy said, "Hey?"

"Hey what?"

"This guy you want to throw off the roof? Your boss?"

"Yeah?"

"What's his name?"

14

IZZY SAID, "Mr. Rubin is expecting you." Which surprised Teddy because he'd heard a lot of stories about Saul Rubin, but he had never heard that he was psychic.

Izzy stood in the opened doorway of Saul Rubin's Society Hill town house with no expression on his face. He seemed bigger than Teddy remembered from his apartment. Rugged, with eyes that looked like they'd seen a lot of sun, gotten dust in them so that they had a little bit of a perpetual squint. But relaxed, too. Standing there, almost filling the doorway.

Izzy was wearing the same outfit as the other day, but without the suit jacket. A black turtleneck with the sleeves pushed up halfway so that Teddy noticed how prominent the muscles in his arms were. He also had a pistol under his left armpit. An automatic in a shoulder holster that he made no attempt to hide or explain.

Teddy pointed at the pistol and said, "What is that?"

"It's a Jericho nine-four-one. A nine-millimeter. Made in Israel."

"I got one too. A nine-millimeter, I mean. I think mine was made in Italy, though. Since I can see yours, you want me to show you mine? We could see who gets theirs out quicker."

"Mr. Clyde, I don't think there's any need for that. You don't look like Clint Eastwood and I don't talk like Mel Gibson. I was going to call you anyway, so I'm glad you stopped by. When I said that Mr. Rubin was expecting you, I really meant that he was hoping the two of you could meet. Talk about things."

"Is that what he wants to do? Talk?"

Still with no expression, Izzy said, "Yes, Mr. Rubin would certainly like to talk to you. And, for what it's worth, I personally think it's a good idea. An idea you should consider carefully. Mr. Rubin does not have too many visitors—who are—"

"Who are of the criminal element?" Teddy laughed in spit of himself.

Izzy shrugged. "I think either you're kidding me or you're being too hard on yourself, Mr. Clyde."

"Maybe. I'm not sure I even know," Teddy said. It was hard to take but something he knew he had to do, stand here and trade bullshit little one-liners with Izzy. Feeling forced to, no, wait, *wanting* to give the performance of his lifetime. It was also harder than hell to talk to Izzy because Teddy felt as if he had to act as though they had this macho gun bond. As of yesterday they were both supposedly stone-cold killers. Maybe Izzy was. Teddy had heard enough about him to think he might be an extremely cold man who could gun down Dominic Scarlotti and not let it bother him afterwards. And now Teddy had killed a man, too. To Izzy it must have seemed like a thing that took no thought. And certainly no remorse. Frankie Morelli had killed Teddy's own brother. Teddy was sure that Izzy had killed for far less. But even though it had happened because Davey had been gunned down in front of his eyes, Teddy knew he would never be the same. Frankie Morelli deserved to die. But Teddy knew he wasn't like Izzy and would never forget the second—frozen in time now—when his blast from the shotgun had caught Frankie Morelli and spun him onto the ground—dead—as if he were a child's toy that got dropped and broken.

Izzy was talking again, and it took Teddy a moment to come out of his reverie to catch his drift. "—did request that I find you. He wanted me to make absolutely certain that you realize that—not only did we not have anything to do with, ah, with what *occurred* yesterday—we both, Mr. Rubin and I, think it was deplorable."

Teddy said, "de*plor*able," as if he was experimenting with the sound of the word. "And Saul wanted me to know that, huh?"

"That's correct."

"Well, since I'm here—why don't we go in and see what Saul has to say for *himself*? Maybe he can help me cope with my grief."

Izzy said, slowly, "I could do that. Take you in to see Mr. Rubin. But if I do, you have to give me the gun you were talking about. The one you have tucked into the back of your pants."

Teddy said, "What've you got, Izzy, X-ray vision?"

Izzy smiled for the first time. "No. But if you want a piece of advice, you're trying to hide the fact that you're carrying a side arm? Try to keep your hand from reaching back there so often. Scratching at it. It more or less gives it away."

"I'll try to keep it in mind"—Teddy smiled right back at Izzy—"but the thing digs into me like crazy sometimes."

Teddy was carrying a small brown bag in his left hand. The kind of thing a mom would pack a lunch into when she sent her child off to school. He didn't particularly want to put it down just yet, but he didn't see how he was going to do what Izzy wanted without doing so. It was rolled up at the top and finally he simply handed it to Izzy as if it was a peanut-butter-and-jelly sandwich and said, "I'm gonna give you my gun," pointing at the bag, "but I want that back."

Izzy felt the bag with a subtle squeeze of his hands and seemed a little confused. "Of course. Why wouldn't you?"

SAUL RUBIN WAS READING a book the size of a dictionary when Izzy and Teddy walked in. He put it aside, stood up and looked at Teddy with a solemn expression on his face. "Mr. Clyde, I want to thank you for coming by." Saying it just as Izzy had, as if he had invited Teddy over. Saul pointed at a chair.

"Please, make yourself comfortable. Would you like anything to drink? Coffee? Something stronger?"

"Do you want to know what I *really* want?" The only chair nearby was an antique that looked like it would collapse if Teddy sat in it.

Saul got a different look in his eyes. The hostess-with-the-mostest gone now and the cunning Jewish man who had survived the Holocaust and probably a lot more creeping through. He said, "I'm certain you want to tell me."

"I do."

"Please do, then."

"What I really want is for you to cut the bullshit." Teddy pointed at the chair. "It's not, Do I want to have a seat? Do I want something to eat? Drink? I didn't come here to chitchat—check up on how I'm handling the idea that my brother—who never meant anyone any harm, got himself whacked by something he didn't even understand. Something that I'm sure was discussed at some point right here in this room."

There was a dog lying on the rug in the middle of the room. A German shepherd with its ears up, looking directly at Teddy. Every few seconds the dog would turn and look back at Saul Rubin. Teddy figured it was checking to make sure Saul wasn't in any mortal danger.

Izzy was standing behind him, his hands clasped in front of his waist and his back to the door. "Benji likes to look at people."

"Yeah? Well, tell Benji I'm not 'people.'"

Saul said something, Yiddish or Hebrew, softly, and the dog put its head on its paws and settled back on the carpet. Teddy looked back at Izzy, still by the door, one of those Marine corporals who stood guard outside of an embassy.

Saul was talking again but Teddy only heard the last part of it, Saul saying, "I know most people think I have a—a what? A checkered past. But the reality is, I'm a legitimate businessman. I'd be lying to you if I told you I didn't occasionally come up against people who aren't legitimate businessmen. But—pardon me, may I call you Teddy?" Saul didn't wait for an answer.

"Teddy, what businessman in this city isn't forced to deal with unsavory characters? In this case, as you know, I'm talking about some individuals— not a representation by any means, though—of Italian descent. And certainly— *certainly*—what happened to your brother was a terrible affair. Not just in the legal sense. I've seen it before, believe me, innocents caught up in a larger struggle. It's a thing I know a great deal about."

Teddy raised his eyebrows. "A terrible affair, huh?"

"Beyond a doubt. Horrendous." Saul said, "Not something I can even fathom, let alone condone. You have my sincerest apologies, for whatever they're worth to you. I don't presume to be able, me, a stranger, to lessen your loss." He leaned forward, speaking with an intensity on his face that surprised Teddy. "But, this—*this*—I want to be absolutely clear on. We"— pointing toward the door to the room—"I'm speaking of Itzhak and myself, had nothing to do with this. Mr. Anthony Bonica is a man, he goes around like . . ." looking at Izzy again, "What is that saying, Itzhak?"

"A bull in—"

Saul nodded. "In a china shop. Exactly. Not at all the way Itzhak and I would've proceeded." Teddy saw it right there—like a light switch being turned on—in the way Saul said, "would've proceeded" and knew the old man still wanted to do business. It was what he'd come here looking to find out.

Saul was on to his next subject—and his next persona—a defense lawyer. "You watch television, I'm sure, Teddy. I imagine you've seen my ads. My three stores. Jewelry and fine diamonds. One here in Center City. One in the northeast and a smaller one—I try to go for the yuppie crowd, if that's what they still call themselves—out in Manyunk." He stopped for a moment and then said, "Most people, they see me, if I ever even go to one of the stores, which I have to admit I don't very often, they think I'm some kindly old shlemiel. An old—an old—"

Teddy said, "An old fart.'"

Saul looked startled and nodded. "That's it." Looking back at Teddy. "That's it, exactly. An old fart. Very good. A bumbling old guy who can't get out of his own way. The truth is I know firsthand that this can be a violent world. Izzy knows it. And obviously, you do too. Am I going to deny that there are times, parts of my, shall we say, other business interests force me to—to *resort* to other means of influence? To most people? Perhaps. But to *you*? After what happened yesterday? No. I'm not going to insult your intelligence. I'm going to say to you that Mr. Anthony Bonica is a *vilde chayea*."

"A what?"

"A savage."

Teddy shrugged. "Aren't we all?"

Saul studied the floor at his feet and then looked up at Teddy, shaking his head again. "You're right. And I'm also an old man who's going on and on. Listening to the sound of his own voice when I should be letting you talk. I should be asking you—especially with what you must be going through—is there anything I can do for you? To help? Is there anything you wanted to say to me? Is there some way we can resolve this—this situation? What Mr. Anthony Bonica did was"—Saul shook his head—"was, I can only say—regrettably stupid. So—please—feel free to say whatever's on your mind."

Teddy looked at Saul for a long time. And then he turned to look at Izzy. He still had the little brown bag in his hand and he held it up for both men to see.

Then he said, "You want me to tell you what's on my mind?"

Saul said into the pause, "Yes."

Teddy was reaching into the little brown bag, coming up with a small black box. Lacquered wood. About half the size of a shoe box. He felt rather then saw Izzy come to even more attention. He was making a slow movement with his hand toward his armpit, getting ready to pull the Jericho out and kill him if he didn't like what was inside the box. Saul noticed and said, "It's all right, Itzhak. I'm sure Mr. Clyde here only wants us to take a peek at something he feels is important."

Teddy said, "That's all I want. You to take a peek at something. How important is it? I believe I'll leave that up to you to decide."

Teddy opened the box without looking at the contents inside because he already knew what it was and didn't particularly care to see it ever again. He turned it so that in a moment Saul would have no difficulty—wouldn't even have to stand up—in seeing what was inside and then he took three steps over to where the old man sat and said, "See, I show it to you. And then, I let you figure out what its impl*ications* are. And then I'll tell you what's on my mind. But the reason I want to show you what I have in the box? It's just so you can be absolutely—*absolutely*—sure that what I'm telling you is the truth." Now he lowered the box.

Saul leaned forward a little and got a grimace of distaste on his face. Then the expression was gone.

Saul let three seconds go by and then motioned Izzy over, pointing at the box and saying, "Itzhak, is that what I think it is?"

Teddy watched Izzy's face, impressed because there was no change to his features. He could've been looking at a flower. Gazing for a moment into the box and then nodding. Turning to Saul. "It's his." Pointing, "I recognize that, saw it the other night. The mark. It's his." He nodded again and gave Teddy a quick look, a different one than he'd ever given him before. Seeing him in a new light perhaps. Then moving back to the door to stand like a statue once again.

"Young man," Saul said, "you've managed to impress me. Not a lot of people do that." Saul was back to being the kindly old man who did nothing more then sell a few jewels out of his three stores. Except for the initial look, there was nothing else that most people would show. No disgust. No fear. Nothing.

And now, with the circus over, Teddy was going to tell Saul Rubin how there could be a way out. A way to resolve the whole mess.

And Saul had better buy into it.

TOMMY INZARELLA STOOD outside the front door of Palisades in a slight drizzle and listened to what Izzy Feldman had to say over the cell phone. The

Jew certainly had a way with words. When Izzy was finished, Tommy told him that he'd think about things and they could talk later. He put his cell phone back in his pocket and made his way back into the club. Anthony was at a table in the back talking to Vicki. Vicki was showing a lot of leg today, even for her standards, dressed in a short, tight leather skirt and a blouse that was made out of some kind of material that was so translucent you could see the ridges on her nipples, seriously, dark brown smudges against the paleness of her tits. She had moved her chair over toward Anthony's right and they were sitting so closely together that it seemed like they were on a bench that was too small for even one person.

Vicki's hand was on Anthony's thigh, her index finger making slow circular motions on Anthony's trousers as she leaned over and whispered something into Anthony's ear. They both burst out laughing and Tommy found himself wondering for a second—seeing Vicki work at it like she was truly going to miss Anthony when she walked away from the table—did Anthony think she, or any broad for that matter, fucked him because they actually *liked* him? Probably. It would never occur to him that the dancers did it only because, A, they made a shitload of money dancing at Palisades and, B, they were scared to death not to.

When Tommy got to the table he said, "Vicki, why don't you go check your makeup."

Tommy looked at the expression on Anthony's face as Vicki grabbed her purse. Shit—Little Anthony actually looked sorry that Vicki had to go. Tommy wanted to snap his fingers in front of Anthony's face and say, "Hey, you mind if we talk business for a second? Or you wanna think about pussy all day long? You run a topless club for Christ's sake, you wanna get laid, all you got to do is *do* it." Tommy himself saw so many tits during the course of any given day that he got tired of looking. But not Anthony. No, he wanted to be known forever as a stud.

He stood there quietly instead, while Vicki stood all the way up—stretching so hard that it looked like her nipples were going to pop *through* her blouse.

Then, turning, she gave *Tommy* a look that Anthony couldn't see because he was behind her now. Running her tongue over her lips like the thing she now wanted to do most in the entire world was pull *Tommy's* zipper down and stick *his* dick in her mouth. Staring at Tommy's face—glancing down at his crotch and then back at his eyes. Christ, an actress. He should send her over to Chuckie Fatelli. Chuckie made skin flicks out of an apartment in West Philly and also out of various motels out in the suburbs. She wanted to go through life eye-fucking every guy she saw, let her put some money where her mouth was.

Tommy knew Vicki's little secret, though. Dumb cunt, did she think that he was Anthony? That he wouldn't? Fuck, Tommy knew more about the day-to-day workings of Palisades than Anthony did. Than *anyone* did. He was the one who saw that the bills got paid, watched the bartenders to make sure they kept their skimming to an acceptable amount, oversaw what trucks got hijacked and when, so that the place had a steady stream of free booze pouring in, free meat, free linen, so Anthony could make even more money when he jacked the prices up. Tommy made sure the girls got medical checkups and didn't scratch each other's eyes out in their fucked-up little catfights. He paid off the health inspector and the fire official—and a city councilman, the greedy prick. Tommy had to deliver it in person to *that* fucking crook because what? It made him feel important?

Tommy sometimes wondered, where did all the hassles get him?

Like right now, eyeball to eyeball with Vicki. She had some kind of challenging, fuck-me-if-you-think-you're-man-enough look in her eyes, and for a second it crossed Tommy's mind to shock the shit out of her and Anthony at the same time. Tell Vicki right now—in front of Anthony—that he knew she and one of the other dancers, Brenda—an Irish redhead who could dance until most of the other girls were ready to drop—were sixty-nining themselves every chance that they got. He could explain to Anthony, "Hey, these two whores, they've been amusing themselves like this since the week they started working together." Tommy could get out of the way afterward, while Anthony went looking to cut Vicki's head off, pull her tongue out through an ear-to-ear slit in her throat so it would be that much harder to use on her girlfriend. Or just cut them up some. The face. Scar them and then make them walk the streets forever after.

But Tommy wasn't going to say a thing. He eyeballed Vicki until she pouted and looked away. Then he sat down, not in the same chair Vicki had been in, no, across the table, so he could look Anthony in the eye.

He didn't waste his time with bullshit either. He sat, moved Vicki's lipstick-stained soda glass out of the way and waited until he had Anthony's full attention.

"Izzy Feldman?" he said, "I just got an interesting phone call from him."

"You don't got to even tell me what that Jew prick said. He—he and Saul Rubin are scared. Fuck, I were them, I would be too." Anthony leaned close to Tommy and used his index finger to make his point, poking it down on the tabletop. "You tell Izzy—he's calling up because he's nervous that Teddy Clyde has a tape or some kinda bullshit can be used against him in a court of law—you tell him, go to Sabbath or whatever the fuck it is. Tell him, don't worry, we got the thing covered. Teddy Clyde? Right now he's so shit-scared, I say 'Bang' and he's gonna drop dead of a fucking heart attack. Shit his pants at the same time."

Tommy kept a straight face. "No."

"No? Whatta you mean, 'no'?"

"Because, see, I didn't have to tell Izzy a thing. He wasn't calling 'cause he was worried."

"The fuck you talking about, Tommy?"

"He's calling us up to tell us that Teddy Clyde, maybe we didn't scare him as much as you thought. Maybe we didn't scare him at all because he stopped by Saul Rubin's house today."

Anthony said loudly, "He did what?"

Tommy held up his hands. "Anthony, I just want you to listen to me. Okay? Teddy Clyde, the reason he showed up, this is according to Izzy Feldman, he wants to make a deal with *them* now."

"The fucker wants to do *what*?"

"Teddy Clyde asked Izzy, apparently because of what happened yesterday at the stadium parking lot, if he turns over the tape—he still wants the money—but get this, he actually asked Izzy to guarantee his, and I'm talking Teddy Clyde's, safety. Izzy said that Teddy doesn't give a shit where we meet, Izzy said he doesn't either, he'll leave that up to us. But according to Izzy, Teddy *did* insist he gets to search us. No guns. No knives. No nothing. Except of course, the money. And nobody shows but you, me and Izzy. Teddy told Izzy that he has the real thing this time. Izzy said he proved it."

Anthony was out of his chair in half a second. Knocking Vicki's glass onto the floor with a crash loud enough so that everybody else in the place, the bouncer, the bartender and close to a dozen girls—all getting ready to open up in an hour—turned and looked at them.

Anthony roared, "The fuck any of you looking at? I pay you for staring?" He sat back down, leaned close to Tommy and jabbed his index finger toward the tabletop without hitting it. "You fucking telling me"—bringing his voice down—"you fucking telling me—I whack this motherfucker's brother—and he's got the fucking balls to go behind my back. Try to sell the fucking thing to Izzy and his Hebe boss? And he wants a guarantee of his *safety*? Motherfucker, Tommy, whatta I look like to you, the fucking pope?"

Tommy said, "Anthony, hey—calm down."

"Calm down? Fuck you, calm down."

"Just listen to me. Listen to what I told Izzy. I told him, Hey, if Teddy Clyde wants to sell the thing to us? He wants to stay alive to spend that money? He wants to pat us down, make sure we're not carrying any box cutters? I said, no problem."

There was a vein in Anthony's neck standing out now. Tommy could check Anthony's pulse just by watching the thing.

Tommy spread his hands and grinned. "Anthony, c'mon. What difference does it make what Izzy told Teddy Clyde? All Izzy's asking us is he wants us to put up half the money. Five hundred grand."

"He's out of his fucking mind, is what he is."

Tommy shook his head, thinking, maybe he should get Vicki back here, the bitch could help explain the obvious to Anthony. He said, "Can I ask you one question, Anthony?"

Anthony was still furious. "What?!"

"What the fuck difference does it make? Izzy calls up here, he already told Teddy Clyde a certain thing. Guaranteed his safety. What the fuck difference does it make *what* we say? Shit, you can tell Teddy Clyde he can have part ownership of this club." Tommy shrugged. "Bottom line, we get the prick somewhere—and I got the idea that the same place we did Dominic, the restaurant you're renovating, is as good a place as anywhere. Especially since Izzy made it plain that it don't matter where it goes down. We put a piece in there. A twenty-two, or maybe something bigger. A thirty-eight. The point is, yeah, we show him we're good guys, put our guns out in the open so no one gets hurt. Meanwhile we hide an extra one. Beforehand. That fuck, Teddy Clyde? He wants to, he can search us all he wants. Then—no matter what we agreed to—we do whatever the fuck we want." Tommy waited for it to sink in. Waited until Anthony was nodding his head and starting to smile.

Then Tommy said, "Hey, if you want, we take out fucking Izzy Feldman at the same time. We make it look right, show up with a suitcase full of money too so Teddy Clyde can get the last hard-on of his life. And we take out Izzy while we're at it. Take *his* fucking money too just because, hey, there it is. Besides, what the fuck is Saul Rubin gonna do about it? Shit, Anthony, it's gonna be the easiest half mil you'll ever make."

Anthony took one breath and went from scowling to laughing. That fast.

15

NATALIE TOOK ONE LOOK at Teddy's face and said, "You're lying to me."

Teddy shook his head. "No I'm not."

She got up from the sofa in her living room, walked across to where he was standing, and put her hands on her hips. Her eyes were flashing and she made him feel like he was a ten-year-old kid who had gotten his hand stuck in a cookie jar.

She said, "What do I do for a living? I expose people. Somebody's doing something shady—he wants to keep it hidden—my job is to write it down, let the whole city know."

"That's what I'm talking about. I do things for a living too. That's why I have to go out. I have to look at a car."

Natalie looked at her watch and said sarcastically, "Oh, right, it's, what, ten-fifteen on a Sunday night? You're a car thief. You're telling me you have to go to work? Tonight? I didn't realize there wouldn't be any more Porsches left tomorrow."

"Jaguars."

"Ex-*cuse* me. So you have to go out, locate the last Jag in the city. And it's got to be tonight. Right now. Did someone else steal all the others when you weren't looking? They on the endangered-species list? Jesus, Teddy, some-times you try my patience. "

Teddy wished she would take her hands off her hips, unclench her fists. "Nat, c'mon."

" 'C'mon,' nothing. You've been running all over town all week. I don't expect that you have to check in with me. But don't come here, look me in the eye and tell me something we both know is bullshit. You're not going out to steal a car."

Natalie walked back to the sofa and sat down. She stared at the floor for a full minute before saying, "Christ, if we had been seeing each other for longer, I'd think you were cheating on me." Looking up at his face now. "But you're not. You're playing hero. Or else you're going after revenge. You don't want to think about it too much. You just want to *do* it. I know they killed your brother. I know that. You think it's going to help if they kill you, too?" She stood. "You're feeling grief over Davey. Is it going to make things right if I have to grieve over you? Huh? Is it? Shit, Teddy, let's you and I just get out of town. Go somewhere—the beach—the Cayman Islands. I'll buy a thong bikini and every day I'll tell you how much I love being with you. You don't have to say a thing back to me. Just be there."

Teddy couldn't believe it. Seeing now that there were tears forming in her eyes. Why couldn't he have just met her *before* all of this crap went down?

He crossed the room and took her in his arms. "Listen to me. You're right. I am going out there to see, once and for all, can I get this situation squared away. I have to live with it, my brother, and, sooner or later if I *don't* do this, it's going to turn me into the kind of person—bitter—who you won't want to be on a beach with, no matter how good the weather is." He wiped her tears with his thumbs, gently, held her and then kissed her on the fore-head. "I promise you—*promise*—I'm going to be back. When I'm gone, you start packing a bag. If you have a thong bikini in it, that's fine. If not, first place we see—I'll buy you a dozen of them. Okay?"

Some kind of mask came down over her face, wooden, as if now she was only going through motions but they didn't mean anything to her one way or the other. Like she didn't at all believe in what she was saying. She stepped back, looked at a spot on the wall somewhere past Teddy's left shoulder and said, in a dull voice, "Okay."

It made him want to give it up. Call Izzy on the phone and tell him he could pick up Dominic Scarlotti's cigarette case someplace in town. A trashcan near City Hall or something. But if he did that it would be as good as telling Anthony Bonica that he could murder a member of Teddy's family any time he felt like it. Plus which, Anthony had to pay. Big time. Either this was going to work or Anthony was going to kill him. And, as far as Teddy was concerned, no one was going to kill him. But that meant he was going to need that money.

So—even though he didn't like dealing this way with Natalie—he wasn't going to give it up either.

He left, knowing—at best—that Natalie thought he was a fool.

FIFTEEN MINUTES LATER there was a knock on Natalie's door. She was supposed to shower and head to Palisades, work the night shift until two o'clock in the morning, but she was too upset about Teddy to even consider doing it. She had enough to write the article, and right now it was the furthest thing from her mind.

She was standing in her kitchen holding on to a cup of lukewarm coffee, staring at nothing but worry. She hadn't taken a sip for the last five minutes and could suddenly picture the grin Teddy would have plastered on his face in the hallway outside her door. Like a little boy who ran away from home and got as far as the corner grocery store, got scared and came back to find out whether his mom had even noticed he had left. Going to give Natalie his Boy Scout look and say, "Aw shucks, Nat, I couldn't do it. Just couldn't." She was going to give him a little piece of her mind but then take him into the bedroom. Hug him for a while before they made love.

She dumped the coffee into the sink, banged her thigh on the corner of the kitchen table, but who gave a damn, and then hurried down the short hall, across the living room and to the door, thinking, the whole time, forget about giving him a piece of her mind, she was going to jump into his arms as soon as she saw him. Maybe pull him down on the carpet and do it right there out of sheer relief and because, why not, they'd already tried out her bed enough to get a little crazy.

The smile plastered on her face disappeared immediately along with any thoughts of jumping into Teddy's arms, losing the sexy remark about to come out of her mouth, too, because it wasn't Teddy at her door. It was two serious-looking men, cops, staring back at her, neither one of them managing to smile.

One of the men, the smaller of the two, had an unruly beard and a badge in his hand that said his name was John Gottlieb and that he was a detective with the Philadelphia Police Department, Twelfth Precinct. But it was the other one who was in charge. The bigger one who stepped in front of his partner, moved past Natalie and into her apartment without being asked and without seeming to worry whether Detective John Gottlieb bothered to follow or not.

As he was passing her, he said, almost as if he was bored, "What we're wondering is, how's Mr. Clyde doing?"

She said, "Excuse me?" with as much nonchalance as she could muster.

He reminded her of that cop in the old television show *McCloud*. Dennis Weaver. He didn't look a thing like Dennis Weaver except possibly they were the same height. It was more the way he talked and acted. His mannerisms. If he'd been wearing a cowboy hat, a Stetson, she wouldn't have been surprised to see him tip it at her and call her "ma'am."

He was dressed in black, a weird look for a detective, unless he was some kind of super-cool undercover narcotics officer. He made his way casually into the living room, first picking up a few knickknacks Natalie had put around, examining them only to put them right back, and was now standing next to the wide-screen TV. Looking around like—Christ—like he was thinking of redecorating the place.

She assumed immediately that they had something to do with auto theft. Her first thought. Seeing for the first time what Teddy would probably call the downside of his work, being hassled by cops. A couple of detectives working a hot-car ring that maybe Teddy had a hand in. She thought about Dominic Scarlotti, but only for an instant because they certainly didn't look like homicide detectives. She'd known some homicide detectives. They were polite but not casual. These men lacked the haunted eyes.

No, these guys were after Teddy for some car that had been stolen, wanting to talk to him or, hopefully not, arrest him. She already knew what she would say, but only if they really pressed, "Teddy Cloud—sorry, Clyde? Wait, wait, sure, a guy I met, a bar. I forget which one. We're getting to know each other." Act as if she wasn't sure she cared too much. Refer to him as a source for an article she was doing. Mention Palisades but sound naive. "Hey, he told me he was a stockbroker."

Or wait a minute—why hadn't she thought of this before? They were here because of Davey-Boy. Good Lord. They'd figured out that Teddy had spent some time with her recently—who knew how—and they were thinking he might still be here, or coming back soon. She took it all back. They *were* homicide detectives.

God, it was crazy, even thinking about it. She had to remember back to two days ago when she felt like a law-abiding citizen.

But before she could say anything she heard a click and turned, realized that the other cop, the one who had flashed his badge, had stepped inside and locked the door after him.

She said, "Hey—" but stopped because the big cop said, behind her, "Is it a problem?"

She turned back and said, putting some serious attitude into it, "Is *what* a problem, Detective? The door?" She stepped closer to the bigger detective; he had seven inches on her, but she was going to show him she wasn't the least bit intimidated. "No, that's not a problem, locking the door like that, because your partner's going to open it back up in *one* goddamned second or *I'm* going to call nine-one-one. I don't know your name but I do"—pointing at the smaller cop—"know his. You're making another serious mistake, not realizing that I can make your life miserable." She took another step closer to the big cop and looked him right in the eye. "If you don't believe me, I can give you a number, *The Philadelphia Inquirer*, where I work. You might want to stop while you're ahead. You might want to ask yourself this: Do you know who I am? I mean, really know? Maybe you're thinking I'm just some woman who's going to be intimidated by you just showing up? I have news for you; it isn't that way at all."

There, that should stop this crap right now. In its tracks.

But, no, all the bigger cop did, calmly, still looking around, was say, "You're Natalie Prentice. You write for the *Philadelphia Inquirer* Sunday magazine." Taking the wind out of her sails. "Lately I heard you were working— ah, undercover at a place called Palisades, going to do a piece on a gentlemen's club." He smiled slightly with no humor. "And now you've gotten in way over your head. Become involved with things that you don't even understand. Now, you want to answer my question: How's Mr. Clyde doing? Actually, *where* is Mr. Clyde?"

Natalie thought, holy hell, who was she dealing with here? She took a breath, holding her face in her defiant mode, but not feeling it that confidently anymore. Feeling like a balloon that had just popped. She managed to say, "I have no idea what you're talking about," and could hear her own voice wasn't the same.

The big cop said, "I know what you're thinking. I don't blame you. You want us out of here so badly I can almost feel it. Right here in the room, it's filling it up. The aura." *What the hell was he talking about?* He shrugged. "Unfortunately, it's not going to do you any good. Wanting us out of here. Where are we going to go? I mean, you're absolutely right, we came here to talk to you. You see what I mean? Because, the problem is, you're thinking this is one thing when, in fact, it isn't. So I want you to concentrate. See if you can help us. Because you aren't even attempting to answer the question. Frankly, to me that means you're also busy trying to hide something. What if we just make this a little easier? You just start by admitting that you actually *know* Mr. Theodore Clyde? After that, we see where we end up."

Now the cop in charge was turning to look around the apartment again. He stood in the middle of the living room, and Natalie watched him the way a sports fan might watch a slow-motion instant replay on TV. The detective's gaze seem to take in everything, lock it away in some part of his brain so that, given the chance or the need, he could sit down with a pencil and paper and draw a blueprint of Natalie's apartment that would make an architect proud.

And then he was looking directly at her again. He had eyes that were so dark they almost appeared black. And suddenly, something in Natalie told her she should see his detective badge—right now—because being looked at by this man was making her head warm and she could feel a sudden spot of perspiration at each of her temples. It felt like she was coming down with a cold. She realized that she had never—forget about Jameel and his bunch of amateur buddies—seen a look that contained such control and deadliness in her entire life.

Jesus Christ. What was going on here?

The detective interrupted her thoughts. "Are you planning on answering the question?"

Natalie said, "Mr. Clyde?"

The detective said, almost gently, "That's right. Mr. Clyde. Teddy. You do know him, am I correct?"

At that moment it hit her, God almighty, Teddy, telling her about walking into Palisades to confront Anthony Bonica and Tommy Inzarella, both of whom Natalie knew because they were the main reason she had taken the job in the first place. Work at a topless bar controlled by the Mob, write an article about it and kill two birds with one stone. Smell Pulitzer just over the horizon.

She could hear Teddy's voice in her head. Talking about a third guy there too, that day. Someone Teddy hadn't expected. She remembered some kind of respect in Teddy's voice that he didn't have when he was talking about Anthony Bonica. A man wearing all black."

She wanted to turn to the door. She wanted to look past the smaller of the two men so that—hopefully—she could see Teddy coming through the door from the other side. Maybe he had forgotten something or else just changed his mind as she had thought he had when these two men had knocked on the door. Sure, Teddy could do that.

Izzy said something, but she wasn't even close to listening.

She was thinking, no, Teddy wasn't going to come back to her apartment, not yet. She was on her own. Teddy wasn't coming through the door. He was out there somewhere on the streets, trying to be a hero or trying to avenge his brother's death. Meanwhile, half the people he was probably looking for—a third of them, at least—were right here. Looking for *him*.

She thought about the shotgun. Teddy had put it back in her bedroom closet. It was there right now. But it wasn't as if she could go get it. She took a deep breath, tried to steady her nerves and look the—the *detective*—right in the eyes at the same time. He knew some things about her, her name and her job? Even the article she was currently working on? What about what *she* knew?

She said, "You're Itzhak, aren't you? Izzy?" and had the slight satisfaction of seeing a quick look of surprise flash across his face. But that's all that happened.

Nothing else.

It certainly wasn't as though Itzhak or his friend went away.

TEDDY TOOK the long way to get to his meeting with Izzy Feldman and Anthony Bonica. He stopped at a 7-Eleven along the way to buy a Coca-Cola and a roll of Scotch tape and then spent five minutes sipping the soda and making one last-minute preparation, putting his sport coat on after and checking to see that he looked okay. He told himself that it was as good as it was gong to get and then drove down Race Street all the way to Second Street, taking his time about it and not worrying was he making the lights or not because it gave him time to think things through. Plan for contingencies.

When he hit Second Street, he took a right, drove a few blocks south until he hit Market and then he took another right. Now he was headed right back to where he had started. But a short block later he took another right, onto Third. After that, he began to drive even more slowly, knowing that the place where they were all meeting—a restaurant that Izzy had told him Anthony Bonica was having renovated—was only a block and a half away.

He crossed Arch Street and coasted to a stop. He could see the restaurant now, under construction and right ahead, a block and a half up on the left-hand side of the street. There was an industrial dumpster out front and construction materials—a stack of four-by-eight sheets of plywood sitting exposed and another stack that Teddy assumed was drywall because it was sitting under a bright blue tarp.

He checked his watch and then looked out the windshield and into all three of his mirrors to see if there was any activity on the street. There wasn't. But just as he was getting ready to check his watch again a sleek black Caddy came down the street in the opposite direction and parked directly in front of the half-finished restaurant.

Anthony hopped out of the backseat and stood on the curb, looking up and down at all the other buildings like he was expecting a SWAT team to appear. A moment later Tommy Inzarella got out of the driver's door and walked around to Anthony. It crossed Teddy's mind to wonder, Did Tommy like his new job? Driving Anthony everywhere while all of a sudden, ever since Dominic Scarlotti had gotten killed, Anthony sat in the backseat? Maybe, if Teddy got the chance, he'd find out. Ask Tommy, "Hey, how's it feel? Anthony's such a big man he won't sit up front with you anymore? You catch some kind of disease?" See what Tommy thought of it.

Tommy closed Anthony's door and stepped to the trunk of the Caddy. He reached inside and lifted out what looked to be the same gym bag as the one he'd had at the stadium lot. Anthony must have spoken to him because Tommy leaned toward Anthony, Anthony moved his lips. Tommy seemed to listen, and then nodded his head. A moment later the two men crossed the street, got up to the front of the restaurant and unlocked the door.

Teddy stayed where he was, trying to make sure that no one else from Anthony's crew showed up. He didn't think he had to worry about Izzy bringing anyone else. He knew that Saul Rubin had a lot more people than just Izzy working for him. But Teddy also knew there was no reason in the world to send anyone else. If Saul Rubin was going to pull a fast one, he didn't need anyone else to do it but Izzy. Shit, if a situation arose tonight—no matter what it might be—and Izzy couldn't handle it, was there going to be anyone else on Saul's payroll who could?

But Anthony was different. Teddy had to be sure that Nicky Migliaro, or someone else connected to Anthony, didn't show up quietly. Teddy was going to give it a few more minutes, and then if Nicky Migliaro or anyone else from Anthony's crew *did* show up, he was going to walk into the restaurant with Davey's Beretta and start blasting away without even saying hello. Try to take Tommy Inzarella out first because he'd be the biggest worry, and then work his way down the list. Get as many of the sonsabitches as he could before they got him.

A light came on inside the renovated restaurant and, from where he sat, Teddy got an occasional glimpse of Tommy Inzarella and Anthony as they walked by the one window in the front of the place that wasn't boarded up. He couldn't tell who was who from this distance, but after watching for a few more minutes, seeing the two men move more and more often past the window, he figured that, sitting here watching, he might just be moving from careful patience to chicken shit. He could sit out here all night. But it wasn't going to accomplish anything.

He pulled Davey's Beretta from underneath the seat, jammed it into the waist of his trousers at the small of his back and put Dominic Scarlotti's cigarette case into the inside breast pocket of his sport coat. He checked his reflection, what he could see of it, in the mirror. He turned the dome light off so it wouldn't illuminate the car when he got out.

Then he took a deep breath and stepped onto the street.

IT FELT WEIRD to Tommy Inzarella, being here, the same place they had clipped Dominic Scarlotti just three nights before. Everything was cleaned up, no bloodstains anywhere, but still, Tommy—helping Anthony drag a sheet of plywood from a stack in the corner over to the center of the soon-to-be restaurant—felt a sense of déjà vu. The beginning of something that had already ended a couple of days ago. A recurring dream that was gonna turn into a fucking nightmare if it wasn't resolved one way or the other tonight.

He and Anthony hoisted the plywood over two sawhorses so that it formed a rough table. Tommy stopped thinking about Dominic Scarlotti and took a Smith & Wesson .38 out of his waistband. The grip of the pistol was wrapped with a few dozen rubber bands and the serial number had been ground down so far it looked like someone had tried to cut the thing in half. He took a roll of duct tape from his pocket and started to bend down under the plywood.

Anthony took one look at him and said, "The fuck're you doing?"

Tommy looked confused. "What's it look like?"

Anthony stormed around the makeshift table and grabbed the gun and the tape out of Tommy's hands. "What it looks like is this: You're planning on doing this fucking piece of work yourself."

"Whaddaya want me to do? You want me to put it somewhere else, so maybe Izzy or Teddy'll see it?"

Anthony said, disgusted, "Nobody's gonna see it, and that ain't the fucking point." Anthony moved back to his side of the sheet of plywood, bent down and started to tear off pieces of tape. While he taped the pistol to the underside of the plywood he told Tommy, "They come in here. We all act like fucking gentlemen. You stand there. I stand here. We smile—fucking what-ever. Put our fucking pieces in plain sight. Right there on the table like we're gonna fucking negotiate. They see what they see and they're gonna be telling themselves things they want to hear. Fuck 'em. Everybody's happy because all the guns're on the table. But if you think I'm gonna let you or *anybody* else take out this fucking Teddy Clyde asshole, you can forget about it. This motherfucker is *mine.* I cap him and he's gonna *know* who does him. Gonna see my face, hear me laughing. It's what he's gonna take to his fucking grave, that treacherous motherfucker. You understand?"

Tommy shrugged. "Anthony, I don't care who does what. You're the boss. Just don't forget, you got Izzy. His pistol, I don't care where he puts it—plain sight or not—you're only gonna have a second or two."

Anthony, finished with the .38, stood up. He walked slowly over to Tommy and shook his head as if Tommy had just told him a joke. And then he said, "Tommy, lemme ask you something. Did I get to be where I am by being a fucking idiot? First thing, Teddy Clyde's standing here looking like somebody peed on his feet, I take that Jew fuck Izzy out. Ba-bing, between the eyes. Same thing as he did to motherfucking Dominic. Then maybe I kneecap Teddy Clyde. Put a thirty-eight right there, let him think about pain for a while before I do anything more."

Tommy said, "C'mon, Anthony, you know I didn't mean it like that. I was just thinking you might want me to do the job. That's all."

Anthony gave a quick laugh. "I know that. Any other time, I'd probably say, no shit, no fucking problem." He shook his head, starting to grin again, but then grimaced and pointed at his bad eye. "But this one? Teddy Clyde? His treachery? This one is fucking *per*sonal."

TEDDY WAS THREE-QUARTERS of the way across the street when a black Lincoln Town Car pulled past him and parked illegally in front of a fire hydrant. Teddy saw the driver's profile, a head partially illuminated by a streetlight. Izzy. Teddy could either keep on walking or wait where he was. He decided to wait, be polite about it so that he and Izzy could arrive together. Maybe one of them would hold the door for the other.

Izzy stepped out of the Town Car and then reached back in to pull out a gym bag that looked identical to the one Tommy Inzarella had been carrying.

When he stood back up Izzy said, without even turning in Teddy's direction, "Your big night, huh, Mr. Clyde."

Teddy said, "We'll see."

"I guess we will."

Neither of them said another word on the way to the restaurant.

JOSEPH STILL hadn't said a word. The only reason Natalie knew his real name, not the one on the phony police badge, was because Izzy had said, "I don't in any way wish to alarm you, Miss Prentice. Joseph"—he nodded at Joseph, who *still* didn't say a word—"is here simply to prevent any unfortunate events from occurring while I go take care of a little business with your friend, Mr. Clyde." Izzy had pointed at the phone and said, "I could do something like ripping that cord out of the wall, but think of the trouble I'd put you to."

"Why don't you just admit that you're using me to blackmail Teddy, Izzy? Cut the bullshit about 'unfortunate events' and try a little honesty."

Izzy had smiled. "I *am* being honest, Miss Prentice. I don't want anyone to get hurt—your friend Mr. Clyde included—so I'm just taking care of any contingencies I can think of."

Natalie thought about Izzy's words. It was revolting, how polite he was. Did he think she wouldn't consider him a thug just because he spoke well? Leaving, Izzy had said something to Joseph, Yiddish or Hebrew, she assumed, because she didn't understand a word of it. Joseph just nodded, maybe he *couldn't* talk, and Izzy turned to look at her one more time, framed in the doorway, one hand on the knob and handsome in his own way. Smiling at her and telling her not to worry, everything would just be fine. Saying, "Joseph is a quiet man, you won't even know he's here, and I'll be back shortly, leave you in peace." The smile still in place as he added, "Perhaps you can write about it when it's all over."

He said something else to Joseph and then nodded his head to Natalie, reaching behind him in one fluid motion to open the door. Even if Natalie had wanted to say more to him, she didn't get the chance because he was gone that fast—a faint trace of cologne the only evidence that he had ever been there.

That, and Joseph.

Joseph now stepped between her and the door. Natalie thought he had watched too much *Monday Night Football* on ABC. He seemed to be impersonating a middle linebacker, waiting for her to make a break for it. A quarterback sneak that would take, not only Joseph, but her front door down as well.

She sat on the sofa like a prim little schoolgirl—hands folded in her lap, back straight and her knees touching each other. She thought about getting up off the couch. She could saunter down the hallway as if she were going to the bathroom, and then duck into her bedroom, pull the sawed-off shotgun out of her closet and come back out here. Ask Joseph, politely, if he wouldn't mind moving the fuck away from the door.

She waited until he took his eyes off her, peering into the kitchen at God knew what. She stood up and began walking nonchalantly toward the hall that led to the bedroom. She had taken three steps when she heard a metallic, ratcheting noise from behind her. She turned around in disbelief to see that Joseph had pulled a pistol out of his jacket, cocked it, and was aiming it squarely at the center of her chest.

In a voice that was so calm it surprised her, Natalie said, "You're going to *shoot* me? I have to use the potty. Is that okay with you or—good Lord—are you going to kill me because of it?"

Joseph finally lowered the gun. While he did, Natalie realized where she had seen eyes like his before. It took a full minute, but then it came to her.

Another reporter from the *Inquirer* had done a feature just a while back. On the Mideast. Gone to Syria with a photographer and brought back pictures of, among other things, the Yarmouk refugee camp, where thousands of Palestinians had fled after the humiliating Arab defeat in 1967. Now they lived there in absolute squalor. That's where she had seen eyes like Joseph's. Flat, dark eyes that had seen too many bad things and had had all the emotion driven out of them. She was sure that's what it was.

When Joseph finally spoke, his voice was the same as his eyes. Flat, with no affect whatsoever. "Whatever you do. It doesn't matter if it's eating or using the facilities. You do it in front of me."

Natalie tried hard to match her own expression to Joseph's. She said, "You want me to go pee-pee in front of you, Joey?" She walked back toward the sofa. "Is that what you want me to do? I take a piss and you want to *watch*?"

She sat down and assumed the same position as before. Then she stared up at Joseph and saw that maybe *all* the emotion wasn't gone from him because there was a reddishness spreading across his cheeks that he seemed to be struggling to stop but couldn't. She let him work at it for a moment and then said, as sweet-sounding as she could, "Well, fuck you, you pervert. You're not watching me do a *god*damn thing."

She looked away from him to stare at the wall opposite the sofa. She had two things on her mind. One, she wished Teddy would be successful at whatever business he had going with Izzy, that he would hurry up and get back here so he could pick Joseph up and throw him out a god*damn* window.

And two, she wished she had never told Joseph that she had to go to the bathroom. Because, now that she had put it into words, she *did* have to pee.

16

ANTHONY BONICA made a production out of taking the gym bag out of Tommy Inzarella's hands, putting it on the table, unzipping it and pulling out a banded stack of hundreds long enough for everyone to take a peek. He turned to look at Teddy and said, "You're gonna have to take my word for it, Teddy, 'cause nobody here has time for you to count the rest of it."

Izzy put his own gym bag on the plywood sheet, unzipped it and showed everyone that it too was full of cash. "I'm sure it's all there."

Anthony said to Izzy. "I know *you* carry a piece. You got that Jew thing—that pistol—under your shoulder. I wanna see it on the table." He walked over to Teddy and said, "*You* I'm gonna search. You make a wrong fucking move, Tommy here is going to take your fucking head off."

Teddy said, without raising his voice, "Tommy, tell your boss, he touches me—he even breathes his garlic breath on me, you won't have time to clear your gun. I got a nine-millimeter behind my back. If you want, I'll take it out. Put it on the table. But"—he nodded at Anthony—"this piece of shit doesn't come near me."

Teddy looked past Anthony—saw that Izzy was putting his own pistol on the table and that Tommy had a pistol in his hands—and waited until finally Tommy gave a small nod.

"Listen to me," Tommy said to Anthony. "I'm gonna put my piece right here. In the center of the table right next to Izzy's. You come back here, do the same thing, and I know Teddy will too."

There was a moment when Anthony couldn't seem to make up his mind. Anthony looked as if he wanted Teddy to do something—anything—so he could use it as an excuse to blow him away. But then he worked a smile onto his face.

"What the fuck," he said. "Tommy's right. We're here to do business. Nothing personal needs to affect that."

Anthony turned around and walked back so that he was standing next to Tommy on the opposite side of the sheet of plywood. Then, as if they'd rehearsed it a dozen times before, Anthony and Teddy each reached behind their backs at precisely the same moment and brought guns out. Anthony's gun looked identical to Teddy's. Teddy wondered if it was. If things kept up, if he got through all of this bullshit, Teddy figured, in another couple of weeks he'd be a firearms expert to go along with being a car thief.

When the pistols were all in a more or less neat pile in the center of the sheet of plywood, Teddy reached slowly into his breast pocket and brought out Dominic Scarlotti's gold cigarette case/tape recorder. He had the satisfaction of hearing Anthony say, "Motherfucker," and hearing Izzy and Tommy take quick, deep breaths. He knew they must all be feeling like idiots because apparently they had seen the thing before and not given it a moment's thought.

Teddy said, "That's right," mostly for effect, "everybody makes a boo-boo now and then."

He put the cigarette case down on the plywood, feeling three pairs of eyes following his every move, pushed the tiny lever that was supposed to be used only to open the thing, and watched the way the three men leaned forward to listen to what must have felt like the voice of a ghost.

The tinny sound of somebody moving, grunting, cloth being pulled, came out of the case and then, as clear as a bell, Dominic Scarlotti was saying, "You mind if I keep this, or are you afraid I'm gonna beat you to death with it?"

On the other side of the plywood table, Izzy closed and opened his eyes slowly. Anthony said, "Jesus." And Tommy said, "Fuck." Anthony looked like he might say something else. Or even reach out and grab the recorder but he was stopped by the sound of Izzy's voice saying, "No, go ahead," from the recorder.

Teddy shut the thing off. "I gotta say, technologically? I'm impressed. I thought this kind of thing was all James Bond bullshit. But these days?"—pointing at the cigarette case—"Nothing surprises me."

Tommy Inzarella was gazing down at the plywood, concentrating, Izzy was looking at Teddy, his composure still in place, and Anthony was bug-eyed, staring at the cigarette case like it was alive.

"Wait, there's more." Teddy said. He had to rewind the recorder three times before he got it right, hit the Play button, and suddenly a new voice came through. Teddy played it for only two seconds, just long enough for the three other men to get confused expressions on their faces, and then he shut off the tape recorder to say, "What you're hearing now is the voice of a federal prosecutor. Donald Shaffer. He's talking to—at, actually—Dominic Scarlotti. As you'll hear, none too respectfully. My point, the reason I'm playing around, rewinding and everything, I want everyone to have a clear understanding of what I have. I hate to put it this way—but I can't think of any other way to say it—I just want to point out how *valuable* this thing is. But, hey, listen for yourself. You decide." He turned the recorder on again and Donald Shaffer's voice said, "Listen carefully, you greaseball pig. This agreement depends *entirely* on how much you fucking cooperate. That, and on whether *I* decide to let it happen."

Teddy stopped the recorder and said to Izzy, "Mr. Shaffer could use a lesson in manners. But, whatever, the way I figure it, just from listening, this prosecutor feels like he had Scarlotti by the balls. I suppose he was thinking, why worry about manners at a time like that?" Teddy turned to look at

Anthony and Tommy. "The way I see it playing out, Dominic must've made some kind of stop on the way over."

Izzy turned, stared at Anthony and once again blinked slowly. It made Teddy want to take him aside, for the hell of it, and ask him how he did it. Hell, just ask him to remember back to the last time he'd shown *any* kind of spontaneous emotion.

Anthony held his hand out. "Gimme the fucking thing." Waiting all of two seconds to say, louder, "You fuck. Give me the goddamned cigarette case," looking like he was going to come around the table.

Teddy made himself smile, trying to let Anthony know that at least someone was enjoying himself. He held up the recorder and said, "You have to wait. It gets better." He pushed the lever on the cigarette case and counted to three, hearing the tiny tape whizzing forward in his hand. Then he pushed the lever in the other direction so it would play again.

Anthony's voice came out at them one more time. There was what seemed like chair legs scraping on a rough floor and then Anthony's voice said, "Hey, Dom, come on, have a seat. We get this thing squared away in a fucking jiffy."

There was one full second of silence and then Izzy's voice, unmistakable, said, harshly, "Enough is enough." It was followed by a sharp bang, the sound coming out of the recorder like it was a phone book being slammed down on a wooden table. Teddy shut the recorder off and said into the silence. "I don't suppose anyone here wants to tell me that was a car down the street having a blowout."

When no one answered, Teddy did the only thing he could think of. He reached out, grabbed the two gym bags, his pistol and held the cigarette case up in the air. He looked at the other three men one by one and said slowly, "I know, I know, this is going to sound like I'm a half-assed bank robber. But nobody moves until I'm out the door." He lifted the cigarette case higher. "I'll put this somewhere right near the front steps. But not in plain sight. So, instead of wasting your time looking for me, I suggest you look for *it*."

He started to back up, trying to watch Izzy, Tommy and Anthony at the same time. He was almost there, reaching behind him and feeling the door handle, when Anthony said, "Fuck this bullshit," and reached under the sheet of plywood. There was a tearing sound and a second later Teddy was staring at the barrel of a pistol that still had a piece of duct tape stuck to it.

He froze. Watched Anthony get a gleam in his eye and then had to stand there, holding onto two bags that contained a million dollars, and listen to Anthony start to laugh.

Izzy was still motionless except that he had swung his head back from looking at Teddy and was now staring at Anthony. There was no expression on his face. Tommy was looking from the gun, to Anthony and then to Teddy.

Anthony said, "Why don't you do this, you prick. Why don't you bring the bags—both of the fucking things—back over to the table. Put your piece back and bring the motherfucking cigarette case too because I don't feel like playing hide-and-seek out in those fucking bushes or wherever. You know what I mean?" Anthony laughed again and said, "Hey, I got an idea. If we got time, you can get down on your knees, beg for your life or do whatever else comes to mind." Anthony cocked the pistol and screamed, *"Now, asshole!"*

Teddy walked back to the plywood table, dropped his gun on it and slowly lowered the bags. Then just as slowly, he placed the gold cigarette case on the same surface and watched as Anthony leaned forward, still pointing the pistol, and grabbed the thing like a bratty kid grabbing his ball and going home because the other kids at the playground weren't playing fair.

He fiddled with the lever but couldn't get it to work. After a moment he said, "Fuck it." He looked at Teddy and said, "But no fucking problem. *I* got the rest of my life to figure it out. Which is more than you got."

Teddy watched the gun barrel move so that it was pointed at his face. He tried to imagine what it would feel like. The bullet coming in, smashing his teeth and then taking the back of his head off. Would he feel any pain?

He tried looking at Anthony's eyes to see if there was anything there. Any hesitation. There wasn't. There was only a dark-brown gleam that Teddy thought hadn't been quite that intense a moment ago. Something else too. Something—shit—something sexual. Some kind of pleasure that Anthony was getting—maybe got—every time he killed somebody. Teddy could see Anthony's finger, whitening on the trigger. And the trigger itself, moving a tiny bit every millisecond, getting closer.

And then Teddy couldn't help himself. He lost his nerve. Closed his eyes because, when it came right down to it, he didn't want to watch the tricks his mind was playing on him, the barrel now seeming to be large enough for a Stinger missile to come out of it. So he closed his eyes. Stopped breathing, too. What was the point? And kept his eyes clamped shut for the whole rest of the time it took Anthony to pull the trigger.

Which was kind of a drag because he really—*really*—would've liked to see the first faint look of surprise on Anthony's face when the hammer fell and the only thing that came out was a distinct click.

TEDDY DID open his eyes in time to see Anthony pull the trigger five more times though. Anthony did it faster than Teddy had ever seen anyone do anything. Speedy Gonzalez. Anthony looking like *some* kind of cartoon character, almost fanning his guns now, with nothing happening. Elmer Fudd banging away at Bugs Bunny, Bugs chewing a carrot, one arm leaning against a tree, looking at his audience because they were in on the joke. Maybe Teddy should walk over and tie the barrel of Anthony's gun in a knot.

Every time Anthony pulled it his face changed, as if he were feeling physical pain, getting a tooth drilled without the Novocain. Moving toward a mixture of complete confusion and rage. He pulled the gun back to look at it as if *willing* it to fire.

"Fuck!" Anthony pointed the gun at Teddy again and pulled the trigger one more time. But he didn't get anything more than he had before. A loud click, which was muffled only by the slight noise Tommy Inzarella made as he took one step toward the plywood sheet, picked up his own gun and held it loosely in his hand.

Anthony grabbed at Tommy's gun, but Tommy moved softly out of reach without seeming to know he was doing it. Anthony yelled, "Shoot the motherfucker! Give me the fucking thing and *I'll* shoot him!"

Tommy stared at him as if he hadn't quite heard. He looked even more calm than Teddy had ever seen him. Holding on to the pistol and slowly bringing it up, slowly swinging his head to watch Anthony. Glancing just one time at Izzy, waiting for a brief moment until he shrugged, a silent message going between the two men that Teddy was fairly sure Anthony didn't even see because he still wasn't up to speed yet.

Teddy was stuck where he was, way too far away from the table to go for his own pistol, way too far away from the door to make a break for it. He had to stand there, the idea in his head that he *thought* he knew what was about to happen. But it wasn't as though he had any certainty.

Tommy rested his gaze on Teddy for an instant, as if he knew exactly what had just gone through Teddy's head. Still not giving anything up as to how this thing was really going to play. Sure, so far everything okay, but there weren't any referees around. No one to throw a flag, wave his arms in a circular motion in front of his chest and charge anyone a five-yard penalty for illegal procedure, still first down but now fifteen yards to go before they moved the chains.

And then Tommy looked back at Anthony, turning to face him squarely, while Anthony *finally* seemed to get his first clue as to what was going on. The look on his face—the rage—was changing. Moving through a flash of disbelief to recognition. Seeing something in Tommy that he, Anthony, had probably given to at least a couple of dozen other guys in his lifetime. A last-time-before-you-die look.

He gave it a try though. Teddy had to admit that. Anthony stared right back at Tommy and said, "Hey, Tommy, c'mon. What are you thinking? Motherfucker. We work whatever you got in your head—you're having a problem—we work it out. Hey, seriously, you whack this asshole"—pointing at Teddy and then turning to Izzy—"and take the Jew out too. Whatever grievances you have, you and I discuss them."

Tommy said, "I got nothing to discuss, Anthony."

Anthony raised his voice. "Jesus fucking Christ. You been listening to someone"—jerking a finger at Teddy and then at Izzy—"one of these assholes? They been filling your head with a bunch of bullshit. No one here can do for you what I can. You got to think this shit through, this action you're taking." He looked closely at Tommy, maybe expecting Tommy's expression to change—he'd start grinning, laughing, any second, tell Anthony, Hey, gotcha. They could laugh more about it after Tommy wasted Teddy and Izzy.

But Tommy's expression didn't change. And finally Anthony realized that what he was seeing was real. He roared, "You treacherous motherfucker. You treach-er-*ous mother*—" but clamped his mouth shut as Tommy raised the pistol so that it was pointed at Anthony's nose, shut up midsentence because Tommy did it that calmly, like he was waving a bug away from his face.

"Izzy's right. You do talk too fucking much, Anthony."

Anthony screamed, "You prick—" rushing at Tommy, clawing at the air he wanted to get to him that badly. A half a second later a bullet smacked into his chest. Teddy, watching, was thinking, what—thousands of feet a second? The force of a fucking charging elephant. Seeing Anthony blown off his feet and punched backward as the *boom* of the gun bounced around the tiny restaurant and through Teddy's head loudly enough that he knew he was going to have trouble hearing for the next couple of hours.

There was dead silence afterwards. A crazy old joke went through Teddy's head just like that, out of nowhere, one guy says, I'm losing my hearing and his friend says, What? A thing he used to do to Davey when they were kids. The joke coming around for a second, lingering just that long and then forgotten, as Anthony landed in a heap and the three men stood where they were, staring at the corpse and breathing in the smoke and cordite from Tommy's gun.

And then Tommy turned to Teddy, not lowering the gun much. "So, sport, what are we gonna do?" He pointed at the gym bags and then at the gold cigarette case. "You think you can get away with this? You think, just because I agreed to go along with my end of your little plan—you think I'm gonna let you walk away with a half million dollars of what is now my fucking money?"

Teddy thought, here it was, the part he knew they'd get to if everything else he'd suggested to Saul Rubin worked out. Showing him what was in the little box first and then telling them what he thought might be a good idea; Izzy listening carefully, Saul asking Teddy in that polite, old-man way, would he mind waiting in the front hall for a few moments while he and Izzy discussed Teddy's proposal. Teddy looking at a Rembrandt near the front door, not even thinking it was real until he realized, Why not? Saul wasn't the kind of guy to put a print of the thing up. The whole house looking like it was a place they ought to sell tickets to. And then the creak of the big door, Izzy stepping out, leading Teddy back in so that Saul could tell him that, Yes, they could certainly see the merits of Teddy's idea. As a matter of fact—Saul's own words—Mr. Anthony Bonica had rapidly become a person that Saul had no more desire to spend time with or conduct any monetary or business transactions with, now or ever in the future. Then Izzy telling Teddy not to worry, he'd give Tommy Inzarella a call, talk to him privately, everything would work out and all their problems, mutually, would be solved once and for all.

At the time, Teddy had been relieved, seen it in as positive a light as he could. A few guys, for a lark, or to increase their luck, go in on a lottery ticket—a three-way split—bowling buddies. Everybody joking around about what kind of yacht they were gonna buy until, bingo, the fucking thing turned up a winner. Suddenly you have best friends plotting murder, wanting it all.

Teddy said, "Tell you the truth, Tommy, I think you *are* gonna let me. Number one, how do you know I don't have a copy? It's not like I'll ever use it if I don't have to. But you have to wonder. Plus, you're not going to ever hear me bragging about how I got one over on you. You know me and you *know* that's not what this is about." He pointed at where Anthony lay dead on the floor. "If you ask me, was there ever a time when I respected that man, then I'd say no. But you? Yeah, I haven't seen you do anything—all the years I knew you—that I didn't at least understand was a matter of business. You got a good future in front of you. Why bother doing something to me that doesn't need to be done?"

Tommy Inzarella seemed to think about it for a long time. Then he nodded. "I tried to tell Anthony he was underestimating you. But Anthony was too full of himself and wouldn't listen." Then Tommy frowned. "But I gotta tell you, I walk outta here, I don't want you to believe that it'd be all right if you show up at Palisades or anywhere else where you might run the chance of bumping into me. Your best bet—I were you—get on an airplane and get out of town." He shrugged his shoulders. "I'm not looking at it, am I *threatening* you. I'm just thinking, I see *too* much of your face, I might end up regretting this decision.

"I don't see it as a threat either. I can understand your point of view." Teddy said, "So I'm gone. Believe me, I'm gone."

Tommy reached across the plywood table one more time. He stared at the gold cigarette case and then looked at Izzy. "I believe the deal was you get to keep this."

Izzy picked up the cigarette case and looked at it. Then he put it back, reached into his jacket pocket and pulled out the miniature cassette recorder he had shown Saul days before. "Tell you the truth, Mr. Inzarella, you can keep it. Appears I have one of my own."

Tommy stared hard at Izzy and for the first time Teddy could remember, actually grinned. "Jesus. All this time?"

Izzy pointed at Dominic's cigarette case. "That was just a loose end."

"Fuck me." Tommy seemed more impressed than anything else. He picked up the gold case, hesitated and then grabbed Davey's Beretta, turning to Teddy to say, "I think, what I'll do, I'll keep this thing. Call it a souvenir."

Looking Teddy in the eye and saying, softly, "You mind?" as if he would give it back if Teddy said he did.

Teddy shrugged. "You can think of it as a gift."

Tommy looked hard at Teddy like he was trying to be sure he wasn't being mocked. Then he laughed. He smoothed the material of his jacket, touched his hair. "Well, maybe you two gentleman have some things to discuss. I don't know. Make it quick, though, because I got a crew coming in an hour, clean this place up and take care of Anthony." He moved toward the door. "Me? I have a girl waiting for me. Woman name of Vicki, dances at the club."

"I know which one."

"Yeah? Well, tonight, this little whore? I'm gonna convince her silly little ass to change her ways. Become a devout heterosexual." He smiled one more time before opening the door and said, "Leastways, I'm gonna give it a fucking try." He pointed at where Anthony lay dead on the floor. "Used to fool the hell out of that idiot. Not me, though. So, if it doesn't work out I'm gonna fire her ass. Fuck her brains out first, though."

And then he was gone.

IZZY FELDMAN said, "So, Mr. Clyde, how does it feel to be rich?"

Teddy said, "I don't know. I told myself, first thing I was going to do, coming in here, I was going to take a close look at the money. Beforehand, I mean. I forgot to, though, what with all the tension. Now I'm wondering, am I dealing with a lot of cut-up newspapers? I mean, underneath the show-me wad Anthony put on top."

Izzy dumped the contents of the bag he'd carried in on the plywood sheet, and Teddy found himself staring at stack after stack of new-looking hundred-dollar bills.

Izzy smiled. "Why don't we see how Mr. Bonica did, shall we?" He upended the gym bag that Tommy Inzarella had left and more stacks of hundreds spilled out.

Izzy said, "Well, hey, that's one worry down. It looks like you *are* going to be a rich man. Welcome to a brave new world, Mr. Clyde." And then he reached into his jacket and pulled out a cell phone. "You mind if I make a phone call?"

"What are you going to do?" Teddy said, "Ruin my day?"

"No, I just want to make a phone call." Izzy punched in a number, listened to it ring and said to Teddy, "Actually, this might interest you."

Teddy felt the hairs on the back of his neck go up a little bit and a thin sheen of sweat start to form under his armpits. He was seeing something here. Izzy's eyes going flat while he held the phone up to his ear and then said, finally, into the phone, "Joseph. How are you? Yes it definitely *is* me. I'll say the word we agreed upon. *Mosque.*" Izzy waited. "Good. Now, I wonder if you might put the woman on the line. Tell her Mr. Clyde wishes to speak to her."

Teddy said, softly, "You prick."

Izzy handed the phone to Teddy carefully and said, "Please, Mr. Clyde, don't take this personally. All this is, a friend of yours seems to be in a bit of a bind. She'd like to talk to you about it."

And then Teddy was listening to Natalie go on about how she'd like to kill some son of a bitch, a guy named Joseph, who was holding her in her apartment, and was some kind of pervert who wanted to watch her go to the bathroom. Her voice kept rising and going soft as she tried to remember all the details of what she'd been through for the last hour and a half and then got louder and louder as she told Teddy how much she'd like to get even.

Finally she took a deep breath and said, "Shit." Another breath, "I made a mistake, didn't check the peephole because I was hoping it was going to be you. Apparently these guys have a thing about making themselves at home in other people's apartments."

Teddy felt himself getting hot. Physically. As if he had a sudden fever. All of the things he'd been put through the past couple of days were racing through his mind. Finding Dominic Scarlotti's body in his trunk. Losing

Davey. Having to deal with people like Anthony Bonica, Itzhak Feldman and Saul Rubin. He realized that he was getting kind of tired of it. All of it.

He said to Natalie, talking slowly into the phone, "I know, it's infuriating. I know." Then he looked up at Izzy. He did not seem to be getting a kick out of this the way Anthony Bonica would have. He told Natalie, "But, the truth? We're almost out of the woods."

"Yeah? I got a guy here, he looks likes he's a member of the Taliban. Got the beard for it. Every time I take a deep breath he points a pistol at me. You want to tell me—explain it to me so I can believe it—how close we are to being *out* of the woods?"

Teddy asked her, "Do you remember what you took from your father?" He said, "Don't say anything except yes or no. Do you remember? And, also, where it is?"

Her voice came back, mad as hell but scared too. "Yes, I remember. If I could go get it I would."

Teddy said, "Well, that's about to stop." He saw Izzy change his expression slightly—a little confusion creeping in there. Maybe Izzy had expected Teddy to panic. Or maybe he thought things were going as planned—that Teddy was going to get Natalie out of the woods by agreeing to whatever Izzy said.

Right now Teddy didn't give a shit what Izzy thought.

"Natalie, I want you to answer me one question. That article you wrote, the one where you took that *thing* from your father—the same thing that's in the closet? Remember the reason you got it in the first place? And the guy's name? That main guy, the head of the group. Just tell me if you remember his name?"

He was watching Izzy carefully. Sure of it now, concern coming over Izzy's face because he didn't know what Teddy was talking about. Izzy leaned forward as if he were going to take a step in Teddy's direction, but Teddy moved backward and Izzy stopped.

Natalie was saying, "I remember."

"Good." Teddy said, "Because, what I'm going to do is this: First of all, in a minute, Joseph is going to leave."

Izzy said, abruptly, "Give me the phone, Mr. Clyde."

Teddy cupped the phone and said, "Izzy, c'mon, after all we've been through, don't you think it's time you started to call me Teddy *all* the time?" He lifted the phone to his face again, shook his head and held up his index finger to Izzy as if he were politely telling a stranger at a public phone booth to hang in there, he'd be off in a minute. And then he went back to talking to Natalie. "Nat, when this Joseph fellow *does* leave, I want you to get that thing in your bedroom. Then I want you to sit on a chair facing the door and if anybody knocks—even *me*—without first saying that gentleman's name—the one you just said you remember—and I mean im*med*iately after the knock— I want you to blow that door off its hinges. Okay? No matter what you hear on this end. Promise?"

"I promise. Are you going to be okay?"

"I'm going to be fine. Now I want you to put Joseph on. I think he and Izzy have some things to discuss."

Teddy held the phone toward Izzy but then dropped it just as Izzy's fingers were an inch away. Izzy instinctively bent down and picked it up and Teddy took a step back, yanked the sleeve of his jacket up, tore away at the Scotch tape he'd wrapped there earlier, and had Davey-Boy's two-shot, couldn't-hit-a-barn-door, .45 caliber derringer out and pointed at Izzy's head from a foot away before Izzy had even gotten halfway back to eye level.

"Your pistol's right over there," Teddy said, pointing to the plywood table behind him, "I can only shoot you twice by the time you get there. I might even miss once. But, I have to tell you, I don't know *all* that much about guns but lately I've been learning more." He pushed the derringer closer to Izzy's head. "But I do know—this thing? It's not a twenty-two and it sure as shit is not a BB gun. Between you and me, the bullets in this thing are huge. Seriously, they're something to see. This close? I don't see *how* I could miss. But hey, you double-crossing fuck, if you want to give it a try—?" Teddy lifted his other hand—palm up—and acted as if he had seen stranger things in his life. "It's up to you."

Izzy didn't move. Teddy grinned. "I didn't think so." He pointed at the phone in Izzy's hand and said, "Now, what you can do, you can tell your buddy—what's his name, Joseph? Tell Joseph to get the *fuck* out of my girl-friend's apartment. Let her go pee in private."

Izzy seemed to pause, as if he were thinking of making some kind of move. Teddy took a half step toward him. "You're not used to coming out on this side of things. The losing side. Letting the Palestinians bomb a café without sending in an air strike afterward. Letting someone insult Saul Rubin without telling that goddamn dog of Saul's to tear them apart. This whole situation must be getting on your nerves. You're telling yourself, *Do something*. Well, whatever it is, forget about it. You don't want to do any-thing except tell your buddy, Joseph, to hit the road. I'm not a violent man, but I hear anything else, you motherfucker, and I swear to fucking God I'll personally carry your corpse into Saul Rubin's house. Dump it onto his lap and watch the old fuck die of grief and a stroke. And if he *doesn't* die? I'll shoot *his* sorry ass too."

Five seconds later Izzy told Joseph to call it a night.

17

GEORGE ABBOT was on an elevator at 615 Chestnut Street—the U.S. attorney general's office. There were four other people on the elevator with him and he knew, without even bothering to look, that they were all staring at him. He didn't give a shit. He was having a great day. Whistling. A grin plastered on his face as big as he'd had the first time he had ever gotten laid. He had gotten fucked all those years ago, smiled like an idiot and hadn't cared? All those times in between, two wives, hookers, pickups in bars—none of them quite equaling his first time? Well, George was finally, once again, about to do some serious first-time fucking.

The elevator door opened and George got out—still whistling—and started down the hall toward Donald Shaffer's office. Savoring every second. Slowing his pace to make each step count.

And then he stopped altogether. Had to. Had to reach inside his breast pocket and pull out the typed piece of paper that had been delivered to him by a messenger service just this morning along with the shoe box he was carrying in his right arm, cradled the way a running back would hold a football—protecting it—so that it wouldn't get stripped by the strong safety coming up on his blind side.

George had already read the typewritten note six times—the first time with disbelief, all the rest of the times with glee. He knew every word by heart but he took this last opportunity to skim it, letting certain names and words stand out in his head.

Dominic Scarlotti
Anthony Bonica
Itzhak Feldman
Saul Rubin
Tommy Inzarella
renovated restaurant
Jericho nine-millimeter
Veterans Stadium
Pier 25 N—medium-sized freighter/Arabic captain

Christ, his boy had done his homework. Gone to a lot of trouble to get enough proof together that George Abbot had the idea that tying the whole case up was going to be a lot easier than it had been to find a girl who was willing to screw him back when he was fifteen and had so many goddamn pimples it was hard to keep track of them.

A janitor was coming down the hall. Wheeling a huge trashcan into which he was dumping the contents of all the smaller trashcans. George walked over and said, "Hey, nice day, huh?" getting a look from the janitor like he was either crazy or a terrorist because it was probably the first time that any-one in the building had said a word to him.

George looked at his big trashcan and said, like he was a complete idiot, "So what, this stuff, you take it all downstairs in the basement? Burn it up?"

The janitor said, warily, "That's right. There a problem?" The guy was black, old enough to sense that he was going to get hassled. A man going about his business and not wanting to talk to this white hard-on even a little bit.

George smiled and said, "Hey, I was just curious. That's all." He crumpled up the piece of typewritten paper and then he tossed it into the janitor's large trashcan from five feet away. "Michael Jordan, huh?"

The janitor looked like he wanted to tell George to go fuck himself.

George didn't care. He had made the shot, fair and square. Didn't matter who thought what about it. Nothing mattered today. He started to walk toward Donald Shaffer's office again. Halfway there, he remembered to whistle again.

INSIDE SHAFFER'S OFFICE things seemed to be the same as they always were at the daily three-o'clock meeting. Shaffer, a serious look on his face—the heavy-duty job of running a ship of fools there in his expression for everyone to see. George wondered, did it come naturally or did Shaffer have to spend time in front of the mirror?

The two FBI agents, standing off to the side, one of them with his hand on his hip so that his jacket looped back to expose a pistol in a holster. The two Philly detectives from the Organized Crime Task Force looked like they were conspiring to shoot Shaffer. James Lacombe glared at George as if he hated him.

George snapped a salute at him and said, "Hey, sport"—grinning politely—"nice suit."

Lacombe said, "Go fuck yourself."

It turned all the eyes in the room in George's direction, though. Donald Shaffer taking a dramatically long time to come out of his thoughts, turn slowly and glare at George as if he were a speck of dandruff.

Shaffer waited another couple of seconds. "Well, well, well—look what the fucking cat dragged in. What a pleasure, Marshal. To what do we owe this—this honor? Why"—he spread his hands wide to include the whole room—"we all thought you might have gone ahead and retired."

George took his time about it, walking slowly up to Shaffer. Let Shaffer have the impression that he *was* about to retire. Or he was someone—better yet—who was going to walk up to Shaffer, drop to his knees and beg Shaffer not to fuck with his pension as he had threatened to do just three days before.

But at the last minute, he simply opened the shoe box and extracted a smaller box—black-laquered wood—and held it out long enough so that Shaffer had no option but to scowl and take it. Shaffer looked at the box suspiciously, back at George and than to the box. George thought it was occurring to him that it might be packed with C-4 explosive.

"C'mon, Donny, open it"

Shaffer snapped, "I'm not 'Donny' to you and never will be."

"Sure. I understand—Donny." George pointed at the box. "I just want you to know I think you'll be pleased to see I've finally achieved some results. The thing about Scarlotti slipping through our hands."

Shaffer seemed to be frozen, uncertain all of a sudden what to do next. So George leaned forward—their heads were only inches apart now—and said, loudly enough for everyone in the room to hear, "C'mon, you pussy, open the goddamn box. There's a message in there for you."

Shaffer slowly lifted the lid of the box that Teddy Clyde had messengered to George just three hours before. He glanced once at George while the lid was only halfway off but then seemed to make up his mind, yanking the top of the thing off, trying hard to let everybody in the room understand that no two-bit, almost retired asshole of a federal marshal could get the better of him.

George had to admit that Shaffer almost pulled it off. He had a serious, I'm-going-to-ream-somebody-out look on his face that stayed where it was until he got his first peek at what was inside the box. But then his face went from its normal, private-prep-school-through-Ivy-League-through-Villanova-Law ruddy-cheeked pallor to pure white. His upper lip started to tremble, and a sheen of sweat popped out along his forehead.

George let Shaffer sweat for another ten seconds—Shaffer seemingly unable to speak—and then said, just as all the other men in the room were getting their first good look at what was in the box, "In case you were thinking about anything *other* then puking, then, yes, I did some checking. It *does* belong to who you think it does. Our Mr. Dominic Scarlotti."

Shaffer tore his eyes off what was in the box long enough to glance at George. George winked and then pulled Teddy's mini-cassette recorder out of his breast pocket. He said, "The same folks—and bear in mind, I have *no* clue who they are"—he flashed back on Teddy Clyde, asking him who his boss was and he almost laughed out loud—"sent me this recorder. I already took the liberty of listening to it. And—even though, unfortunately, a fingerprint check came up negative—believe me"—George put his face close to Shaffer's again—"I'll stake my eighteen years in law enforcement against the time you spent sucking on your mama's tit that this recording is taken directly off the cigarette-case recorder you so graciously provided to Mr. Scarlotti the night he got whacked."

Shaffer stared at the mini-cassette and then lowered his eyes to peek one more time into the box he was holding. To George it seemed as if Shaffer was seeing the thing for the first time even though it wasn't something anybody could overlook if they had even glimpsed it for a second.

George played the mini-cassette just long enough to hear Izzy Feldman's voice say, "Enough is enough." And for the flat, tinny sound of a bang to fill the room and jolt every other man in the office into instinctively reaching for their guns.

George laughed. "Hey, it's a fucking recording. Don't shit your pants."

Donald Shaffer was busy trying to hand the box back to George as fast as he possibly could.

"Hey, no, no thank you. I already saw it. It's yours." He took a step back from Shaffer—a parent looking at a child with concern. "Hey, you know something, *Donny*, you don't so good."

George could picture what was going on in Shaffer's head. A dilemma. If he tried to make it to the bathroom, he probably wouldn't. It was out the door, down the hall and it was kept locked at all times. Shaffer had a key, but George didn't think his hands were steady enough to unlock the thing in time. If he tried to open a window he'd find out that, not only were they sealed shut, even if he did somehow get one open he'd being raining puke down on people hundreds of feet below—be bound to draw *somebody's* attention. George thought, What's a poor boy to do, as Shaffer finally looked down at his own desk, at the trashcan that was next to it. Shaffer suddenly dove for it.

George said into the stunned silence that followed, "Hey, Donny, you mind if I use your computer? Appears I got to write up a couple of affidavits for some search warrants." He looked at Shaffer, who was concentrating on holding on to the trashcan and pulling wildly to loosen his tie. "Never mind, you go ahead with what you have to do."

When Shaffer did begin to puke, the sound made everyone else in the room turn away and groan. A couple of them started to laugh.

George did neither. He flipped Shaffer's computer on and spent the time—while it was warming up and the arrogant prick of an assistant United States attorney threw his guts up on the floor a few feet away—looking down at what had now fallen completely out of the wooden box and lay on the floor. Everyone else in the room could see what it was and the laughter that had started a moment ago stopped abruptly.

Yep, there was no doubt about it. The ring on the pinkie was Dominic Scarlotti's. And George had to give Teddy Clyde credit—even though the spot where the hand had been severed from the wrist looked like something out of a Frankenstein movie and the thing was beginning to smell god-awful—folding all the fingers into a fist except for the middle one?

It was a nice touch.

18

THE MARRIOTT Grand Cayman had a stretch of beach that was as long as the hotel was wide and about twenty feet deep. There weren't any tides or currents to speak of, just crystal-clear azure water. But you had to wear flip-flops or sandals because the beach was made up of pebbles and ground-up dead coral. Besides being very hot, it tore at your feet. There were larger pieces of coral, loose, cinder block size, in the water once you got above your knees. They made wading difficult and, farther out, a hundred feet from shore, a tiny reef, the size of a couple of semi trucks, the top of it jutting to a multicolored point just below the level of the water and contrasting nicely against the blue of the Caribbean sea. Skin divers paddled around it, their flippers, blue, red, black or mixed, resembling the tail fins of exotic fish, their snorkels like miniature submarine periscopes. Teddy had been out there the day before. The reef wasn't much, some live coral on top of a larger mass of dead coral, the stuff almost falling apart in your hands if you touched it, a few parrot fish, angels, sergeant majors and one small grouper all swimming lazily around as if they wished they were somewhere else. Sea urchins everywhere, like tiny seawater porcupines, and some wild-looking, slug type of thing that Teddy later learned was called a sea cucumber.

Every few days they'd go visit some local touristy place. The Stingray Farm, a place on a reef that you traveled to on a boat and then got out in waist-deep water to feed and actually touch the big eagle rays and stingrays that were so used to humans they probably wouldn't know what to do if folks stopped coming. They'd gone to the Iguana Refuge, the place alive with parrots and lush trees and almost hadn't seen those smaller versions of Jurassic Park because you could walk right up to one—the thing so immobile and so well camouflaged that you didn't know it was there unless it blinked or suddenly scrambled for the bushes, scaring the hell out of Natalie and Teddy, but then making them laugh with delight.

They'd spent a fair amount of time in the capital, Georgetown. The Switzerland of the Western Hemisphere, Natalie shopping while Teddy scouted the banks, recognizing names, Girard, Citicorp, Mellon—setting up a series of numbered accounts for when he was ready to funnel the rest of the money down here, keep from paying Uncle Sam anything because, seriously, where had Sam been when Anthony Bonica had been pulling the trigger of that gun—never mind that it had been empty.

Natalie bought about as many duty-free items as she could carry, some of them for her but enough of them for Teddy so that they had a good time looking at them back at their hotel room.

But mostly they hung out near the hotel on Seven Mile Beach, enjoying the sun, the sound of the small waves and the sight of the gulls fighting like mad over any scrap of food they could find. Roasting themselves until they began to look like they lived there all year round. They were feeling good, saying exactly that every once in a while, "You feel it?" The other one nodding. "Yeah, I do." Neither having to ask, What? because they both knew they were talking about their relationship. Three and a half weeks into it now—kissing each other every time they sat down for a meal or just for the hell of it, out of the blue. It seemed as though they'd known each other—in a good way—forever.

———

TEDDY HAD STARTED to put sunblock, SPF 45, on Natalie's back a full two minutes ago, taking his time about it because her skin felt that good under his hand. She was lying on her stomach, the top strap of her bikini unsnapped, and he had been forced to drape a towel over the front of his bathing suit to hide what was happening there—the reaction he was getting just by putting the oil on her skin. Every once in a while, if he got the chance, he'd slide his fingers a tiny bit down the side of her chest, under her armpit, and touch the side of her breasts.

Each time, she sighed elaborately. "You want to cut that out?" When he finally did run out of lotion she looked up, grinned and said, "Well, *now* what? The other half of my body fries while you sit back in your chair, have a cigarette and tell me what a good time we just had?"

He said, "I have no idea what you're talking about."

"No? Well I dare you to stand up." A smile lit up her face as she said it.

He smiled back at her and rearranged himself on his beach chair. He'd been reading *Time* magazine, and now he went back to it as she resnapped her top, stood up, rummaged through a large green-and-white canvas bag on the spare chair and then looked up at the hotel.

She said, "Damnit."

Teddy marked his place and put his magazine down. "What?"

"I thought I had more. Sunscreen, I mean." Giving him a look. "Just in case *somebody* got carried away with it." She looked up at the hotel. "I'll be back."

"You want me to go?"

"No, that's all right. I have to pee anyway. You want anything?"

"No. I'll get us something to drink. Maybe have a quick one first before you get back." He reached back to where his spare towel lay rolled into a tube, pulling it apart and bringing out a bottle of sun oil. "Or hey, you can use mine."

"No, thanks. It smells like coconuts and, plus which, what is it? Level four? No, see, I'm not actually looking forward to getting skin cancer."

Teddy said, "Can I tell you something? Growing up—"

"I know, I know. Growing up, all you had was Coppertone or baby oil. You were a deprived child. I think we've had this conversation before. Actually, I think it was this morning." She slid her sandals on. "I'll be right back."

Teddy watched her butt as she walked up the beach to the hotel. He saw two more guys, one of whom he would've sworn was asleep ten seconds before, prop themselves up on their elbows and watch as she walked past. Teddy couldn't blame them. He was thinking, If he wasn't *already* sleeping with her he certainly would want to sleep with her.

A minute later he caught the attention of a hotel waiter whose job was to wander the beach and make sure none of the guests died of thirst. The waiter's name was Henri, pronounced "on-*ree*." He kept a pleasant smile on his face no matter how dumb the questions got, and Teddy had made a point of doubling up on the tip from the very first day so Henri would keep an eye out for them and serve them first if he had to make a quick, competitive decision. Teddy told Henri that a margarita and a Heineken would be swell, and then he grabbed his *Time* magazine, stood up and looked in Natalie's beach bag. The first thing he saw, sitting right there between a tube of lipstick and a copy of *Vogue*, was a tube of sunscreen, SPF 45. He picked it up, looked at what the ingredients were, got scared and then put it back exactly where it had been.

HE WALKED past the Marriott's swimming pool and up a flight of six steps to a second level, which continued underneath an alcove and ended at an outdoor bar. It was ten degrees cooler here than down on the beach. A cute blond girl who looked to be all of eighteen years old, wearing ripped blue jean shorts and a tank top with a seaside print on it, was shaking a martini pitcher as four sunburned guys watched every move she made. She smiled and waved at Teddy as he went past. She'd been smiling at him every day now for almost three weeks, but he knew it didn't mean much. She was one of three blond bartenders who worked the bar, and their looks made him believe the Marriott had made a worldwide search; they could've been triplets. Hip-looking, California good looks, fashion-model smiles. All with the same-length blond hair that actually looked like it was the real thing and a snappy way of talking without ever saying anything. Teddy had told Natalie that, secretly, he thought they switched name tags every once in a while as an inside joke.

Natalie must not have heard him correctly because she said, giving him a funny look, "And *when* was it you had so much time to study the problem?"

There was a courtyard between the bar and the hotel itself and another bar inside where the dress was more formal. The hotel restaurant was farther in. Between the two was a Steinway grand piano where a guy named Steven stopped by every day at cocktail hour and banged out show tunes like he'd rather be playing Rachmaninoff. The courtyard had a fountain at one end, a waterfall just after that which bubbled nicely and emptied into a stream that snaked back and forth under two bridges to disappear into a tunnel on the opposite side of the outdoor bar where an electric pump shot the whole thing back underground to begin all over again. There were several small pools placed along the stream surrounded by lush tropical plants and soft low-wattage track lights. Schools of koi swam lazily through the water with no worries except staying out of range of several large turtles that also lived in the water.

Teddy stopped before he got to the rear entrance of the hotel and spent several minutes counting the fish. There was a large softshell turtle nearby, alien-looking, motionless, and Teddy wanted to see if it was going to take a shot. Go for one of the koi. The thing looked big enough; Teddy had seen them before, in the Everglades. Knew they had necks on them like a snake, one minute close to their heads, the next, extended six inches out, mouth wide open, looking for something to bite.

When he saw Natalie step out of the elevator just inside the entrance of the hotel he looked in the opposite direction, past the cute bartender and back toward the ocean.

If Natalie came back through the door, straight, and walked fifty feet, she would bump into him and he'd take her hand, walk her back to the beach and they could have their drinks. Or they could stay right here and place bets on how long the turtle could stay underwater without coming up for air.

Instead she turned left, walking away, purposefully, her legs moving quickly while she kept something clamped underneath her right arm, a flash of manila, striding past the Steinway. Without looking around at all she hurried in the general direction of the front entrance of the place.

She had changed into a pair of jeans but still had the bra of her bathing suit on. Black against denim. A typical teenage look being pulled off nicely by a woman in her thirties. Looking, from where Teddy stood and if you didn't know any better, like an eighteen-year-old girl, early June, college three short months away. Going to spend one last glorious summer down at the New Jersey shore. Stay high and sleep with guys she normally wouldn't even talk to. Margate, Stone Harbor, maybe Longport. Someplace like that. Drive a sharp-looking convertible her old man had gotten her because she'd been brilliant enough to pass high school without doing anything more dangerous than snorting cocaine and sleeping with her algebra teacher because he was, well, cool and—the main reason—older. Swearing her friends to secrecy afterward so that word would get around that much faster.

It made sense. Except, of course, this was Natalie. A woman who had probably never done an airheaded thing in her life.

Teddy stopped thinking about high school and began to make his way to the back entrance of the Marriott. By the time he got to the door he could see Natalie again. She was over by the front desk, talking to the clerk. She still had something in her hands and was waving it in front of the face of the clerk like the guy was giving her a hard time.

———

NATALIE WAS HAVING a little trouble with Paul, the desk clerk. She knew his name because he had a little gold name tag on his jacket similar to the one she had worn at Palisades. But Paul had also gone to the trouble of introducing himself—smiling like a Cecil B. DeMille Latin lover—the very first time Natalie had appeared in the lobby without Teddy nearly three weeks ago, eyeing her from head to toe long enough that she had wanted to snap her fingers in front of his face to see if he was in a trance. When Teddy came down a minute later, Paul had taken one look at him and a mask had seemed to come over his face. All smiles from then on: Yes, sir, Mr. Clyde. Absolutely, sir.

Since then, Natalie had learned that Paul owned three suits. Two black ones and a charcoal-colored one. Right now he was wearing one of the black ones. She could picture him after work, wearing a Hawaiian shirt and shorts, the island native look—the shorts J. Crew but faded to show that he was a true insider. Hitting on tourist women from America, Britain, Australia— wherever. Overdoing the accent even though he was white under his dark tan. Like he was doing right now to her. "Sure, Nat'lie, I can mail de t'ing." Jesus. She thought he probably did fairly well with American women from the Midwest: "Take you to behind dee scenes, Sugarcane, we see how dee real islan' happen." Dance them into the night and right into his bed because they couldn't tell a fake when it was between their legs. He was good-looking in a kind of disco way, and Natalie figured he was successful at his pursuits a reasonable number of times. So far she'd been unable to convince him that she wasn't the woman of his dreams.

Now was a perfect example. All she wanted was for Paul to mail something for her. Quickly. She said exactly that and knew right away it was the wrong thing to do. "Quickly? What you wan' do any'ting quickly for? T'ings be slow, tha' way you lean back, enjoy them, hey?" He couldn't seem to take his eyes off her chest long enough to listen to more than half of what she was saying.

She leaned a little bit over the counter, thinking that maybe he'd see the light if she talked to him as if he was the child he was. She said, very slowly, "See if you can understand me if I do it this way. Airmail," spelling out the letters. "A-I-R-M-A-I-L. Okay? Does that help out? You've heard of it, I assume."

Paul took the package and somehow managed to let his hand touch hers for a couple of seconds. Natalie had to fight the urge to yank hers away but thought, if he mailed the goddamn thing, what was the point? He said, "Airmail, hell, for you, sugar, I take the t'ing there myself."

Natalie said, "Jesus. Do you think—instead of that—do you think you could just *weigh* the thing? Lose the *Saturday Night Fever* thing and the accent—just this one time—and tell me how much it costs?"

Paul scrunched up his face, playing sad boy, but the look faded as his gaze slid past her. A shadow fell over the desk and she thought, thank God, another guest, maybe even the hotel manager. She could get out of here in one piece and before the sun went down.

Paul seemed confused for the first time since she had first met him.

Then a voice, from behind her, said, "Bond. *James* Bond." It was said in a better imitation British accent than Paul's crappy Caribbean one and it made Natalie wince. She thought, Shit, and turned around.

Teddy was smiling broadly, too. She realized how tan he had become because his teeth were strikingly white. He pointed at the package that Paul was holding in his hand and said, "Is there a problem with my wife's package?" She had no idea how he did it, but he managed to sound polite and intensely threatening at the same time. A bead of sweat appeared on Paul's forehead.

"Ah, no sir, ah, Mr. Clyde. No problem at all."

Natalie touched Teddy's arm. "Teddy, listen, it's not worth—"

But it was as far as she got. Teddy said, "Excuse me, sweetie pie," to her and then stepped up to the counter.

When he spoke to Paul his voice had the same nice/deadly quality as a few seconds ago. For the first time she wondered if that was how he'd been the night that Itzhak had left his friend Joseph to watch her. The night he'd come back with all the money and told her that it had been no big deal, everything had gone according to plan. She thought, *whose* plan? Wondered who had been the recipient that night—besides Izzy, probably—of the tone of voice she was hearing now. Tough but quiet. Pinning Paul behind his desk as if he were some kind of bug. And the killer was, anyone walking even ten feet away would have no idea what was happening here.

But Paul knew. Recognized the real McCoy when it was right in front of him and knew that he was in danger of being dragged across the desk and thrown into the ocean. Natalie looked carefully at Teddy's face as he stepped closer to Paul and couldn't tell if he was serious or not. She was *fairly* sure he was only kidding. Unless—oh, hell—unless he was furious about the package too?

But he didn't seem to care about the package one way or the other. All he did was put his arm around Natalie in the most affectionate way possible. Then he said, as if he were asking for directions, "Paul—kiddo—*are* you giving my wife a hard time? Is that what I'm seeing?"

The package slipped out of Paul's hands and landed with a thump on the desk. Paul didn't even seem to notice. He was too busy wiping sweat off his forehead and saying, "No. Ah—no—certainly not. I was—I was—Mr. Clyde, honestly, if I've—"

Teddy said, "Shut up," and Paul acted like he was dead. Natalie almost felt sorry for him.

Teddy picked the package up from the desk and handed it to Paul. Paul took it as if it were full of anthrax.

"Paulie, do you think it would be possible for you—*personally*—to get this thing down to the post office and mail it? Hey, I have an idea, why don't you pay for the postage yourself? I'll write a letter to your boss, tell him what a considerate thing it was."

Paul was holding the package in one hand, treating it like it was fine china and grabbing a set of car keys at the same time. Opening his mouth to say something to Teddy about, He could count on him—but then stopping because Teddy had already turned around with Natalie and begun to walk toward the rear door, looking at her jeans and saying, with no change of expression on his face, "You know what? You remind me of a girl I knew in high school. Only she looked older than you."

Walking through the courtyard on their way back to the beach, Teddy put his arm around Natalie again and Natalie took the opportunity to finally say what was on her mind. "How long have you known?"

Teddy looked up at the sky and then glanced at his watch. "Well, tell you the truth, I didn't think you had ever stopped."

Natalie glanced at his face. It was unreadable. She said, "You can be pompous, you know that."

Grinning at her and pointing a finger at his own chest, he said, "Me?"

"Can I ask you something?"

"Sure."

"That guy, Paul. What you said to him."

"About buying the stamps himself? Sure, why not?"

"No. The other part. You referred to me as your wife. What was that all about?"

Teddy looked out at the ocean. There was a one-man sailboat two hundred yards offshore and past that, maybe a half mile, a cruise ship headed away from the island.

"I'm waiting."

He turned to her. "I'll tell you what. I'll answer your question if you answer one of mine."

"Fair enough. What's your question?"

"What's my name?"

She put a hand flat on his chest and looked him squarely in the eye. Going for surprise. "In the—"

"Yes. In the piece."

She said, "See that? You and I think alike. I had the same question. What do I call you? I couldn't come up with an answer. You look like a 'Teddy,' and that's a fact."

"Maybe that's why my mom and dad named me what they did."

"Probably."

He stared hard at her. "You're running a *huge* risk here. If you don't tell me what I want to know, I won't sleep with you today."

She went over to him, relieved that he was going to have fun with it. Wrapped her arms around her chest as if she was scared and said, "Oh. Is that a threat?"

He smiled more. "Yes, it is." Shrugging. "I don't know if I can stick to it. But I'm going to try."

"It comes out next summer. The article. June probably."

"Nat, answer the goddamn question. I won't get mad."

"Yes you will."

"I won't."

"Promise?"

"Na-ta-*lie*."

"You have to promise."

"All right. I promise, I promise."

"Jameel."

He looked at her for ten full seconds without saying anything and then he glanced at the entrance to the hotel.

"No way. No goddamned way."

Natalie gave him a look, wide-eyed innocence with a touch of humor. "You're mad? My goodness."

"I'm not mad. I'm—I'm just—"

"You're mad. You won't admit it but what you really want to do is walk right back in there and take it back away from that guy. Paul."

"Your boyfriend."

"Only when you're not around."

"Jameel? *Jameel?* How could you do that?"

"It's all I could come up with."

"I *am* going to get the package. I'd rather you used my real name."

She shook her head. "You can't."

"Well, I'm serious. I'm *not* going to sleep with you. You blew it. You have to realize that. Never again.

She ran her hand up his arm and then put it on his cheek. "What if I went upstairs with you? Right now? I could torture you. I'll make you succumb."

"You'd never be able to."

She stared at his eyes.

He said, "It would take days."

She kept looking.

"Hours."

She stared.

He said, "Shit." Looking around, the waterfall, the ocean behind him, back to her and then down at the small fish pool by his feet. "You want to know the truth? I don't think that turtle'll mind if we do it right *here*."

She said, "I don't know about that. But I think my days of having sex in hotel courtyards are over. So maybe we better not be too adventurous."

"Adventurous? Us?" He smiled. "Never."

What the hell is that?" She was pointing at the magazine in his hands. "An instruction manual?"

Teddy looked down at the *Time* magazine. He'd forgotten about it. "It's nothing." He put it down on a nearby table and came back to Natalie. Taking her hand in his he said, "Lead on, sweetie pie. Heaven awaits."

Walking with her back to the entrance of the hotel he wondered, when they were finished, would he come on back, maybe grab a drink at the bar, and finish the article about two would-be international gunrunners, one Saul Rubin and one Itzhak Feldman being caught by the FBI with a freighter full of armaments headed for Palestine?

Maybe.

Or maybe he'd see if he was still as young as he once was.